REFUGEE SMITH
AND OTHER STORIES OF THE RING

COLLECTED WORKS, VOLUME III

Copyright © 2022 by Eustace Cockrell
*All world rights reserved.*

No part of this book may be reproduced, stored in a retrieval system, or transmitted in any form or by any means electronic, mechanical, photocopying, recording or otherwise, without the prior consent of the publisher.

Readers are encouraged to go to www.MissionPointPress.com to contact the author or to find information on how to buy this book in bulk at a discounted rate.

Published by Mission Point Press
2554 Chandler Rd.
Traverse City, MI 49696
(231) 421-9513
www.MissionPointPress.com

Edited by Roger Coleman
Cover Illustration: William Meade Prince, American, 1893-1951.
Illustration for "One By Land" by Eustace Cockrell, Collier's,
   April 29, 1944, oil on canvas, 22 x 17 in. (55.9 x 43.2 cm).
   Ackland Art Museum, University of North Carolina at Chapel Hill.
   Gift of Mrs. William Mead Prince (William Meade Prince Collection), 62.27.54

ISBN: 978-1-954786-81-3
Library of Congress Control Number: 2022902111

Printed in the United States of America

# Refugee Smith
## and Other Stories of the Ring

**Mission Point Press**

# EUSTACE COCKRELL

(1909 – 1972)

*They all told me that writing is nice work if you can get it,
and I always was gullible. Well I still think it's nice work
— if and when you can get it.*

To Francis (Frank) Cockrell,
older brother and mentor
to Eustace.

# Contents

**ix**
INTRODUCTION

**2**
THE LORD IN HIS CORNER
*Collier's*, April 13, 1940

**8**
MARCHING AS TO WAR
*Argosy*, October 5, 1940

**14**
THE DIVINE RIGHT
*Argosy*, October 26, 1940

**19**
RETURN OF THE NAIVE
Unpublished

**23**
COMPLIMENTS OF R. SMITH
*Collier's*, December 28, 1940

**29**
WILLIE WURTZEL'S WAY
*Collier's*, April 19, 1941

**34**
THE EMPIRE CITY ANGEL
*Collier's*, September 6, 1941

**40**
IT AIN'T NO SIN
*Collier's*, September 27, 1941

**46**
SHOESHINE BOY
*Collier's*, December 20, 1941

**50**
LOVE CAME BORROWING
*Collier's*, June 20, 1942

**55**
REFUGEE AND MR. WILLIE
Unpublished

**59**
FIRST CLASS MALE
Unpublished

**63**
REFUGEE RETURNS HOME
*Collier's*, August 15, 1942

**70**
ONE BY LAND
*Collier's*, April 29, 1944

**75**
SPELLING BEE
Unpublished

**81**
THE RECONSTRUCTION
OF REFUGEE SMITH
*Argosy*, June 1946

## Other Stories of the Ring

**88**
RIGHT-HAND MAN
*Blue Book*, July 1936

**99**
GLOVES FOR THE GOVERNOR
*Argosy*, January 14, 1939

**114**
THE LAST FIGHT
*Blue Book*, April 1939

**121**
SWEET-TALKIN' MAN
*Argosy*, July 15, 1939

**128**
RESERVATION ON QUEER STREET
*Argosy*, February 10, 1940

**133**
A FIGHTER HAS TO FIGURE
*Argosy*, April 12, 1941

**139**
FOURTH MAN IN THE RING
*Blue Book*, June 1945

**144**
THE RIGHT GUY
*15 Sports Stories*, March 1949

**149**
COUNT OF TEN
*American Magazine*, May 1950

**155**
THE EAGLEBIRD
*Argosy*, January 1957

*Movie poster from the MGM drama,* Tennessee Champ *(1954), based on "The Lord in My Corner" and other Refugee Smith stories by Eustace Cockrell.*

# INTRODUCTION

Eustace Cockrell published his first short story, a "story of the ring," in 1932 at the age of 22. It was co-authored with his older brother Frank and appeared in **Blue Book,** a leading pulp fiction magazine.

Cockrell could not have known then that his future would be intimately tied to this initial tale. Over the next 25 years, often working with his brother, he was to become a major contributor to pulp fiction publications including not only **Blue Book** but **Argosy, True Detective, Adventure, 15 Sport Stories** and **All-American Fiction**. While his themes covered a spectrum of fiction categories – detective, adventure, romance and even science fiction, Cockrell was also a prolific writer of sports stories, "the ring" being his favorite setting.

In addition to pulp fiction magazines, Cockrell's stories were to appear in many of the "slicks" including **The American Magazine, Collier's, Saturday Evening Post, Coronet, Redbook, Cosmopolitan** and **Esquire.**

It was one of his boxing stories that introduced Cockrell to Hollywood and eventually led to his more recognized career as a pioneer television writer. (While under contract with Warner Brothers, he contributed scripts for many of the early westerns including **Have Gun Will Travel** and **Gunsmoke.**

He also wrote episodes for such television classics as **Alfred Hitchcock Presents, Philco Playhouse Theater, The Loretta Young Show, The Web, This Man Dawson, Two Faces West, Man Without a Gun, Cheyenne, Damon Runyon Theater, Walter Winchell File, Target** and **Naked City**.)

In 1940, **Collier's** published Cockrell's short story, "The Lord in My Corner." This narrative introduced one of the first African American fictional heroes in the person of Refugee Smith, a young Black man who, thinking he has killed someone while gambling, escapes by jumping off a paddle wheel steamboat into the Mississippi River. Here he was rescued by another man on the lam, small-time boxing manager Willie Wurtzel.

Cockrell went on to write a total of 16 Refugee Smith stories, 12 of which were published between 1940 and 1946 in **Collier's** and **Argosy** magazines. (Four stories were unpublished.) In 1942, MGM bought the movie rights to the series and invited the author to help with its production. At the time, Cockrell was serving as a consultant for MGM in the filming of **Cabin in the Sky**, one of the first movies featuring an all-Black cast. **Cabin in the Sky**, a musical, was released in 1943 and starred Ethel Waters, Eddie "Rochester" Anderson, Lena Horne and Louis Armstrong.

The long-time drama critic for the **Los Angeles Times,** Edwin Schallert, announced MGM's purchase of the Refugee Smith series in his September 12,

1942 column. Schallert wrote *"With* **Cabin in the Sky** *maturing, Metro-Goldwyn-Mayer expects to undertake more films concerning colored types. This is indicated by the studio's purchase of the 'Refugee Smith' stories, written by Eustace Cockrell, which have been running in a national weekly magazine. The author himself is to come to the Coast to supply adaptation. Series, which has been attracting much attention, revolves around a young Negro prizefighter who is very religious. It is likely that some of the players now in* **Cabin in the Sky** *will be recalled for this feature."*

While it may have been the intent of MGM to produce more films featuring African American actors, something happened between the 1942 observation by Schallert and the eventual 1954 release of **Tennessee Champ**, the MGM movie based on Cockrell's Refugee Smith character. The film featured Shelley Winters and Keenan Wynn with the boxer, Refugee Smith, played by white actor, Dewey Martin.

One contributor to this change in casting can be found in the attacks by Senator Joseph McCarthy on Hollywood actors, writers and producers, whom he accused of being communist sympathizers. Sen. McCarthy's "red scare" tactics began in the late 1940s and continued through the mid-1950s. The fear created by Sen. McCarthy began to alter the climate in Hollywood, with producers, concerned about being blacklisted, becoming less likely to take on "message films" like those prominent in the early 1940s. Too, there was the growing assumption in Hollywood that white audiences only wanted to see white characters. Movies, like theaters, were segregated.

Another of Cockrell's stories, "Rocky's Rose" (**The American Magazine**, April 1949) was also purchased by MGM. The resulting movie, **Fast Company**, a story of the horse track rather than of the boxing ring, appeared in 1953 starring Howard Keel, Polly Bergen and Marjorie Main. Prior to this, Cockrell was the ghostwriter for **The Stardust Road**, an autobiography of songwriter Hoagy Carmichael, published in 1946.

Money for those in the movie industry was sometimes tight. On one occasion, prominent New York theater producer and later Hollywood movie producer, Jed Harris (**The Light Touch, Night People** and **Operation Mad Ball**), gave Cockrell his Bentley to drive until Harris could come up with the cash to pay Cockrell for one of his scripts. Cockrell, according to his daughter Leacy O'Hanlon, promptly drove to Las Vegas, receiving a speeding ticket on the way.

Cockrell began writing a half-hour series for Armed Forces Radio in 1950. A photo recently added to the National Archives Catalog shows Capt. John Quinn on board the *USS Norton Sound* with "famed writer" Eustace Cockrell. While on the *USS Norton Sound*, Cockrell reported on "Project Reach," the highly secretive testing of the Viking rocket and the only test performed aboard an actual vessel.

In 1953, while managing editor of **Fortnight Magazine** in Los Angeles, Cockrell was part of a team nominated for an Academy Award in the documentary category. On the **Fortnight** staff with Cockrell was novelist and close friend Richard Matheson, author of the science fiction classics **I Am Legend** (1954) and **The Shrinking Man** (1956).

INTRODUCTION

## II

Eustace Williams Cockrell was born in 1909 in the small mid-Missouri town of Warrensburg. His was a distinguished family. His grandfather, Francis Marion Cockrell, was a brigadier general in the Army of the Confederacy and later served as U.S. Senator from Missouri for five terms from 1875 to 1905. Prior to this, F. M. Cockrell was a practicing attorney in Warrensburg. His law partner, Thomas T. Crittenden, went on to become governor of Missouri and was most famous for rounding up Jessie James and his gang of bank robbers that had given Missouri a national reputation for lawlessness.

Eustace Cockrell's parents were Ewing and Leacy Williams Cockrell. Like his father, Ewing was an attorney. He later became a circuit court judge before moving to Washington, D.C. and then to New York. Judge Cockrell was nominated for the Nobel Peace Prize on three occasions for his work in developing the Federation of Justice, an organization formed in 1928 to promote successful court practices throughout the United States. In 1939, Ewing Cockrell published **Successful Justice** (Michie Publishing, Charlottesville, VA), a major resource for law school curriculums.

In 1936 Eustace Cockrell left Warrensburg to join his brother Frank in Los Angeles. Here he met his future wife, Betty Barnett Garrett, another writer, while she was working as an extra on a movie set. The two traveled back to New York to live briefly with Judge Cockrell, before returning to Los Angeles where they were married in 1939. Eustace and Betty had four children: Leacy, Geoffrey, Frederick and Elizabeth.

## III

Since the "golden age" of boxing – the 1930s and 1940s, even up through the early 1950s – interest in the sport has greatly diminished making it difficult to understand today the significance boxing once held for the public. For almost 25 years, however, boxing reigned as America's most popular sport second only to baseball.

Following the Great Depression, boxing began to grow in popularity as many sought to fight for limited or even "volunteer" purses and sometimes just for the passion of the sport. The sport appealed to many levels of society. It offered a social outing for those who could afford to attend live events and it provided an escape for those suffering from the economic hardships of the Depression with neighbors often gathering to listen around their radios.

The 2005 movie, **Cinderella Man** directed by Ron Howard, captured the impact of the Great Depression on boxing and the sport's ethnic flavor that led to its broad popularity. The film was based on the life of boxer, James J. Braddock, played by actor Russell Crowe. Braddock, an Irish American, earned the name "Cinderella Man" for his rise through the boxing ranks from a poor kid in New York City to eventually becoming heavyweight champion of the world in 1935.

Cockrell would have been familiar with Braddock's story both because of his love for the sport and the fact that he lived in New York during the time Braddock was fighting. It was not Braddock, however, but more likely boxer John Henry Lewis that provided the inspiration for Cockrell's famous fictional fighter, Refugee Smith. Lewis fought as a light heavyweight champion from 1935 to 1938, winning over contenders who often outweighed him by as much as 25 pounds. Lewis was fighting in St. Louis about the same time as Refugee Smith's first fictional bout in "The Lord in His Corner," set in that same town.

Partly because of its focus on gambling, boxing was a sport filled with unsavory characters including shady managers, swindling promoters and behind the scenes mobsters. Such portrayals only encouraged the sport's popularity and the image of young boxers as working-class heroes. It also provided great plots for writers like Eustace Cockrell and others who regularly filled the pulp magazines with narratives that fed the imagination of the multitudes following the sport.

John Dinan has compiled a record of pulp fiction sports stories published between 1923 and 1943 (**Sports in the Pulp Magazines**, McFarland & Co, Jefferson, NC, 1998). During this period, boxing with 363 stories ranked second to baseball with 478 stories. Track was third with 281 stories. Eustace Cockrell was among the more prolific of these writers with over 50 sports-related stories written between 1932 and 1957.

Cockrell's initial Refugee Smith story, "The Lord in My Corner," did not appear in pulp magazines like **Blue Book** or **Argosy,** however, but in **Collier's**, a more mainstream publication. Including the story of an African American in a prominent publication was significant. Times were changing and magazine editors were becoming increasingly aware of the importance of African Americans in society and the growing popularity of boxers, many of whom were Black. Boxers, as World War II approached, were the new American heroes, especially those who promoted or joined the war effort. Champion fighters like Joe Lewis and Sugar Ray Robinson were household names and held in great esteem by the American public.

Both the Refugee Smith series and Cockrell's other "stories of the ring" contained in this volume reflect the world of boxing from the late 1930s until the mid-1940s. It is a world that gives flesh and blood to the stereotypes surrounding the sport itself. Only one story, "Eaglebird," was published after 1950. This is Cockrell's single narrative that recognizes the influence of television on the sport. While television, with programs like the "Gillette Cavalcade of Sports," was to create larger audiences and superstars like Rocky Marciano and Floyd Patterson, it was also to signal the sport's demise in popularity. Television could attract tremendous audiences but the media's focus on a few great boxers led to a decrease in local boxing clubs and local participation.

Mob control also contributed to the sport's decline as the criminal element became more visible in the late 1940s and early 1950s. Thrown fights and scandalous decisions were commonplace. This criminal element is depicted in **Raging**

# INTRODUCTION

**Bull: My Story,** a memoir by boxer Jake LaMotta that became the basis for the 1980 movie **Raging Bull,** directed by Martin Scorsese and starring Robert DeNiro as Jake LaMotta.

## IV

Cockrell's collection of 26 boxing stories is divided into two parts – "Refugee Smith Stories" and "Other Stories of the Ring" – to reflect the different approaches used by the author to introduce the reader to the behind-the-scenes world of boxing.

While it is correct to categorize the Refugee Smith stories as boxing narratives, they are much broader in scope than most traditional sports stories. Cockrell adds significant detail to the portrayal of Harlem society in the early 1940s as well as the boxing culture along New York's W. 49th Street. Much of the action takes place, for example, not in the ring, but amidst settings like Senate "Slippery" Ellum's Eatmor Fish & Chips Shoppe; Mazda Brown's hamburger stand, The Igloo (Come in and chew the fat); and the Yellow Front Cabaret and Nite Club.

Among the more colorful reappearing characters in Refugee's world are Freewheeling Johnson (Freezy), the shoeshine boy; local gamblers Hardhat McGee, Three-Story Gooch, Infinite Sanders and Sunday Sheehy (so named because he never collected his markers on Sundays); and enticing women with sometimes ulterior motives like Arselia Toogood and Annabelle Divine. Several of the stories, "Love Came Borrowing," "Refugee Returns," and "Spelling Bee" do not include fight scenes at all but incidents that provide further insight into the characters of Refugee Smith and his manager Willie Wurtzel.

The relationship between Smith and Wurtzel remains central to every story. Beginning with the classic, "The Lord in His Corner," in which Refugee is saved by Willie from drowning in the Mississippi River, Refugee believes Willie to be an angel of the Lord. Just before he is pulled into Wurtzel's rowboat, he makes a promise: *"Get me outta dis ole River and I'll carry de Word to de multitudes. I'll go up an' down de lan'."* This promise and its implementation under the crafty tutelage of fight manager Willie Wurtzel forms the basis for the entire Refugee Smith series. Whether Cockrell intended this to be a series from the beginning or whether he simply built on the popularity of the initial story remains to be known.

Looking back, it was really Refugee who saved Willie Wurtzel since Willie, also seeking to escape a gambling experience gone sour, is floating in the river with no ability to paddle. Refugee gets him safely to shore. This begins a series of episodes in which Refugee, with his great faith and his tremendous strength, continues to pull Willie Wurtzel, his Jewish manager known for his gambling and self-serving interests, out of deep water.

It is his promise to the Lord, however, that leads Refugee forward as a fighter along with the promise by Wurtzel that Refugee will find more sinners in the boxing world than any other place. *"Where I'm goin',"* he said, *"there's sinners thick as fleas. Miserable sinners."*

Religion and scripture are consistently used by the Jewish Wurtzel (who is not particularly religious) to motivate his fighter. In "Willie Wurtzel's Way," for example, a hex has been placed on Refugee by his Haitian opponent, Frankie Blood. Refugee is losing his bout with Blood and is upset that Wurtzel will not let him carry a pouch prepared by a voodoo woman to ward off the hex. Instead Wurtzel places a small purse around Refugee's neck that contains the wording *"Thou shalt not make unto thee any graven image, or any likeness of anything that is in heaven above, or that is in the earth beneath, or that is in the water under the earth." (That also goes for phony voodooers. W. Wurtzel.)* After winning the fight, Refugee responds, *"Lord, God forgive me. I knowed not what I done."*

In "The Reconstruction of Refugee Smith," Smith has returned home from fighting in World War II. He has lost his faith in the Lord, and therefore his strength, because of the suffering witnessed during his enlistmen. To help restore his faith, Wurtzel hires Three-Story Gooch to flash the neon image of a harp at the top of Madison Square Garden so that Refugee, as he is fighting, can see that the Lord is still in his corner. It's this type of intervention by Wurtzel that brings out the best in Refugee with the interplay between the non-religious boxing manager continually reminding his fighter of the need to "carry de Word to de multitudes." Wurtzel's motivation is not clean, however. He knows that without Refugee believing the Lord is in his corner, he does not have the strength to continue pursuing the middleweight championship.

In addition to creating a social setting for Refugee in Harlem and using Refugee's religious faith as the basis for his strength and motivation, Cockrell also develops unique cultural dialects for Refugee, Willie and his other characters. The language of religion and the language of the pugilism center along W. 49th Street often leaves gaps, however. In "Compliments of R. Smith," for example, Refugee involves "Slippery" Ellum in a plot to find out what Willie would like for a Christmas gift: "Didn't he say he wanted somethin'?" Refugee asked.

"Yeah," Slippery said. "He said he wanted the winner of the second at Sunnyside Downs."

"What dat mean?" Refugee asked.

"Sunnyside Downs is a horse park down in Florida," Slippery said. "He meant he wanted who was gonna win the second race down there tomorrow."

After much discussion, the trusting Refugee determines that Willie must really want a horse for Christmas. He and Slippery fly down to Florida and purchase the winner of the second at Sunnyside Downs and, on Christmas Eve, Refugee presents Deuces Wild to Willie Wurtzel, Compliments of R. Smith.

It is easy to be critical of Cockrell, writing in the early 1940s of life in Harlem, of African American religion and using African American and ethnic dialects for Refugee and his Jewish manager. Dr. Judith Weisenfeld (**Hollywood Be Thy Name: African American Religion in American Film, 1929-1949,** University of California Press, 2007, p. 294, n43) notes that it was Cockrell's short story,

"Compliments of R. Smith" that brought him to the attention of Allen Freed in Hollywood. Freed was told: *"This boy knows how to write negroes better than anybody I've read in a long time and judging from these stories ... he has a great sense of humor. He would be worthwhile remembering when you get to* **Cabin in the Sky***."* As mentioned earlier, Cockrell was later brought in to assist with the "dialect" of the all-Black **Cabin in the Sky** cast.

White writers like Cockrell and film makers in Hollywood understood the importance of religion in African American culture. Because their interpretations often portrayed the believer as childish or backward, it would be easy to label their writings as discriminatory and insensitive. The issues, however, are much more complex as Dr. Weisenfeld points out. Rather than placing such presentations in a negative context, she suggests instead that these portrayals of African American culture by white writers, directors and producers become the basis for further discussion and dialogue about race and American identity.

Whatever shortcomings may be placed on Cockrell's portrayal of African American and Jewish culture, his creation of the boxing duo of fighter Refugee Smith and manager Willie Wurtzel continued to feed the growing desire for personal narratives about boxers, especially those who could rise above the limitations of poverty, unethical promoters and fight-fixing gamblers to become heroes in the eyes of the American public. Refugee Smith was foremost a hero. Too, his religious beliefs were not always that childish.

In the story, "It Ain't No Sin," Arzelia Toogood, the girlfriend of gambler Infinite Sanders, has dripped paint on Refugee's head. Just prior to his fight, she cuts off his hair to remove the paint. Having heard the story of Sampson and Delilah, Refugee believes his strength has been taken away. Willie glues a patch on Refugee's head during the fight and convinces Refugee that his hair is growing back. Refugee goes on to knock out his opponent with Willie responding, *"One rock was enough for David and one round was enough for you."* *"Yes, sir,"* Refugee said, *"De Lord he do things differently in de Yankee Stadium than he do em in Gaza but hit looks like hit work out to de same thing."*

"*Amen,*" said Willie Wurtzel.

In addition to the 12 Refugee Smith stories published in **Collier's** and **Argosy** magazines, four unpublished stories have been provided by the Cockrell family for inclusion in this volume. One of these, "First Class Male," offers an alternative account of Refugee's enlistment in the Army during WW II. It is dated April 1942. A published story of his enlistment, "Refugee Returns Home," appeared later in **Collier's** on August 15, 1942. These two narratives plus the fact that several other stories in the Refugee Smith collection are related to Refugee and Willie's military service, further highlight the importance of boxers in recruiting and supporting America's war effort. Refugee was a man of his times and, in very human terms, reflected the best of a boxing world, a world increasingly at war with the mob and those seeking to subvert its popularity for personal financial gain.

## V

Along with the Refugee Smith stories, ten additional "stories of the ring" written by Cockrell are included in this volume. These stories represent more traditional sports narratives. Most of the action takes place either in the ring or preparing for the fight. The story line is often very simple. In "Fourth Man in the Ring," for example, fighter Joe Wilder, a WW II veteran, is losing badly to his opponent Arnold Baronski. As the bout progresses, Wilder begins to hear voices. Much of the dialogue during the fight focuses on trying to understand what these voices are saying. Finally, he figures it out. It is the voice of his Army captain, the man he helped rescue but who later died from his wounds. The captain was calling him to do his best – not for his daughter or for his wife – but for himself. *"A man can love his country, and his daughter and his wife. And a man can almost love himself if he always does his best."* The conclusion offers a reconciling moment for Wilder because he finally gets the chance to express to the captain how much he loved him.

Cockrell's story, "Right-Hand Man," speaks more to the fight-fixing and unethical activities prevalent in the boxing world. Seven years prior, fighter Jocko Humboldt, managed by Ace Finley, had red pepper rubbed in his eyes with a towel by a ring handler hired by gambler Joe Mordesti. Jocko won the fight but was badly cut in the process. As Jocko prepares for his final fight, Finley recognizes that this will be his last chance to get revenge against Mordesti for the red pepper incident. Much of the story involves an elaborate scheme to convince Mordesti that Jocko has broken his right hand in training and will not be able to use this powerful weapon in the upcoming fight. Mordesti falls for the trap and bets everything and more on Jocko to lose. When this doesn't happen, Mordesti, unable to pay off, is run out of town by the very mob that had supported him. Again, the little guy wins and the bad guy is brought down, a theme consistent throughout Cockrell's boxing stories.

Perhaps the greatest of Cockrell's boxing narratives is the classic, "Reservation on Queer Street." "Queer Street" is the boxing term used to describe those fighters who have been so badly beaten that they hear voices and are often no longer in touch with reality. Mike Sutton is one such boxer. He is the brunt of jokes as he is allowed to hang around the training camp of fighter Louis Arnovich, a cruel man who plays on Sutton's fears and irrationality, especially his fear that "some day they are gonna get you. They come for you in uniforms, not like coppers, but gray uniforms and they take you away to the booby hatch." Such statements drive Sutton into the woods to hide overnight until someone comes and convinces him that the men in gray uniforms are gone.

In his dressing room, as Arnovich prepares to enter the ring, he turns to Sutton and says, "Don't let anyone get you while I'm gone." During the fight, however, two ushers in gray uniforms enter the dressing room causing Sutton to rush out of the room and down the aisle toward the boxing ring yelling, "Champ, Oh God,

# INTRODUCTION

Champ, don't let 'em take me!" As Arnovich turns to look at Sutton, his opponent, Baby Face Gannon, drops him for a count of nine and then when he gets up, Gannon drops him again. Arnovich is saved by the bell.

Back in the dressing room, Arnovich begins talking to Sutton, his eyes wild and pleading, "Mike," as he shook his head back and forth, "what's it like?" Arnovich is now on equal terms with Sutton. He has become a resident of Queer Street.

Cockrell is a master craftsman of the sports story. His boxers enter the ring for a variety of reasons. It may be for money or self-respect. It may be for revenge. It may be to raise money needed to pay medical bills for a wife or a friend. Regardless, these stories provide the reader with an understanding of the intricacies that motivate boxers, intricacies often invisible in the straightforward world of watching two men slug it out in the ring.

Discovery of these motivations and the personalities behind the desire to have one's hands lifted high at the end of a fight is what makes Cockrell's tales relevant in a world where boxing no longer holds the attraction it once held for previous generations.

*Roger Coleman*
Edenton, North Carolina

# Refugee Smith

Refugee Smith turned dutifully around on the highway. They continued thus for perhaps forty-five minutes. Then Willie started showing Refugee how to lead, how to stand.

# THE LORD IN HIS CORNER

**If he couldn't fight a lick he'd still be a sensation.**

**REFUGEE SMITH** got from his knees to his feet and up to a half crouch in one smooth, flowing motion as the dice from the cup rolled to a stop in the blob of yellow light from the lantern above the kneeling circle of gamblers. His left hand, coiled into a black, knotty fist, moved in a long arc and hit with a sharp, metallic sound against the chin of the man who had the cup. Then with the right hand, on an arm long enough so that he didn't have to bend over, he groped for the dice, found them and stepped back.

The man with the cup had fallen over on his face, the leather cup still half clutched in a passive hand. Nobody moved.

Refugee held up one of the dice to the light and turned it over slowly. The dice had three fives on it. He reached out then into the circle and with a quick movement grabbed the two dirty dollar bills lying there.

"Top dice," he said, and waited. "Don't nobody top off Refugee."

The man who held the cup pushed himself back up to his knees and was reaching into some inner recess of his coat when Refugee sprang. In an instant he had the hand that was reaching for the gun. The others faded against the walls into the darkness as suddenly Refugee leaped back. In his hand he held a gun.

He didn't hold the gun as if to shoot. He held it by the butt but his finger wasn't in the trigger guard. He held it like a club.

The man across from Refugee was bigger than Refugee, much bigger, and he was a lighter color, a dirty coffee color. Refugee could hear him breathing hard, through his nose.

"Put dat gun down, boy," the big man said. "Put de gun down."

Refugee stood swaying on the balls of his bare feet. "I'm gonna put de gun down," he said. "I'm gonna put de gun down yo' th'oat and pull your gizzard out wid de sight." And he moved a half step closer.

The big man saw he wasn't going to be shot and came to meet him, charging with his head down. Refugee Smith leaped and swung the gun. There was a flash of metal in the light, a crunching sound and the big man went past Refugee, charging on, his head going lower and lower until finally it drove into the floor. Then he lay still, blood making a little pool beside his still head.

There was a long silence. Then a voice from out of the darkness came through: "You've kilt him, Refugee. The Man ain't gonna like dat. Even if he went to th'ow in dem crooked dice, the Man ain't gonna like dat."

Refugee Smith stood perfectly still, looking down at the man on the floor, then he leaned down and put the gun on the floor and straightened up and let out his breath in a long sigh. "I never went to clear kill him," he said. He looked around him wildly for a moment. "I don't aim to go wid de chain gang."

A hoarse bellow that shook the boards of the floor sounded from above. "The Man blowed for a landin'," the voice from the outer darkness said.

Refugee Smith took two shotgun shells from the breast pocket of his ragged overalls and put the two dirty bills in the telescoped shells with his matches. Then he turned and started for the steps that led to the deck of the steamboat.

"Can you swim?" a voice queried.

The steamboat whistle sounded again, twice. "Some," Refugee Smith said, and disappeared up the steps.

**WILLIE WURTZEL** laid the oars down in the bottom of the boat and just drifted. His hands were raw, and as far as he could see he was as far from shore or succor as he had been an hour before.

It was the rowing machine, Willie reflected. That was the trouble. If it hadn't been for the rowing machine he'd have gone for the hills.

The rowing machine had been a purchase made some years before when Willie was managing Harper Wilde and Harper had the title. Somebody had said something derogatory about Willie's paunch and it was fashionable in that day to have a rowing machine. He'd worked on the rowing machine one morning for about ten minutes but it hadn't seemed to make him any slimmer so he'd pushed it under the bed. However, the ten minutes had fallaciously demonstrated one thing: rowing was a cinch. The only trouble was, a 49th Street hotel-room floor didn't seem to have much in common with the Mississippi River. There hadn't been any oars on the machine. Just nice little handles. These real oars would just as soon jump out of their locks and slug you in the kisser as not.

Willie was on his way home. Home to 49th Street and the Garden, where a man might make a strike, even in tough times, to carry him through. Willie had gone to New Orleans to look at a fighter. It turned out that it wasn't a fighter Willie had gone to look at. Willie didn't have a fighter and it was only in desperation that he'd left 49th Street. Willie had to have a fighter to live. Sometimes he had had fighters where it was vice versa so to speak, but usually Willie and a reasonably good fighter were a money-making combine. Willie was two days out of New Orleans and a vague guess at the geographical contours of the Southern states, coupled with a rough estimate of the river, told Willie that in about two days he would be back at New Orleans or rather drifting past New Orleans going south. Willie had had enough of going south to last him several lifetimes.

**WHEN** Refugee Smith had said that he could swim "some," it was an overstatement. True, he could and had dog-paddled around in the pond back of the cabin where he was born and he hadn't drowned, but to dog-paddle to shore from some place near the center of the Mississippi River was another matter.

Refugee was strong. Strong and enduring and game but the old River was trying to suck him down and he had turned from being afraid of the chain gang to being afraid of drowning and now he wasn't even afraid much of that.

"Lord," he said aloud, throwing the blame squarely onto shoulders more competent than his own, "hit looks like You was fixin' to drowned me." He struggled a few more weary strokes.

"Lord," he said, "You seen for Yo'self, them crooked dice he th'owed in on me, and I didn't go to kill him, I just was of a mind to punish him some." The river lapped at Refugee's chin inexorably and he tried to kick his feet a little harder.

"Lord," Refugee Smith said for the third time, "if Yo' is fixin' to gather me to Yo' bosom, gimme a sign so I can let up on this paddlin', 'cause I'm weary, Lord." His legs were like lead.

"Lord," he said finally, and his voice was cracked now with real fear, "if You succor me out'n this ole River, I'll sin no mo', I'll lead a good life." Refugee Smith raised his voice in one final appeal: "Get me outta dis ole River and I'll carry de Word to de multitudes. I'll go up an' down de lan'."

The Lord's answer floated back in the voice of one of the chosen who was born near Brooklyn Bridge. "Over here," the voice said, and Willie Wurtzel took up the oars once more and struggled toward the voice he had heard.

"Lord be praised, it's a deal," Refugee Smith said, and divine energy flowed into his body as he struggled through the warm muddy water toward the sound of clinking oar locks.

**WILLIE WURTZEL** sat in the back and looked at the black man sitting facing him in the boat. The moon had finally fought its way through the clouds and it was light out on the water now.

"Can you row?" Willie asked.

"Yes, suh, I can row. Wait'll I get my wind an' I'll row us to shore," Refugee Smith said, covertly studying this rather odd agent of the Lord.

"What were you doin' out here?" Willie asked.

Refugee made his face blank, searching his mind for an adequate story. But suddenly he remembered his contract. "I won't bear no false witness, Mr...."

"Wurtzel," Willie said. "Willie Wurtzel."

"I can't tell no lie, Mr. Willie. I was roustaboutin' on the Mary Jane an' we was shootin' craps below deck when a big coffee-colored fellah th'owed in a pair of crooked dice, so I taken his gun away from him an' hit him wid hit an' they do say I kilt him. So I went over the side 'cause the Man wouldn't like that."

"Maybe you didn't kill him," Willie said.

"I hit him a right smart lick," Refugee said truthfully.

Willie Wurtzel only grunted, studying the black boy facing him. The big hands, the long heavy arms. The sloping shoulders.

"Which way do you want me to row?" Refugee asked.

Willie pointed to the shore away from whence he'd come. "That way," he said.

Refugee Smith picked up the oars and the boat leaped like a live thing for the distant shore of the river.

After a moment Willie spoke, "It's funny," he said. "I was hitch-hikin' north and I get in this little town and I'm settin' in a restaurant scoffin' a cup of coffee when somebody says there is a game in the back room and I go back to watch." He paused a minute watching the play of muscles under Refugee's skin as the boat skimmed over the water.

"Hmmm," Willie went on. "I went back to watch and finally I faded somebody and they threw in these tops."

"Watcha do then?" Refugee asked, straightening up.

"I got tough," Willie said, "and they kind of beat me up for objectin' to gettin' cheated."

Refugee rowed on silently.

"I lammed down to the drink," Willie said, "and I saw this boat and jumped into it and took off. I thought I could row," he concluded.

"It's kinda funny, Mr. Willie," Refugee said finally, convinced beyond any contradiction that the Lord had ordained it thus, "about them dice. I mean yo' dice and my dice. Both bein' tops."

"Yeah," Willie Wurtzel said. "It must be an old Southern custom."

Refugee angled the boat in expertly, climbed out in the shallow water and beached it. Willie watched him all the time, watching the way he moved.

"How'd you like to come up north with me?"

Willie asked finally, casually. "We might pick up some change."

Refugee Smith ran a black hand over his face. "I gotta carry de Lord's Word to de multitudes," he said, "up an' down de lan'."

Willie Wurtzel's face remained blank. "Where I'm goin'," he said, "there's sinners thick as fleas. Miserable sinners."

"I'll go where yo' tell me to go," Refugee said, " 'cause yo' was sent to save me on a special deal, 'twist me an' de Lord, an' yo' must be a good an' holy man."

Willie Wurtzel's eyebrows went up. "God almighty!" he said finally.

Refugee tied the boat carefully to a shrub. "I knowed hit!" he said contentedly.

**THE NEXT MORNING** found Willie Wurtzel and Refugee Smith on the highway. During the night Willie had outlined his plan. He, Willie, would undertake to make a fighter out of Refugee and during the process he would guarantee to keep Refugee in constant contact with a great many people who were absolutely a yard wide and all wool when it came to being bona fide sinners. In fact, Willie said, this part would practically take no doing at all. The other, the learning to be a fighter, that was another matter.

"You walk backward, you run a little backward every once in a while," Willie directed as they trudged up the road. "That teaches you to go away from a man easy, without worryin'. The best of 'em have to go away sometimes."

Refugee Smith turned dutifully around on the highway. They continued thus to the amazement of sundry by-passers for perhaps forty-five minutes. Then Willie started showing Refugee how to lead, how to stand, how to use his right hand and still not leave himself unprotected. Slowly he accustomed Refugee to moving correctly, keeping his elbows in and his right shoulder high to protect his chin. They were shadowboxing up the road when they came to a little restaurant, divided as they are in that part of the country for both colored and white trade. Willie took a few worn bills out of his pocket. He peeled off one of them. "You order three three-minute eggs," he said, "four slices of whole-wheat bread, toasted, two slices of bacon, a big glass of orange or tomato juice and coffee if you want it. I'll be outside when you get through."

Refugee repeated his menu. "Okay, Mr. Willie," he said. "But I don't need yo' money. I got two dollahs of my own."

Willie told him to keep his two dollars and went into the other side of the restaurant. There he called the town where the steamboat had landed and talked to the sheriff. He came out of the phone booth grinning. Then he took a dime from his pocket and bought a cup of coffee and an apple. The apple he put in his side pocket for lunch. He drank the coffee and went out to wait for Refugee. Soon they were on the road again.

That noon it took some doing in the place they found themselves but Refugee Smith lunched on spinach and a lamb chop, dry toast and tea. Willie Wurtzel ate his apple and bought a cigar. That afternoon he found two rocks and Refugee shadowboxed with them in his hands.

"There ain't no substitute," Willie Wurtzel explained, "for a sparrin' partner or two and the heavy bag and the light bag, but we ain't got 'em so we'll do the best we can."

"I'll do what you say," Refugee said.

"I'm gonna get you a fight," Willie said, "when we get to St. Louis. We got to make a strike."

"Yo' mean wid gloves like yo' tole me about?" Refugee asked. "Gee, that ought be kinda fun. I seen some fellahs once at a carnival play fight like dat. They wore little pants," he added irrelevantly.

"You'll have to get right in the ring without knowin' nothing," Willie said. "So all the time you play like you are fightin' in the ring with someone with gloves, like you are practicin' here along the road. When we get to St. Louis, we won't have any money."

"I still got my two dollahs," Refugee said.

"St. Louis," Willie Wurtzel said, "is a hell of a town for two dollars not to last very long in."

The two dollars never reached St. Louis. It went to feed Refugee Smith in Memphis but they caught a truck there and it took them to St. Louis.

Willie Wurtzel climbed down from the truck behind Refugee, took a ring from his finger and looked at it a moment. It was a medium-sized diamond ring with a well-cut stone. He looked up and down the St Louis street, saw the three hanging balls that he sought and set off in that direction. As he walked, he took another ring out of his pocket and put it in the palm of his right hand. It was an exact duplicate of the one he'd taken off his finger except that its stone was well-cut glass. In the pawn shop he laid the real diamond on the counter. Refugee stood fascinatedly eyeing the guns, cameras, banjos and silver knickknacks in the showcase before him.

The man behind the counter examined the ring through a little thing screwed in his eye. He and Willie argued briefly. Willie picked up the ring in high dudgeon, called the man behind the counter various uncomplimentary names, then in one final burst of impassioned oratory in defense of the rights of the defenseless, tossed it back on the counter. "Okay," he said. "Okay, but I've got a hundred on it many a time."

The man behind the counter picked up the ring, labeled it and took it back to his safe. He came back and gave Willie three ten-dollar bills.

Willie faded quickly from the store.

In another pawnshop he bought Refugee a suit, shirt and shoes. Refugee scorned socks. He had, he pointed out, never worn socks. Willie didn't argue with him. He bought him ring trunks and boxing shoes, a worn silk bathrobe with a golden harp on its faded green back. Then he took Refugee and planted him in a pool hall with explicit directions to talk to no one and not to go away. Then Willie took his last ten dollars in his hand and walked to the curb. "Take me to Tom Packer's office. Tom Packer, the promoter," he told the cab driver.

**WILLIE WURTZEL** came up the aisle behind his fighter without a thin dime in his pockets, carrying his own water bucket because he couldn't pay a boy two dollars. If Refugee won they would have fifty. If he lost they would have nothing.

The announcer got Refugee's name wrong, called him Refuse Smith but stated the other facts correctly: that Refugee weighed one fifty-eight, was fighting four rounds to a decision against one Western Mahoney and that Refuse was a substitute for the popular Eddie Andrews who had broken his hand while training.

This got a tolerant chuckle from some acquaintances of Eddie Andrews and Willie took Refugee Smith by the arm and led him to the center of the ring for his instructions.

Back in their corner, Willie leaned over. "Remember about your left hand and keep your shoulder up and…." The bell rang.

Refugee Smith walked out to the center of the ring, wound up with his left hand to the delight of Western Mahoney who beat him to the punch by several miles and cut his cheek with a crashing left hook. The round was a shambles, though Refugee never went down. Willie couldn't look.

Refugee came back to his corner at the bell and sat down. He looked puzzled. "I can't remember all what yo' tole me, Mr. Willie," he said. "I try to remember an' he hits me."

Willie Wurtzel rubbed blood from his face. Refugee's heart was beating slowly. He wasn't hurt.

"Look out there," Willie hissed. "All those people. What'll they think of the Lord if His servant gets beat. They'll think the Lord is layin' down on the job. That's what they'll think." He paused.

"Refugee," he said impassionedly. *"The Lord is in your corner.* Go out and smite him hip and thigh but don't hit him really that low because you'll lose on a foul. Forget everything I told you."

Refugee Smith's face creased into a grin. "Hot dog," he cried, and he left his corner with a big joyous bound as the bell for the second round sounded.

**NOBODY** was ever quite sure what happened. Willie didn't know, and it was plain that Western Mahoney never had time to get the faintest glimmer. But Western Mahoney was laying on the canvas from one of an avalanche of blows that came from all the unorthodox directions they should not have come from and Refugee Smith was standing at the ropes shouting to the crowd as the referee counted.

"Repent," he yelled, "for the Day of Judgment's comin'! The Lord gives me strength for I've seen the light."

The rest was drowned in delighted cheers. A reporter at the ringside started a story: "The Lord and Willie Wurtzel were in the corner of a colored middle-weight named Smith last night. Between them they seem to have something."

**WILLIE WURTZEL** dragged his feet into the pawnshop where he'd hocked his ring and laid down thirty-one dollars and sixty-eight cents. He laid a ticket down beside it. "I want to redeem that glass I give you," he said.

The man behind the counter picked up the ticket and went back to the safe. He came forth with the ring.

"Yeah," Willie said. "It's glass. I palmed the McCoy."

The pawnbroker screwed his glass into his eye and looked at it. Then he looked up, scratched his head under his little cap and sighed.

"Why did you come back?" he asked.

"I guess I got … I dunno. I — well — this boy here. He thought he killed a man and that I saved him and he believed so strong in me and the Lord that he made us fifty dollars and I thought … I dunno. Gimme the ring."

The pawnbroker took the money. He looked at Refugee Smith standing feasting his eyes on a pearl inlaid harmonica. "I give you the harmonica," he said. And he reached in and handed it to Refugee. Then he turned to Willie Wurtzel. "Keep this glass ring," he said. "You can always get thirty dollars on it here."

Refugee Smith blew a soft blast on his new instrument. "Where we go now, Mr. Willie?" he asked.

Willie Wurtzel looked up at Refugee Smith. "In a roundabout way," he said, "we are headin' for Madison Square Garden. When it's full," he added, "it holds eighteen thousand sinners, miserable sinners." He reached over and patted the old man behind the counter on the arm.

"Where is the nearest synagogue?" Willie Wurtzel asked under his breath.

———————————————

Refugee Smith had gone down twice. And then, when Diamond was coming in at him again, he heard those voices in the topmost gallery: his congregation.

# MARCHING AS TO WAR

**Up an' at 'em dark-skinned boy. This here's a good fight you're fightin', an' the congregation of righteousness is sure-nuff behind yo'. And remember: the cat did not get up until he heard the man say nine.**

**WILLIE WURTZEL** jiggled the sliding weight on the bar and held his breath. The bar stayed up. Willie let his breath go in a long sigh and with a finger that trembled with reluctance moved the weight one notch to the right. Still the bar stayed up.

Willie looked up at the big black man on the platform of the scale, moved the weight still another notch to the right and watched it bring the bar down to balance.

Refugee Smith, standing nearly naked on the platform of the scale, looked down at Willie Wurtzel with a little frown creasing his forehead. "I feels right ga'nted, Mister Willie. Can I have a drink of water?"

Willie Wurtzel looked at the ground. "Go up to the house," he said, "and get you a half a glass of water outta the tap and drink it real slow and while you're drinkin' it suck you a lemon."

Refugee Smith grinned wanly. "It's a good thing I don't crave to spit," he said stepping down from the scales, "'cause I couldn't get it done."

When Refugee had gone Willie Wurtzel turned and looked at the round little man across the scale from him. "Well, Sudsy," Willie said, "that's that."

Sudsy McGuire pushed his derby back and mopped the sweat from his brow with the back of a pudgy hand. "Hunnert sixty-two," Sudsy said. "Today's Satdee. Monday mornin', eleven o'clock the boy makes hunnert sixty or it costs you a gee what you've posted. He's drawed too fine now. If we steam it offen him he won't be able to hoist his hands."

"What the blazes you tellin' me that for?" Willie snarled. "I got you up here as a trainer not to tell me a bunch of stuff I already know too well."

"There ain't but one thing we can do," Sudsy went on. "We got to get him in a rubber suit and put him over the road tomorrow and then we got to keep him dryin' out 'til Monday mornin'. That won't weaken him so bad as the steam."

**WILLIE WURTZEL** shut his eyes, shaking his head from side to side. "I can't put that boy through that," he said. He paused. "Sudsy," he went on passionately, "I picked that boy up out of the river and I kept him from bein' a preacher like he wants to be by tellin' him that if he gets to be a champion he'll have more of a swing with his congregation. I can't hardly bring myself to make him take such a beatin' as he'll have to take if he makes sixty."

Sudsy McGuire, who in Willie Wurtzel's opinion was the best trainer and second in the business, took off his derby hat and fanned himself with it. "He's a natchal light heavy," Sudsy said logically. "What did you get him on with Daisy for?"

"Daisy's a big name," Willie said. "And this boy of mine is hot in River City. I've fought him sixteen times, the last four here. He's murdered their local hopes and ain't drawed a deep breath. If he beats Daisy he'll be the contender."

Sudsy's mouth fell slightly more ajar than it usually was. "You don't mean you're shootin' with the eight ball, Willie?"

Willie Wurtzel's face took on a slightly pained look. "Listen, Sudsy," he said ominously. "Me an' Refugee Smith, we're strictly on the level, see. That gee I got posted, that's strictly the mahoskey. We're tryin' to win 'em all. I've changed, Sudsy."

Sudsy McGuire let this penetrate for a moment. "Well," he said finally, "that's different. I natchally thought that the Daisy's crew had it set. Why, Daisy's tryin' to get a record. Didn't they say nothin', didn't they? . . ."

Willie Wurtzel walked over to the door of the barn where the indoor ring was and looked down the hill at the house. He could see Refugee Smith sitting on the steps of the porch.

Refugee held an empty glass in one big hand, a limp lemon in the other. He looked dusty black. He wasn't sweating even in the heat.

"Yeah," Willie said, not turning around. "They come to me, Sudsy, but we didn't deal."

"Jeepers," Sudsy said, "I'd a thought they'd of tried to see it before they signed."

"Refugee hadn't beat nobody," Willie Wurtzel said. "He ain't fought but sixteen times. They didn't think it worth while 'til he kicked over Frankie Kline." He walked on out the door and toward the house. Sudsy followed.

**IT WAS** hot up in the country, and nobody was there but Willie and Sudsy and Refugee Smith. The sparring partners had gone down the day before.

*The* sparring partner, rather. Willie had been able to afford one spavined welter-weight for Refugee to work with the one week he took him to the country to train for his first big fight.

Willie was doing the cooking. The farm he was getting rent free from a friend who had alternately run a training camp and gambling store on the property; but that had been back in the days when River City and its surrounding country was run by another political faction.

Willie Wurtzel walked up the steps, reached down and ran his hand through his fighter's thick black hair. "Only two more days, boy," he said, "and then we'll drink a gallon of beer and eat steaks two inches thick."

Refugee Smith looked up and licked dry lips. He summoned a grin. "Mister Willie," he said, "I woulda thought it a most kindly thing 'iffen you hadn't said about them things you said about."

Willie walked on into the house and picked up his typewritten sheets. The carbon he kept, the other, again out on the porch, he gave to Refugee.

"Okay," he said. "Let get at our home work."

Refugee reached out and took his sheet and an eagerness came into his face. Willie settled himself beside him on the step. "The rat was a hooker," Refugee read haltingly, "but the cat held his left paw out in front of him and kept his left — left shooder . . ."

"Shoulder," Willie said.

"But c-o-u-l-d," Refugee protested, spelling out the word, "spells cood."

"It's screwy," Willie said sympathetically, "but it ain't my fault."

". . . shoulder up hiding his chin and hooked his right paw to the body when the rat put a left jab to his heed."

"Head," Willie said.

Sudsy McGuire appeared from the door. He had a toothpick in his hand and was wielding it in conjunction with loud sucking noises when it proved unequal to its task. "Sunnay school?" he inquired good-naturedly.

"Mister Willie," Refugee said reverently, "is ateachin' me to read writin'."

"What's this about the cat hookin' his right?" Sudsy went on.

"I'm teachin' him to read," Willie said, "and I got a lotta books and they was all about the cat and the rat so I just figured I'd write my own and learn him a little about fightin' as he went along. Might as well," he added apologetically.

"Readin's a great thing," Sudsy opined, drifting casually toward the door and the kitchen. He chuckled reminiscently. "Didja see L'il Abner this mornin'?" But Refugee Smith wasn't listening. He was crouched over his paper. "The cat was c'nocked down —"

"Knocked."

". . . knocked down but he did not get up until he heard the man say nine. . . ."

**WILLIE** came out of the house the next morning and he had the rubber suit and the sweatshirts in his hand. He looked at Refugee lying in the porch hammock.

"Refugee," he began haltingly, "I hate to tell you this but you gotta hit the road today."

Refugee Smith looked up and he didn't smile. "But it's Sunday, Mister Willie."

"I know," Willie said, "but you got to. You got to take off a coupla pounds."

Refugee Smith set his face bleakly. "I can't work on Sunday, Mister Willie. It's wrote down in The Book."

"But, but—" Willie Wurtzel looked down at his fighter's face and stopped. He walked up and down the porch. "But preachers work on Sunday!" he shouted. "That's their hardest day."

"Preachin's different," Refugee said inexorably. "That's the Lord's work."

Willie Wurtzel took a couple of more turns up the porch. Finally his expression of deep gloom lifted a little. "Would you preach?" he said. "Would you give a little sermon if I got you a congregation up here?"

Refugee Smith jumped out of the hammock. "You reckon I could do it?"

Willie Wurtzel said slowly: "You won your first fight not knowin' nothin' about fightin'. You gotta start with prelims in any racket. You could kinda take a trail fight up here in the country and if you didn't do so good you could train some more just like for a fight."

"Oh, boy!" Refugee exclaimed. "Lemme get to thinkin'."

Willie Wurtzel disappeared into the door in search of Sudsy. He found Sudsy at the refrigerator. He gave Sudsy the last money in his wallet. "This'll be enough to get 'em all gallery tickets and hire the truck," he said. "Now this is what I want you to do."

Willie talked fervently and explicitly for five minutes. Sudsy nodded dazedly.

"And don't forget the coat," Willie finished as Sudsy set off down the back steps for his car and River City.

**IT WAS** several hours later when Johnny Tirandelli ran into Sudsy. Johnny Tirandelli found Sudsy in a bar where Sudsy was having a couple of beers after the somewhat arduous task of rounding up a Prince Albert coat, nineteen indigent colored men, and a truck owner who would haul them all up to the farm.

Sudsy was pleased. He had gotten the coat from a friendly undertaker for nothing; and since he had thus saved the two dollars Willie had given him, he felt entitled to spend it on beer.

But Johnny Tirandelli found him; and thus it was that Johnny Tirandelli — who managed Daisy Diamond, middleweight contender, and who spoke in terms of a *hundred* dollars — made a deal with Sudsy McGuire and assigned Sudsy McGuire a task in event of emergency.

The deal between Sudsy McGuire and Johnny Tirandelli was closed, ironically, at the exact moment that Refugee Smith climbed into the ring of the sweltering training shed and gazed happily down at the faces of nineteen apathetic gentlemen of his race, who had come up to listen to him on promise of a gallery ticket to his fight.

Beaming, clad in wool pants, high collar, and Prince Albert coat, Refugee allowed that he was going to preach on "true frenship and prayer." His voice was husky with emotion.

As the fighter swung into his work, Willie Wurtzel watched anxiously for any sign of moisture on that black and shinning brow. But among Refugee's other listeners there was a quickening of interest from another source.

Refugee Smith was giving them everything he had. He recounted in graphic pungent phrases his own experience of jumping from a river boat thinking he'd killed a man in a dice game, and swimming until he could swim no more, and praying until he could pray no more, and finally of vowing to give his life to the ministry if he was saved.

". . . and the Lord sent Mister Willie and Mister Willie pulled me out. And the Lord was in my corner the first time I fit and I smote the man down. And ever after the Lord and Mister Willie has been in my corner and whilst I has learnt to box some better . . ."

The truck driver standing beside Willie Wurtzel leaned over. "Pal," he said, "is that there the real McCoy?"

Willie Wurtzel looked up. "Yeah," he said. "I'd got in a little argument and they was fixin' to go over me so I run down and jumped in a boat and I rowed out in the river and found that boy and I've had him ever since."

And Refugee Smith just then, for the first time, struck audible spiritual pay-dirt. A small brown man, at the rear of Refugee's sparse audience gave in. "Amen!" he chanted.

Refugee walked to the edge of the ring and took the top rope in his hands, hunched his shoulders in his black coat and gave. And Willie Wurtzel, watching tensely, grinned.

A single drop of sweat rolled down Refugee Smith's blunt nose, teetered there a moment, then dropped. And as if by signal, prearranged, the fattest sleepiest member of Refugee's audience shook the rafters with a fervent "Hallelujah!"

Willie Wurtzel walked out of the barn and to the house. Sitting there on the porch, two hours later, he heard the booming, heart-tightening strains of *Onward Christian Soldiers* sung by men of voice who were at that moment, anyway, willing to man the front line trenches in that army.

The next morning at eleven o'clock a gaunt, thirsty and happy Refugee Smith weighed in for his fight that night. He weighed one fifty-nine and three-quarters.

**WILLIE WURTZEL** leaned over, felt Refugee's gloves, patted him once on the shoulder and said: "What about it?"

Refugee Smith grinned. "I feels frisky," Refugee said. "That eatin' and drinkin' you lemme do done cured me up. I feels hostile."

"All right," Willie said. "This Daisy is very good. He'll box you daffy; but crowd, bull him around, lean on him, rassle him, and hit him in the belly. I'll tell you when to go to work on his head."

Sudsy McGuire busied himself with his bottles and towels, not looking up. Sudsy felt a little poorly. He hoped fervently that Daisy would box this colored boy silly and he wouldn't have to do what he knew now, looking across at Johnny Tirandelli in Daisy's corner, that he might have to do.

Johnny Tirandelli looked very grim; and sitting at the ringside under Daisy's corner were two other characters who looked as if they kind of hoped Sudsy would try to cross Johnny Tirandelli because he was such a round little man and so easy to hit with something, like say a bullet.

The bell broke his thought.

Daisy Diamond was a good fighter. A good boxer; fast, smart, strong. He bewildered Refugee for a couple of rounds, stabbing him, marking his right eye; but Refugee Smith bulled in and he got a couple of shots at Daisy under the heart and Daisy moved a little slower there-after.

Willie Wurtzel was pleased. In the minute between the fourth and fifth round, he asked Refugee again: "What about it, boy?"

"I'm getting' my second wind," Refugee said. "I feels right coltish."

"Has he hurt you?"

"Nawsir. But I'm fixin' to hurt him."

"Go on like you been goin'," Willie said. "There's six more rounds."

Sudsy scrambled down with Willie at the bell. "That smoke is bull-strong," he said a little nervously, "but Daisy stabbin' him silly."

Willie Wurtzel grinned.

Sudsy McGuire reached back and fingered the small clean towel in his hip pocket, and he looked up to see the black man crowd Daisy to the ropes, take a jarring hook on the chin but still ram home both hands solidly to the white man's body.

Daisy Diamond's mouth flew open and he boxed his way out to the center of the ring through sheer instinct. The black man followed him stolidly. Sudsy McGuire stole a glance at Daisy's corner and Johnny Tirandelli nodded emphatically. The bell found Daisy walking to the wrong corner.

Willie Wurtzel leaned down. "Okay, boy," he said. "Come up."

Refugee Smith leaned back, and let Sudsy wipe his face and expertly close a cut. He straightened up a little with the ten-second buzzer; and Sudsy McGuire reached into his hip pocket with trembling hands, bent over and unfolded the towel, then drew it quickly across Refugee Smith's eyes.

The bell rang. Sudsy McGuire was half-way up the aisle.

**REFUGEE SMITH** stood up and whimpered like a puppy. Both his hands were at his eyes and he was standing there, not moving.

Willie Wurtzel half jumped, half climbed to the ring apron, stood up and screamed something; but his scream was drowned by the bellow of the crowd as Daisy hurrying across swung his left, and pivoting, his right. Refugee was down.

Refugee Smith got his hands away from his eyes and the tears were streaming out of them and the muscles of his face and cheeks were twitching with the pain.

And then Willie Wurtzel — watching him, cursing the referee, Sudsy, and the man who discovered pepper — saw Refugee start moving his lips; and Willie Wurtzel knew what he was saying.

". . . the rat knocked the cat down but the cat did not get up until he heard the man say nine . . ."

Refugee Smith climbed to his feet. He was trying now to keep his eyes open, and part of the time he was successful. He still moved his lips. ". . . the rat was a hooker but the cat held his left paw out and kept his left shoulder up hiding his chin . . ."

Daisy Diamond set himself, feinted needlessly and slammed his right glove deep into Refugee's body. As Refugee's hands came down involuntarily Daisy dropped him with a whistling left hook.

Refugee Smith took "nine."

Willie Wurtzel was screaming. "Grab him, grab him!"

Refugee moved down along the ring holding to the top rope with one glove, and Daisy Diamond came in. Then — above the screams of Willie Wurtzel, above the feminine screams to stop the fight — from the highest gallery came nineteen male voices in one concerted reverberating, full-throated expression of militant hope.

The members of Refugee Smith's first congregation were pulling all the stops. *"Onward Christian soldiers, marching as to war . . ."*

Refugee Smith turned, and with both arms wide out lunged. He caught Daisy Diamond around the waist, and his rush carried them both to the opposite ropes.

Then Refugee started moving. Holing, pushing, taking blows, fighting against the referee's efforts to make him break, he worked Daisy Diamond into a corner.

Refugee Smith got his legs wide apart, pulled back his hands and started swinging.

*. . . going on before . . .* Daisy went into his shell, ducked, and tried to butt his way out. Refugee brought him up, blood spurting from his nose, held him a moment, pushed him back into the corner and let go with both hands for where he thought Daisy Diamond's jaw ought to be; and this time it was there.

**REFUGEE SMITH'S** congregation was still singing when Willie Wurtzel led him up the aisle behind the men who were carrying Daisy Diamond. "I'll kill Sudsy, boy. I'll cut his heart out. We'll get that pepper out of your eyes soon as we get to the dressing room. And I promise you I'll kill Sudsy for you. He'll never do—"

Refugee Smith gripped Willie Wurtzel's arm.

"No," he said, "don't do that. We'll find him some time. I allow he's a real hard case."

He gripped Willie's arm a little harder. "I craves," Refugee Smith said, "to prove myself, and the way I aims to prove myself is to lead him up to Grace."

And suddenly it seemed that every one in the big hall was singing and the singing could be heard a long way off. Three blocks, anyway; because Sudsy McGuire, waddling as swiftly as he could up a side street, heard it; and his flabby face twitched.

Then there were footsteps. Sudsy darted up the steps, tugged at the door and was inside. Only the candles were there for light and he was alone. And still he heard the singing.

Carefully he bent over and took off his shoe. Then he took the new hundred-dollar bill and went over to the mite box. When he came out of the church he felt good. It was fine not to be afraid of footsteps in the dark.

It was good.

He turned and headed back toward the Coliseum.

---

# THE DIVINE RIGHT

**Presenting again that peerless fighter with a conscience, Refugee Smith. The text for today is this: As David swung his slingshot so shall ye swing the right that is divine!**

"**HI, LOOK!** Hiiii, lookee lookee!" the man on the platform chanted, beating on a cowbell with a stick. "Lookee lookee lookee."

Refugee Smith tucked his recently won porcelain cat under one arm, and put his pennant — emblazoned in gold letters *Excuse My Dust* — in his pocket and looked. "Hurry! Hurryhurryhurry!" the man shouted beating on his cowbell.

Refugee obediently quickened his step, walking down the midway toward the tent with leopard-skinned supermen painted on its front under the faded legend: *Athletic Arena*.

Most of the people along the carnival midway were stopping in front of the tent now and two men had appeared on the platform on either side of the barker, who had laid his cowbell down and had picked up a sheaf of dollar bills which he was waving.

The two men beside the barker bore scant resemblance to the pictures above them or to each other, one being short, wide and blond with the thick neck and gnarled ears of a wrestler; the other a slack-muscled Latin, his face laced with scar tissue.

The barker laid down the money, freeing both his hands of his harangue, and gave tongue. Refugee caught part of it.

". . .Have you got a rassler down there? If you have, here's his chance." He pointed to the wide

- 14 -

blond man beside him. "This here is Ole Olson, the Scandinavian Scourge. If there is a rassler down there that can stay fifteen minutes with the Scourge without his shoulders bein' pinned — with your own referee officiatin' — I'll give him fifteen dollars. A dollar a minute, folks. That ain't hay."

The Scandinavian Scourge flexed his impressive muscles and sneered good-humoredly. The barker turned to the other man on the platform. "And this is One-round Scinelli, folks. If there is a fighter down there that can stay four three-minute rounds with One-round without gettin' knocked out, we'll give *him* fifteen dollars. A dollar and a quarter a minute, folks. Easy money."

Refugee Smith nodded his head in agreement. It would be easy money. Mr. One-round, judging by his face and general appearance, was what Mr. Willie would call a round heeled bum. Refugee Smith sighed. He sure wished Mr. Willie hadn't told him not to tell anyone who he was; for fifteen dollars was a month's wages chopping cotton.

The barker was holding a brief consultation with a large party in sweat stained overalls who had climbed up on the platform.

Of course, Refugee reasoned he didn't have to tell anybody who he was and it really ought to give these people a thrill to see a real fighter who was going to fight two nights from now in Madison Square Garden. He could just tell them his name was Smith. Lots of people, black and white, were named Smith.

Refugee sighed again and remembered Mr. Willie's stern admonitions and tried to dismiss the whole thing from his mind. He looked back at the platform — still eager.

The large gentleman in the overalls had accepted the challenge of the wrestler. The barker turned to the crowd. "You all know this man, folks. Pete Perkins, your local blacksmith; and a brawny man is he. If the Scourge don't pin him in fifteen minutes he gets fifteen dollars."

Refugee couldn't keep his eyes off of One-round Scinelli. He knew One-round couldn't hurt him in four rounds. He turned and cast his eyes over the crowd. There was a little knot of colored folks on the outer rim. They were looking at him, at his loud jacket and his white shoes.

Refugee felt his chest swelling. A brown-skinned girl in a purple hat smiled a shy smile.

". . . Now ain't there a fighter out there? Ain't there anybody out there that thinks he is proficient in the manly art of self defense? Ain't there anybody at all in Hyattsville that needs fifteen dollars? Ain't there. . ."

**IN THE** parlor of a farmhouse in the hills above Hyattsville, Willie Wurtzel was entertaining those members of the press who had come up to see Refugee Smith, middleweight contender and erstwhile roustabout, in his last full workout before his debut in Madison Square Garden two nights later.

When Willie Wurtzel stood up to replenish a couple of glasses, it could be seen that Willie's torso had a prosperous bulge to it, a bulge that would doubtless have been still greater had not Willie been lashed across the front with a double-breasted waistcoat. This garment had a hue and quality that would tab Willie Wurtzel the length and breadth of West Forty-ninth Street as a fight manager: One with a fighter who not only could fight but could do so in a manner that people would pay to see.

When Willie Wurtzel sat down, he picked up his monologue where he had left off.

"Sam Langford was before my day," he said, "but this boy must be a carbon copy. The Black Blitzkrieg, that's what they called him in Denver. In St. Louis he climbs in the ring without never havin' a glove on in his life and stops Western Mahoney in two. He beats Sammy Stein just a month ago in Pittsburgh in the third. . . ."

One of the reporters interrupted Willie. "This afternoon he looked fair. Maybe he can fight. But anyway it goes, you've done a wonderful job on the boy. That story about finding him in the middle of the river and how he thinks the Lord is in his corner because you saved him from drowning; that's wonderful stuff. And you handled it just right."

Willie Wurtzel was hurtly silent for a moment. "Yes," he said coolly. "But that's not what I'm talkin' about."

His voice began to regain some of its fervency. "We been up here workin' for three weeks. Nobody knows where we are until you come up today. Now, today, you see Refugee box the last time before the fight and you can see he is sharp as a razor. And," he said disgustedly, "you say he looks *fair*. Why —"

"Frankie Boomer isn't a sparring partner," one of the reporters pointed out, "nor yet a Sammy Stein. He is about the smoothest middleweight around. I think your eight ball is in for a bad night."

"He's done everything I asked him," Willie said. "He's won all his fights. He'll take Frankie. He's got a sweet a left hook as. . ."

**TEMPTATION** in the form of a shill sidled up to Refugee's side, nudged him in the ribs. "Why don't you get up there, boy?" the shill said. "You'd be pretty proud of yourself if you won that fifteen dollars, wouldn't you?"

"Dat's sinful pride," Refugee said weakly.

The shill took a cautious glance over his shoulder. "That gal in the purple hat is watchin' you mightiy close," he said craftily.

"I oughta go home," Refugee said uncertainly. "I oughta go home right now."

"It won't take but a little while," the shill said. "Ain't you got any pride at all? That gal'll think you're scared."

"I'll bet that big colored fellow down there ain't afraid to get up here," the barker taunted studiedly from his platform. The shill gave Refugee a little push.

"You don't have to shove me, white boy," Refugee said.

"Here he comes," the barker shouted triumphantly.

Refugee was on the platform now, look-down at the excited faces before him. Out of the corner of his eye he saw the admiration in the faces of the colored folks out at the edge of the crowd. He banished his last twinge of conscience and grinned down at them cockily.

Two more figures appeared on the platform from inside the tent: Pete Perkins, grinning self-consciously in ill-fitting tights, and the Scourge.

"In a minute," the barker shouted, "we are goin' into the tent. These two boys are gonna fight four rounds or less." He made a gesture that took in Refugee and the carnival boxer. "And these two are gonna rassle fifteen minutes or less. These two big matches can be witnessed for the price of one. One quarter of a dollar, a lousy, measly, two bits, folks."

The barker continued in this vein for a few minutes more, then moved over to the ticket booth. At his direction, the four men moved into the tent.

"It would seem to me," one of the reporters said, "that your dark angel should be in bed by now." The reporter looked at his watch.

"He'll be in in a minute," Willie Wurtzel said uneasily. "I let him go down to the village. A carnival made a pitch down there this afternoon. I wanted him to get his mind off the fight."

"You let him run around loose?"

"I can trust him," Willie said.

Refugee Smith climbed into the ring in the tent and looked across at One-round Scinelli. Refugee was a little worried. His hands weren't taped like Mr. Willie always taped them and the gloves were old with uneven padding in them.

And he just didn't feel right. Pride had got him in here, sinful pride. He couldn't expect the Lord to be in his corner tonight, though from the looks of his opponent, he surely wouldn't need any help.

Still, he wished at least Mr. Willie was in his corner. "Lord," Refugee muttered placatingly under his breath, "all I ask is dat You don't pay no heed to this fight one way or the otheh."

**WILLIE WURTZEL** heard the buzz of the crowd up in the Garden and it sounded like capacity. But he was troubled. He threw down a half-chewed cigar, took another from his pocket.

His fighter lay before him on the rubbing table, his lean black length honed to a razor edge of fitness. But there was something the matter. Refugee Smith acted funny. Willie talked, forcing confidence into his voice.

"There's sinners up there, boy," he said, "lots of 'em. You got to go tonight, boy. You ain't fought anybody as tough as this Frankie; you'll take him all right. You gotta take him. You gotta remember your duty up here in the Garden."

Refugee Smith lay on his back. A heavy frown creased his brow. He didn't answer. "I guess it's kind of got to you, this bein' in the Garden," Willie went on half to himself, "because you sure have been actin' funny the last coupla days. But it's just another fight. You know what to do. It won't be like it used to be before you learned how to fight. It's just another fight."

Willie Wurtzel looked at his watch. "Gimme your hand," he said, picking up length of gauze and putting his tape nearby.

Refugee Smith crossed his right hand over his chest and gave it to his manager.

"Naw," Willie said, not looking up, "the other one." He reached over and took the colored boy's left hand. Suddenly he looked up. Refugee winced.

Willie Wurtzel felt his heart stop beating and then bound on heavily. He fingered the hand gingerly. "How?" he asked in a half whisper, letting his breath go out in a long sibilant sigh, seeing all his hopes and plans dissolving before him.

Refugee Smith looked at him, his eyes wet. "I was afraid you'd be mad," he said in classic understatement. "But I got the fifteen dollahs an' I don't want none for myself, not none of it."

Willie Wurtzel walked over and listened a second at the door of the dressing room, then bolted it and walked back. "Whatcha talkin' about?"

"I boxed de man at de carnival you lemme go to an' I neveh tol' 'em who I was an' I knocked de man out an' dey gimme de fifteen dollahs. I got hit all. De gloves was kinda old and when I hit Mr. One-round wid my left han' he didn't get up but hit hurt my hand most powerful an' I was afraid to tell you. I thought maybe de misery would go outen hit befo' tonight."

"You fool," Willie said, helplessness strangling his voice, "it's broke! You gotta broke metacarpal bone." He reached into his little bag and took out a hypodermic syringe and picked up the hand.

"We can't call it off now," he said. When he replaced the needle in the bag he added tonelessly, "Keep him from findin' out about it as long as you can but don't hit him with it."

Refugee Smith tried to summon a grin. "If I nevah know whose han' dat was," he said as the anaesthetic took effect, "I would swear hit warn't mine, 'cause hit sure is dead."

"That's ain't all about you that's dead," Willie said in a flat voice.

There was pounding on the door and Willie picked up his bag. He pointed to the door, not able to speak.

**FRANKIE BOOMER** was a pale ghost that Refugee couldn't find. His hand was coming to life, now, and it hurt. He hadn't tried to use it; but just holding it out, feinting with it had got it hit. It hurt but that hurt was not the worst. The voice of the crowd hurt Refugee Smith the most.

Frankie Boomer went around him like a cooper around a barrel and Refugee was bleeding from above one eye and his mouth was cut. But the cries of the crowd cut deeper. The Lord wasn't in his corner and the crowd knew it. "Knock his halo off!"

"Kill the eight ball!"

"Slug him one for the heathen, Frankie!"

Willie Wurtzel leaned down at the end of the third round. "Don't go out with the bell, boy. Don't go out."

Refugee Smith tasted the salty taste of his own blood, "you mean quit, Mr. Willie?"

"Yeah."

"I can't do dat, Mr. Willie."

"He'll just cut you to pieces."

Refugee Smith looked down at the floor. "Lord," he muttered to himself, "I done sinned a double header. I sinned when I let my sinful pride get me in dat ring wid One-roun', an' I sinned when I neveh tol' Mr. Willie about my han' but I guess you know dat, Lord, 'cause You an' Mr. Boomeh are sure punishin' me."

The bell for the fourth round sounded and Refugee climbed to his feet and walked out to his punishment.

Frankie Boomer came in behind a long left hand, moving smoothly, and flicked Refugee's flat nose, clubbed a right to his belly and moved away. Refugee pawed the air with his left hand and moved in trying to find an opening for his right. Boomer tied him up, laughing. After a while the bell sounded.

Refugee Smith came back to his stool. Willie cleaned his face, whispering, his voice laced with pity: "Don't go out, boy. Don't go out."

Refugee Smith put his two gloves together in front of him, shut his ears to the voice of the crowd and in a whisper of resigned humility asked: "Lord, just don't pay no 'tention to me. But Lord, Mr. Willie ain't done nothin'. You know dat, Lord."

Willie Wurtzel, listening, felt his throat go tight.

"... He fed me whenst I'se hungry, teached me to box, an' ..."

Refugee Smith went out with the bell; and Willie Wurtzel, activated by long habit, gathered his stuff and scrambled from the ring. He looked up, watched Frankie Boomer spear Refugee's bad eye with a long left and move away.

Frankie stabbed the colored boy again, pulling his head back out of range as he struck. Refugee's frantic right whistled through the air in front of Frankie's face.

One of the reporters who had been up at Refugee's camp called to Willie. "Why don't you quote him a little scripture, Willie?"

Willie heard him, watching Frankie Boomer hit Refugee with a left lead and pull his head back. And suddenly Willie Wurtzel's face changed. He cast deep into his boyhood memories.

The bell rang.

**WILLIE WURTZEL** climbed into the ring. He rubbed the blood from Refugee's face, leaned down and closed his eyes in the effort of concentration. *The God of my rock; in him I will trust; He is my shield, and the horn of my salvation, my high tower, and my refuge ... Thou savest me from violence."*

Refugee Smith wheeled on his stool. "Dat's de Word," he said. "Dat's straight from de Book."

Willie Wurtzel looked at the light in the colored boy's eye and racked his brain. *He brought me forth also into a large place: He delivered me, because He delighted in me.*

"Dat's me!" Refugee exclaimed. "Dis here is de 'large place'."

*He teacheth my hands to war; so that a bow of steel is broken by mine arms.* Willie Wurtzel quoted from desperate memory.

Refugee Smith took a deep breath. His eyes under his bloody brows were bright.

Willie gave once more, freehand. "When he leads his left, swing your right a *foot behind* his head, boy. With all your might. As David swung his slingshot so shall ye swing the right that is divine!"

The bell sounded.

It was a sucker punch, winging from some place near the floor; going around Frankie Boomer's neck. But Frankie Boomer, careless with confidence, drew his head back heedlessly as he had drawn it back all night. He drew it back a foot.

Refugee Smith heard the drone of the referee's count; he felt his left hand, a red hot agony, jump with pain with every beat of his heart. But he didn't hear the crowd. The jeers of the crowd were stilled: suddenly, profoundly.

He was walking slowly to his own corner, his hands at his sides with the palms of his gloves turned forward; and under the ring lights his eyes shone white as they stared into the upper reaches of the great amphitheater filled with the gallery gods now silent.

His back was to the referee and he heard the count reach *eight* over his stricken opponent; and he heard no sound of movement of the canvas of the ring.

"Lord," Refugee said through battered lips, "much obliged."

Down under the apron of the ring Willie Wurtzel watched his fighter. Suddenly he heard a voice muttering. It was his own voice.

"Lord," Willie Wurtzel said, "if I did wrong, forgive me." He paused a moment hearing the roar of the crowd as the referee reached *ten*. Then as he scrambled into the ring, he added:

"If I misquoted, Lord, please forgive me for that, too."

# RETURN OF THE NAIVE

**WILLIE WURTZEL** squinted his beady black eyes into the darkness of the house away from the ring lights. Up in the ring Refugee Smith, leading middleweight contender, was giving a benevolent boxing lesson to a local hope.

Willie Wurtzel had come upon Refugee Smith in the long ago, in the time that "mighty atom" was a sportswriter's synonym for a classy bantamweight. But Refugee Smith was very young then, and he seemed as ageless as Joe Palooka — perhaps because Refugee had an abiding faith in the Lord and kept in shape.

The bell rang signaling the end of the third round and Willie clambered up in the ring as his fighter came back to the corner. Refugee was breathing easily; in fact more easily than Willie. Willie was suffering from asthma and prosperity and as a result was somewhat short winded.

Willie wiped his fighter's face off, handed him a water bottle. "Jeest," Willie said. "This River City is a good fight town. The joint's strictly S. R. O."

Refugee gargled some water, stretched two long muscled cabled black arms out on the ropes and grinned. "This Mr. Shorty ain't suchamuch as a fighter," he said. "Seem like his feet ain't in touch wid his haid."

"There's eight thousand people in this joint if there's a quorum for a crap game," Willie Wurtzel said. "And we're cuttin' thirty seven and a half percent of the gross take."

"Shouldst I let him have hit this roun', Mr. Willie?" Refugee asked. "Ain't any use of him gettin' hisself scarred up."

"Any time," Willie said. He peered out into the darkness. "Everybody's in this hall can get in."

"Okay, Mr. Willie," Refugee said as he heard the ten second warning buzzer, "I'll turn his damper down."

Willie Wurtzel turned and watched. Even the exciting and satisfying pastime of counting a packed house couldn't compete with watching a real workman work at his trade.

Refugee Smith, a hundred and fifty nine pounds of somnolent black efficiency advanced with the bell. His chin was cuddled behind his left shoulder and his right hand moved in aimless circles though his right elbow, close against his side, didn't move.

Shorty Rowan, the class of River City, came to meet him. Refugee twitched his right hand in a feint, jabbed with his left for the head, and as the punch started, Refugee dropped his shoulder and the left became a left hook for the belly.

It landed. Shorty Rowan dropped a tardy guard with a painted grunt just as Refugee put the big muscles of his back into a right cross. Refugee came back to his corner.

"Mr. Willie," he said, "what does S. R. O. mean?" Willie Wurtzel scuffled his way into the ring, looked up at Refugee, grinning. "As I was usin' it," he said, "it means standing room only. For Mr. Shorty, as you call him, it means sleep right on."

**GABRIEL EINSTEIN** is the fight promoter in River City and in common with another of the same name — though no relation — Gabriel had a facility with figures. "Okay, Wurtsburger," Gabe said the next morning. "thirty seven and a half percent of the gross. Here's your check."

"Wurtzel," Willie said automatically, not interested in his own name so much as the check he was reaching for. He looked at the check; his face darkened.

"Wurtzel!" he screamed. "My name is Wurtzel, and how the hell do you get this way?"

Gabe looked at Willie, took a cigar out of a box on his desk. "I made it out to Wurtzel," he said.

"Yes you did," Willie screeched. "For twenty two hundred and eight dollars!"

"That's right."

"Right! Why you, you dirty double crosser, you scaled the house from five dollars to fifty cents and you had better'n eight thousand people in there and you tell me two yards two gees is thirty seven 'n a half percent."

Gabriel Einstein leaned back in his chair, his face bland and untroubled. "Now, now. Keep calm. We have a lot of passes we have to give out, there's the workin' press, politicians. . . ."

"You're tellin' me!" Willie cut him off. "I been managin' fighters for twenty-five years. I know how much paper goes into a house. . . ."

G. Einstein lit his cigar, took a couple of tentative connoisseurish puffs. "Have a cigar, Wurtsheimer. If you think I'd cheat you, why didn't you put a checker on the gate?"

Willie's face turned a slightly darker shade of purple. "Wurtzel! Wurtzel! Wurtzel!" He screamed. Then, honestly, he answered the query. "I didn't know anybody I could trust in this town," he said.

The upshot of the whole thing was, as the upshot of all such matters are, that Willie Wurtzel got his check for twenty two hundred and eight dollars and not a thin dime more. Panting and hoarse he stamped out of Gabe Einstein's office, down the hall and out onto the street. There he caught a cab, went by and cashed the check, then down to Refugee Smith's hotel.

He found Refugee snoozing in his room. He shook him awake. "Let's get packed, boy," he said in a thick whisper, "we gotta be in Denver tomorrow night."

Refugee got up, grinned, stretched. "I kinda likes this fightin' ever' week," he said. "I loves to ride them railroad cars." He paused, yawned. "'Specially on de cushions," he said.

"Well," Willie said, "I figure we might just as well barnstorm acrost the country, make some money and keep you in shape."

"Okay, Mr. Willie," Refugee said. "I trusts you to do de right thing."

"Well I done a wrong thing in this town."

"Speak fuller."

"I got us beat out of some money. I don't have a checker on the gate and the promoter cheated us."

"Cheated you, Mr. Willie?" Refugee asked.

"Yes, me," Willie said bitterly. "But," he added, "I got a memory long as a country clothes line on stuff like that and there'll come a day."

"Don't carry no malice in your heart, Mr. Willie," Refugee said gravely, "De Lord will take care of de righteous."

"I ain't carryin' no malice in my heart," Willie Wurtzel said, "I'm carryin' it in my pocketbook. And the Lord needn't bother about this matter if I ever get a chance I'll take care of it myself."

In Denver Refugee Smith won in three from a good tough boy. He compassionately outboxed an old trial horse in Los Angeles, stopped a loud mouthed youngster in the first round in Frisco. That was the last fight Willie had scheduled and it was the morning after that fight that Willie got the wire from G. Einstein.

G. Einstein offered Refugee Smith a fight. He offered twenty five hundred dollars or thirty seven and a half percent of the gross gate receipts. The fight to be scheduled a month from even date, opponent not yet selected.

Willie Wurtzel, to whom the wire came, read it carefully. Then he sought out Refugee and read it to him. "I guess us won't take hit will we Mr. Willie," Refugee said. "You is mad at Mr. Einstein, ain't you?"

"I ain't mad at anybody twenty five hundred dollars worth," Willie said.

"Then us'll take hit?"

"I'll try to lift him five hundred," Willie said, "and take a guarantee."

"I don't want to tell you nothin' about managerin', but don't you think dat'n if you took de percent this time, Mr. Einstein would be honest wid you?" Refugee asked.

Willie Wurtzel looked at his charge pityingly. "That Gabe'd steal your vest if you took off your coat."

"Dat's hit," Refugee said. "De Good Book say, do they steal your overcoat don't say 'whoa up' when they reach for your jumper."

"I don't know no book teaches you how to manage a prize-fighter," Willie said. "In that business it's dog eat dog."

"Okay, Mr. Willie," Refugee said. "I was just tryin' to help."

Willie Wurtzel smiled a knowing and superior smile. "Ref, boy," he said. "If we get three thousand for the fight and he fills his hall, why still we'll be getting' a shade better'n thirty seven and a half percent of the gate."

"Maybe he never cheated you last time, Mr. Willie."

"Maybe the sheep will kill the butcher," Willie said. He paused a moment. "You so strong for the percentage, how about you takin' eighteen and three quarters of the gate for your share?"

"I don't unnerstan, Mr. Willie."

"Well, we split right down the middle. I take half and you take half. And half of thirty seven and a half percent is eighteen and three quarters percent. If we took the percentage that'd be what you got."

"Okay, Mr. Willie, I'll do dat, an' I leave de fixin' to you."

Willie Wurtzel went downstairs and sent a lengthy wire, collect. In it he asked for a three thousand dollar guarantee.

To Willie's acute dismay Gabriel Einstein wired a prompt acceptance to this proposition, and named Refugee's opponent as one Whitey Welch. Under separate cover, Gabe informed him, he was sending the contracts for Willie's signature.

Willie dismissed the matter from his mind, took Refugee to Portland where he picked up a small purse by disposing of an ambitious lad of that region, and three weeks later they rolled into River City.

There Willie found Gabriel Einstein had beat the drum with consummate skill. Whitey Welch was particularly impressive in his work-outs and the papers had heralded this fact. Refugee off of his last showing was a prime favorite and Gabriel had the papers full of prominent men picking the winner.

The night of the fight the big Convention Hall was full. Willie ran a practiced eye over the house coming down the aisle behind his fighter. In the ring he leaned down. "Ref, boy," he said. "You takin' a percentage, you'll do pretty near as good as I will at that. The joint's sold out again."

Refugee Smith didn't look up. His mind was on the business at hand and he went out for the referee's instructions with a little frown on his face. In the center of the ring Willie Wurtzel looked up and examined Whitey Welch closely for the first time. He let out a scream. "That guy's a light heavyweight," he said. "And. . . ."

"Pipe down," the referee said. "It's an over-the-weight bout. You know that."

"I didn't sign to fight no Blondy Bellows, a damn good light-heavy," Willie said, looking closely, "and that's who this guy is."

"He's Whitey Welch to me," the referee said, "and he can come in over the weight."

"Hell, he weighs one eighty if he weighs an ounce," Willie Wurtzel said. "My boy was signed to fight a local middleweight."

"Well, he'll fight here tonight or I'll have him barred in every state in the country," the referee said.

"Oh," Willie Wurtzel said, "so they got you fixed, too, along with the scales. This guy is a ringer."

"Go back to your corner," the referee said, "and come out fightin'."

Refugee Smith turned around and walked back to his corner, shrugging out of his bathrobe. Willie followed him, still screaming.

"Watch out, Ref, boy, watch out! There's some kind of coop here. There's been a lot of money bet that this guy stays or somethin', watch out for tricks."

Refugee Smith looked up and his face was set like black jade. "They tryin' to do you a unfair thing, Mr. Willie?"

"No, no. It's you. It's me, too. But it's you I'm worryin' about."

"Don't worry about me, Mr. Willie. I'll show that big man a trick he don't know nothin' about."

The bell rang.

Refugee Smith walked out to the center of the ring, both hands dangling from his sides. Blondy Bellows, almost a head taller came after him. Refugee backed up, backed up, backed into a corner of the ring; Blondy came in after him. Refugee leaped, grabbed him like a wrestler and threw him, spun Blondy Bellows to the right, rolled him down the ropes one full revolution with the fury of his shoving, wrestling spin. And when Blondy Bellows, dizzy, upset, confused, came out of his turn, facing the ring, two big black cannons exploded in his face. He didn't even try to get up, though it took the referee fifteen seconds to count ten.

Willie Wurtzel walked into Gabriel Einstein's office the next morning. "Okay," he said. "Let's have the money. Three grand," he added grimly.

"I'm sorry about last night," Gabriel Einstein said, "I signed the guy in good faith, I never knew." He handed Willie the check.

"You didn't know the referee was fixed either, I guess?" Willie said sarcastically.

"No," Gabe said. "I didn't."

"Well," Willie said. "The fight's over now and it come out all right. I'll believe you." He started for the door. "Oh, there's one more thing. What was in last night?"

Gabe looked up. "I offered you a percentage," he said. "I know, I know. . . ."

"We gross sixteen, five 0 six," Gabriel Einstein said, looking at a slip of paper on his desk.

Willie Wurtzel gulped. "Sixteen thousand!"

"Yeah, I doubled the scale of prices, you know. Your boy is very popular in this town."

Willie Wurtzel slumped to a chair. "Oh," he groaned. "I gotta pay my boy eighteen and three quarters of the gross. I made a separate deal with him. It'll cost me money outta my pocket."

Gabriel Einstein smiled an oily smile. "Listen," he said. "You didn't know I doubled the prices, he wouldn't know, surely. They say he can hardly read." He paused. "Why don't you just keep your mouth shut."

Willie Wurtzel got up slowly. "You mean you want I should cheat my boy?" he asked softly.

"Well, not; well. . . ."

That was as far as Gabriel Einstein got. Willie Wurtzel rose from his chair and as he rose he took off his coat.

**WILLIE WURTZEL** came into Refugee's hotel room, made his way to a chair and slumped into it. "Boy," he said, "you were right about the percentage, they doubled the admission and you made over three thousand dollars for yourself last night."

Refugee looked up, looked again. "Gee whiz, Mr. Willie what happened to you? Look like you haided off'n accident for sure."

"That Einstein made a crack I didn't like and I tried that trick on him you used on that tow-headed ringer last night."

Refugee grinned. "Did he spin, Mr. Willie? I learnt dat trick fightin' them tough roustabouts up an' down de Mississippi in de old days before I seen de light."

"He spun fine," Willie said, "but I forgot what to do then." Willie lifted a battered misshapen face. "You know," he added, "that guy would have whipped me if I hadn't beat him to the paperweight. But anyway," he finished, "I did beat him and I figure him and me are even now."

"Don't worry about de money, Mr. Willie," Refugee said, seeking balm for his manager's wounds. "Us splits de money, come what ever."

"Listen," Willie Wurtzel said harshly, "you get the money, see? Just like we agreed. I don't want to have no trouble with you."

"Okay, Mr. Willie. I was just tryin' to ease you a mite." Willie didn't answer and a sly grin came over Refugee's black face. "I see you done one right thing," he added.

"What's that?"

"Mr. Willie," Refugee said innocently, "goin' from your looks I would say dat for one time you turned de other cheek."

# COMPLIMENTS OF R. SMITH

**Concerning a certain wonderful Christmas present such as never saw the inside of a stocking on land or sea.**

**THE SURF** doesn't roll against Jacobs Beach because Jacobs Beach is on West 49th Street and it isn't a beach at all. But it is the nerve center of the pugilism business and you can hear sounds there not unlike the sounds of the wild waves, for they are, in common with the surf, constant in pitch and largely unintelligible.

It is here, against this background of double negatives, double talk and double crosses, you might pick up, piece-meal, the story about the Christmas present Refugee Smith gave to Willie Wurtzel, his manager. But it would probably be garbled and so for your convenience I will give it to you straight.

**REFUGEE SMITH** is a coal-black baby. He's got hands like Dempsey and big, heavy, sloping shoulders and a lean waist and enormous feet. He is twenty-three years old and he can make one fifty-nine. He is a hell of a fighter, for he has, along with his natural equipment and the skill that Willie Wurtzel has imparted to him, an exclusive in the prize-fighting business, and that is backing of the Lord. At least that is Refugee's conception of the matter, and who can blame him? One minute he was a drowning crapshooter telling the Lord that if He saved him he would carry His word and the next minute he was in a boat with Willie Wurtzel. But that is another story.

It has been more than a year since Refugee Smith, gloves on his paws for the first time, was taking a beating in a four-round preliminary in St. Louis and was being told by Willie Wurtzel, crouched in his corner, that for a servant of the Lord to lose to a stumblebum would put the Lord in very bad repute in the St. Louis area. And so

Refugee Smith marched out in the next round, with his heart filled with faith and his gloves with dynamite, and to this day he hasn't lost a fight.

He has won twenty-two straight, as a matter of fact, and it is simply a matter of time, according to the experts, until Refugee Smith clears up the middleweight situation and inaugurates a one-champion rule in that much confused division.

But on the night of December 15th, this future problem had no place in Refugee's mind. Refugee was sitting in the Eatmor Fish and Chips establishment of Slippery Ellum, trying to think of what he would give Willie Wurtzel, his earthly deity, for Christmas.

Slippery was sitting in the booth with him and his own slightly lighter brow was creased in helpful concentration. "You can't give him no jewelry, no gewgaws," Slippery said, "'cause 'cordin' to you he's got a gang of that stuff."

"It's gotta be high class," Refugee said.

"No gewgaws, no jewelry, but high class," Slippery said.

Refugee Smith put his elbows on the table, hunched his big shoulders and hid his chin in his hands. "He's gotta ceegar case, he's gotta closet fulla clothes." He paused a moment. "Forty vests," he added, "all different."

"I wouldn't give him no vest," Slippery said.

"No, hit's gotta be a surprise," Refugee said.

"Whyn't you ask him what he wants?" Slippery said logically.

"Hit wouldn't be no surprise, then."

"Give him a box of ceegars."

"How'd you like to getta box of ceegars for Christmas?"

"I don't smoke 'em," Slippery said.

"Hit's a caution what to get him," Refugee said sadly.

"How much money have you got?" Slippery asked.

"Money," Refugee said, "is no objection."

"You can't hardly take him down to a store and have him ast Santy Claus what he wants," Slippery said.

"He'd catch on to dat," Refugee agreed. "He's sharp. Powerful sharp."

"Well," Slippery said, "be a little more pacific. How much money you got?"

"I gotta gang of hit," Refugee said. "More'n a hundred, more'n a thousand. Hit's in de bank."

"You'd spend it all?"

"Look at my clothes. Look at de shoes on my feets; an' socks. I never even had no socks till Mr. Willie pulled me outen de river." Refugee paused. "Money is no objection," he said again.

"Hmmm," Slippery grunted, "maybe you should get somebody to call him up that's voice he didn't know and ast him what he wants. They could say they was Santy Claus," he added in a burst of inspiration.

"I wonder whose voice he wouldn't know whose it was?" Refugee said, brightening.

"I dunno," Slippery said.

"He wouldn't know your'n," Refugee said.

"Santy Claus is from way up north," Slippery said. "I talk like from Montgomery, Alabama. He'd know I'se not Santy Claus."

"How do you know how Santy Claus talks?" Refugee asked.

"He must talk like a Yankee...."

"Santy Claus," Refugee said positively, "jus' *couldn't* be no Yankee."

"What's Mr. Willie's number?" Slippery asked.

Refugee Smith told him. He reached in his pocket and got out a nickel. "Here's for the call," he said.

**WILLIE WURTZEL** pulled himself out of bed, walked over and looked out of the window and saw the familiar sights of 49th and Broadway. He shucked himself out of his gay pajamas, went into the bathroom. He viewed his reflection in the mirror with disgust. He opened his mouth, looked at his tongue, rubbed his hand over his bald head. Shivering a little, he stepped into the shower, adjusted the water.

The telephone rang.

"Damn," Willie Wurtzel said. Then: "To hell with it."

The telephone kept on ringing. Willie picked up the phone.

"Hello," the voice said. "This Mister Willie Wurtzel?"

"Yeah," Willie snarled.

There was a pause. "This is Santy Claus," the voice said meekly.

Willie said things into the phone that would have melted a hole in a thick igloo. "I'll Santy Claus you," Willie finished. Then he added: "This Refugee?"

"No, sir!" the voice said. "This here is Santy Claus. An' iffen you been good you're gonna get what you wants for Christmas."

"No," Willie said, "you ain't Refugee." He lapsed into more profanity. The voice on the other end of the wire insisted deferentially that it was straight from the North Pole and was strictly Santy Claus in person. Esquire.

"All right, Santy," Willie shouted. "You got a pencil. Write this down. Okay, then. I want…."

Slippery sat back down in the booth.

"What'd he say?" Refugee asked.

"Mostly," Slippery said uneasily, "he cussed."

"Didn't he say he wanted somethin'?" Refugee asked.

"Yes," Slippery said reluctantly.

"What?"

"He said he wanted a brief case," Slippery said.

"We'll get him de fanciest brief case ever was," Refugee said. "What's a brief case?" he added.

"It's a little satchel, like," Slippery said sadly.

"Didn't he say what kind he wanted?" Refugee asked.

"Yes," Slippery said, "he said. But you can't give him that."

"Why not?"

"He said he wanted a black one," Slippery said. "He said he wanted a black one made out of my hide."

"Oh," Refugee said. He looked critically at Slippery. "How much hide would hit take?" he asked finally.

"Too much," Slippery said hastily.

"Didn't you tell him you was Santy Claus?"

"I told him."

"Then how come he knew you was dark folks?" Refugee asked accusingly.

"I dunno."

"Didn't he say nothin' else?"

"Yeah," Slippery said. "He said he wanted the winner of the second at Sunnyside Downs."

"What dat mean?" Refugee asked.

"Sunnyside Downs is a horse park down in Florida," Slippery said. "He meant he wanted who was gonna win the second race down there tomorrow."

"You mean he wants a hoss?" Refugee asked.

"No," Slippery said, "he means he wants to know who was gonna win the second race down there tomorrow, so he could bet on him."

"He couldn't mean dat," Refugee said, "'cause even Santy couldn't tell a man who was gonna win a hoss race."

"That's what he meant, all right," Slippery said.

"He couldn't," Refugee said. "He means he wants a hoss."

"What would he want with a hoss?" Slippery asked.

"He could ride him in de park," Refugee said. "When I'm runnin' in de park in the mornin' I see lotsa hosses."

"It don't seem right to me," Slippery said.

"Hit's right," Refugee said. "Could you go to buy dat hoss?"

Slippery got up and came back with a paper. He turned it to the well-thumbed racing section. "It's a cheap race," he said. "I reckon you could go to buy the hoss iffen you had plenty cash money and was there on the spot."

"What spot?" Refugee asked.

"The race track," Slippery said. "But that wantin' a hoss, that is kinda a sayin' like. I still don't think he wants no hoss, really, in the skin."

"Mr. Willie never say nothin' he don't mean," Refugee said positively. "But I couldn't go clear to Florida an' get dere tomorrow."

"Sure you could," Slippery said. "You could go down by plane."

"What you mean?"

"Plane," Slippery said. "You could fly down in a airplane."

"Uhuh!" Refugee said. "If de Lord had wanted me to fly he'd've gave me wings."

"If he hadn't've wanted you to fly, he would've not let 'em make no airplanes," Slippery said.

Refugee pondered this a moment. "I could go with you," Slippery said slyly. "You found out now what Mr. Willie wants. It's only fair you gets it for him. I could go along with you an' help you."

"How long's hit take to get down to Florida in a airplane?" Refugee asked.

"We could leave tomorrow mornin', get there tomorrow night, get the hoss and come back the next day. We could send the hoss back on a train. He'd be here easy by Christmas."

"Well … " Refugee began.

**IF YOU WILL** consult the chart on the second race, December 16, 1940, at Sunnyside Downs you will see that Deuces Wild won it, driving, by a head. In the Racing Form dated December 18, 1940, you will find a one-stick story to the effect that one Senate Ellum purchased Deuces Wild for the sum of one thousand dollars and shipped the horse north. And as is the expensive custom of race horses, Deuces Wild rode back north in the expensive ease of a baggage car. With him rode two very sleepy Negroes.

"Sure was lucky I could trade dem airplane tickets in for cash," Refugee said, "or us'd never got dis hoss back to New Yawk."

"That old Deucy hoss is a train-ridin' fool," Slippery said. "Look at him bat them eyes happylike."

"Le's take de blanket offen him an' look at him again," Refugee said. "Boy, he's a pretty hoss, for fair."

"Pretty nice that fellow give us the blanket with him," Slippery said.

"He's a wonderful present," Refugee said. "A real sure 'nough wonderful present."

**CHIEF FLYING CLOUD,** born Eddie Bernstein, was red hot in Boston. He was a stump of a man with short, heavy arms, a square chin and a pointed head that were all, apparently, completely impervious to punishment. In Boston they thought he could take Garcia and Overlin in one night, but Willie Wurtzel signed Refugee for him for Monday night, December 23rd, with no qualms whatever. Willie Wurtzel had as implicit faith in Refugee Smith as Refugee Smith had in the Lord.

He told Refugee as much as they were riding up to Boston on the train, "You can take this phony Indian," Willie said, "slick as an eel in a barrel of oil." He paused, chewed on his cigar a moment. "It's short notice," he went on, "but Addy Mann had Billy Johns signed for the Chief and Billy went and broke a hand in trainin'."

"Yes, suh," Refugee said abstractedly. "I ain't worryin' about de fight, Mr. Willie. I figures us can whup anybody needs to be whupped." Refugee peered out the window for a moment. Then, with casual uneasiness, he added: "Mr. Willie," he said, "you is a Jewish gent'man, ain't you?"

Willie Wurtzel looked up, surprised. His cigar just didn't fall out of his mouth. "I ain't no Swede," he said. "Listen here, Refugee, what's the matter with you?"

"Nothin'," Refugee said brightly, uneasily. "I was just wonderin'."

"Don't get to wonderin' too hard about nothin' but that Flyin' Cloud," Willie said, going back to his paper, "or he'll rain right on you."

There was a long silence. Refugee gazed out of the window. "Mr. Willie," he said finally, "does…." He lapsed into silence.

Willie Wurtzel looked up at his fighter. "What's eatin' you, Refugee?" he asked.

Refugee Smith's dark brow was creased with unhappy lines. "Nothin'," he lied unhappily.

**REFUGEE** wasn't right. He was in a corner, and Chief Flying Cloud was under his arms, and he had belted Refugee a couple that had hurt. Refugee boxed his way out of the corner, a look of pained preoccupation on his face. Somebody high in the gallery gave him a lusty South Boston bird. Refugee worked his way to the center of the ring, caught a roundhouse right and was holding on at the bell.

Willie Wurtzel was mad. "What the hell is this?" he said. "You act like you ain't woke up. Left-hand that boy, stay away from him…."

"Mr. Willie," Refugee said, "does Jewish folks go to church on Sunday?"

"Gee!" Willie Wurtzel almost screamed. The bell rang.

The Chief came in faster this round. Refugee hadn't hurt him.

Willie Wurtzel heard Addy Mann's voice in his ear. "I thought your guy could fight," Addy said.

Willie turned to the promoter. "I never saw him act like this," he replied truthfully. "Don't suppose he could've got doped, do you? He's talkin' crazy as a bedbug, in the corner."

"They'll wanta lynch me," Addy said, "puttin'

this fellow on for Billy Johns." The bell found Refugee moving a little unsteadily to his own corner.

The referee came with him. "I don't want to ask the commission to hold up your boy's purse," he said meaningly to Willie Wurtzel.

Willie Wurtzel stabbed in his most vulnerable point, let out an agonized cry. "Refugee," he pleaded. "What's the matter?"

"Mr. Willie," Refugee said finally between battered lips, "does Jewish folks have Christmas?"

Willie Wurtzel put down his sponge, tried unsuccessfully to grip his scanty fringe of hair. "Say," he said, "what's that got to do … ?"

The bell rang.

Watching Refugee Smith, Willie felt his eyes smarting. "He's blew a fuse," he muttered. "He's jumped his trolley and he's gettin' murdered."

**THE CHIEF** was putting on a little pace now. Blood showed in tiny rivulets on Refugee's upper lip. Willie had him with the bell before he got to his corner.

"Lemme throw in the towel," Willie said.

"Mr. Willie," Refugee said with weary trouble in his voice. "I heard Jewish folks don't pay no heed to Christmas. They told me dat dey have New Year's Day way back in October."

Willie Wurtzel didn't say anything. He looked at Refugee Smith trying to fathom this twist of his mind.

"Is dat de fact?" Refugee asked desperately.

Willie Wurtzel read near-terror in Refugee Smith's voice and none will know what went on in his mind. Perhaps he thought of the fight, maybe the purse, perchance for a little while and vaguely of the great stretch of time that was 5,700 years on the calendar of his people.

But he looked at Refugee Smith and shook his head. "No, Refugee," he said gently, "it ain't so."

Refugee Smith's face broke into a grin. "When's de nex' train to New Yawk?" he asked.

Willie Wurtzel glanced at the clock up in the end of the great hall.

"Fifty minutes," Willie Wurtzel said, puzzled.

"Us'll catch it," Refugee Smith said. "I'll clear up de Cloud right now."

Refugee Smith came out of his corner and his feet looked a little flatter on the canvas and his shoulders looked like they were hunched a little higher. On his face was the slight, intent frown that Willie Wurtzel knew reflected a profound concentration on the task at hand.

Chief Flying Cloud came in as he had before. Refugee Smith stabbed him twice with a left hand sharp as an ice pick and as the Chief came on, doggedly, let him come, dropped his own arms and beat him to the punch with a left hook to belly that made Chief Flying Cloud speak the only Indian word he'd ever spoken. They could hear it in the galleries. It was "Ugh!"

Refugee turned, walked to his corner, bouncing, watching Willie Wurtzel.

Willie Wurtzel held up his right hand, and his thumb and finger made an O; his nose quivered and his face split into a grin.

Refugee Smith turned, his back in the neutral corner, draped his long, heavy arms out on the ropes and listened to the referee count.

At "ten" he bounded out to help Chief Flying Cloud's handlers get him to his corner.

**THE SEA WAS CALM** at Jacobs Beach, that cigar store on 49th Street. The waves of sound were little waves. Willie Wurtzel stood leaning against the counter. It was eleven-thirty on Christmas Eve, and there was a lull. Willie Wurtzel was almost alone. A cab pulled up in front of the store and stopped. A yellow coat got out of the cab, propelled from within its super-richness by a black, grinning Negro. He came into the store and Willie looked up.

"Come'n get in de cab, Mr. Willie," Refugee said. "Us wants you to go for a little ride."

Willie walked out of the place glumly. He climbed into the cab.

"What for you so sad?" Refugee asked. Then added hastily: "This here is Slippery Ellum."

"I was standin' in there," Willie said, "Christmas Eve and me standin' in there by myself." He sighed, shook his head and lit a cigar. He summoned a grin, "Gonna have a big Christmas, Ref?"

"Yes, suh," Refugee said. Craftily he added: "Member when Santy Claus called you on de telephone?"

Willie Wurtzel frowned, then grinned. "That your rib? I was in the shower with a hang-over.

I guess I cussed a lot. But it wasn't your voice," Willie added.

"No, suh. You'd have caught on," Refugee said. "It was Slippery, here."

Slippery bobbed his head sheepishly under Willie's stare.

"Member what you said you wanted?" Refugee asked.

"No," Willie admitted.

The cab was rolling toward Central Park now.

"Member when I sent dat telegram from Boston town after de fight? I was telegrammin' Slippery here, to go ahead."

"Go ahead with what?" Willie Wurtzel asked.

"I boughten you a present," Refugee said, "for Christmas an' then I heard somebody say Jewish folks don't pay no heed to Christmas."

"I wouldn't know about that," Willie said. "I ain't what you'd call strictly orthodox."

"Well," Refugee said. "I was worried about hit an' I just couldn't fight for worryin' about hit. That's what's ailed me in Boston town."

"I see," Willie Wurtzel said, not quite seeing.

"So, I telegrammed Slippery to go ahead with de wrappin' when you told me what you told me."

Willie would have liked to have asked some questions at this point but the cab had stopped and his hosts were hustling him into what looked like a stable. It was a stable.

**THEY LED HIM** back to a lighted stall and there stood Deuces Wild, a five-year-old gelding, who on the 16th of December had run and won as a thousand-dollar plater at Sunnyside Downs. On his back he wore a blanket and into the blanket was worked a legend.

"He de one dat won de second at Sunnyside Downs, dat day you told Slippery dat's what you wanted. Merry Christmas, Mr. Willie!"

Willie Wurtzel stood looking at the inscription and various things pieced together in his mind. The horse looked at him and he looked at the horse, then he read once more the green embroidered inscription:

**MERRY CHRISTMAS
to
MR. WILLIE
Compliments of
R. SMITH**

"I never knew how to spell your name," Slippery said, "or it'd come out evener."

"Dat's all right," Refugee said.

Willie Wurtzel turned and looked at Refugee Smith and on Refugee's face he saw a look of terrible expectancy and pride. Willie turned, hiding his face for a moment as he composed himself, and looked into the eyes of Deuces Wild. It was a vicious face, as Willie saw it. But he remembered how Refugee looked and he pumped real fervency into his voice as he turned.

"It's just what I needed," he said.

Then he reached into his pocket and took out a box. He handed it to Refugee.

Refugee Smith opened the box and saw the big stone. Refugee tried to say something but it stuck in his throat.

Slippery looked over his shoulder, saw the stone. "Oh, Lord!" he said.

"Yes, Lord," Refugee whispered. "Many happy returns of the day."

# WILLIE WURTZEL'S WAY

**The effects of black magic on a very black boy named Refugee Smith.**

WILLIE WURTZEL taxied up Lenox Avenue with peace and contentment pervading his soul. He had just signed his fighter, Refugee Smith, to go ten rounds or less with one Frankie Blood at Madison Square Garden. The fight was to take place approximately one month hence, with the Wurtzel-Smith percentage of the gate of such a size that Willie's original demand for same had brought many a screech of anguish from the promoter.

Willie leaned forward in the taxi and pushed the glass aside. "Turn left," he said, "at a hunnert-thirty-fifth." He paused a moment, then innocently added: "Did you ever see an ebony fighter, name of Refugee Smith, fight?"

The taxi driver halfway turned his head. "Ya mean the one 'at t'inks tha Lord is in his corner?"

"Yeah."

"Yeah," the taxi driver said. "I seen him. I seen him flatten Kid Coco in t'ree heats out in Queens, onct. I don't see what he needs tha Lord in his corner for with that right of his'n."

"He's a great fighter," Willie said. "He got religion," he added slyly, "when his manager saved him out of the river, one time. He thought God had sent him."

"Yeah," the taxi driver agreed. "I heard that. A shame a good man like that hadda get took in by one of them Broadway Yiddishers, ain't it?"

Willie Wurtzel swallowed slowly. "Pull up here," he said finally, indicating the Eatmor Fish & Chips Shoppe.

The driver stopped, climbed out and opened the door. He looked full into the saturnine Semitic face of his fare. "Gee, mister," he said, "I'm sorry. I didn't know you was a Jewish gent. . . ."

**WILLIE** stopped him with an imperious wave of his hand. He reached into a pocket of his colorful double-breasted vest and extracted the two-dollar counterfeit bill he had been carrying since acquiring it in a stuss game some months before. "Don't let it bother you, Buddy," he said. "Just gimme my change. *All* of it." He turned and stumped into the restaurant. Senate "Slippery" Ellum, proprietor of the Eatmor Fish & Chips, friend and confidant of Refugee Smith, sat in the first booth with Refugee. Willie came over to the booth and sat down. He greeted Slippery, turned to his fighter. "Refugee," he said, "I just signed you for the Garden, a month from Friday. You fight Frankie Blood."

"Yes, suh, Mr. Willie," Refugee said. "I was frettin' wid de idlements."

Willie Wurtzel, out of the corner of his eye, saw Slippery's features assume a strange, half-fearful look.

"He's a Haitian," Willie said. "A good, tough boy but we'll take him."

"Us better git to trainin' tomorrow," Refugee said, pleased with the prospect of work. "Though I feels hits de truthful fack I don't need to feel no better."

"Do you *have* to fight Refugee against that boy, Mr. Wurtzel?" Slippery asked. "He's a bad man."

"Who's a bad man?" Willie asked.

"Frankie Blood," Slippery said.

Refugee Smith laughed. "I'll gooden him up some," he said.

Slippery looked at Willie Wurtzel. "He works with a *conjur man*," he said in a hoarse whisper.

Willie looked at him blankly.

The words tumbled from Slippery's mouth: "The second. The second that always works with him. He makes a little doll outen clay that looks like who Frankie's fightin' and he sticks a pin in its chest." He pointed to his heart. "Right there!"

Willie Wurtzel laughed a relieved laugh. "Oh," he said. "A hexer, like Evil Eye Finkel? Well, Ken Overlin has beat Evil Eye seventeen straight and Ken's champion. What do you think of that?"

"I don't know nothin' about Mr. Evil Eye," Slippery said. "But Frankie's second, he's a *conjur man*."

Refugee Smith laughed too, but his laugh was strange and forced.

**REFUGEE SMITH** couldn't read. That is, he couldn't read well. He learned, though, that two men that he had fought — knocked out — had come back to fight again. He knew, too, that these two men, subsequently meeting Frankie Blood — the Haitian Hurricane — had fought no more; had languished, walking on their heels, sick and losing weight. One of them had disappeared. Thus the fear that is almost unbeatable came into the mind of Refugee Smith. The fear of the unknown. He laughed. He laughed as best he could, and he tried to trust the Lord because the Lord had saved him. But, in Stillman's Gym two weeks before the fight, a stitch caught him in the side, cut across in front of his heart. He dropped his hands, walked out of the ring.

Willie Wurtzel, who had been watching, was waiting for him. "Ah, you coward, you dirty, yellow coward," he said before Refugee could speak. "The boogie-woogie man has got you. I know what's wrong with you. Well, I'll tell you something, you big stupe. I'm asking, I'm standing here asking — with my arms wide open — for a man, black, white or tan, to put the hex on me. To do *anything* to me!"

Willie Wurtzel was middle-aged. He lived high when he had a fighter who could fight, and he loved to stretch his gaudy waistcoats with those viands dear to the palate of the gourmand but anathema to the gastric juices. And it was coincidence, horrible coincidence, that when Willie Wurtzel, his passion draining much needed blood from his digestive organs — in grease-locked struggle with a cargo of ill-cooked matzoth balls — uttered the words "*. . . anything to me,*" he turned a bilious green and shakily sought a chair.

Refugee Smith grabbed him. "What'sa matter, Mr. Willie?"

Willie Wurtzel gripped the edge of his chair,

straightened himself, punctuated a belch with a groan and said, "Nothing."

"Oh, Mr. Willie," Refugee moaned, "de conjur man done taken you at your word."

"I got indigestion," Willie said, struggling up.

"What made de pain grab at my heart too," Refugee asked, still trembling, "if hit wa'n't de conjur man?"

Willie Wurtzel looked up into the fearful face of his fighter, reached into his pocket for a soda mint. "Well," he said, "I guess you got a little cramp for a minute. It ain't botherin' you now, is it?" he added comfortingly.

Refugee took a deep breath. "No," he said doubtfully. "But I ain't boxin' now."

"You think the hexer, he only works when you are boxin'?" Willie asked.

"I dunno," Refugee admitted.

That night Refugee saw Slippery. "I kind of got a little pain in my side today," he said, "whilst I was workin'."

Slippery pointed to his heart. "It was right there, wasn't it?" Refugee thought of telling him about Mr. Willie's digestive brush with the supernatural but thought better of it. "Just about," he admitted.

"They is an old woman," Slippery said, "lives up on Lenox. They do say she's a hundred years old. She sells dream books to the policy players, but she do a little voodooin' on the side."

"I don't want to have nothin' no more to do with voodooers," Refugee said hastily.

**"THIS** lady," Slippery said, "could, chances is, brew you up a little somethin' that'd taken the spell off of you!"

"You think dat other man — dat conjur man dat Frankie Blood has got for a secont — has put a spell on me?" Refugee asked, well knowing the answer.

"Why sure he has," Slippery said. "That's his natural occupation."

"Let's us kind of stroll up an' see dis ole lady," Refugee said.

The crone, Refugee admitted to himself, looked as though she could do the job, if anyone could do it. She may have been only a hundred but she looked older and her eyes, in the dim light of her little room, glittered like stones. Slippery, as spokesman, had guardedly stated the case and the old woman was now filling a little leather bag with various objects, over which she was mouthing unintelligible incantations. She sealed the bag, affixed a little string to it and gave it to Slippery.

"Have him wear this around his neck like a necklace," she said. "It'll keep off any spirit ever was."

Slippery took the bag and handed it to Refugee. "We aims to pay you," Refugee said gratefully. "I aims for you to," the old woman said, and her black parchment skin crinkled. "Twenty dollars."

**WILLIE WURTZEL** bustled into the dressing room, took a quick look at Refugee on the rubbing table, opened his bag and started checking his equipment.

Upstairs, the faint sound of cadenced hand-clapping told of the progress of the semiwindup. Willie, chewing a dead cigar, his hands fast and sure, laid out his collodion, sponges, tape. With half an ear he heard the beginning of faint strains of the Merry Widow Waltz whistled in concerted off key. He sterilized a razor blade with a match, put it beside the cotton and walked over to Refugee. "Who died?" he asked.

"Died . . .?"

"Don't you smell nothin'?"

"No, suh," Refugee said, moving a black hand slyly toward the little bag suspended from his neck.

"What's that under your hand?"

"Nothin'," Refugee said, looking at the ceiling.

"Move your hand." Refugee Smith reluctantly moved his hand.

Willie Wurtzel leaned down and sniffed. He lifted his head, spit out his cigar. "Gee," he said, "you are . . ." He stopped, straightened up and a gleam of understanding came into his eyes. "You can't wear that in the ring, boy," he said.

Refugee Smith sat up. "I can't wear dis in de ring?"

"It'll work," Willie said, thinking fast, "just as good out of the ring. I'll hold it in my hand."

"I'm a blowed-up Hindu," Refugee said. "I'm a goner."

A head appeared in the dressing-room door. "Let's go," the head said. "You're on."

**FRANKIE BLOOD** was short and square. A freak that resembled, both in the fury of his attack and his imperviousness to punishment, the great Joe Walcott. Five feet four, wide, heavily muscled, tough. And with him always in his corner, a lean, wizened second with eyes like those of a catfish. Refugee Smith moved a helpless hand across his bare chest, looked once at the second as he listened to the instructions from the referee and dragged himself back to his corner.

He came out with the bell from habit, with his long left hand out, from habit, and when he caught the swishing hook with which Frankie opened hostilities, he groped into a clinch from habit.

Willie Wurtzel washed his eye, held the smelling salts under his nose, and threw a pint of cold water down his neck, but Refugee Smith went out for the second round with a little cramp catching across the front of a heart filled with fear.

Frankie Blood was careful and implacable. Refugee Smith came back to his corner after the second round with his nose billowing mushroom of pain.

"Lemme touch my little bag," he muttered. "Lemme touch my little bag."

Willie Wurtzel expertly closed the cut under his fighter's eyes. "Next round." Willie said. "Next round I'll give it to you."

That was enough. That was enough to carry Refugee through. That and a jaw like iron and a young, superbly conditioned body.

McGovern, the third man in the ring, grabbed Frankie Blood after the bell. Frankie Blood had Refugee in a corner, groggy, bleeding. Refugee made it to his own corner, walking on his heels, coughing the blood out of his windpipe, his eyes fearful.

Willie got him. Willie Wurtzel got him, had him on his stool, had the blood cleared from his eyes, had an ounce of brandy down him, had him breathing free.

Refugee Smith looked across at the set, cruel face of Frankie Blood, looked across at the cold, weird eyes of Frankie's second, heard the ten-second whistle.

Willie Wurtzel reached down into his pocket and took out something. He tied it around Refugee's neck. "Okay, boy," he said. "You're unhexed."

Refugee Smith climbed up from his stool, felt the bag bob against his chest, felt the pain go out of his heart.

He moved out, and his left hand was out. Frankie moved to him, whistling a left hook for the body out of his shell of elbows and shoulders. Refugee sucked in his stomach and stabbed viciously at the two square inches of Frankie's exposed face. It brought the Haitian up for a second, and it left a portion of his prognathous jaw exposed. Refugee rippled the right cross up from his heels, felt the dead, stinging impact of a clean shot, wheeled and walked calmly to his corner. He expanded his chest, felt the little bag bounce against it. He turned, looked down at Mr. Willie Wurtzel, and grinned.

**REFUGEE** was lying on the table. He was covered with a blanket, his cuts were mended and Willie was bustling around the room chewing on a cigar. "Mr. Willie," Refugee said unhappily, letting his hand move up to the little bag on his chest that his manager had strung around his neck, "hit's a good thing I went an' got me a little ole charm, now, ain't it?"

"Is it? Willie said flatly. "You gonna wear that thing the rest of your life so's all can see you believe stronger in voodoo than you do in the Lord?"

"Oh, hush, Mr. Willie," Refugee said almost tearfully.

Willie Wurtzel came over to the table. His bright vest was unbuttoned and his cigar was lit and he moved uncertainly. He reached down and broke the string around Refugee's neck, handed him the bag. "Okay, boy," he said.

**REFUGEE SMITH** looked at the little bag and a strange look began creeping across his face. The little bag was an old-fashioned purse, bought, obviously, from a five-and-ten many years ago. The string which held it was a shoe-string. Refugee sat up and looked at Willie Wurtzel's feet. One shoe had no string.

Willie looked at his fighter.

Refugee Smith unsnapped the little bag, took out the contents slowly. A lead slug, fashioned in the size of a nickel; a broken locket with the picture missing, one of a set of dice — obviously a six-ace flat — and a little piece of wrapping paper. A little piece of wrapping paper with fresh pencil marks upon it. Slowly, with much moving of the lips Refugee read:

*"Thou shalt not make unto thee any graven image, or any likeness of anything that is in heaven above, or that is in the earth beneath, or that is in the water under the earth." (That also goes for phony voodooers. W. Wurtzel.)*

Refugee Smith looked up at Willie Wurtzel, smoking his cigar, with that look on his face which it had when the gate had been good and the purse had been fat. Refugee let his legs slide off the table until his knees touched the cold concrete. He lifted up his battered face and opened his mouth. "Lord, God," he said, the words rumbling from his heart, "forgive me. I knowed not what I done."

———————————————

Refugee Smith meant no harm when he gave Willie Wurtzel a race horse. How could Refugee know that Willie would ride it straight to the cleaners?

# THE EMPIRE CITY ANGEL

**WILLIE WURTZEL** wandered disconsolately into Honest Mike's Smoke Shop and leaned against the counter. Mike reached down and brought forth a box of three-for-a-dollar cigars. Willie waved them back, took three cigars from another box and threw a dime on the counter. "Now don't get smart, Mike," Willie said. "I know you've heard"

"Heard what?"

"You know."

"I ain't heard a thing," Honest Mike said, holding up his right hand, "Honest."

"If you ain't heard," Willie said, slowly, "you are the only man between here and the Brill building that ain't. Also, it is a story I do not get no pleasure from giving with. But if you ain't heard…."

"Honest," Mike said. "I ain't heard a thing."

Willie Wurtzel clipped his cigar, lighted it. His face wore an expression of acute pain. "You know my man, Refugee Smith, he gives me a bangtail for Christmas last year?" Willie said finally.

"Yeah, name of Deuces Wild."

"Okay," Willie said, mentally bracing himself. "I am boarding this hide on the Island and it cost just two percentage points less'n if they was feeding him salad, catered outta Twenty One, alla cart. "So," Willie went on, "I figure I will get some Joe to sharpen him up and knock down a small purse with him out to Empire. They tell me that around Lindy's that there are trainers that train for maybe three, four guys at once; one-horse guys like me."

Willie paused, rubbed his brow with a damp hand. "I get all registered up and it ain't bad; the Whitney stable, the Vanderbilt stable, the Wurtzel stable; that's all right, see? I get my colors offa the vest I buy when Refugee stops Jimmy Stiller and we cut up twenty-seven gees. Purple, blue-trimmed in — but you seen it."

"Yeah," Mike said, "That's one thing I *did* hear."

**"THEY AIN'T** any use in drawin' this out," Willie said grimly. "I gotta trainer name of Ringo Harness. This Ringo he hires him an exercise boy and he gets his Deuces Wild readied up and so we enter him in a race. It is strictly a cinch, see? A six-panel sprint with a bunch of dogs ain't fit to carry Deucy's water bucket."

Willie's cigar was out now and little beads of perspiration clouded his brow. "Deucy is a price, and by now I am Wurtzel the big sport of kings man and I know that if I chunk it in heavy at the trace, in the mutuels, it will cut the price and hurt my take; so I lay it around with the handbooks. A gee here, five yards there. And Mike … "

"Yeah?" said Honest Mike.

"I never told nobody this. This strictly can't get no farther…."

Honest Mike piously crossed his heart with a blunt forefinger.

"I chunked in all I had," Willie Wurtzel finished thickly, "an' the money I was supposed to have started Refugee's annuity with besides. I was gonna give him a break."

"What happened?" Mike asked.

"I put it on to win," Willie said, "and Deucy run a second with a sponge stuffed up his nose."

"Ohhhhh…."

"That Ringo Harness," Willie said, "the stewards caught him and he got barred for life but they don't give you no refunds. Anyway," Willie added, "you know good and well them books fattened up that Ringo plenty. I'd have broke half of 'em."

Honest Mike dusted his counter, clucking sympathetically.

"When Refugee give me that horse," Willie said sadly, "I was on top. I never thought it would be like this again. Why I give him a rock I paid better'n two gees for … " Willie Wurtzel stopped and his brown eyes narrowed. "That diamond ring," he said half to himself, "Two gees, two yards…."

"Hey," Mike said, "who's after you, Willie?"

**BUT** Willie Wurtzel was gone.

He found Ed Delaney in front of Lindy's. Ed Delaney looked at Willie, a faint smile on his face. "How, Willie," he said. "What gives?"

"Where was you last week, Ed?" Willie asked.

"While the boys were taking you," Ed Delaney said, "I was visiting friends at Delmar."

"Ed," Willie said, looking up at the big commission man, "I been knowing you a long time, you are all right, Ed. And to you don't it look like my horse can run, comin' in second with a sponge stuffed up his nose so he can't even breathe but half good?"

"He wouldn't run twice that fast without the sponge," Ed Delaney said, "but he is a fair plater. He is out of Wild Widow by Joker, and Joker has sired solid sprinters, being out of Hit Me by Baccarrat…."

"Ed," Willie said, "do not give me the begats. He is a fair sprinter, okay. I want a trainer who will get him sharp again and drop him into a spot."

Ed Delaney sighed, watching the passing cars a moment as they boiled up Broadway. "I will give you a note to Billy Venders," he said finally, "who is a trainer who you can trust. When he says enter the horse you enter him." Ed Delaney wrote briefly on a slip of paper, handed it to Willie. "Next time," he added, "you *know* a fighter is going to lose, you let me know."

"And Ed," Willie said, "say do I get a grand together, would you lay it around for me, among them guys that took me — the ones you know for sure will pay off?"

Ed Delaney gave the nails on his right hand a searching inspection. "Yes, Willie," he said. "I'll do that for you."

"Thanks, Ed," Willie said. He leaned over, spoke softly, briefly into the lowered ear of Ed Delaney.

"You sure?"

Willie Wurtzel put his hands above his head in the classic pose of the diver. "The fix is strictly in," he said.

**TWO DAYS LATER** Willie Wurtzel was in Harlem in Senate "Slippery" Ellum's Eatmor Fish and Chips Shoppe sitting in the first booth talking to his fighter, Refugee Smith.

Refugee Smith was black. Black as the blackest cat and every opponent that had stepped in front of him in his fighting career had been beset by luck of a very evil nature. Refugee moved a good deal like a cat in the ring, he had the finest right cross in the business and a jaw imperious to punishment. But beyond this, in the heart of Refugee there was an abiding faith that the Lord had saved him, working rather surprisingly through the pudgy and ofttimes grasping hand of Mr. W. Wurtzel, prize fight manager, W. 49th St., N. Y. City.

Thus Refugee Smith with the Lord and Willie Wurtzel in his corner, had fought his way from the ranks of the preliminary boys to the status of leading contender for the middleweight championship of the world. He had fought Willie Wurtzel into a bank roll, himself into the makings of a tidy annuity. Even last Christmas Refugee had been prosperous enough in his own right to buy Willie a horse. A horse named Deuces Wild.

"Refugee," Willie Wurtzel was saying, holding his face straight, "that ring I give you, what you done to it? The mountin', looks like you bent it some. Here, lemme see it a minute."

Refugee took off the ring and handed it to his manager. Willie Wurtzel, looked at it, took a handkerchief out of his pants pocket, polished the ring with it, looked again at it, handed it back to the fighter. "Naw," he said. "Ain't anything the matter with it, must be my eyes." He watched Refugee slip the ring back on his finger, his face blank, his round dark eyes still in his olive face.

"I got Deuces Wild trainin'," Willie said. "I run him the other day; he run second."

"Ole Deucy's never winner?"

"Naw," Willie said. "But," he went on grimly. "I know a little more, now. He'll win the next time out."

"Sho he will," Refugee agreed, "I ain't no first-round fighter myself."

"Speakin' of fightin'," Willie said, "we ain't gonna have a fight very soon, it don't look like. I'm workin' on one but we've about fought ourselves outta competition for a while, anyway."

"You take care of dat, Mr. Willie, I is keepin' in shape."

"Okay."

"Ole Deucy gonna run again soon?" Refugee asked. "I'd sho admire to see him go. You know, Mr. Willie, I ain't never seen him even trot through de park."

"I ain't had much time to do no personal equesting," Willie said. "But I'm gonna run him again for sure, now. I'll let you know."

"Thank you, Mr. Willie."

"And Refugee; you got plenty of money?"

"I got enough to run me for a while," Refugee said, "I is livin' cheap 'cause I loves to think of dat ole cash money ridin' up into dat 'nudity."

**"THAT'S THE WAY,"** Willie said gruffly, looking down. "I guess I better be goin'." He got up and hurried out of the door heading for the 135th Street subway station. Inside the kiosk he stuffed a nickel that Honest Mike had refused as phony into the slot, caught a downtown local.

Disgorged at 50th Street, Willie walked over to Eighth Avenue, and into the small building that sheltered the house of Eisenstat & Eisenstat, Collateral Loans A Specialty. He walked over to the counter under the daylight bulb, took out his handkerchief and unwrapped Refugee's diamond ring.

"Put the glass on that, Abe."

Abe Eisenstat looked up, saw Willie, smiled. He screwed the magnifying glass into his eye, looked at the stone. "What do you wanting?" He asked.

"All I can get."

"Six five O, be making you happy?"

"Twenty-two hunnert it cost," Willie said. "Do I look happy?"

"They are paying high rent on Fit' avenya," Abe said. "You pay part of that when you are buying there." He looked at the ring again. "Eight hunnert," he said.

Willie picked up the ring started wrapping it up

in his handkerchief. "Twelve hunnert," he said, "no less."

"I'm lending you a t'ousant," Abe said. "Hokey, make out the ticket one t'ousant?"

"Make out the ticket a thousand," Willie said.

The money was crisp in his pocket and Willie held his hand on it making his way toward Lindy's on Broadway. He found Ed Delaney standing on the curb reading a Racing Form.

Willie beckoned him aside, took the ten crisp hundred-dollar bills out of his pocket, handed them to Ed Delaney. "Venders says it'll be two, three days," Willie whispered. "Get me the best price you can."

"Trust me," Ed said.

"I got to," Willie Wurtzel said, turned and walked away.

**REFUGEE SMITH** came into Slippery Ellum's place, mopped his brow with a gaudy handkerchief, did a little jig from sheer exuberance, called to Slippery. "Mr. Willie call me; Ole Deucy go today, the fourth race out to the Empire City hoss track; you want to go out with me?"

Slippery Ellum looked up, saw Refugee, came around the counter. "I might," he said, but his face his face was troubled.

"Shorten up your face, boy," Refugee said, "this here smilin' weather. It gives to mind old Mississippi."

"You was in Mississippi when Mr. Willie pulled you outta the river, wasn't you?" Slippery asked obliquely.

"I was half in Mississippi," Refugee said, grinning, "an' half in Luzyanna, but mostly I was plumb in de center of de ole river hitself." He chuckled to himself. "I was a drowndin' man dat time."

"Mr. Willie," Slippery said, "he didn't have nothin' when he found you, did he?"

"He didn't have nothin'," Refugee said. "Us hiked hitched to St. Looie an' I fought for fifty dollars. But we rolled good since den."

"I gotta miserable fact to tell you," Slippery said. "Mr. Willie he ain't holdin' no better now than he was when he pulled you outta the river."

Refugee's face went completely blank for a moment, then his grin returned. "You is foolin'," he said.

"No," Slippery said. "Mr. Willie done lose his entire bank roll abettin' on that old Deucy hoss, the other day."

"How you know dat?"

"My brother, he wait table at the Cotton Club and a bookie told him that Mr. Willie bet thousands of dollars around town with bookies on old Deucy, and the bookies they pay Ringo Harness that is trainin' Deucy, and Ringo he do somethin' to the hoss so the hoss he lose. They say it broke Mr. Willie."

"When he was up here de other day." Refugee said, "he act awful down-mouthed now dat you remember hit to me."

"You still want to go out to the track?"

Refugee Smith creased his brow and the sweat popped out a little more profusely on his long upper lip. "Yeah." He said finally. "But first I wants to stop off down aroun' Fifty Street. I done got me a notion."

"What the notion?"

Refugee Smith was smiling now. "Why, man," he said. "I take dis little ole ring down dere an' I pawns hit. Den I takes de money out to de track and I bets hit on ole Deucy an' den I pays Mr. Willie back what he loses an' everything is fine."

"What if the hoss lose?"

"De Lord," Refugee Smith said. "Hits right funny about de Lord. He let a sinner sin, all right. Once, maybe. Den when de sinner he start to sin again de Lord He hauls off an' let's him have de back lash from his first sin. He'll bring ole Deucy in."

"I don't see how the Lord can find time to be watchin' no hoss race with all the big sinnin' goin' on in the world," Slippery said dubiously.

"Why," Refugee said scornfully, "de Lord got angels, plenty angels. I bet he got a angel don't do nothin' but kinda look out for de Empire City hoss track."

"If it's a fact," Slippery said, "that angel got fine hours 'cause they just run somethin' like thirty days outta the year at Empire and he get his mornin's off then."

"Dat's what bein' a angel gets you," Refugee said. " 'Leven months vacation with pay."

**REFUGEE SMITH** walked into the building on Eighth Avenue that sheltered the house of Eisenstat & Eisenstat, Collateral Loans A Specialty. He took off his ring and walked over to the counter under the bright light. He laid the ring down. "What you gimme on dat?" he asked.

Abe Eisenstat looked at the ring briefly. "You wanting to sell it?"

"No, suh, just a temporary loan."

"I can't loan nothing. I'm giving you six-bit, you selling."

"I wouldn't sell hit," Refugee said. "Anyways, seventy-five dollars; hits worth a lot more'n dat. Look how big hit is."

"Seventy-five *cents*, I'm giving. Mine you, that ring is glass."

Refugee Smith stood perfectly still for a long moment and his face didn't change expression. Then he turned slowly and looked at Slippery with un-seeing eyes and started walking stolidly toward the door. He walked like a man carrying a great weight in each hand and his brown eyes were dim with tears.

**WILLIE WURTZEL** bustled into Slippery Ellum's Eatmor Fish & Chips Shoppe, resplendent in his gayest waistcoat. He turned around, didn't see Refugee, turned to Slippery sitting silent behind his cash register. "Where's Refugee?" he asked. "We just got time to catch the last race train. Old Deucy is gonna run today."

Slippery Ellum looked at him woodenly. "Refugee at Bobo Lincoln's crap game," he said coldly.

Willie Wurtzel looked at Slippery. "What you givin' me boy. That Refugee, he don't shoot no craps."

"He shootin' craps now," Slippery said. "Drunk."

"Drunk?"

"You hear what I say." Slippery Ellum got up from his stool, walked down and stood across from Willie Wurtzel. "He heard you was broke, and he went down to pawn his ring to bet the money on Deucy to try and help you. If'n he can get drunk and shoot a few dices and forget about you and the Lord and everything he's a lucky boy."

Willie Wurtzel stood perfectly still, feeling his heart thumping against the last button on his vest, feeling his stomach tighten into a hard, cold knot.

"He never believe in but two things." Slippery went on inexorably. "You and the Lord. And he believed in them together. Now he don't believe in you and he don't believe in the Lord neither-wise. If you'd told him the ring was glass when you give it to him he wouldn't have cared. But when you lie to him it's like the Lord lyin' to him. Now it'll pleasure me for you to get outta my place and not come in it again."

Willie Wurtzel took a deep breath. "Slip," he said. "I gotta go now, but I'll be back. Don't let him get to fightin', don't let him break no hand. I'm goin' but I'll be back. I...."

"Get out!" Slippery Ellum said.

Willie Wurtzel went out on the street, turned into a drugstore, picked up a racing sheet and checked the post time on the fourth race. He looked at his watch, felt his pulse. "I can't go out there and watch that race now," he muttered. "It'd kill me." He started walking methodically downtown. Every few blocks he would look at his watch.

It was a long walk, a long, long walk for a man who didn't walk a half a mile a day. At 110th Street Willie's feet felt like two large blazing corns, but he hit into the park, grimly, glad his feet were hurting. He checked his watch. The first race would be over now.

He came out on Columbus Circle and he couldn't stand it. The fourth would be over. There was a drugstore near where they'd have the results. He walked in, bracing himself, muttered his question to a man standing there, heard the three words: "Flamingo win it."

He never knew how he got out. Never knew how he got back to 49th and Broadway. He was like a sick animal crawling to a familiar habitat to lay him down and die.

He felt a hand on his shoulder, looked up. Ed Delaney was standing there, his big pink face bland, his hand reaching in his pocket. He drew back when he saw Willie's white drawn face, the misery in his eyes.

"What gives, Willie, you look like you been poisoned."

Willie let his head fall, grunted.

"It was a close one," Ed said, "but it oughtn't to get you like that. It come out all right."

"What?" Willie managed, not caring.

"The fourth. Flamingo bumped your horse and

they disqualified him. Deucy won. I got you mostly fourteen, fifteen to one. Here's your dough, fifteen thousand, four hundred. Haven't you heard?"

When the average man faints away they throw water on his face. But Ed Delaney knew Willie Wurtzel over many years. He knelt down beside Willie's inert form, took a sheaf of crisp bills in his hand and fanned Willie's face with them. Willie Wurtzel came up. He grabbed the money, yelled something that sounded like "Thanksed-I-thank-God!" And bolted.

Out in the street he skipped in front of a cab, around the corner, heading toward Eisenstat's pawnshop. Inside he laid down a ticket, peeled off a thousand dollars, plus interest, and with the ring and money clutched in a hot pocketed hand struck a waddling run toward the subway. Thirty minutes later he was in Slippery Ellum's place.

"Where's Bobo Lincoln's crap game?" he said.

Slippery looked at him, his face blankly contemptuous. "Leave that boy alone, he said.

Willie Wurtzel advanced on two feet that shot pain clear to his ears. "Where's that crap game?" he said softly.

Senate Ellum took one look at Willie's face, torn with anguish, streaked with sweat and worry. "Two doors to the right and upstairs," Slippery said.

**WILLIE WURTZEL** pushed the guard aside from the door and walked in. Refugee Smith was shaking the dice, his face twisted meanly with drink, his voice hoarse. "Who fade twenty?" He shouted.

Willie Wurtzel summoned his voice: "Refugee!"

Refugee Smith looked up. He saw Willie Wurtzel standing there, saw his familiar brightly colored vest, saw his white face. Refugee sneered at him. "Go on 'way from me Mr.... go on away from me, Willie Wurtzel."

Willie Wurtzel walked over, reached down, his courage at the sticking point and took Refugee by the arm. "Come out of here," he said harshly. He looked around at ten ominously belligerent faces. "Don't nobody try to stop him."

Refugee came.

On the street Willie turned to him: "What's the matter with you, Refugee?"

"A seventy-five-cent ring. You tole me hit was a diamond."

Willie Wurtzel reached over, pulled the ring off of Refugee's finger, jabbed in into a vest pocket. He hailed a cab, shoved Refugee in it, climbed in after him. "Fifth Avenue and Fiftieth Street," he barked.

In the store he dragged Refugee, subdued, and only staggering a little, through the luxurious depth of the carpet to the diamond counter. He pulled a ring out of his pocket, threw it down before the startled morning-coated attendant. "What's that ring worth?"

The clerk looked at, smiled. "Oh," he said. "I remember now, you are Mr. Wurtzel, you bought the ring here." The clerk looked apprehensively at Refugee, disappeared for a moment.

"You paid two thousand and two hundred for it, sir," the clerk said when he came back, "but of course the price of diamonds is advancing...."

Willie Wurtzel took the ring from the counter, held it out to Refugee. "Put it on," he said.

Refugee's brown eyes were wet as he reached for the ring. "They told me hit was glass," he said, groping for the ring.

"Who told you it was glass?" Willie asked.

Refugee's voice broke completely answering. "A man named Mr. Eisensomethin' over on Eighth Avenue."

**WILLIE WURTZEL** led Refugee out of the store, holding him by the arm. "Refugee," he said gently, "there is persons around this town you cannot trust. And it looks to me...." Willie summoned all his histrionic ability, holding his voice paternal. "It looks to me like some dirty guy was tryin' to beat you out of your ring."

Refugee nodded his head. Then his face brightened. "Ole Deucy winner?"

"Easy," Willie said absently, mentally calculating he could replace all of Refugee's money in the annuity and still have enough to send the Jewish Welfare Fund an anonymous hundred.

"I guess," Refugee said, "dat Empire City angel was so busy out to de track he let ole Satan slip up into Harlem."

# IT AIN'T NO SIN

**Our favorite destroying angel does a few whirlwinds in the Yankee Stadium and righteously reaps the harvest thereof.**

**REFUGEE SMITH** sat in a booth in the Yellow Front Cabaret and Nite Club contentedly surveying the neatly demolished remnants of a large, expensive and succulent pig's knuckle.

In the back of the club a languid, ocher-colored party took a drink from the glass beside him on the piano, picked his cigarette off low C and tucked it between his lips. He hit a couple of experimental chords, the drummer on the platform beside him sawed off a small riff, and the saxophone gave a pleased squeal. The piano player boogie-woogied into Beat Me Daddy, Eight to the Bar, and the tiny floor of the Yellow Front immediately seethed with dancers.

Arzelia Toogood sauntered purposefully away from the bar toward Refugee's booth. When she reached it she slipped into the empty seat opposite him, flashed her white teeth in greeting. "Hello, Big Shot," she said.

Refugee looked up. Arzelia Toogood had a chassis sheathed in yellow satin that matched her last name, limpid brown eyes and red lips. "How do," he said.

"How's about us dancin' a dance?" Arzelia asked.

Refugee Smith pulled his gaze up to Azelia's face, and a tiny change in the sheen of his black face told of his blush. "Thank you, Miss — Miss . . ."

"Arzelia."

"Thank you, Arzelia, but de truthful fack is I don't reckon I could cut de mustard. Leastwise not like dat." Refugee nodded toward the floor, packed with expertly gyrating couples, who continued on and on, miraculously not maiming one another.

"Well," Arzelia said, hiding her surprise at Refugee's ready cordiality, "if'n you can fling you feets in time to the music I can follow you."

Refugee smiled reminiscently. "Was a time," he said, "I could do de Jump Jim Crow, and dey do say aroun' de river packets dat I was a natchal Natchez Shuffler."

Arzelia Toogood stood up and sent a rhythmic ripple down her yellow dress. "Come on, Big Shot," she said. "Ain't no shuffle I can't shuffle along with." Over Refugee's shoulder she winked briefly at a fat brown man standing at the bar.

When the music stopped and they were back in the booth, Arzelia said, "You kind of low-referenced yourself when you says you was a natural shuffler, Big Shot."

Refugee looked across the table, beaming. "You is mighty handy yourself," he said. He paused. "How come you calls me Big Shot?" he added. "My natchal name is Refugee."

"Why?" Arzelia said, still panting slightly from her recent exertions. "I knows your name is Refugee. Refugee Smith, the famous prize fighter. Everybody in Harlem knows you. But me, when a man is a big shot, I reckon he ought to be called Big Shot."

Refugee shuffled his large feet in embarrassment and his grin became even wider. The fat brown man at the bar finished his drink and walked out into the night.

"How's about buyin' me a drink?" Arzelia said, beckoning a passing waiter and ordering whisky and soda.

"I'd be pleased," Refugee said politely. "Gimme a bottle of strawberry pop," he added to the waiter.

"Ah, you can't get sent on no soda pop," Arzelia teased. "Why'ncha have a little snort?"

"I don't drink no whisky no more," Refugee said. "I don't figure hit no natchal sin but I gotta keep in shape."

"Oh, yes," Arzelia said as if suddenly remembering. "You're the fighter what was saved and aims to get to be a preacher."

"Ise saved, all right," Refugee said. "De Lord sent Mr. Willie clean to de center of de ole river to save me, an' I mostly done what he says ever since an' I ain't lost a fight."

"Done what who said?"

"Mr. Willie," Refugee said.

"Who's Mr. Willie?" Arzelia asked.

"Mr. Willie Wurtzel," Refugee said. "My manager."

"You set a right smart store by Mr. Wurtzel, don't you?" Arzelia said.

"I sets a heap," Refugee said simply.

"Well," Arzelia said, "it ain't no sin."

The music started and Refugee's shoulders twitched. Arzelia stood up. "Let's us get in the groove," she said.

**WILLIE WURTZEL** strolled out of Lindy's restaurant, flicked a stray fragment of smoked herring off his tightly stretched multicolored vest and bit the end off a long black cigar.

A large, well-dressed man standing at the curb contemplating his fingernails hailed him: "How, Willie? What gives?"

Willie walked over to the curb. "Hello, Ed," he said. "Nothin' much. How's things with you?"

"Okay. How's your fighter?"

"All right," Willie said casually. "I just signed him for an outdoor show with Jimmy Stiller."

"Stiller's a nice boy."

"What kinda price you make me on the fight?" Willie asked.

"Dunno yet," Ed Delany said. "But I'll make you a price."

"Be Stiller money around," Willie said. "He's a Fancy Dan."

"I'll let you know," Ed said. "I'd guess it'd maybe be eight and five and take your choice."

"I'll take two and a half G's of that right now," Willie said.

Ed Delaney looked at him in mild and hurt surprise. "Why, Willie," he said. "You know I don't bet my money. I'm a commission man."

"Well," Willie said, "lemme know."

"That's my business," Ed Delaney said, and went back to the contemplation of his nails.

Willie walked on over to the corner and disappeared into the subway kiosk, caught an uptown train. At 135th Street, he climbed out and made his way toward Senate "Slippery" Ellum's Eatmor Fish and Chips Shoppe.

Inside, he sought out Slippery. "Where's Refugee?" he asked.

Slippery Ellum looked up from his position at the cash register, shook his head. "He ain't been in yet," he said. Then, lowering his voice, he went on, "He was at the Yellow Front last night with Arzelia Toogood."

"Sounds like a candy bar," Willie said. "What is it?"

"It's a gal."

"Gal?"

"Yes, sir, Mr. Willie, a gal. Infinite Sanders' gal."

"Sanders, the gambler?" Willie asked, a slight frown appearing on his face. "The fellow used to bank policy?"

"That's right."

The door opened and Refugee appeared. He was yawning hugely. Willie glanced at his watch. "Hello, boy," he said.

"How do, Mr. Willie," Refugee said. He turned to Slippery. "How's de ham an' eggs?"

"Give him lamb chops and spinach," Willie Wurtzel said.

"Us has got a fight?"

"Jimmy Stiller," Willie said. He paused impressively. "Outdoors."

"Hot diggety dog. Dat's de big money, ain't hit, Mr. Willie?"

"If it draws," Willie paused. "How you getting along with your readin'?"

"Pretty good," Refugee said. "I done tackled de Good Book."

"Where are you at?"

"I done made hit through Genesis an' I'm buckin' into Exodus."

"If you get time," Willie said pointedly, "skip over to Judges and read about Samson."

"De strong man?"

"He was stouter'n John Henry, till somethin' happened to him."

"What?" Refugee asked. "I disremember."

"He got to runnin' 'round with a gal. A wrong gal. Named Delilah." Willie looked off out of the window. "Do three easy laps around the reservoir in the morning and be down to Stillman's at two o'clock."

"Yes, suh, Mr. Willie," Refugee said but he was looking at the floor.

**A WEEK** before the fight, Infinite Sanders, middle-aged, rotund and on the light tan side called on Arzelia Toogood in her apartment. He embraced her perfunctorily, lit a cigarette and dropped into his favorite chair. Bluntly, he asked: "How you doin'?"

"I ain't," Arzelia said sulkily.

"What's the matter? Don't he like you?"

"Oh, he likes me fine," Arzelia said. "He gimme that watch yonder on the bureau and he taken me to the picture show the last three Sattiday nights, and two Sundays he taken me to church," she added a shade unsteadily. "He likes me fine."

"Five'll get you eight if Stiller beats him," Infinite said. "We could win a wad of dough, did Smith lose."

"I don't know what to do," Arzelia said. "He got more will power'n a river bottom mule."

"Lemme think," Infinite said, folding his soft brown hands across his paunch. "If we can't get him outta shape we gotta run another angle. You gonna see him this week?"

"We's goin'. . ." Arzelia hesitated a moment. "We is goin' to prayer meetin' Wednesday night."

"That's two nights before the fight," Infinite said. "You couldn't maybe have him come over here the night before the fight."

"I dunno," Arzelia said. "I reckon I could. Why-for?"

"He's *real* religious, ain't he?" Infinite went on.

"He's a good man," Arzelia said, frowning. "He's a four-square fellow."

"He read the Bible, don't he?" Infinite asked. "I guess a guy like that'd be a Bible reader, wouldn't he?"

"He ain't what you would call a strong reader," Arzelia admitted, "but he workin' on the Book. He whup off maybe a page a day, he say."

Infinite Sanders's shrewd brown face twisted into a smile. He got up, walked into the tiny kitchen, looked at the ceiling. "Your kitchen ceilin'," he said enigmatically, "it need paintin' right bad. I 'spect that dumb boy would help you paint it did you ask him, wouldn't he?"

"I speck he would," Arzelia said.

"And he'd get thirsty paintin', don't you reckon?"

"Uh-huh."

"Okay," Infinite said. "This here is the layout. And I don't want no slip-ups."

**WILLIE WURTZEL** walked down Broadway from Stillman's gym where he had watched Refugee's last limbering workout before the fight. He found Ed Delaney in Dempsey's.

Willie worked his way into the bar beside Ed, ordered a drink. "What's the price?" he asked. "Still eight to five?"

Ed Delaney didn't turn his head. "Nope," he said. "There's a big play on Stiller. I can lay you even money."

"I'll take three thousand," Willie Wurtzel said.

Ed Delaney penciled a slip of paper briefly, pocketed Willie's six five-hundred-dollar bills. "You've made a wager," he said.

"Where's the play from, Ed?" Willie asked. "Stiller's a Brooklyn boy. Is it from over there?"

"Nope," said Ed Delaney, moodily contemplating his burnished nails. "Harlem."

"Harlem?"

Ed Delaney nodded, then asked: "What's the rush, Willie?"

"I just thought of somethin'," Willie Wurtzel replied over his shoulder.

**WILLIE** arrived at Slippery Ellum's Eatmor Fish and Chips Shoppe slightly breathless from his walk from the subway kiosk. "Where's Refugee?" he asked Slippery.

"He over to Arzelia's," Slippery said.

"He ain't been goin' out late at night with her, or drinkin' or nothin', has he?" Willie asked.

"Nope," Slippery said. "He been getting' to bed early."

"Ain't really any my business," Willie said, worriedly. "If he keeps in shape I ain't got any right to tell him what he does. But there's somethin' mighty funny some place."

"What you getting at Mr. Willie?" Slippery asked, worry creasing his chocolate brow. "I done bet a hundred dollars on Refugee."

"There's some smart money up here in Harlem thinks he's gonna lose," Willie said.

"Uhhhh, uh!"

"Yeah," Willie said. "I figure it must be Sanders."

"Ohhh!"

"Refugee be here tonight?"

"He generally stops by for a minute."

"I'll wait if it's all right," Willie said.

"You can set over there in the first booth," Slippery said. "I'll get you a newspaper to read."

There are a lot of ways to put the fix in on a fight, Willie knew. Sitting waiting for his fighter, he sifted the several score he was intimately familiar with through his mind. He shook his head, lit a cigar. "I don't get it," he said half aloud.

Refugee came in at nine-thirty. "Gimme a glass of milk," he said gaily. "I gotta get to bed."

Slippery nodded his head, pouring the milk and Refugee turned. "How do, Mr. Willie? What you doin' way up here so late?"

"I wanted to talk to you a minute."

Refugee came over and sat down in the booth. "Yes, suh."

Willie fumbled for words. "Miss — er — Miss Toogood. Arizona . . ."

"Arzelia," Refugee corrected politely.

"Arzelia. She ain't . . . she ain't said anything about you helpin' her poor old mother or nothin' by losin' the fight, has she?"

"Naw, suh. She hope I win."

"You ain't gonna see her no more. I mean that is before the fight tomorrow night?"

"Naw indeed, Mr. Willie. I been doin' just like you says." Polite as he was, there was a slight chill in Refugee's voice. Willie Wurtzel, acute to nuances of mood in his fighter, caught it.

"Okay, Well, I don't want to bother you none, boy. I just got to worryin' about you. I was engaged to get married up once myself. Her poppa paid the dowry with a rubber check . . . . Uh, sorry, don't want to bother you. I'll get along on home."

Refugee Smith didn't get up; instead he ran a black hand over his brow, sighed, took off his green pork-pie hat and fanned himself with it.

Willie Wurtzel looked down at him and his mouth flew open. Refugee Smith's head was as bald as an eight ball, and his color was muddy. "Boy! What they done to you?"

Refugee raised an apologetic hand, rubbed his head. "You mean my haid. I was adabbin' a little paint on Arzelia's kitchen ceilin' and she spilt some in my hair. . . ."

Slippery Ellum from across the little restaurant let out a wail: "She done shore him, Mr. Willie. She done shore him!"

Willie Wurtzel tried to stop Slippery, but Slippery's eyes were on Refugee and the words poured from his mouth: "Ref, you feels all right? You feel like you got your full stren'th?"

"I feels a little tired," Refugee began. He stopped.

Willie Wurtzel saw the whites of his eyes as he rubbed his head and comprehension stole across his face like a slow and horrible shadow. "I'se been done outta my stren'th like Samson," Refugee Smith said in a voice laden with doleful conviction.

Willie Wurtzel's voice rose into a near scream: "That's a lie!" He grabbed Refugee's wrist, felt his pulse. "You drink anything over there, boy, after you got done paintin'?"

"Nothin' but a glass of water," Refugee Smith said. "An' now I feels so weak I couldn't whup Mr. Tom Thumb with a baseball bat."

"Listen to me," Willie said and his voice was harsh. "It didn't do nothin' to your strength to have that gal cut your hair. She give a pill in that water to make you feel weak for a little while. You'll be all right in a little while."

"Ise sorry, Mr. Willie," Refugee said slowly. "But I am afeard you are mistook, 'cause I just natchally feels destren'thed."

"And I," Willie Wurtzel moaned, "*I told him to read about Samson.*"

**WAITING** for the bell, Willie made one final appeal. "The Doc told you that your hair didn't have nothin' to do with it. And he told you that that little thing you drunk has done wore off. So please, boy, get out there and fight your fight."

Refugee looked around at his manager. "You don't unnerstan' Mr. Willie," he said, "I is . . ."

The bell sounded.

Refugee, the whites of his eyes shining, went out slowly. Jimmy Stiller, blond and wiry, moved in, stabbed him sharply on the nose, danced away. Refugee followed him almost meekly.

When the bell brought Refugee to his corner Willie was hissing in his ear before he was on the stool. "Bull into him, boy, work on his belly." But Willie Wurtzel's voice carried no more conviction than Refugee's padded hands. Refugee didn't answer.

Infinite Sanders twitched a knob on the radio, placed within easy reach of his favorite chair in Arzelia's apartment. The announcer's staccato words were pleasant in his ears: *Stiller stabs Smith with a right to the face. Stiller hooks his left twice to the head. The colored boy misses with a right. His right eye is nearly closed. And there's the bell that ends the seventh round.*

Infinite Sanders looked over at Arzelia. "We's in the bag, baby," he said. "Stiller's got the fight won by a mile."

Arzelia didn't look at him. "Refugee might knock him out," she said in a faint voice. "Refugee might go for to knock him out."

"Naw," Infinite said. "Long as Smith thinks he ain't got no stren'th he ain't got any." He lit a cigarette and the squinting of his eye where the smoke rose to it gave him a faintly evil expression. "Your share of this'll be plenty potatoes, honey."

Arzelia looked at the floor.

**WILLIE WURTZEL** wasn't watching the fight. Down under the ring apron he was rummaging frantically through his little black bag. "If it'll only work," he muttered to himself. "If only it ain't lost its strength."

Long ago, for a purpose somewhat brutal and completely nefarious Willie Wurtzel had bought a tube of stuff. On the tube was written: Deado: an anesthetic ungent.

Willie Wurtzel found the tube, turned to his one-hundred-fifty-dollar plush overcoat that he was afraid to leave in the dressing room, and grabbing up a sleeve, braced himself and tore it out by its roots. With a penknife he hastily finished his work. He climbed back into the ring with the bell.

Refugee came to his corner, slumped onto his stool. Willie Wurtzel disregarded his fighter's puffed and bleeding eyes, squeezed a generous portion of the stuff from the tube into his hand

and under cover of a cold sponge, rubbed it into Refugee's shining head. "Stall through this'n, boy," he pleaded. "An' things'll get different."

"They can't get no diff'unt, Mr. Willie," Refugee muttered brokenly, "till my hair grows out."

"Stick out this round," Willie begged. "I ain't gonna quit," Refugee said, "do he beat me blind, but my haid done gone deader'n a doorknob."

Willie Wurtzel slipped the plush from his pocket, up Refugee's neck, anchored it with two swiftly pressed pieces of tape. "I don't wonder," he said, and his voice was dripping awe.

"How come, Mr. Willie?"

"I guess maybe," Willie Wurtzel said with tense casualness, "it's because you've sprouted a head of hair."

Refugee Smith didn't move for an instant. Then slowly, carefully, fearfully, one leather-clad hand moved toward his head. It stopped there for an instant, then descended in the lush cloth from Willie Wurtzel's plush coat. "Lord, Mr. Willie!" Refugee whispered, "You've give me back my stren'th!"

"Yeah, boy!"

"But Mr. Willie, he done won de fight. I can't stop him."

"Why not?" Willie's voice was hoarse and pleading.

"I can't see him."

Willie stopped the flow of blood above the right eye, moving with the speed and skill of a prestidigitator, grabbed his sterile razor blade. All the time he talked. He talked six thousand dollars a minute: "Refugee, boy. They done tricked you but 'member old Samson. He slew more them Philistines when he's blind than any other time and he slew a herd of 'em. Well I'm fixin' to fix you so you can see. I want you to go out there and tear this guy apart."

"Amen!" Refugee Smith said grimly.

Willie leaned down, slit the lump that kept Refugee's eye closed, and worked efficiently with collodion and tape. Refugee Smith came out fast in his old crouch. He had his chin tucked behind his shoulder and his hands cocked low. He bulled Jimmy Stiller to a corner, taking a couple of lefts, hooked his own left and right twice, crowding in, his head down, slugging.

Jimmy Stiller's mouth flew open with the second left and he fell, disjointedly, like a rag doll, forward slowly on his face.

Refugee Smith walked slowly to his own corner. His face, battered and bloody, was grave. He stood there, still, while the referee completed the count. Willie Wurtzel in the ring with *ten*, reached up and tore the plush patch from his fighter's head and threw it down out of the ring.

"Boy," he said, "believe me. They'll tell you I put somethin' on your head and you thought it was hair. But your strength came back to you, didn't it?"

Refugee rubbed his bald head. For a long time he stood there; but finally he grinned. "Mr. Willie, all at onct I felt surely full of them black corpuscles and maybe de Lord done growed me just a smidgin of hair to last me out one roun'."

Willie Wurtzel grinned back at his fighter, looked across the ring at the still inert form of Jimmy Stiller. "One rock was enough for David," he said, "and one round was enough for you."

"Yes, sir." Refugee said. "De Lord he do things different in de Yankee Stadium than he do 'em in Gaza but hit looks like hit work out to de same thing."

"Amen," said Willie Wurtzel.

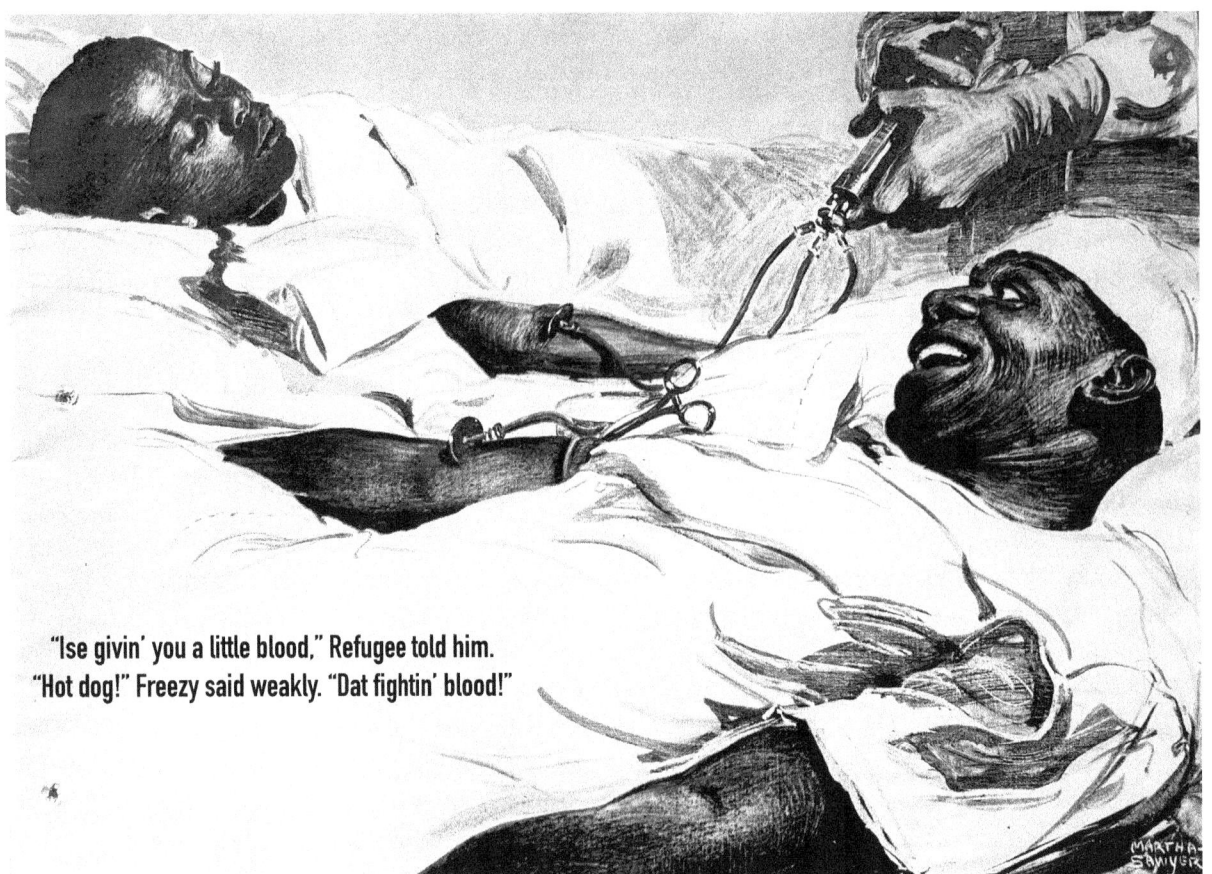

"Ise givin' you a little blood," Refugee told him. "Hot dog!" Freezy said weakly. "Dat fightin' blood!"

# SHOESHINE BOY

**Loyalty comes in all colors, and black, it seems, is by no means the least common of these.**

**THERE** was a little boy who worked on 135th Street, around off Lenox Avenue, usually in the vicinity of Senate "Slippery" Ellum's Eatmor Fish & Chips Shoppe because people around there would sometimes give a tip. The little boy was named Free Wheeling Johnson, having come upon the scene roughly coincident with the automotive device of the same name.

At the moment he was shining the shoes of Refugee Smith and they were some shoes, indeed.

"Mistuh Smith," Free Wheeling said, "I oughtta charge you ten cents for dis shoeshine."

Refugee Smith standing with his right foot on Free Wheeling's box looked down. "How come dat?" he asked.

"At five cents a shoeshine," Free Wheeling said, grinning, "hit comes to two an' a half cents a foot, don't hit?"

Refugee thought this over a moment. "Freezy, boy," he said finally, "dat's a natchal fact."

"Dem shoes of yours," Freezy said, "look to me to be at leas' two foot long. Dat makes four foot, an' four times two an' a half makes ten centses." Free Wheeling Johnson laughed immoderately at his own wit, sloshed four drops of his *Dazzle Gloss Finisher* on each of the long toes of Refugee's shoes and whipped them up to a mirror finish. Refugee's answer was even longer in coming this time. "You is a 'rithmeticin' fool, Freezy," he said at last, taking a quarter out of his pocket and giving it to the boy. Yes, suh, you is a paper'n pencil 'rithmeticer right outta your haid. Hit do beat me."

Freezy shoved the quarter in his ragged pocket, looked up at the towering black man with frank adoration. "Mistuh Smith," he said, "is hit a fact you is gonna fight Johnny Revolt for de chance to fight de champeen?"

"Hit's de fact," Refugee said. "Mister Willie signed for de fight two days ago."

"Do you reckon you'll wax him, Mistuh Smith?"

"I keeps my faith in de Lord," Refugee said, "I keeps in shape, an' I does what Mr. Willie tell me to do."

"An' you ain't never lost a fight yet," Freezy said triumphantly.

Refugee Smith stretched his long black arms, yawned. "Mr. Willie," he said, "he do de worryin'. I just has to fight ever' once in a while; but Mr. Willie he worry constant, so I lets him worry for both of us."

"Mistuh Smith . . ."

"Yeah, Freezy."

"If'n I shined your shoes free would . . . do you reckon you could get me. . . ?

"Get you a ticket to de fight?"

"You done read my mental mind, Mistuh Smith," Freezy said.

"How long would you go to shine my shines for nothin'?"

Freezy Johnson's eyes got big and round with the ecstatic prospect of seeing the fight. "Ever' day," Freezy said fervently. "Forever!"

"That," said a voice in the accents of deep south Brooklyn, "is a bad deal, son."

Freezy Johnson looked up, saw a small rotund man in a gaudy double-breasted waistcoat whose blue, fat-creased cheeks were dominated by a bold nose. "Shine 'em up, Mister?" Freezy said automatically.

Willie Wurtzel spoke to Refugee Smith, bent his head and looked at the 5c mark Freezy had scrawled on the side of his box. "You shine shoes for a nickel, son?" Willie Wurtzel asked.

"Yes, suh, but I does a ten-cent job."

"How come you don't charge a dime, then?" Willie asked.

"De natchal truth is," Freezy said, "I don't figger hit's worth more'n a nickel."

"Can you get him a ticket to de Revolt fight?" Refugee asked his manager. "He's a pal of mine."

"I'll see about it," Willie said, "but that ain't what I come up here for. This Revolt is a hell of a tough boy. I seen him fight down to Philly last night. I want you should get yourself down to Stillman's gym this afternoon at two o'clock. I'll see about gettin' you some boys to work with later."

"Yes, suh, Mr. Willie," Refugee Smith said.

**THE** days passed and from the waist-line of Refugee Smith there passed six pounds and four ounces. It left the waistline of Refugee Smith hard and ridged like a washboard and it left Refugee Smith weighing one hundred and fifty-nine pounds and sharp.

The passing days also brought small comfort to Willie Wurtzel. For Willie Wurtzel had come back from Philadelphia — where he had seen Johnny Revolt club a smart, tough boy into insensible submission in three rounds — a worried man.

Johnny Revolt was a man who fought with a controlled but implacable fury, with a deadly destructiveness such as Refugee had never faced.

**THE** passing days passed in subglacial tempo for Free Wheeling Johnson. For Free Wheeling Johnson had his ticket for *the* fight, secured in his watchless watch pocket with a safety pin where he could reach down and take it out and look at it any time he wanted to.

That's what Free Wheeling was doing when he stepped from behind the car at the curb in front of the cab. Fumbling the ticket out to look at it.

Refugee Smith came into the Eatmor Fish and Chips Shoppe of Senate "Slippery" Ellum the morning of the fight. "Where at Freezy?" he asked. "He ain't between here an' Lenox."

Slippery looked up, came around the counter. "Ain't you heard?" he asked.

"Naw," Refugee said. "Heard what?"

"He done collide with a taxicab," Slippery said. "He layin' in the hospital, dog-sick."

"He bad hurted?"

"He dog-bad hurted," Slippery Ellum said. "His sister lookin' frantic for somebody to give him some blood of what they call the three kind."

"Three kind?"

"Yes, man. That's the kind o' blood little Freezy's got — such as he got left — an' he need some fresh of the same number an' the three kind folks is scarce."

Refugee Smith was running when he hit the door. It took five or six minutes for him to get to the hospital and it took them fifteen minutes more to type his blood. But he was a type three, all right, and Freezy was conscious during part of the transfusion. "Hello, Mistuh Smith," he said. "What you doin' up here?"

"I'se givin' you a little blood," Refugee said.

"Hot dog," Freezy said weakly. "Dat fightin' blood I'm getting. I'll be all right, now."

One of the nurses quieted him but Freezy managed one more sentence. "I sho hated to miss de fight," he said.

Refugee Smith walked out into the hall, feeling a little funny. He went on down to the desk.

"De little colored boy," he said there. "I'll pay up his bills when dey come due. He a friend of mine."

"And who are you?" the man behind the desk asked.

"I'se Refugee Smith," Refugee said. "De middleweight prize fighter. Mr. Willie Wurtzel is my manager."

A doctor tapped Refugee on the arm. "The boy is apt to need another transfusion tomorrow," he said. "He is badly hurt."

"He dat bad?"

The doctor nodded. "We have no professional donors available of the right type," he added.

"I'll find somebody," Refugee said. "I'se busy tonight but I'll look in this afternoon and in de mornin'."

Refugee Smith came back to his corner from the center of the ring where he had stood with Willie Wurtzel and received his instructions. Willie Wurtzel threw a practiced and accurate eye over the house, noticed the empty ring-side seat. "Where's your little pal?" Willie asked.

"Who?"

"The shoeshine boy?"

"Oh," Refugee said. "He got hit by a taxicab. He in de hospital. By de way, Mr. Willie, you ever give anybody some blood?"

"Yeah," Willie said. "I give a rabbi a transfusion once." He grinned at the recollection.

The bell rang and Refugee went out. He went out languidly and Johnny Revolt was on top of him and moving in, slugging for Refugee's belly, his bright blue eyes expressionless. Refugee boxed with him, going away, but Johnny Revolt scored with a left hook and Refugee was in trouble at the bell.

Willie Wurtzel got him back to the corner. "Boy," he said, "if you wasn't so black I'd think you looked pale. Do you feel all right?"

"I feels a little peaked," Refugee said, "but maybe I'll warm up."

"Go to his right," Willie Wurtzel said, "this guy is very sharp with his right hand."

**THE** second round brought no comfort to Willie Wurtzel and it brought a welt above Refugee's right eye and a thin trickle of blood from his nose.

"What you doin', boy? You gotta *fight* that guy, he's mean."

"I'se tryin'."

"You feel all right?"

"Naw, suh."

"What you been doin' today."

"I ain't done nothin' 'cept go over to de hospital an' give little Freezy some blood. I been restin' since den like you tol' me to."

"*Blood!* Say, boy, you didn't give that kid a transfusion?" Willie Wurtzel's voice rose in pure anguish.

"He bad need de blood," Refugee said. "He might go for to die but for it."

"How much? Oh, it don't matter. You're thirsty and you're weak and you're in there with Johnny Revolt and if you beat him you get the champion only you ain't gonna beat him . . ." Willie Wurtzel's voice trailed off in a wail of pure pain.

"I'll keep tryin', Mr. Willie."

Willie Wurtzel started to say something but the warning buzzer caught him. He clambered out of the ring and watched Refugee go back, almost go down once, stagger back to his corner, with the bell.

"Boy," he said into Refugee's ear, his voice dripping passion, "what'd you want to know about my blood for?"

"He need some more tomorrow, the three kind."

"Type three?"

"Yes, suh."

"Listen, boy. You go out for this guy. This round, you go out for him. You won't get no stronger. You go out for him this round and I'll give the kid some of my blood tomorrow. I remember now. I'm type three.

"You do dat, Mr. Willie?" Refugee Smith said.

"Yeah. And Refugee. What if that boy's listenin'

on the radio, it'll kill him to hear Sam Taub say you lose."

"Dat a fact, Mr. Willie. I'll go out."

"Okay, boy."

"Mr. Willie. Did dat rabbi get well?" Willie Wurtzel scanned the crowd, found a bearded man that looked healthy visible in the ring light. "I'll say he did," Willie lied. "There he sets."

Refugee Smith bowed down his head. "Lord," he said, "I ain't askin' you to help me, but don't put no props under Mr. Revolt does I get to him."

Freezy Johnson didn't hear the fight, of course. Freezy Johnson was hovering someplace where the only thing that he was apt to hear was Gabriel's trumpet. But a lot of people heard it, and seventeen thousand of them sitting in Madison Square Garden saw it.

Refugee Smith came out of his corner and he carried his hand down, cocked, and he took a left that cut the welt above his right eye, to fire a sucker right from his hip. It was a winging, awkward punch and it caught Johnny Revolt too high to hurt him, but the very impact of it threw him slightly off balance and into the left hook Refugee had sent following the right.

Johnny Revolt was a tough, game boy. He got up and he came in. He didn't know anything to do but to come in and Refugee came in to meet him and they were both swinging and Refugee's head flew back and he was down. But he didn't take a count, he came up swinging, coming in to meet Johnny Revolt and Johnny Revolt came in, too.

They were screaming. Seventeen thousand people can scream, and they were screaming. They weren't seeing anything that remotely resembled the art of self defense, manly or otherwise. They were seeing two men, one black, one white, who wanted to do away with each other in the shortest possible time. The difference was with the black man. The black man's jaw had an ounce more iron in it, and while the black man's heart may have been pumping a pint less blood than the white man's heart the black man's heart carried a pity for a little boy lying in a hospital, and a pity, channeled into action, is — for a round at least — worth a pint of blood.

Johnny Revolt went down from one of those rights, and he pushed up on his hands and knees but he couldn't make it up inside the count and Refugee bent down to help him to his corner, and Refugee Smith fell down, too.

**WILLIE WURTZEL** came out of the room and the doctor came out of the room with him. The doctor was smiling. "I think he'll make it now," the doctor said. Willie Wurtzel walked over and got a drink of water and slumped down in a chair. "How you feel, Mr. Willie?" Refugee asked, his face anxious under his bandages. "I don't feel like fightin' no Johnny Revolt," Willie said.

A nurse came out of Free Wheeling Johnson's room and nodded to the doctor and the doctor went back in.

"How come," Refugee asked, "you know I'd stop that fellow if'n you tol' me you'd give Freezy some blood?"

Willie Wurtzel took a cigar out of his vest. "Aw," he said, "you're just that kind of big stupid ape."

"But you given him some blood, too. You didn't have to."

"Hell," Willie said. "I'd naturally want to keep a guy alive that'd shine my shoes for a nickel. Blood don't cost nothin'."

Refugee grinned, started to say something but the doctor came back out of the room. "He's conscious now," the doctor said. "He talked a little."

"What'd he say?" Refugee asked eagerly. "Did you tell him I won de fight?"

"Yes," the doctor said. "I told him and he was awfully pleased."

"But what'd he say?"

"He said," the doctor went on, smiling, "that this all must cost a lot and that he thought he would raise his price to a dime when he got out. I don't know exactly what he meant."

"He's a shoeshine boy . . ." Refugee began.

"Well, I'll go to hell," Willie Wurtzel interrupted, his voice rich with wonder. "That blood of mine has gone to work already."

# LOVE CAME BORROWING

**Refugee looked at Hard Hat McGee, the whites of his eyes hidden.
"Give Mr. Willie his paper," he said softly.**

WILLIE WURTZEL — manager of Refugee Smith, leading contender for the middleweight crown — had a heart as big as a shriveled pea. At least that would be the impression one would gain through consultation with his associates, though there were among these some who would contend this was too generous an estimate by half, and then some.

However, at the moment, this organ of moot dimensions was beating in a fashion to impart a perceptible quiver to the third button on Willie Wurtzel's gay waistcoat, for across the table from Willie sat Annabelle Divine.

In the economically lighted bistro where they were, Annabelle Divine was indeed a vision, although there was also some debate about what kind of vision she would be at 10 A.M. Eastern War Time, out in the pure sunlight.

Long ago love had come to Willie and its consummation was being duly arranged through a reliable broker in those matters when the dowry check his betrothed's old man had put up had proved to be ersatz. This had somewhat shaken Willie's faith in love and marriage. It had left him something of a cynic which, withal, was a handy attitude in the prize fighting managing business.

But love had come again to Willie Wurtzel, and when Annabelle smiled sweetly at him and said, "Do you know what today is?" Willie, bemused as he was by this tenderest of all emotions and six brandy-and-sodas, saw no harm in admitting it was Tuesday, the seventeenth.

"And," said Annabelle archly, "do you know what *next* Tuesday is?"

Willie told her that he hoped it would be Tuesday the twenty-fourth.

"I hope so, too," Annabelle said. "Because that's my birthday."

"Birthday?" said Willie.

"Birthday," said Annabelle.

Willie smiled weakly. "In such a case," he said, "I guess I should come up with a slight knickknack."

"No," Annabelle said.

"No?" said Willie in relieved disbelief.

"You don't have to worry your head about it at all," Annabelle said. "I have it all picked out."

Willie Wurtzel squirmed. "What," he said cautiously, "have you all picked out?"

Annabelle stood up. "Come on," she said, "I'll show you. It's not far."

It isn't far from the vicinity of Sixth Avenue and 52d Street to some place around Fifth Avenue and 52d Street, but when 52d gives way to Fifth Avenue a change takes place. Where before there were night clubs, there are now stores which very definitely don't give away to anybody.

In front of one of these stores Annabelle stopped. Willie stopped, too, took one fleeting glance into the window and cringed. In the window, in solitary state, was a coat. It was a fur coat and it was worn by a plaster lady of cold hauteur. Against one of the lady's slim ankles was propped by a discreet card.

"Isn't it too, too, grand!" Annabelle said rapturously. Willie looked at the card again. "Three," he corrected in a hollow voice.

**HARD HAT McGEE** was a character of some repute, all ill, who would lend you a few bucks did you pledge a pound of flesh and more than legal interest — and no fast ones about blood not being flesh, either. Hard Hat had come by his cognomen through the simple expedient of never having been seen except under an ancient derby in a couple of decades of leaning against the same building, and he was known in his own sphere as a very fast man to a dollar. So fast, indeed, that there was some talk at one time of putting up a monument to Mouser Bergen — Mouser having shrewdly succumbed to pneumonia while owing Hard Hat a small sum and thus becoming the only man on record who ever beat Hard Hat out of that which he owed him.

And it was to Hard Hat that Willie Wurtzel came, Willie having found that Ed Delaney was out of town and that other friends were severely in the shorts. Willie wanted to borrow three thousand dollars.

"Ah, Willie," Hard Hat said. "You're extravagant. You drink and gamble and take show girls around, and though your colored boxer makes you lots of money, you come to me."

"That's right," Willie said.

"How much do you want?"

"Three gees for thirty days."

"And what makes me think you'll pay me back the thirty-three hundred in thirty days?" Hard Hat asked.

"My boy, Refugee Smith, has got a fight in Philly thirty days from yesterday. We're gettin' eight grand. I'll have my four the next mornin'."

"What security have you got?"

"Security?" Willie said. "At them interest prices?"

"You might die," Hard Hat pointed out from the green and bitter memory of Mouser Bergen's betrayal. "Aw," Willie said, "I'm healthy as a horse."

"Okay," Hard Hat said. "You got life insurance?"

"Naw."

Hard Hat McGee tilted his derby back a shade and scratched his brow. "Well," he said finally, "I think I have thought of a way I can help you. I think I have thought of some security you can put up."

"Yeah?"

"You make me out an assignment of your

fighter's services, contract, et cetera et al," said Hard Hat, who figured a few ets might dull the edge of his proposition, "in event you die — or don't pay me back in thirty days."

Willie Wurtzel backed up a step. "Aw naw," he said. "Not that."

"It's just formality," Hard Hat said casually. "It will be in plain print you can redeem the assignment do you pay me back inside of thirty days, and you'll have your four grand thirty days from now."

Willie pictured Annabelle unwrapping the coat. "Well. . ." he began doubtfully.

**A WEEK** later Willie Wurtzel was standing in the apartment of Annabelle Divine, unwrapping a box. On Willie's face was a look of rectitude and sacrifice. Annabelle's face was blank, poised for elation or disappointment.

Willie fumbled willfully with the strings. Finally in one grand gesture, he broke the string, threw open the box. He stood back and watched Annabelle.

Annabelle's face stayed blank. She picked up the coat, felt it, threw it over her shoulders, walked to the mirror. Then, finally, she turned. "Oh, Willie!" she cried.

Four weeks and one day later Willie got a long distance phone call. It was from the Philadelphia promoter and it told of injury in a motor accident to Refugee's opponent of the *following* night. The promoter further told Willie that the fight would not be held. The fight was off. There would be no fight.

Willie, standing in his hotel room, heard the voice squeaking over the wire with a slightly uneasy feeling.

The promoter was additionally explicit. No fight. No purse. No nothing. Willie Wurtzel reached for his coat with the same motion with which he hung up the phone. "I gotta get out hustle up that three gees," he muttered to himself as he hurried out the door.

Across 49th Street, down Eighth Avenue, back across to Seventh, into Broadway and up to 52d. A hundred people spoke to Willie and with fifty of them Willie stopped and talked.

It was very, very funny. Willie Wurtzel, thirty years in the neighborhood, raised sixty-two dollars and eighty cents.

*I'm sorry, Willie: Rent due, the horse ran out, throwed ace deuce with it all ridin', business has fell off, the income tax, me brudder's in de hospital.* It was a chant.

It was four o'clock in the morning when Willie got his break. A bookie, conveniently and strangely broke at the moment, told him Ed Delaney would be in from Santa Anita the next afternoon on the five o'clock train.

Willie went to his room and to bed. Ed would let him have it.

**THE** next afternoon far up in Harlem, Senate "Slippery" Ellum held dolorous conference with Refugee Smith.

"It was a shame, a bad, bad shame that that fight down to Philly was called off," Slippery said, easing into the booth in the Eatmor Fish & Chips Shoppe where Refugee sat.

"Hit surely was," Refugee said, "dat fellow I was gonna fight, he was bad hurted."

"I wasn't thinkin' about him," Slippery said.

"Don't waste no sorry on me," Refugee said, grinning. "Hit kinda flatten you out some, you train for a fight and de fight don't happen. But I'll get over dat."

"I wasn't thinkin' 'bout you, neither," Slippery said.

"Who den you sorryin' over?" Refugee asked, frowning.

"Mr. Willie," Slippery said succinctly.

"Mr. Willie? Hit don't make whatfor to Mr. Willie, 'ceptin' his cost him some," Refugee said, smiling once more.

"It make a heap of difference to Mr. Willie."

"Get de Devil from behin' dat stump," Refugee said. "What you drivin' at, boy?"

Slippery Ellum's long face got longer. "Mr. Willie done sold you outright for a mess of partridge," Slippery said dolefully.

"I ain't in tune wid you, Slip," Refugee said. "Speak fuller."

"Well," Slippery said, "Miss Annabelle Divine, that Mr. Willie's gal, she wanted a fur coat for her birthday and Mr. Willie he didn't have enough to buy it, so he borrowed three thousand dollars from

Mr. Hard Hat McGee for thirty days, and he give Mr. Hard Hat your contac' for security."

Refugee digested this information for a while. "How come you know dat, Slippery?"

**WILLIE WURTZEL**, waiting in the Grand Central Station, collared Ed Delaney as he got off the five o'clock train from the west. Briefly and dramatically Willie told the big commission man his tale.

Briefly, dramatically, almost tearfully, Ed Delaney told Willie Wurtzel that he didn't have the money. Willie made his way blindly to the bench and sat down. His ample brow was damp with sweat and his heart felt like an old indoor baseball. Into his fevered vision crept Hard Hat McGee, armed with a sharpened dollar sign and riding an iron-bound contract. Ed Delaney sat down beside him. In a dull, lifeless monotone Willie told his friend of his efforts to raise the money.

Ed Delaney pursed his lips. Finally he said: "Willie, there's something funny there." He paused again. "I figure it like this. Hard Hat wants your fighter. He's worth a hundred grand. And when the fight was called off he gets his chance. Every one of those guys you hit up for money, why, Hard Hat he has got a note of theirs, or they have to do business with him sometime; anyway, someway or other he's got 'em in the nine hole so he sends out the word: 'Don't let Wurtzel have a dime.'"

"Yeah," Willie said finally, "I guess you're right." He looked around him with unseeing eyes. "Well," he said, finally, "I guess I better go up and see Refugee. I gotta tell him. He's gotta find it out from me."

"Want me to go with you?" Ed Delaney said.

"I'd like that," Willie said dully. "Thanks."

But they couldn't find Refugee. They looked at Slippery Ellum's, they looked at Refugee's apartment. They looked and asked everywhere they could think of but there was no Refugee to be found. And finally, at eleven o'clock, Willie headed back for his hotel. Up in his room Willie picked up the phone, tried Annabelle Divine's apartment. He got no response.

"What are you calling *her* for?" Ed Delaney asked.

"It ain't any chance," Willie said, "the way things are, but I thought if I could get hold of that coat and maybe get a grand or so on it I might give that to Hard Hat and he'd gimme a little more time."

Ed Delaney hid the look of pity in his face. "It wouldn't help anyway, Willie," he said.

"I know it wouldn't," Willie said. He looked up at a clock on his dresser. "Hard Hat'll be over soon," he said. And for the next fifteen minutes he sat silent, his face wiped clean of expression by the numbing impact of that which was to happen.

Hard Hat McGee, when he did arrive, came straight to the point. "Willie," he said, "I've come for the money."

"Yeah," Willie said.

Hard Hat looked at Ed Delaney, sitting across the room. Had Ed let Willie have the money?

"I ain't got it," Willie said, and Hard Hat let his breath out in relief.

"Well," Hard Hat said, "I guess that's that. My option becomes a contract at twelve o'clock tonight."

Willie Wurtzel looked at Hard Hat McGee, tried to say something, then looked down. He was looking at the floor when the door opened and Annabelle Divine came in.

"Willie, darling," she said without preliminaries. "I hocked the coat, and some rocks I had around. I got eighteen hundred. Will that help?"

"Baby," Willie said in a whisper, "how did you know?"

"I got a couple of friends," she said. "Hard Hat couldn't keep it to himself."

"Hard Hat," Willie pleaded. "That's more'n half. I'll get the other up. Will you hold off?"

Hard Hat McGee looked at the clock on the dresser: It said seven minutes to twelve. His eyes narrowed a little. "No, Willie," he said. Then gloatinly, he added, looking at Annabelle. "Your doll has got you in a spot, now, hasn't she? A greedy doll."

Willie half rose from his chair, his face pale. Ed Delaney pushed him down. Ed Delaney took a ring off of his finger. A ring he had bought thirty years before with the proceeds of the first big parlay he ever put over in his eighteen hundred, and this — this ring, will you give Willie his paper? The ring's worth fifteen hundred."

Hard Hat looked at the clock. "No," he said.

The door opened.

Framed in the doorway was a big black man, wrapped up in a plush coat as yellow as the big man was black. He grinned, said: "How'do, Mr. Willie, Miss Deevine, Mr. Ed."

Willie Wurtzel tried to look up at his fighter, tried to look into his fighter's face, but he couldn't do it. He said nothing.

Nobody said anything. It was still.

Refugee Smith advanced into the room, walked over to the bed, reached his hand into the side pocket of his coat and brought forth an enormous clump of crumpled bills. He looked at Hard Hat McGee, and the whites of his eyes were hidden. "Give Mr. Willie his paper," he said softly, very softly.

Hard Hat McGee reached into his inside pocket, his hand moving mechanically, and extracted a legal document. He handed it to Refugee.

"Count de money," Refugee said.

Hard Hat counted the money.

Refugee Smith handed the paper to Willie Wurtzel, not taking his eyes from Hard Hat McGee. "Mr. Willie," he said, still in the soft voice. "Write out a recipe for de money. Thi'ty days for three thousand dollahs, three hundred dollahs in'trust."

Willie Wurtzel picked up a pen and wrote. Refugee Smith took the slip of paper from Willie, handed it to Hard Hat McGee. He loosened his coat, flexed his big arms. "Sign de recipe," he said to Hard Hat McGee.

Hard Hat signed. Refugee took the paper and gave it back to Willie.

"Now," Refugee said, "you have done signed a confess dat you is a uzzerer. De law in dis town don' like your kind. Iffen you ever puts the muscle on anyone anytime, we gives de recipe to de law." Refugee took off his coat, laid it on the bed. "Goodbye, Hard Hat," he said ominously.

Willie Wurtzel looked up at his fighter, rubbed the tears from his eyes. "Boy," he said brokenly, "how did you know?"

"Miss Deevine," Refugee said, "tol' Slippery."

"Where," Willie asked, "did you get the money?"

Refugee Smith looked down at the pudgy little man who was his manager, his one-time life saver. "I got a dollah six bits from Freezy Johnson." Refugee began, "I got five hundred and fifty from Hank Robinson, I got five hundred from Slippery, I got three hundred and twenty-five from Sam White. . . ."

"What did you tell 'em?" Willie Wurtzel asked.

"I could've got hit all from most any one of 'em," Refugee said, "only de banks was done closed down for de day. I got four hundred and sixty-two fifty from Infinite Sanders. . . ."

"The gambler that tried to frame you once?"

"Yessuh, Mr. Willie."

"What'd you tell 'em?" Willie Wurtzel asked helplessly.

"I tol' 'em I needed hit an' dat I wouldst pay hit back."

**WILLIE WURTZEL** looked up at Ed Delaney, and then he looked at Annabelle Divine. "I got two friends," he said, "in thirty years around here."

"That's two more than most have," Ed Delaney said.

"But that boy," Willie Wurtzel said, "he's got hundreds; that trust him."

Refugee Smith said, "They trust me 'cause I trust de Lord."

"It'd cost you a hundred thousand bucks if that boy hadn't showed up," Ed Delaney said.

"They wouldn't've handled him right," Willie said in a low voice, "he'd have been unhappy."

Annabelle Divine looked at Willie Wurtzel and she knew then that Willie Wurtzel had been thinking of his fighter and not of the money and she walked over and took one of Refugee's big black hands in hers. "I'd like to shake hands with you," she said.

"You'll never shake a better hand," Willie Wurtzel said in a tight voice, "in a glove or out."

# REFUGEE AND MR. WILLIE

**WILLIE WURTZEL** came down from Stillman's Gym and walked toward the subway. He caught an uptown train with a swift and practiced absence of gallantry, elbowed a route to a single vacant seat, beating out an elderly lady handicapped by poor vision and an encumbering cane.

At 135th Street he disbarked into the teeming maelstrom of Harlem and started across town. He passed Mazda Brown's The Igloo ("Come In And Chew The Fat"), gave a gruff and monosyllabic answer to Free Wheeling Johnson's glad greeting. The little shoeshine boy watched, puzzled, as Willie's figure disappeared into the Eatmor Fish and Chips Shoppe.

Senate "Slippery" Ellum, the proprietor of that establishment and a long time comrade in arms and peace of Refugee Smith, greeted Willie warmly and ushered him to a booth.

Willie sat morosely waiting while Slippery served a customer. Slippery finished and came around the counter and sat down across from Willie.

"Whatsa matter, Mr. Willie?"

Willie signed. "Aw, it's that boy — that Refugee," he said. "Damn if I can't get into more trouble with that boy! Sometimes I wish he drank and chased women like a regular box fighter. . ."

"He used to," Slippery said. "But when you save him that time the Lord purely got to him. An' when the Lord got to him, He got clean to him."

"Yeah," Willie said sorrowfully. "I know that."

"You got a fight comin' up," Slippery said, "that ought to profligate you both; I don't figure how come you is so downmouthed."

"It's like this," Willie said wearily. "I need help. I gotta figure an angle."

"I is two-earin' you," Slippery said.

"Well, I sign him all right," Willie said. "And you know me and that boy. I'd sign him with Superman if Supe would come in at a hunnert sixty."

"Be a good fight," Slippery said absently.

"Yeah," Willie said. "Anyway, while the singin' was goin' on, Uncle Mike he kept sayin' Cap'n this and Cap'n that, about this Johnny Early that we was signin' up with."

"Cap'n, huh?" Slippery mused.

"Yeah. Least that's what I thought," Willie said morosely. "Today it come out in the blats," Willie went on removing his cigar for emphasis, "that the guy was a Chaplain, or supposed to be. 'The Fighting Parson', Johnny Early."

"Ah, ah. . ."

"Correct. You know as well as I do Refugee's kinda partial to a legitimate sky pilot, and I can see the news workin' on him today."

"You think he may carry this Early 'cause he's a Chaplain?"

"Carry him, hell! He's liable to blow the nod."

"He kinda softish, all right, toward the strickly pious," Slippery agreed.

"I put a private dick on him, the Early guy," Willie said. "But you know them lads — take 'em a few days to find a elephant in a one-ring circus."

"You think Early is a phony?" Slippery asked.

"I don't care," Willie said. "I just want Refugee to fight his fight."

"And you is afraid he won't?"

"You ain't jestin'. Hell, I bet my end of the purse. Laid evens he'd chill the Rev. in three heats."

Slippery pondered this for several seconds. Finally he beamed. "Hire you up a girl," he said, "and have her borrow a baby somewhere — a nice young one — then have her run down the aisle hollerin' Mr. Early is its poppa."

Willie thought about this for a minute. "Nope," he said. "That wouldn't work. Refugee wouldn't know what was goin' on before the cops throwed her out."

"Can't you find out nothin' 'bout Early?"

"Not nothing. Not in time anyway. He's been fightin' out on the coast a little bit since the war."

"He a good boy?"

"Damn right, fast and shifty. It's a bad bet for me. With everything right, Refugee mightn't catch him in three."

"How came, then, you wagered the bet?" Slippery asked, surprised. Willie wasn't in the habit of giving himself the worst of it.

"I needed the money."

"What so bad for?" Slippery pressed him.

"It's a long story, kind of stupid. . ."

"Tell me it."

"Well, you know I shipped in the Merchant Marine for awhile and I was in England one time and I guess I got kind of drunk and I don't know just how it happened but it seem like I signed up to put a coupla Jewish refugee kids through growin' up or somethin'."

"Clean up to adultery?" Slippery asked wonderingly.

Willie grinned weakly. "Naw, but quite awhile. Seemed it run four hunnert apiece and I'd kinda talked like I owned the ship instead of bein' secont cook on it and it looked like the price was right. So I give 'em a couple of C's then and signed to send the big chunk when I got home and lined up."

"I see," Slippery said.

"You don't either," Willie said petulantly. "I signed up to pay off in some kind of damn pounds and when the tab came in from The Foundation, it was for near four grand. I thought that two hunnert price was out of line. Anyway, I got dumber and give a guy a marker for the dough and sent it along."

"Who'd you give the marker to?" Slippery asked.

"Sunday Sheehy."

"Funny name; how come he got that name?"

"He got that name," Willie said slowly, "because they say he ain't ever knocked off nobody on Sunday for not pickin' up one of his markers." Willie felt the cool sweat on his brow. "But I know for a fact he slipped up twice when daylight saving time was on."

"Ohhhh. . . ."

"You said it, boy. And I gotta win that bet to pay him off. I hadda give them three frame terms to lay it at all."

"Have you told Refugee about it?"

"Naw. He's dead against gamblin' — anyway, it ain't he won't try! It's just he can't try his best does he have a suspicion he's sluggin' the Lord's servant. It ain't but a hundredth of a secont separates a champion and a trial horse."

"Ain't much separates you from the beeyond. . ."

"Hush. Don't talk like that. Think for me."

"I done thought," Slippery said. "If'n it happens again, I'll call you."

The fight approached. Willie Wurtzel worried, tried a couple of three horse win parlays without success. Refugee seemed to train well but a spark was missing.

Slippery Ellum thought. And finally, discarding the devious, he struck on the idea of telling Refugee Willie's plight.

Refugee stopped by the Eatmor, going down to weigh in the day of the fight and Slippery told him the story of Willie's drunken gesture in England.

Refugee pondered a long time, flexing his hands. Then a big grin split his face. "The Lord done give us a opportunity," he said, "to teach that Mr. Willie a powerful lesson."

"Whatcha mean?" Slippery said.

Refugee smiled again. "Hit's like this, Slip," he began, and for five minutes he outlined a plan to his friend. When he was finished, Slippery roared his delight.

"Okay, Ref, boy, I'll do it."

Willie Wurtzel, in the dressing room before the fight, pleaded desperately. "Maybe he ain't a real Chaplain," he said.

"He wouldn't say he was a Reverent," Refugee told him, "if'n he wasn't. He's be afraid to."

"Anyway," Willie said, "won't you please go out there and beat him to death right offa the bat."

"I'll try," Refugee said lugubriously.

"It might save my life," Willie pleaded. "I bet you'd stop him in three."

"Ah, Mr. Willie, hit's wrong to gamble. This'll be a lesson to you."

"Lesson!" Willie screamed. "You don't want nobody breakin' no commandments — anyway not breakin' 'em on me, do you?"

"Which one?" Refugee asked with real interest. Willie counted on his fingers, gave up. "I don't know which one, by number. But it's the one about murderin' people."

"Who's gonna murder anybody?" Refugee said blandly.

"Ain't anybody gonna murder me if you beat this guy in three heats."

"What if I don't. . . .?"

"I ain't gonna be responsible," Willie said darkly. Then suddenly he caught himself and his voice went up. "I ain't gonna be. Period."

"Tsk, tsk," Refugee clucked. "That's a real shame."

"Refugee," Willie begged, "what's the matter

with you, boy? You never treated me like this before. Your heart done hardened against me solid?"

A man stuck his head in the door and called out to them and Refugee turned to his manager. "My heart done hardened against sin. And gamblin's a sin."

Willie grabbed up the tools of trade and followed his fighter up the aisle.

Through habit he gave the house a quick appraisal and climbed into the ring. The announcer, in few well-chosen redundancies, announced "Johnny Early, Chaplin in the Air Corp, etc. etc. etc." Then he introduced Refugee. "One hundred and fifty eight pounds, undefeated middleweight contender, recently of the United States Army. . ." Warming to his work he took three agonizing minutes to say they would fight ten rounds to a decision. With a short biography of the knock-down timekeeper, he concluded. The ring was cleared and Willie went out with his fighter for instructions.

The instructions from the referee were as terse as the introductions had been long. Refugee went back to his corner.

He came out with the bell, moved in from habit and Willie immediately knew all his fears were well founded. Refugee exhibited a reluctance, a barely perceptible reluctance, that was quickly apparent to Willie's practiced eye. Johnny Early was a smoothly operating wraith behind a long left hand. He moved from Refugee's right and stabbed him silkily.

Willie took his eyes from the ring, cringing from what he saw therein, and glanced down. Slippery Ellum sat in a ringside seat, his face wreathed in an ill-suppressed grin. Near him sat Sunday Sheehy pale and implacable.

The first round was dull. Refugee gave the impression he was trying, but it was a blurred impression. Something seemed to stay his hand for a split instant when he had an opening and it made him look clumsy, his timing bad.

Willie, one eye on Sunday Sheehy, pleaded eloquently between rounds. "Get mad," he begged. "Bull him into a corner, get close; he can't hurt you." But something told him he was talking to hear his own voice. The old phrase 'Whistling in the graveyard' came to his mind with a poignancy beyond belief.

"I'se tryin', Mr. Willie."

The bell rang and Refugee, unhurt and breathing easily, went lethargically forth. Willie Wurtzel looked mutely down at Slippery and heard Slippery's loud comment. "Seem's like old Refugee is strickly neutral, don't it?"

The second round was a bad imitation of the first. Refugee lost it by a mile, not landing once solidly.

When he came back, Willie gave him the last pitch. "Ref, boy, I saved you. Please save me. Go out there and stop this guy. Get offa your feet and give him the business. . ." The ten second buzzer sounded.

"Mr. Willie," Refugee said slowly. "Sinnin' don't pay."

"But —"

"Ain't no buts, the jig is up. I couldn't hurt that boy if'n I tried my best."

"Oh, Refugee, please. . ."

But Refugee had shuffled to the center of the ring. Johnny Early was a little careless now. Obviously this highly touted black boy with the big shoulders had left his fight in Italy. Johnny jarred him experimentally with a right cross and got away unscathed. Refugee's counter punch was wild.

Refugee shuffled after him, his face creased in concentration and Willie heard somebody laugh. He looked down and saw it was Slippery. They'd both, he supposed, have hysterics at his funeral if Sunday's boys didn't take care of the interment, too.

The bell rang. The fatal bell.

Refugee came back and slumped in his corner. Gone was Willie's bet; gone down the river. And speaking of river, maybe that's where he, Willie, would soon be.

But he was a fight manager, a fine second and he had a real love for his fighter. "Ref," he said. "Listen, boy, I may not see you after tonight, but lemme have somethin' to take with me. Not a big clown letting a preliminary boy stab him silly. You're a great fighter, greatest I ever saw, and if you can't hurt this boy it ain't your fault. But lemme have something to remember. . ."

Refugee turned to his manager. His eyes, then, were damp. "You learned your lesson, Mr. Willie, but it won't do no good. . . It just won't help any, you is saveless and. . ." The bell rang.

Refugee went forth. But over Refugee had come a subtle change. It wasn't noticed by the ringsiders, and it wasn't noticed by the erstwhile Chaplain, who, Willie had discovered that afternoon was genuine. But Willie Wurtzel noticed it and he forgot his early demise and he felt the little hairs that graced his neck, rise up.

Out there now was Stanley Ketchel with a black polish job. Joe Gans grown bigger. Out there was his fighter.

Johnny Early led a silky left, moving toward his right away from a clumsy left hook. And that was the end.

Johnny Early's head was attached to his shoulders by a very serviceable neck. This was fortunate, otherwise his head would have been the object of search in the twelfth to twentieth row. As it was, it flew back sickeningly with the impact of Refugee's right cross, then dangled limply as his knees, his waist, his shoulders folded gently to let him collapse on his face.

Willie Wurtzel's moan was heard above the crowd but he didn't quite collapse. He stumbled down the aisle after his triumphant fighter. Bitter tears burned his eyes. It had come one round too late. They cleared the dressing room for them. All but two were gone. One was Slippery Ellum. One was Sunday Sheehy. Willie stood still, watching Sunday's hand creep to his inside pocket. Sunday, he thought vaguely, was getting rather crude. . . right here in the Garden.

"Here's your marker, Willie," Sunday said and he held out the fatal piece of paper.

Willie reached, his hand nerveless, speechless with surprise. Slippery laughed and Willie saw the grin that creased Refugee's face. "It was a lesson to him," Refugee said. "A fine lesson."

"These two," Sunday said, "they told me what the score was about the little kids on the other side. . ."

"An' you're gonna pay for 'em? You gimme the marker for free!"

Sunday Sheehy let a grin split his somber face. "Not exactly for free," he said. "So long." He went on out.

Willie turned. Refugee was grinning. Slippery was, too.

"I'll take my part of the purse," Willie said fervently, "and send it along. Take care of another kid, that'll make three. . ." He paused. "What did you do to Sunday?"

"I posted bond with him," Refugee said. "I posted bond with him that I'd stop Mr. Early in exactly the fourth round. I figured if he knew exactly when the fight was gonna end, he could make hit pay."

"Boy, I thought you'd let me down. I'll never. . . ." Willie stopped. He'd still have five hundred bucks left even if he sent enough off for another refugee, and there was a beetle going tomorrow at Belmont was a shoo in. "I'll never forget this," he finished lamely.

---

# FIRST CLASS MALE

**REFUGEE** Smith ambled down 135th Street, his black face grave. He turned automatically into Senate "Slippery" Ellum's Eatmor Fish & Chips Shoppe, pushed down on the latch of the door. Nothing happened. He backed up and looked at the door, through its dingy glass. The Shoppe was locked; nothing was inside. Refugee noticed the note on the door, then, leaned over and slowly spelled out its brief message.

*Gone to open brunch in Tokyo.*
*S. Ellum.*

Refugee Smith walked a few doors down and turned into The Igloo. (Come in and chew the fat.) The Igloo was a small hamburger stand, presided over by one Mazda Brown, a dark woman of indeterminate age and ancestry. He ordered a bottle of pop, looked at it a minute, then said slowly, "Ole Slip done joined up wid de army?"

Mazda Brown looked over Refugee's head. "He set and sull like a possum, listenin' to de radio sence Pearl Harbor. Yesdidy he give away all his stock, hone up his Yazoo City sabre, and run don't walk to de nearest recruitin' station."

"Ole Slip," Refugee said. "Gone to perish by de sword."

"Man live to die," Mazda Brown said contentedly, "an' I 'spect he's fixin' to nullify some of de enemy 'fore he perish off hisself."

Refugee Smith left his pop untasted, got up and walked out on the street. He started aimlessly toward the subway. "Shine 'em up!"

Refugee stopped, looked down, saw Freezy Johnson and grinned.

He walked over and put one big shoe on Freezy's box. Freezy Johnson picked up his rag and beat out three dots and a dash. Refugee looked down at Freezy Johnson's kinky hair, and saw neatly mowed therein a V.

"Dat's some haircut you got, Freezy," Refugee said.

"If de war last five years," Freezy said, "I can get in hit. I'm buildin' up my moral."

Refugee Smith didn't say anything. On his face was a look of gravest preoccupation.

"Ole Slip was fixin' to join up wid de Marine corpse if he could," Freezy Johnson said, making conversation, "but when he learn they call 'em corpse he say hit give him a kinda squeepish feelin'. Said when he got to be a corpse he kinda wanted hit to take him by surprise."

Refugee pulled his foot down off the box, dropped a dime and started down the street. One shoe was unshined. Freezy called after him but he didn't hear. Lounging in the doorway of the Yellow Front Cabaret and Nite Club, he saw Infinite Sanders, the gambler.

Infinite Sanders had once tried to fix a fight against Refugee, and though Refugee didn't know about that he had an instinctive distrust of Infinite. "Hi, Smith," Infinite said.

"How'do," Refugee said guardedly. "How de policy bank runnin'?"

"Runnin' good," Infinite said. "I don't take nothin' in play but Defense Stamps an' I pays off with Bonds. I done fattened up Mr. Whiskers plenty."

Refugee walked to Lenox Avenue, turned downtown. On a window to his right he saw a soaped sign: "We are Pearl Harboring a Grudge."

"Seem like folks' madder'n a suck-aig houn' wid a door knob," Refugee muttered to himself. He turned into his apartment house and made his way to his flat.

There, with a deep frown on his face he paced back and forth. And as he paced his lips moved. "Lord," he said, "in case you ain't been payin' 'tention to de details, hits like this: I gotta contrack wid you and I've strove to keep hit. I've tried to be a good boy sence you saved me out'n ole river; and whilst I'se on de subjeck — much obliged, Lord."

Refugee made two more trips up and down the room. He loosened his collar, rubbed a big black paw over his face and continued. "Lord, you sent Mr. Willie to save me an' I gotta contrack wid him; I prizefights for Mr. Willie, Lord, an' wid Your help I done coldcocked a few tough boys, Lord, an' I ain't never lost a fight."

Refugee stopped, sat down and took of his shoes and socks. The carpet felt prickly and good on his bare feet. "I hope I ain't wearyin' you, Lord, wid de small talk, but Lord, I gotta fight tomorrow night, and to tell you de truth, Lord, dat fight don't seem like hit amount to a wart on a elephant to de other fight."

"Lord," Refugee said. "I wants to know what to do."

For a long time Refugee Smith walked up and down him room. "Lord," Refugee said, "I gotta notion. I ain't expectin' You to answer me in person . . . ." Refugee's eyes rolled fearfully. "Fack is, Lord, I'd just as lief you didn't do dat. But de notion I got is this."

Refugee thought a minute; he wanted to make his explanation clear. "Lord," he said, "I got twenny dollars in my pocket. I'll take hit an' I'll go down to Bobo Lincoln's crap game. If I runs it up to forty I'll figure you figure hit's all right for me to join up wid de Army. If'n I goes broke I'll figure You wants me to stay civil, an' I'll wait 'til de draft catches me."

Then Refugee, because he was an honest man, made a confession to his Maker. "Lord," he said, and his eyes were closed and his voice was terribly earnest. "De truthful fack is I'd mightily like to get at me some Axists, wid a good straight-edge Charleston pistol. Maybe I ain't got but a thin skim of religion after all."

Refugee walked over and sat down in a chair. He felt pleased with his idea, and mightily relieved. He put on his shoes and socks, buttoned his collar. "Lord," he said, in afterthought of naïve bribery, "In case I gets dat forty dollars I'll give hit all to de Salvation Army."

Bobo Lincoln's place hummed with activity. Many who had been on relief for years were working, now. Refugee elbowed his way into the crap table. Bobo himself was handling the stick at the dice game.

"What's cookin' boy?" Bobo asked, hiding his surprise at seeing Refugee.

"I just come up to shoot a few dices," Refugee said innocently.

"Well," Bobo said cordially, "glad to 'commodate you."

A gangling tannish lad next to Refugee had the dice. He banged the leather cup on the table. "Hot up, dice," he implored fervently. "Give 'em stab-in-de-back day. De seventh day of de 'leventh month. Uhhhhh, wham!"

The boy threw the dice out on the table. They came up four-ace. "Dice! I didn't say nothin' 'bout de year. I just wanted de day or de month. Four-ace or trey-deucy, I ain't particular, diceys. I'm gonna join de Army tomorrow, get me a little ole fever, dice."

The boy rolled a six-ace and handed the cup disconsolately to Refugee. Refugee took out his twenty dollars, threw it over to Bobo and got twenty chips in return. Five of these he laid on the DO line.

He rubbed the dice in his hair, dropped them in the cup. "Dice," he said piously, "'member who you're workin' for." With a flourish he rolled out two aces.

"Jap eyes," Bobo Lincoln said. "The man crapped out. Double up and beat 'em, boys." With a dark and dexterous hand he gathered up all the chips on the DO line, paid the field and the DON'T line.

Refugee looked at the dice for one unbelieving instant, then slowly picked them up. He dropped them in the cup, placed ten chips on the DO line.

"Natchal 'em, dice," he plead. "How many days in de week?" Refugee rolled the dice out, bouncing them against the wall around the table. They fell back on two sixes.

"A Mussolini communick," Bobo said. "More craps. Get on the line, boys. He's still firin'. He ain't lost nothin' but his money."

Refugee Smith put his last five chips down. "Lord," he said silently. "I trust You." Slowly he put the dice in the cup, slowly he drew back his arm. Swiftly he threw the dice. His head was bent and he didn't watch the dice, instead he looked down at the table, his head bent in supplication.

Bobo Lincoln's cheerful voice came through to him. "And the men throwed acey-deucy. Three messes of craps in a row! Old Refugee done throwed the Axis."

Refugee looked up at the dice, confirmed Bobo's announcement, let the cup fall from his hand and turned away.

"Need some money Refugee?" Bobo Lincoln asked, concerned. "Naw," Refugee said sadly. "I never really come up to gamble." He turned and walked toward the door. The gangling youth who had stood beside Refugee gave his pants pockets one more hopeless inspection and followed Refugee out of the room. Downstairs on the street, Refugee stood a moment. The boy beside him said: "I reckon I might as well get on down to de recruitin' office."

Refugee looked up, past the boy, saw the finger of Uncle Sam from a poster in a window pointing directly at him. "I WANT YOU" the legend read.

"Please forgive me, Lord," Refugee Smith said humbly.

"What'd you say?" the boy asked.

"I said I believe I'll just go along wid you," Refugee Smith said desperately.

Refugee Smith sat on the rubbing table, his face in his bandaged hands. Willie Wurtzel, his coat off and his brightly colored vest unbuttoned paced frantically up and down the little room.

"What the hell is the matter with you?" Willie wailed. "Just because this guy outweighs you is no sign you should go into a coma."

"I ain't worried about dat, Mr. Willie," Refugee said sadly. Somebody called at the door and Refugee pulled his bathrobe tighter around his shoulders and stood up. "I couldn't whip a bantyweight, tonight," he said, and walked out of the door.

Up the aisle they came, Refugee in the old bathrobe that Willie had bought him in St. Louis for his first fight. It was faded and green and on its back was a harp and as usual it got a laugh. But Refugee Smith's face remained doleful and Willie Wurtzel, behind him, thought about a bet he'd laid and his face was doleful, too.

The referee called the fighters to the center of the ring and for the first time Refugee noticed the man he had to fight.

Sergeant Jebby, on special leave for this fight, was a big man, bigger than Refugee by twenty pounds and he had a streak of cruelty in him that was an asset in the ring.

"How come you ain't in the army, Smith?" Jebby said with a sneer.

"Flat feet?"

Refugee didn't say anything. The referee finished his instructions and the fighters turned and went back to their corners.

"Knock the big horse's neck loose from his teeth," Willie said angrily.

Refugee heard the bell and came out of his corner.

Jebby bulled him into a clinch, said in his ear. "This is the first time you ever been in the ring with a real fighter. With the laces of his right glove he scored Refugee's cheek going out of the clinch.

Refugee pawed with a left, caught a left hook to the belly that made him grunt. Jebby's winging right was too high, but it threw his head back and Willie Wurtzel from the ringside saw the thin trickle of blood start from an old cut above Refugee's eye.

Willie was in the ring with the bell and got the bleeding stopped.

"Boy," he plead, "Tell me what's the matter with you?"

Refugee looked up at Willie Wurtzel and he formed the words slowly. "The Lord ain't in my corner," he said.

Willie Wurtzel spoke gently. "Why ain't He, boy?"

"'Cause I done promised to join up wid de Army, an' de Lord, he good as tole me not to."

Willie Wurtzel cringed. He had known this day was coming. He had known it a long time. And the idea of his meal ticket being gone hurt. Financially, it hurt. Willie started to say something, the warning buzzer caught him. Willie thought of the bet he had laid on this fight as he scrambled down from the ring.

The second round was worse than the first. Refugee Smith, black and bloody, was a pathetic spectacle. Willie Wurtzel, white and bleeding at the purse was a pathetic sight, too.

Refugee made it back to his corner under his own power with the bell but it was an obvious effort. Willie Wurtzel, scrambled into the ring, disregarding physical ministrations he leaned down and shouted in his fighter's ear.

"How'd the Lord tell you that?"

Through puffed and bleeding lips Refugee sketched briefly his round with the dice at Bobo Lincoln's crap game. Before Willie could answer the buzzer sounded and then the bell.

Willie Wurtzel scrambled under the ring apron, out of his little satchel he plucked a Bible. Hastily, he flipped the pages to the Proverbs. There was nothing like the Proverbs to prove a point. "I gotta keep him outta the army," Willie muttered to himself, "as long as I can . . . ." Suddenly as he thumbed the pages he saw a line. It leaped up at him and he saw it. *I called upon the Lord in my distress: The Lord answered me and set me in a large place.* Willie glanced uneasily around the vast reaches of the Garden. He flipped hastily to the Proverbs.

Up in the ring Refugee, battered and bloody was trying to stall out the round. Willie Wurtzel looked down at the Bible and another line came up to him. *These things doth the Lord hate . . . . . A proud look, a lying tongue and hands that shed innocent blood.*

The bell rang and Willie scrambled back up, helped his fighter to the corners. "It's all right," he said into Refugee's ear. "The Lord wouldn't be hanging around no crap game . . . And the Lord hates them Japanese, all right. Listen!" — Willie read aloud.

"Dat de Book, Mr. Willie?"

"Yeah. And listen . . . . . *with good advice make war.* That's a coupla pages on over. Right outta the book."

"Okay, Mr. Willie," Refugee said and his voice was mightly relieved. "I'll get out and lower de boom on this fellow 'cause I takes my examination in de mornin' an' I want to get a good nights sleep."

Willie Wurtzel looked across the ring at Sergeant Jebby and he felt an instants tiny pity. "You know," he said slowly, "That Jebby's kinda got a proud look on his puss." Then he turned his head away to hide his eyes. Me a Jew, he thought and him a black man, and we do all right. That's what he wants to fight for . . . . He scrambled down from the ring. "A grand'll get you four hunnert my boy wins," he said to a gambler at the ringside.

---

Willie heard a voice call to the Lord. He leaned over and picked up Refugee Smith, the finest middleweight he'd ever seen.

# REFUGEE RETURNS HOME

**Harlem's miracle worker, Refugee Smith, revisits the past, and brings it up to date.**

**IT WAS** a languid day of sun and shadow, and Harlem was out in force. Refugee Smith, blazing in a fancy coat and bright yellow shoes approximately the length and breadth of violin cases, lounged into the Eatmor Fish and Chips Shoppe, a toothpick dancing in his wide, good-humored mouth and a great hunger in his mind, if not in his stomach. Senate "Slippery" Ellum, proprietor of the shoppe, looked across the counter at Refugee and said: "I can't put up with it no longer. I done bought up a bunch of deefense bonds and I done got a job air-raid wardenin', but it won't do. I craves to get me in razor range of some of them Axists and I ain't likely to get there just settin' here in Harlem."

"You fixin' to recruit?" Refugee asked.

"Enlist," Slippery corrected him. "The recruitin' office is where you go to join up and they call that enlistin'."

Refugee Smith pondered this a moment. "I reckon they ask you a lotta asks when you go to enlist?" he said.

"I guess they do," Slippery told him.

"Like if you ever stole nothin' or killed nobody or anything like dat?" Refugee said with studied casualness.

"Oh, I reckon they don't inquire as to if you done a little totin' if you worked for somebody. Course if you done kilt off someone and run off they might not like that."

"Reckon they'd put you on de chain gang."

"If you done a little light totin'? Why, no —"

"Naw," Refugee said, "if you'd kilt off somebody."

Slippery Ellum leaned over the booth and his face was creased with concern. "Ref, boy," he said, "you *ain't* kilt nobody, have you?"

The hard-held blandness of Refugee's voice melted under the scrutiny of his friend. "Slip," he said slowly, "you is de bes' friend I got outside Mr. Willie, and Slip, de answer to de ask is —"

"What?"

"I dunno," Refugee said.

"You dunno," Slippery said slowly. Then, his voice tinged with pride at his knowledge, he added: "Did you put a mirror at his mouth? If they's dead hit don't fog up."

"I never taken de time," Refugee said. "I done been working on de Mary Jane for two years but when I seen de blood on de floor of de engine room I resigned over the side." Then briefly, his eyes pleading for understanding, he told Slippery of the old days on the Mary Jane, roustabouting up and down the Mississippi, and his long battle with the river until Mr. Willie pulled him out.

It had been almost three years ago and a colored boy named Refugee Smith got in a crap game. The time was night, the place was the boiler room on the Mississippi steamer Mary Jane someplace off a little town called Woodland, not far from Natchez.

Refugee was a roustabout on the Mary Jane and Sixty Jubal was also a roustabout on the Mary Jane and they were, with others, shooting craps. Sixty Jubal threw in a pair of funny dice and Refugee caught him at it and took Sixty's gun away from him and slugged him over the head with it and the last time Refugee saw Sixty Jubal, Sixty was lying in a widening pool of his own blood, if not as good as dead at least the best Refugee could do with one lick.

Refugee didn't stay to find out if Sixty was dead or to help with artificial respiration if he wasn't because in Refugee Smith's mind was a picture of a chain gang, or maybe a rope. So Refugee Smith went over the side into the Father of Waters and therein gradually was drowning. In fact, he was so definitely drowning that he called on the Lord to save him and he made a deal with the Lord that if he was saved he would lead the good life thereafter.

So Willie Wurtzel, cast upon the same stream in a rowboat he couldn't row and by circumstances he couldn't circumvent, saved him. Willie Wurtzel was a prize-fight manager without a fighter, so he took this black man from the water and made a fighter of him and to this day Refugee Smith had never lost a fight.

Slippery whistled admiringly. "Ain't no wonder you is so devoteful to Mr. Willie."

"De Lawd, too," Refugee said. "He's de One."

"I reckon so," Slippery said. "I reckon He just juggled Mr. Willie around for you that night."

Refugee was silent for a moment, then he wrenched his mind back to the original question. "But dat ain't tellin' me would they pick me up for killin' Sixty did I try to enlist?"

"Well," Slippery said judicially, "it's this-a-way. Uncle Sam he got a long arm and when it ain't reachin' out for you I wouldn't tickle the palm."

Refugee thought a long moment, then haltingly, while little beads of sweat sat on his brow, he said, "I got know 'bout Sixty."

Slippery sat and thought. "Call Mr. Willie," he said finally, "he'll give you the straight facts."

Refugee's face cleared with relief. "He's de very one," he said. He fished in his pocket, found a nickel and walked over to the phone. Presently he came back. His face was grave again. "He done gone to Atlantic City wid Miss Deevine," he announced.

Slippery's face fell, then brightened. "You is a right famous prize fighter, boy, and if'n they's gonna pick you up they'd done it before now."

"Hits a long ways down there," Refugee said. "An' de high sheriff he mighta just racked it up in de book to throw me into de jailhouse did I pass his way."

"That's a fact," Slippery agreed, "and you get to messin' with the guv'ment it might be a different story."

"Wid a sadder endin'," Refugee added. He paused, licked his lips. "But since Pearl Harbor I'se set and studded about hit an' I'se like you, Slip. I gotta get in de Army if'n I can."

"What you fixin' to do?"

Refugee Smith straightened up and his face was set. "They ain't but one thing to do," he said. "I gotta go down there an' find out if'n they's lookin' for me."

Slippery Ellum looked at his friend, looked around his little place. "I 'bout sold out my stock," he said slowly. "And you've been a good friend to me."

"Yeah . . ."

"And we'll join up together, when we unlaws you."

"I ain't . . ."

"I is goin' with you," Slippery said. "Two heads is thicker'n one."

"Slip, boy, I don't want you to do dat," Refugee said, his eyes clouding.

"Shut up, boy," Slippery said. "Let's get in the icebox and see if we can eat up all the perishers."

**WILLIE WURTZEL**, with the aid of a lightly tipped redcap, shepherded his companion into a cab at the station, and saw her off. Then, his eyes bright, he walked out onto Eighth Avenue. He had been gone a week and he was homesick. He started walking up toward the Garden, smelling the familiar smells, viewing with a fresh delight the tawdriness and brutality of this city where he lived. A cab hastening to the station with a fare tried craftily to crush him lifeless to the pavement. Willie avoided this fate with casual dexterity and the curses he hurled meaninglessly at the back of the taxi were genial.

At the Garden he stopped and read in detail all the posters in the entrance that told of coming events. Finishing this pleasant task he turned east on 49th Street and from there to Broadway he spoke to half the people he met. Willie Wurtzel was home.

He stopped in at Jacobs Beach, exchanged casual insults with half a dozen denizens therein, got all the gate receipts and fight results of the last week, manfully resisted a two-dollar touch, and made his way to the phone booth.

He dialed Refugee's apartment, got no answer and when he hung up he got back two nickels. He discovered that the nickel he had gotten back with his own was lead and used it to call Slippery Ellum's Eatmor Fish & Chips Shoppe. Again he got no answer. With the lead nickel in his hand he made his way toward the uptown subway kiosk. The day was especially fine; the air was nicely diluted with carbon monoxide and the Giants were ahead in the sixth.

At 135th Street he got off the subway and made his way to Slippery's place of business. He tried the door, found it locked, then looked down and noticed the penciled note pasted to the door.

*Gone to Tokyo — and not to pull no ginricky nether.* S. ELLUM

Willie grinned. He walked down two doors and turned into Mazda Brown's The Igloo ("Come in and Chew the Fat.") Mazda herself, a large black lady of indeterminate age, was occupying most of the space behind the counter.

"How do," Mazda greeted him.

"I'm Willie Wurtzel," Willie said. "Refugee Smith's manager. Do you know where I could find him?"

"No, sir," Mazda said.

"Have you seen him lately?"

"No, sir, I ain't."

"How long," Willie said, "since you have seen him?"

**MAZDA BROWN** turned around and consulted an alarm clock crouching between two empty beer cases on a shelf behind her. "'Bout a week," she said.

"A week," Willie repeated in slight alarm. He changed his tack: "Old Slippery gone to join the Army, I guess."

"No, sir. Not yet."

"Just leave, did he?"

"No, sir. He been gone 'bout a week, too."

"You don't know where I could find him, do you?"

"No, sir."

"Could you tell me where he lives?" Willie asked wearily.

"He used to live over his place," Mazda said.

"But he ain't there any more?"

"No, sir, he's left."

"And you don't have any idea where he went?"

"No, sir," Mazda said, "'cept he went with Refugee."

"Refugee?" Willie said and his voice held real alarm. "Ohhh! I got him signed for a fight three weeks from now. Three weeks," he said again and his voice was anguished. "And I already posted the forfeit money."

Mazda Brown said nothing.

Willie Wurtzel reached into his pocket and took out a dollar bill. He laid it on the counter.

Mazda Brown picked it up and rang up fifty cents. "I can't tell you no dollar's worth," she said.

"Tell me what you can," Willie pleaded.

"They done went south," Mazda Brown said.

"South," Willie said, anguish in his voice. "But why, when?"

"They left 'bout a week ago," Mazda Brown said. "And what ole Slip said didn't make no sense."

"What'd he say?" Willie said. "Tell me."

"He say they was goin' down south to defrost Refugee's conscience," Mazda Brown said. She looked out of the window a moment. "An' if dat boy' conscience needs defrostin' why, most ever'body in Harlem is froze up solid."

Willie Wurtzel turned and walked out onto the street. The carbon monoxide was rank in his nostrils, and on a newsstand he automatically noted the box score on a late edition. The Giants had lost in the ninth to the Phillies. His mind went back.

Long ago, almost three years ago, he had gone down to New Orleans to look at a fighter that he had a chance to sign. The lad he'd gone to see hadn't been a fighter and would never be a fighter.

And in New Orleans, Willie Wurtzel had gone broke. And broke, he was as popular as a boll weevil. So, wearily, with a few dollars in his pocket, on foot, he'd started north. He longed to hear an *r*. If not familiarly used as in *boil*, at least in a word where it was plainly written down.

With four dollars and three bunions he had made it into a village known as Woodland and, stopping there for coffee and what passed in those parts for human companionship, he had heard in the rear of the restaurant the click of dice, whose accents never vary. Idly he went back, and was welcomed to the fray. He faded a man a dollar and the man rolled out a pair of obvious tops, those crooked dice so-called because they have the same number both on tops and bottoms and with which it is impossible to lose.

**NOW** the world over when a man catches another cheating at gambling he immediately has the undivided support, in any ensuing contention, of all the other players. Willie snatched up the money, called the man, accurately, a dirty crook and other things. But in Woodland the ground rules were different. Willie erupted from the restaurant at a full gallop and turned onto the main stem, downgrade for the sake of added speed, with the entire quorum of crapshooters, cheater and cheatees alike, in loud pursuit.

Down the hill he sped, increasing his lead with every leap. He topped a rise, and catapulted down. And there the street ended, and the Mississippi River began. Willie threw a quick glance in each direction, saw a small rowboat, leaped into it and pushed off. A whirling eddy took him out and soon all sound died except the moan of a steamboat whistle far downstream. Willie moaned softly in reply, took up the oars and learned he couldn't row in one long, hard lesson. Finally with oars awash and hands afire, he heard a splashing and a negro voice calling to the Lord. Willie paddled over and picked up Refugee Smith, the finest middleweight he'd ever seen. Refugee had hit a man over the head with a gun and jumped off the boat. . . .

Willie Wurtzel shook himself, looked up and down the Harlem street and knew in his heart what he must do. He hailed a cab, went to his bank and got out all his cash and headed for the airport. He could get to Woodland from New Orleans, and planes went to New Orleans though he didn't know why.

**REFUGEE SMITH** and Slippery Ellum approached Woodland with prudence and caution. They had detrained at Memphis, taken a happy tour of Beale Street and then sold their good clothes and acquired two pairs of old overalls, two hickory shirts. After a few miles they gave their shoes away.

"We get into Woodland dressed up good," Slippery said. "They'd th'ow us under the jailhouse for stealing the clothes."

Refugee squeezed the warm dust of the road between his toes. "I 'spect dats a natchal fack," he said. "We oughtta be makin' hit into Woodland pretty soon." he said. "We done hitched an' hiked four days since Memphis."

"When we get close," Slippery said, "I'll go into the town and reconsider. You lay up out'n the town an' I'll come back and tell you which way the wind blows."

They spent that night in a small cabin. Slippery told the owner, an aged black man with a soft hand on a harmonica, that they were going south to hoe cotton. The old man told them that Woodland lay ten miles ahead and that he hadn't been in since the flood which he thought was back in nineteen twenty-seven. They had rounded up every man in the county then, to work on the levees to save the town.

"Seems like a shame," Slippery said, thinking all this would have been avoided had Woodland washed away.

"Hit war," the old man said. "But he ain't in no hurry," he said beckoning with his head toward the river. "He'll git hit one day. Woodland jes' a pimple on his aidge. He'll squish hit off one day." He paused. "I got a catfish pole baited," he said, "an' a trotline out. You boys better stay for breakfus."

The next morning after breakfast Slippery called the old man out and Refugee hid a five-dollar bill where he wouldn't find it too soon and they took their departure.

A mile from the town Refugee marked a spot on the river's bank where he would be and turned off. Slippery went on into the town.

Late in the afternoon he came back. "Ain't no pitcher of you in the post office nor the depot," he told Refugee. "They gotta new high sheriff since you was swimmin' down this-a-way." Slippery paused, then added with slow relish: "Old one got drunk and shot hisself with his own gun."

"Did you ask aroun' de warehouse and de landin'?" Refugee asked.

"Yeah. I asked. They say maybe some river-boat hustler get kilt and buried here, maybe they ain't. Seem like a dead roustabout don't cause no more commotion'n varmint gettin' a shoat."

Then across the water came a long eerie sound. Refugee jumped up. "Dat's hit!" he said. "Dat's de Mary Jane an' de man is blowin' for a landin'. Come on!"

"Where you goin'?"

"We's gonna get down to de landin' and see if dat Sixty's on there. If he on there we're goin' back to New York town. If he ain't on there, you can go aboard an' ask after him."

"Okay," Slippery said. "I guess they don't know you in this town noway."

They got to the landing at the same time as the boat. The gangplank came down. Two roustabouts, strange to Refugee, wrestled a barrel down onto the pier. The gangplank started back up.

Refugee shouted, "Cap'n, you going south?"

"I ain't goin' across country," the captain yelled. "Get aboard, you two! I got rush stuff here for New Orleans and you all look stout."

"Come on," Refugee said. He took Slippery by the arm and they went up the gangplank. A bell rung someplace, the whistle blew and the pilot started taking the boat out to the channel again in the gathering dusk.

Refugee started below decks and his heart beat in his throat. Slippery didn't care for water much and the boat vibrated alarmingly.

**WILLIE WURTZEL** pulled into Woodland in his rented car, hot, tired and dirty. He found the main street, turned down toward the river, more slowly than he'd made it last time. He turned the car into the curb at the street's end, got out and walked down to the shore. Far out on the river he could discern the idling lights of a boat. He walked stiffly down to the landing.

There was a faded white man lounging there in an ancient motorboat tied to the dock. "You see anything of a couple of strange colored boys around here lately?" Willie asked.

"Cap'n took on a couple of roustabouts," the man said. "Dunno whether they's strange or not. One negro looks pretty much like 'nother'n at night."

"What boat was it?" Willie said, knowing the answer, feeling the answer before it came.

"Mary Jane," the man said. "Fer N'Awlins."

Willie looked at the man's boat, patently unseaworthy. He looked at the fading riding lights of the Mary Jane. He took a deep breath. "I wantcha to take me out there," he said. "I gotta get aboard tonight."

The man looked at Willie, spat over the side of his boat. "Be ten dollars," he said.

Willie crawled timidly into the boat, and the man fiddled with the engine and it roared to life.

"Better pay me now," the man said, "never kin tell about this danger thing."

Willie handed the man a bill.

The boat sputtered on into the darkness, too loudly for conversation, but in half an hour they caught the Mary Jane. The man cut the motor and Willie gave a hail.

"What you want?" the captain hollered down.

"I want aboard," Willie said.

"Go on away," the captain said, "'fore I drop somethin' on you."

**WILLIE WURTZEL**, long used to shouting above the din of a prizefight crowd, filled his lungs. "I'm Willie Wurtzel," he screamed, "from N'York and I gotta hand fulla money. And I want aboard."

He heard the paddle wheel chunk into reverse and a light come on and the ladder unrolled down the side. Willie climbed up.

"Okay," the captain said. "I'll have that fare now. Where do you want off?"

"I . . . I dunno," Willie said. "I'm looking for them boys you took on at Woodland."

The captain looked at him more closely. "Well," he said, "when you figure where you're goin' come on up to the wheelhouse. I'll be there."

Willie looked out at the river. 'I ain't gonna run off," he said.

"The roustabouts stay down in the engine room," the captain added over his shoulder.

Willie groped his way toward the center of the boat. "Oughta be a door around here someplace," he muttered. He stopped. That was Slippery Ellum's voice, raised in exultation:

"Hit him on the head when he ducks, Ref, boy!"

Willie Wurtzel felt the cold sweat break on his ample brow. He tried to yell, broke for the door from which the voice had issued.

Willie Wurtzel's entrance into the arena stopped the fight, because Willie Wurtzel had opened the door and rushed through it and the door opened on a pair of extremely steep stairs. He felt Slippery pick him up and help him back. He looked up. Nothing could be heard but the steady throb of the engines, unattended now.

There in a glob of light stood Refugee Smith and a large, heavily muscled coffee-colored man who Willie guessed weighed two hundred. He was all man and all mad and as Slippery pulled Willie back the big man rushed at Refugee.

Refugee stabbed him delicately on the nose and let him go by and turned and waited, a coiled black spring.

"Don't hit him!" Willie screamed. "Your hands ain't taped and there ain't no purse and you got a fight comin' up soon!"

Refugee Smith glanced up. "How'do, Mr. Willie," he said without surprise. "I'll be th'ough in a minute."

"What you fightin' him for?" Willie wailed. "Besides for nothin'?"

Refugee watched his man. "Dis here is de fellow I thought I kilt dat time an' come clean down here to fin' out. I'se so glad to see him I put out de han' of frenship an' whilst we's shakin' hands and goodbyin' bygonners, he whup out a razor and try to carve me loose from my lights."

"Don't hit him with your bare hands," Willie pleaded. "I'll get him jugged for pullin' a razor on you." He turned to the circle of silent watchers. "Stop it," he begged. "That boy's hands are worth fifty grand."

Nobody moved except Sixty Jubal. He came back, came back low, swinging, trying to get his man down, to make it rough and tumble. Refugee cut his eye with a sharp left jab, and moved Sixty's nose across his face with an accurate held-in right cross. He sucked in his stomach, moving like a toreador, and let his man go by.

Willie Wurtzel, watching this beautiful product of his tutelage, yelled: "Straighten him up with a left hook and let him have the right downstairs." It was his fighter out there and this was a fight. Willie Wurtzel forgot all else.

Refugee Smith nodded. Sixty Jubal came. Refugee moved, raked his knuckles through Sixty's bloody features, straightening him and the right whistled. Sixty Jubal went down writhing. He rolled over on his side, looked up at Refugee. "Okay, Ref," he managed. "I'll do hit."

Willie Wurtzel, habit still on him, ran out, grabbed his fighter. "Your hands all right, boy?" he asked.

"Yes, sir."

Willie Wurtzel heaved a sigh, then his indignation rose in him. "What you want to risk your hands on a lug like him for, just 'cause he pulled a razor on you?"

"Why," Refugee said, "I wasn't fightin' Sixty cause he tried to cut me, Mr. Willie. I was just showin' him de light."

"Light!" Willie Wurtzel screamed. "Why, wouldn't no church take that guy . . . not even in a box. . . ."

"But," Refugee said, "I wasn't tryin' to lead him into de fold, Mr. Willie, I was persuadin' him to join up wid de Army. When he say *okay*, he was agreein' to enlist when he got to N'Awlins. Course I'se fixin' to keep an eye on him till den."

Willie Wurtzel looked at Refugee. "But what does the Army have to do with it?" he fumbled.

"Slippery an' me," Refugee said patiently, "we come down here to see if I had kilt him off or not dat time I hit him wid his gun, but when he pull dat razor on me I figure he oughta be in wid us."

"With you?" Willie Wurtzel said dazed.

"Sho. Me an' Slip's gonna join up," Refugee said, his face wreathed in a happy smile, "now that I ain't got no law lookin' for me. An'," he finished, "I figures dat Sixty such a snake in de grassed dat he be de very one to fight dem Japs."

"But," Willie began, "I got a forfeit posted . . ."

**HE LOOKED** up and saw Refugee's beaming face and bit back his words after a moment — he reached out and took one big black hand between his two pudgy ones. He turned and made his way blindly to the stairs that led up to the deck.

At the rail he stopped and looked out over the water. The moon had come between two clouds and he saw the bank. Below, the Father of Waters rolled unheeding to the Gulf. He wants to join the Army, Willie thought; he wants to fight for God and country, for Jews and Negroes and . . . a light blinked out from the faraway shore. "And that guy over there," he said aloud, "who just blew out his light."

Suddenly Willie Wurtzel grinned. "Gosh," he muttered. "*He's never lost a fight.*" He started for the wheelhouse. Maybe the captain knew a joint in New Orleans where they would lay a man a price on how the war came out.

"Remember out in St. Louis, your first fight," Willie whispered, "I told you the Lord was in your corner and to go out swingin'."

# ONE BY LAND

**"Go out there and smite him, boy," Willie Wurtzel said, "smite him."
And Refugee Smith, the long-lost meal ticket, went out and smote.**

**WILLIE WURTZEL**, late of 49th and Broadway, erstwhile manager of Refugee Smith, Middle-weight Contender, sat in the boat and heard the lapping of the waves.

Once, long ago, he had sat in a little rowboat and heard the lapping of the waves. That time he had been in the middle of the Mississippi River and the waves were small and tepid and that time from the darkness had come the rich brown voice of a poor black man calling on the Lord for succor. Willie had saved him. And *he* had been Refugee Smith, a lean, big-boned black man with grace in his soul and a natural right cross laden with anesthesia.

Refugee was in the Army now. Now these many months. And Willie Wurtzel in his haste to get the war over and get his meal ticket back had signed on a freighter as a cook, second class, a position which turned out to give him sole charge of the dish-washing department.

But right now Willie didn't think of that, he heard the lapping of the waves, the waves that were quite high and vigorous and cold, waves that mayhap sloshed down from Greenland in route to warmer climes. He heard the waves and they became in his mind the waves of the gentle Mississippi lapping warmly at a little boat long, long ago. And Willie sat up and looked out into the blackness, striving to hear the sound of the voice that had once called to the Lord for aid.

He heard it, not loud, but clear enough, and for that lapse perhaps he is excused for Willie Wurtzel, along with the others in the boat, heard many things they hadn't heard the first few nights.

The Skipper heard the clanking of a windmill, a sound he hadn't heard for fifty years and the third mate heard the singing sound of a wagon wheel on freezing snow. But Willie heard a voice that sounded like Refugee's and the voice said: "The Lord is in your corner, Mr. Willie. Keep dat chin up."

Willie Wurtzel grinned to himself thinking: These rations made that chin deal easier. I ain't got but one, now. Aloud he said to the boat at large, "Five'll get you eight if we ain't picked up tomorrow." He reconsidered; those odds were out of line even with a hint at divine guidance. "Even money," he said, "even money we get picked up tomorrow."

But nobody answered him.

**MIKE GOLDEN**, in his smoke shop on 49th Street, stood behind his counter and wondered whether he ought to call up Ed Delaney, the commission man, and tell him the news, or wait until Ed came in and save a nickel. Ed Delaney ought to know, but Ed probably would find out anyway. Mike moved the cigar from his mouth deftly from port to starboard, took a cloth, polished his glass counter, and glanced up. In the door stood a big black man in a big brown uniform. Behind him stood a smaller, lighter man in the same garb.

"How'do, Mr. Goldie," Refugee Smith said, beaming. "I is lookin' for Mr. Willie. I got fifteen days of liberty from last Monday an' I admire to find that Mr. Willie an' su'prise him."

Mike Golden came around the counter and shook Refugee's hand. "Wurtzel?" he said.

Refugee nodded, then added, "This here is Slippery Ellum, Mr. Goldie. Me an' him been soldierin' together. We joined up the same day."

**MIKE GOLDEN** shook Slippery's hand. "Willie's in the hospital," he said without preliminaries.

"Hospital?" Refugee said blankly.

"Yeah. Exposure, scurvy, malnutrition, sunburn, incipient pneumonia."

"Lordy," Slippery said. "He gonna recupe?"

"Yeah," Mike said. "He shipped out on a freighter and they tie with a torpedo. They was around in one of them little boats for quite a while before they get picked up."

"I be dogged," Refugee said. "I been soldierin' aroun' in Arizona without no more danger than getting' maybe shot as a error and Mr. Willie he done gone out and heroicked."

"I don't take no credit from Willie," Mike said, "but he was tryin' to get the war done with so's he could get you back and cut some of them fat purses. Fact was he was broke."

"Broke?" Refugee said. "Me'n him made lotsa money, me fightin' an' him talkin'. . . ."

"Oh, yeah," Mike said. "But Willie always hadda good change of pace with a buck did he have it, and he ain't cut no purses since you been gone."

"What hospital he in?" Refugee asked. "I'll git up there an' see him."

"I don't know the name," Mike said. "It's the one up on the park. . ."

"Hold on," Slippery said, "I done ideaed up a idea."

"Not go see Mr. Willie?" Refugee said blankly.

"Not yet," Slippery said. "Not until after the fight; then when you goes up to see him you has got a pocketful of money for him. What'd help him recupe quicker?"

"Nothin'," Mike said.

"What fight?" Refugee asked.

"Your fight. You gets a fight, you is in good shape, you cuts the purse sideways and takes Mr. Willie his share."

"Not let Mr. Willie know about hit?"

"That's right."

"Why, why I ain't boxed none for pretty near two years," Refugee said. "An' without Mr. Willie in my corner . . ." He paused. "But dat'd really su'prise him. . . ."

"I'll manage you," Slippery said. He turned to Mike. "What kinda fighters you got aroun' now?"

"I ain't been to a fight since they started callin' the Garden the 4-F tango academy."

"You mean they ain't no good fighters around?" Refugee asked. "Maybe even in the shape I'm in with my timin' all off . . .?"

"Sure," Slippery said. "Like Louis took Smellin'."

"There's one good boy in your class around," Mike Golden said. "Name of Walker. He's got a busted eardrum — he's 4-F."

"Well bust the other'n," Slippery said, "does he choose us."

"I'd stay away from him," Mike said, "if you're rusty."

"Let's go promote with the promoter," Slippery said. "You take a bundle of rustlin' money in to Mr. Willie he'll rise outta that bed like a hello gyro."

"*What?*" Refugee said.

"You heard what I said," Slippery announced. "Let's go see the promoter."

Mike watched their uniformed backs out of the door. "Tell me how you come out," he called after them. He turned back to his counter. "He's a good fellow," he said aloud. "I hope he don't fumble himself into Walker."

"Who's Walker?" Ed Delaney said from the door.

"Hello, Ed. Dummy Walker, the fighter," Mike said. "Hear about Willie Wurtzel?"

"Yeah," Ed said. "I was up to see him."

"How does he do?"

"He don't look like he used to but he ain't gonna die."

"He know you?"

"He offered to lay me a price he got picked up tomorrow."

Mike Golden shook his head. "His boy, Smith, is in on fifteen-day furlough."

"Yeah. I didn't see him up at the hospital."

"Him an' another man name of Ellum have gone over to try to get a fight. They figure to get a fight and take Willie a cut. Surprise him."

"H'mm," mused Ed Delaney. "Only other guy to see Willie was a kid name of Free Wheeling Johnson, shoeshine boy from Harlem."

"Freezy Johnson. Willie and Refugee give him some blood once, saved his life," Mike Golden said.

"Yeah," Ed said. "I remember. Refugee give him a coupla gills right before a fight. I like to lose a package on that one."

"Good boy," Mike Golden said. "That Smith."

"What about Walker?"

"If Smith gets a fight I hope it ain't Walker. He's sharp."

"Refugee boxed any?" Delaney asked.

"Naw."

"Smith'd draw. He was a great fighter," Ed Delaney said.

"Yeah."

Ed Delaney looked at his fingernails, shined them off his cuff. "They won't give Willie no papers to read for a while."

"He wouldn't know about it," Mike Golden said.

"He ain't gotta radio in his room," Ed Delaney said.

"Stick around," Mike said. "They'll be back pretty soon."

**ED DELANEY** looked at his watch and nodded. They weren't back soon, but eventually they were back.

Slippery gave them the results. "We done signed," he gloated. "Ref vs. Walker, ten rounds to a incision, winner gits 37 ½ percentage, the loser gits 12 ½ percentage. The fight's next Friday night. We catches the train the next mornin' and gets to camp on time."

"Mr. Jakes, he talk on de long-distant telephone to my commandin' officer an' he say hit all right if'n I give my share to de Army Relieve. I talk wid him, too, an' he say hit all right 'bout Mr. Willie's share. I can give hit to him," Refugee added. "An' dat suits me, causin' I is drawin' good wages. Natchel fack of de matter is if'n you don't shoot no dice yo' money kinda backs up on you."

"Well," Ed Delaney said. "You got a fight. Now all you gotta do is win it. That short end ain't gonna be much."

"Why, what you talkin' about?" Slippery demanded. Refugee ain't *never* lost no fight."

Mike Golden polished his counter aimlessly "He ain't never been in there without Willie in his corner, neither."

"De *Lord* is in Refugee's corner," Slippery said finally.

"Don't go worryin' de Lord wid dis piddlin' little fight," Refugee said hastily.

"I ain't worryin' de Lord," Slippery said. "I guess de Lord can letcha have a angel for one night — a apprentice angel, anyways."

"Guess I'll go up to Mr. Stillman's and see if I can find someone to work wid me a little," Refugee said. "I got my faith but I'd like to git sharpened up a little, too."

Willie Wurtzel lay on his bed and gazed at the ceiling. His mind was clear, now, and when the nurse let the little colored boy in he knew him. "Hello, Freezy," Willie said. "How's the business?"

Freezy started to say something, stopped himself. "Pretty good," he said. "You getting' well?"

"Yeah," Willie said. "You been up to see me before, ain't you?"

"I come ever' day," the little colored boy said. "I ain't forgot how you and Refugee gimme dat blood dat time. But dey say you didn't need his back."

"Them was the days," Willie said. "What's the matter, kid?"

Freezy Johnson's face looked anguished. "Nothin'!" he said. He picked up a package he had at his feet. "I brung you a radio," he said. "Borrowed hit."

**WILLIE** looked at the battered little portable radio, smiled. "Thanks," he sighed. "You know, Freezy," he reminisced, "the first fight we had was up in St. Louis, me'n Ref, was up in St. Louis for fifty clams winner-take-all and he hadn't never been in the ring before. I tried to tell him how to box and he like to got murdered the first round and when he come back I told him to get in there and swing, that the Lord was in his corner. He stopped the guy next frame."

Unobtrusively Freezy set the radio on the table and twitched a dial. He hid his face, his lips twitching.

A voice from the radio said: *Smith was down twice in round one. His timing was off and he missed badly. He's not the Smith we used to know.*

"Fight, huh?" Willie said brightly. "An' some guy usin' Ref's name. Oughtta sue him."

The bell sounded.

*Refugee comes out, he looks confused. Walker stabs him twice . . .* "REFUGEE!" Willie screamed.

Freezy Johnson had two tears in his eyes. "I didn't tell you," he said. "I didn't tell you, did I? I didn't tell you. They told me not to tell you but I was scared . . ."

Willie Wurtzel sat up in bed. His head reeled and he could feel the blood go out of his face but his mind was working. And no mind worked faster than Willie Wurtzel's.

"Walk down the hall," he said to Freezy. "Walk in the first door that's a little open and take the bell offa the pillow and stick a pin in it so's it stays down. I don't care who's in the bed just so they don't look like they're dyin'. Then get out in front and get a cab; have one waitin'."

Freezy nodded dumbly, moved toward the door. *Smith is bleeding from the cut over his left eye and Walker is picking away at it. Walker tied him up and shook the colored boy with a left hook. . . .* Willie Wurtzel stumbled over the radio and it went off as he stood tentatively upright beside his bed. He moved toward the door, peered out. A man in a white suit, with white rubber boots, moved down the hall. He carried a mop and pail.

"Come here a minute, Mac," Willie whispered. He moved back toward the bed.

The janitor came in. Willie placed his hands on each lapel, whispered, "I want you to do me a favor." Suddenly he jerked both lapels and the white coat came half-way off. The man's arms were pinioned at his sides and Willie took careful aim behind his ear with the bed pan. It made a slight clank.

He walked all right. The boots helped, nobody walks so good in rubber boots. He walked past the desk all right and down the stairs holding to the rail. He walked right out the front door and climbed into the cab. Freezy Johnson's teeth showed in the gloom.

"The Garden," Willie said to the driver. "Fast."

He had trouble getting out of the cab and he didn't have any money and there was the beef at the gate 'til someone came who knew him, and he had an arm around Freezy's neck by now and he had trouble walking but it wasn't the boots.

He came into the big cavern of sound that was the Garden and saw the black length of Refugee Smith on the canvas. He thought he was running but he was moving slowly and Freezy was beside him or he would have fallen. Refugee got his knees under him and got up at "six"; his eye was closed and Dummy Walker, a smooth automaton was measuring him when the bell rang.

Willie got to the ring apron and held on to it

and moved up the little stairs. "What's the round?" he said to someone that he knew but couldn't recognize.

"Tent' comin' up," a voice said.

Refugee sat slumped on his little stool.

Willie tried to get through the ropes, fell and bounced his chest on the second rope and clung to it. He pulled his face over.

"Boy," he said into Refugee's puffed black ear.

Refugee didn't turn his head. He didn't seem to think it strange that that voice should be in his ear. Then finally he grinned.

"Mr. Willie," he said.

Willie Wurtzel's voice was soft. That was the only way his voice came out — no matter what he tried to do his voice was soft — so he got as close to Refugee Smith as he could and whispered: "Remember it in St. Louis, your first fight . . . ya tried to box the guy because I told you to and he like to killed you and then I told you the Lord was in your corner and to go out swingin'."

"Like a apprentice angel . . . all in white," Refugee said, turning his head.

"Naw, boy, I ain't no angel, I'm a sick Jew. But Ref, boy, remember that fight when you give blood to Freezy an' you never had but one good round. You always got one good round, boy. Okay, boy, this is the good round."

Refugee blinked the eye that he could blink and a little tear squeezed out in the blood. "Mr. Willie," he said again.

"You go out there," Willie whispered, "and forget you ever tried to box. Go out there and smite him, boy, smite him!"

"Okay, Mr. Willie," Refugee Smith said and he moved out with the bell, flat-footed, and Dummy Walker came to him — a mistake.

Willie Wurtzel didn't see that round. The round that Refugee Smith came out nine down and one to go, one eye closed, rusty, swinging wild. But swinging! Willie Wurtzel had fainted.

But you don't beat guys like Dummy Walker with faith alone. Maybe Refugee was lucky. He threw twelve right hands, twelve right hands too short, and he took twelve sharp lefts in his face to throw them. But he remembered something Willie Wurtzel had screamed at him one time and the big one, the last one, he threw a foot back of Dummy Walker's chin.

Dummy Walker moved his chin back twelve inches that time and when the count was over and Refugee leaned down to try to help him to his corner he almost fell himself.

**WILLIE WURTZEL** lay in his bed under the cold and forbidding eye of a nurse who didn't read the sports page, though of large and athletic build. Refugee Smith stood at the door.

Suddenly he thrust his hand in his pocket and stuck the check out, laid it on the table. "Goodbye, Mr. Willie," he said trying to grin. "Gotta catch them railroad cars; dis here's your share."

Willie Wurtzel looked at the check, looked at the big black man with the bandaged face. He tried twice to say something, twice failed. He put his hand up, put his thumb and forefinger together. Finally he said, "Goodbye." The door closed.

Willie picked up the check, groped for an envelope and stuck the check in it.

*Sailors Relief Fund*, he wrote shakily. He added the address, sealed the letter. "Mail this for me pal," he said to the nurse.

The nurse looked at it, blew her nose, "Okay," she said.

*So now I'm still broke*, Willie thought. Then he grinned. *When I offered to bet them guys we'd get picked up next day they was probably in as bad shape as I was. When I get up I'll look 'em all up and tell 'em they bet me twenty apiece on it. Them forgetful sailors will probably pay off and it'll tide me over until I ship out again.*

# SPELLING BEE

ED Delaney, the big commission man, studied the list once more. It was, he concluded, a reasonable morning line. He had clocked the entries and the line looked all right from here. It was, of course, subject to sudden drastic change, but as a morning line it looked all right. It read:

Barber 7-2
Moscovitz (Mrs.) 4-1
Moscovitz (Mr.) 30-1
Abrams 5-1
Clancy (Miss) 4-1
Clancy (Mrs.) 20-1
Clancy (Mr.) 100-1
Minelli 10-1
Bollinger 12-1
Smith 11-1
Daniels 6-1

He stood in the front of the Forrest Hotel, idly looking at his list, doing small arithmetical calculations in his head. He was standing there when Willie Wurtzel came up.

Now Willie Wurtzel was a small pudgy man, given to loud double-breasted vests and a profound distrust in values that couldn't be counted between thumb and forefinger and weren't a lovely green in color; but also Willie was a man that would take a chance. Especially if the chance involved his fighter, Refugee Smith.

For when he took a chance of Refugee — in the ring, at least — he was hardly taking a chance at all for Refugee was a hundred and fifty-eight pounds of undefeated dark brown middleweight, with a trust implicit in the Lord and atomic potentialities in each big black fist. Willie was Refugee's manager.

Ed Delaney looked up and saw Willie and spoke. "How, Willie," he said, "what keeps with you?"

"Hello, Ed. I'm anglin' Refugee a go. Haven't froze it yet, though."

"How's he doin' in school?" Ed Delaney asked innocently.

"Terrific. You know the army done a lot for that boy. Hell, he can read as good as me." Willie paused and thought a moment, then in a sudden burst of candor, added: "Better."

Ed Delaney raised his eyebrows. "I visit up to his class the other night. Adult education, they call it. Twelve in the class."

"And Refugee's the smartest one," Willie said.

"Oh, I wouldn't say that. That Mrs. Moscovitz is pretty sharp."

"Bah. . ." Willie began.

"They are havin' a spelling contest — his class is — up at the school tomorrow night. The winner gets to keep a little silver cup till the next contest," Ed Delaney said.

"That's the cup Refugee's been talkin' about," Willie said. "I didn't understand what he kept talkin' about a cup at school, for."

"I lay twelve to one he don't win it," Ed Delaney said.

"Twelves for you. Eleven for the trade."

"You makin' a book on a spellin' match?" Willie asked, incredulous.

"Horses don't run in the winter in this town."

Hardhat McGee came around the corner, his wealth-stuffed threadbare suit shining under the light. His derby was a green thing, second-hand in 1923. Willie yelled:

"Hardhat!"

Hardhat McGee, once outsmarted by Willie and Refugee in the old days, stopped. "He lays a big prize against my boy — spellin'," Willie added. "Want a piece of the field?"

Avarice lighted Hardhat's eyes and he approached Ed Delaney cautiously. "What. . ." he began.

"Three Story!" Willie hollered. "Whatcha doin' out? Ed lays a price against my boy."

Three-Story Gooch sidled up, unobstructive, colorless in the crowd. "Big Ed bails me," he answered the first question. "What price?" He rubbed his hands together. "Don't pay," he said. Then added seriously, "Crime."

A big yellow coat showed then, down Broadway came the coat — big, yellow, moving like it had a tiger inside of it, sleekly smooth, like a big two-footed cat took a coat for a ride down Broadway. Enormous shoulders sliding people from them

— deferential shoulders, polite shoulders, but great big shoulders.

"Ref!" Willie yelled.

The big yellow coat moved to them.

"Yes, Mr. Willie — How you doin', Mr. Ed?" Refugee Smith ignored Hardhat.

Ed Delaney showed the list. "Come off tomorrow night," he said. "Here's the price."

"On what?" Hardhat asked.

"Spelling bee," Delaney said.

Three Story Gooch probably going up for the "remainder of the natural" when he came to trial said excitedly, "A C note on Clancy."

"Which Clancy?" Ed Delany asked.

"The hunnert to one shot," Three Story said.

"Mr. Clancy." Ed Delaney said slowly. "Ten thousand dollars against one hundred dollars. Mr. Clancy."

Eight Ball Ballinger, coming from the Strand Pool Room, saw the crowd, moved in. "A thousand on Moscovitz, the Mrs. Moscovitz."

"Fifty on the black boy."

"Two yards goin' on Minelli."

"Five hundred on Abrams. . ."

Ed Delaney, calm above the hubbub, made his book, balanced his book, kept his book round.

"Ummm," Willie Wurtzel said, "town is fulla nothin' but money."

"Horse tracks closed down for the winter," Hardhat McGee said, "Government lookin' mighty sharp for big bills, see if they was come by on the level. Boys kinda bet it around amongst their selves."

"Mr. Willie," Refugee took his manager by the shoulder and pulled him aside. "Mr. Willie, don't you get foolish now and bet on me in that spellin' contest. There is better spellers than me in that class."

"Middleweight?" Willie said, indignation rising in his voice.

"Naw, the adult education class I'se in, -I'm in."

"But twelve to one," Willie said, "against you!"

"I ain't fightin' them people, Mr. Willie. . . This is purely mental."

"Tomorrow night," Willie said to himself. "What's the teacher's name?"

"Ellinwood, Mr. Herman Ellinwood."

"Okay, boy, I'll lay offa ya," Willie said.

He stood and watched as people came up to the little knot of men around Ed Delaney and laid their bets. "Ho hum," he said elaborately, "I guess I'll be goin'."

It took Willie Wurtzel quite a while to find the right Herman Ellinwood. In fact it wasn't until the following day that he was able to track down the proper one. But find him, he did. Mr. Ellinwood proved to be a small gray wisp of a man whose eyes twinkled when they lit on Willie's bright vest.

"I'm Willie Wurtzel," Willie opened, a little nervous.

"Ah, yes, Mr. Wurtzel. Refugee Smith's manager. Refugee has spoken of you often. The answer is no. You are, by the way the sixth one to come here seeking the words that are to be used in tonight's contest." Herman smiled benignly. "Sit down, sir."

Willie sat down, not knowing what else to do. His conversation legs having been shot from under him, his real legs felt rather weak, too. "I never wanted the words," Willie lied. Then gaining momentum, "Hell, my boy, Refugee, wouldn't be no partner in a gyp anyway."

"I doubt very much if he would," Mr. Ellinwood said softly. "If, however, you didn't want the words, what did you what? And I am sorry if I've misjudged you."

"I just wanted to find out how Refugee was doin' — there's nothin' wrong tryin' to get a line on a boy when he's comin' up to a — a contest. I just wanted to know how he was trainin'."

"I'm not prepared to say, relatively speaking," Mr. Ellinwood said, "but he is extremely conscientious, and a very fine gentleman, certainly."

"But how good can he spell?"

"Better than some," Mr. Ellinwood said, "not as good as others."

"You talk like a horse handicapper in the paper," Willie said accusingly. "Very indefinite."

"There is an element of chance."

"Yeah," Willie said, "that's what I don't like. Well, I'll be seein' you." He moved off toward the door and out into the street. "There ought," he muttered to himself, "be some kind of a angle."

But he didn't think of one. Not a single angle. However, burned there such a faith in the heart of Willie Wurtzel in connection with his boy that he hunted up Ed Delaney and laid a thousand dollars on Refugee's short black nose.

He then hied himself to Harlem and with the aid of a dictionary gave Refugee a rough workout.

Refugee was sweating in the final round but he had

stopped Knowledge, Virtue, and Synthetic with one punch and Willie beamed.

"Knock 'em over like that, boy, tonight, and you got the cup on your hip."

"Did you bet on me?" Refugee asked worriedly.

"Naw," Willie lied, "I just want to see you win that cup so I can borrow it."

Refugee looked at him narrowly. "Okay, Mr. Willie," he said. "I'll be tryin'. But they is lots better spellers in the class than me. Mrs. Moscovitz and Miss Clancy and. . ."

"Don't you worry about them," Willie said magnanimously. "We'll take care of them."

"I'd pretty near rather win that spellin' than the title. . ."

"You'll win it, boy. Trust the Lord." Willie said.

"Don't aim to bother the Lord but I sure aim to exertion myself," Refugee said seriously.

Now where Willie Wurtzel had failed to think of an angle, Hardhat McGee, untroubled by any semblance of scruple, had concocted one. He simply went around to all the contestants — found by dint of great perseverance in the short time he had — that were priced at five to one or shorter, and bought them off. Twenty-five dollars a head for misspelling the first word they were given. Thus he laid out to contestants Endicott, Barber, Abrams, Mrs. Moscovitz, Miss Clancy and Daniels a sum of one hundred and fifty dollars. He then bet heavily through agents and in proportion to their odds on each of the other contenders, except Mr. Clancy, whom Miss Clancy assured him was asleep in the back end of a Third Avenue saloon and an extremely doubtful starter.

However, such was the character of Hardhat, that on the off-chance that Clancy might show up and stumble in a winner, after his bets were down he decided to plug this last tiny loophole. He hunted up Mr. Clancy in the designated bistro and asked him if he intended to attend his education that night.

Mr. Clancy assured him profanely that he was. Thereupon Hardhat offered him ten dollars to misspell the first word he was given. Mr. Clancy accepted the proffered money readily, then called Hardhat many unprintable names for suggesting he would throw a spelling contest and staggered to the bar with this Heaven-sent windfall.

Hardhat watched Mr. Clancy absorb three double whiskeys and left feeling his mission accomplished.

Mr. Clancy, whatever his moral rectitude, would obviously soon not be able to spell his own name.

As it happened, Willie delayed by a traffic jam, and Mr. Clancy delayed by having to detour around various reptiles, arrived at the same time, barely in time.

As they made their way into the building together, Willie heard Mr. Clancy muttering to himself what sounded like "Tried to buy me off, green hatted basket."

Willie grabbed him by the arm, his mind spinning tightly. "Who?" he said.

"Green hatted bastard," Mr. Clancy said, jerked loose from Willie and staggered into the door that led to Refugee's class.

Now Willie Wurtzel, thirty-five years on Broadway, was a man who didn't have any callouses on his hands and he didn't have any rusty wheels in his head, either. He had survived, and largely prospered, in that deadliest of jungles by being able to get four quickly adding two and two; and also, if occasion demanded, get more difficult answers from more complex problems. Thus, from Clancy's mutterings, and the well-known hue of Hardhat McGee's derby, he made a swift deduction.

"Hardhat put in the fix," he said to himself. "He'd queer every short price in the field and spread it on the long shots." He smiled. "Except Honest John, there — who don't look like a threat." He grinned happily to himself and went on into the class room. This turn of events obviously enhanced Refugee's chances considerably. Another G would definitely be in order.

Inside a strange sight met his eyes. Mr. Ellinwood, was sitting at his desk, calling the roll. Ten pupils sat in front of him in a row. They became eleven as Mr. Clancy hung his hat in the air and fell into the end seat.

In the back of the room were grouped twenty or so men. These were hard-faced, narrow-eyed men, who talked in sibilant whispers. They had names but not addresses, money but no bank accounts. In their center sat Ed Delaney, a small slate on his lap.

"Scratch Mr. Clancy," a voice hissed, when the roll had been completed.

Ed Delaney rubbed out a name, changed his odds a little and accepted a couple of bets whispered to him. Willie came up and looked over his shoulder.

Smith — 11-1.

"Another Grand on Refugee Smith," Willie said softly.

Ed Delaney made a note, rubbed out Refugee's price and replaced it with 7-1.

Mr. Ellinwood cleared his throat. "We will," he said, "proceed with our program as we had planned. However, in view of the fact, that we have a rather large group of er — visitors, I shall conduct tonight's contest in a slightly different way than usual." He took two quart size paper containers and placed them on the desk. Into one he dropped a number of white slips of paper, and into the other he dropped a handful of small red squares.

"On the white slips," he went on, "are the names of the members of the class. On the red slips are the words that are to be spelled. I draw a name, announce it, then draw a word. The person whom I have named will endeavor to spell the word. If he is unsuccessful he will move into this section over here." Mr. Ellinwood gestured to a group of seats beside his desk. "If he spells the word correctly he remains where he is. I then draw another name and another word. The last remaining person remaining is the winner."

Three Story Gooch's hysterical whispers came into the silence. "Scratch Clancy — give 'em the saliva test, he ain't a fit entry. . . I want my money back. . ."

"He's at the post," Ed Delaney said softly, inexorably.

Willie leaned over his shoulder and whispered something. Ed Delaney scrubbed again on his slate.

"Mr. Barber," the teacher said. "Crimson. His blood was crimson."

Mr. Barber stood up, glanced nervously around. "C-R-I-S-O-N. Crimson."

There were sharp snarls from the rear of the room and Mr. Ellinwood frowned. "That is incorrect," he said. Then he lifted his eyes and looked at the group around Ed Delany. "Any audibly remarks, coaching, or otherwise, will result in the disqualification of the contestant." He smiled a wintry smile and drew two other slips.

Mr. Clancy's snores broke the silence and Mrs. Moscovitz shook him. "Smith," he said, "Worry. A fighter not in condition will worry his manager."

Refugee stood up and Willie could see the dampness on his brow. But he went for the word confidently. W-O-R-R-Y. Worry."

"That is correct. Remain seated where you are."

"Hell, I thought it was W-E-A-R-Y," a voice came from the rear.

"Mrs. Moscovitz," the teacher said, drawing a slip of paper. He plucked another. "Foreign. The man arrived in New York from a foreign country."

"F-O-R-I-E-G-N," Mrs. Moscovitz muttered, looking at the floor.

Mr. Ellinwood's eyebrows shot up. "That is incorrect," he said. He drew two more slips, suppressed a smile.

"Mr. Clancy, the word is alcohol. Alcohol is — er — a — a stimulant."

Mr. Clancy leaped to his feet, glared wildly around him and swiftly and clearly said "A-L-C-O-H-O-L."

"That is correct, remain where you are," Mr. Ellinwood said superfluously, Mr. Clancy having collapsed in his chair.

Three Story Gooch gave a small yip of pleasure and dreamed of hiring a big time mouthpiece when he came to trial with ten thousand dollars in his pants.

Abrams went down on Curious. Endicott faltered on Squeeze and there were ugly rumblings from the back of the room. Ed Delaney was constantly changing his slate now, rubbing out, changing odds, but with the genius that was his, keeping his book so regardless of the winner, Ed Delaney would be winner, too.

Miss Clancy failed on Business and there were sharp howls from the back of the room from a segment who felt they were getting the same.

Minelli kept the atmosphere electric for ninety seconds spelling Metropolitan; Mr. Minelli developed a naturally fine stammer into a much better one under pressure. There were groans of relief.

After quiet was restored, Daniels, a middle-aged man of mild mein and obviously badly shaken went down on Turmoil.

Mr. Moscovitz stayed in the running on Destiny, though it is doubtful if the teacher's patient explanation of the word's meaning ever became clear to him. Bollinger almost faltered on Embarrass, but reluctantly put in both R's and stayed in looking surprised.

The field was now reduced to five contestants, and Mr. Ellinwood felt that there was something definitely wrong but could think of nothing to do about it. Three Story Gooch was damp with perspiration, Willie Wurtzel looked enigmatic and Hardhat McGee looked like a horse player with the third horse of a three-horse parlay winging down the stretch with open daylight behind him.

Several players had left and two had quietly torn their hats in two and left the pieces on the floor.

Mr. Ellinwood drew two slips. "Mr. Clancy," he said.

Mr. Clancy jumped to his feet, his hands extended in a fighting pose. Refugee calmed him down and he was given Technical, which he ripped of swiftly and correctly.

Little doubts gnawed at Refugee's mind. Unwanted doubts that he tried to put aside. But they gnawed. "We'll take care of 'em." That's what Mr. Willie has said about the good spellers falling from the ranks so strangely. Mrs. Moscovitz missing Foreign, that was funny. Had Mrs. Moscovitz been took care of. . . .?

Hardhat McGee looked slightly alarmed but regained his composure as Refugee, grinning, spelled Doubtful. Bollinger's luck failed him and he bogged down badly on Biscuit, and Minelli took two minutes to spell Establish.

Mr. Moscovitz, getting confusing signals from Mrs. Moscovitz, messed up Despicable almost beyond recognition and there were cries and counter cries of "Foul!" from the rear and Mr. Ellinwood had to issue stern threats to restore order.

Refugee spelled Genesis, with ease from his training on the Good Book and Minelli took three and one quarter minutes missing Consultation.

And then a terrible thing happened. Refugee Smith looked out and he saw Willie Wurtzel's beaming face. He saw Three Story Gooch's white drawn face. He saw Hardhat McGee's slightly green face and the little doubts crystallized and became a conclusion. A horrible conclusion, reluctantly arrived at. But it seemed inescapable. Mr. Willie had put the fix on the best members of the class and then bet heavily on his fighter. Naturally Clancy would not be worth fixing, Clancy's performance so far being in the nature of a miracle.

"Oh, Mr. Willie," Refugee moaned to himself, "after all I done to show you righteousness pays cash money."

He remembered Willie's stern practice session of the afternoon. He remembered Willie's moral flabbiness where money was concerned. "We'll take care of 'em." The words haunted him.

He made a desperate decision. He would purposely miss a word and bring his scheming manager once and for all into the fold of honest men. And, too, he had seen Three Story make his bet. It would bring Three Story a large sum of money. A large sum of money might clear Three Story. Three Story said he was innocent. Mr. Willie was guilty.

"Mr. Smith," Mr. Ellinwood's voice was crisp. "Spell Synthetic. As 'Our new tires are made largely from synthetic rubber.'"

Refugee Smith swallowed, glanced at the little cup gleaming on the table. Then he glanced Heavenward, his lips moved and then he looked straight at Mr. Willie. "S-I-N," he said clearly. "S-I-N-T-H-E-T-I-C."

"That," the teacher said, is incorrect. Mr. Clancy is the winner."

Mr. Clancy leaped to his feet at his name. "I was robbed," he bawled.

Hardhat McGee stumbled from the room and Refugee Smith stole a glance at his manager. Willie's face was still wreathed in smiles!

Ed Delaney smiled, too. He had made a nice thing of this, and a couple of pretty nice guys were the winners. Three nice guys, Ed Delaney was all right. He turned and gave Three Story ten crisp thousand dollar notes. Then he turned to Willie. "How'd you figure it, Willie?"

Refugee said almost tearfully. "Forgive me, Mr. Willie . . . ."

"Skip it, boy." Willie held out his hand. Ed Delaney counted bills into it.

"You win, Mr. Willie?"

"Sure."

"But I threw you down because I thought you fixed the good spellers. . ."

Little Mr. Ellinwood stood and watched Willie put more money in his pocket than Mr. Ellinwood would make in two years, but he smiled and there was no envy in his smile.

"Naw," Willie went on, "Hardhat put the fix in, and I learnt it from Clancy. Clancy wouldn't hold still for Hardhat."

"An' you bet on Mr. Clancy?"

"You don't think I'd let one from the cold sod go to the post at a hundred to one if I knew he was tryin'?"

Willie riffled the bills and a smug unrighteous smile split his dark greed-filled face.

Refugee Smith, of the ebony skin
and pure heart,
who believed in the right
and could also knock your head off with his left—
Refugee Smith had lost his faith.

# THE RECONSTRUCTION OF REFUGEE SMITH

**WILLIE WURTZEL** needed a miracle. Not a big full-dress miracle; just a small token miracle would do, one that would convince Refugee Smith that the Lord still took a personal interest in him.

For Refugee Smith, late of the United States Army, undefeated contender for the middleweight crown, owned and operated by W. Wurtzel — Refugee Smith, of the ebony skin and pure heart, who believed in the right and could also knock your head off with his left — Refugee Smith had lost his faith.

In the long ago, Refugee Smith had been a roustabout on a Mississippi packet. Just an average roustabout who would look on the mule when it was white, toss the pockmarked cubes of chance, and sin generally in a manner average to his type. But that was in the long ago.

Willie Wurtzel had saved Refugee's life and he had saved it when Refugee had just concluded a desperate pact with the Lord. Refugee had promised the Lord that if his life was spared, he would carry His Word to the heathen multitudes. And just then Willie Wurtzel, fighterless prize-fight manager, had saved him. Refugee reasoned that the Lord had heard and had closed the deal. Willie reasoned that Refugee could get in touch with more sinners to the square yard in the prize-fight business than any other — besides, he needed a fighter — and he convinced Refugee of this and so became his manager.

And the talent that laid money on Refugee's opponents — well, as the saying goes, Refugee made Christians out of them. Because he had it. He was a natural. Heavy-muscled and fast, impervious to punishment, dead game. With Willie's wily brain behind him and the Lord here in his corner, and his faith a shining shield.

But now the faith was gone. Gone with the blood of his comrades in the blood-soaked Italian soil. Gone with the agony and death of those he felt deserved not to die. He said so to Willie standing on the bustling corner where 49th Street bisects Broadway.

"I don't understand hit, Mr. Willie," he said patiently, "but I can't put no abidin' faith in the Lord since He let all that sufferin' happen."

"Whyn't you blame Hitler?" Willie asked, desperately fingering the contract in his pocket. "He was the one —" "The Lord made Hitler," Refugee said with cold logic.

"Anybody can have an off day —" Willie began. He stopped hopelessly.

"Look," he said. "He pulled you through, didn't He?"

"Yeah."

"And me — when I was with the Merchant Marine and we got torpedoed?"

"Was you any better'n some that was drowned?" Refugee said.

Willie stopped and came in from another angle. "Look," he said, "let's leave the Lord outta this. I just come from signing you for a tenner with One-Round Burke. All you gotta do is get up to Stillman's and get in shape and fix it so One-Round lives up to his name."

"I'll do my best," Refugee said, "but I ain't gonna do no good unless I got my faith —" Refugee's black face was creased with doubt and suffering. And that's when Willie thought of the miracle. The thought was vague in his mind but he said, "Don't worry, Ref, boy. The Lord'll give you a sign."

"A sign?"

Willie, who could plan campaigns between the ten-second warning buzzer and the bell, thought fast. "Yeah," he said, "He'll give you a sign." The plan was forming in his mind. "You see, it's like this. The Lord, He's gonna need more people now than ever before and He don't want to lose you, see? So He'll give you a sign."

"I sure hope so," Refugee said feelingly. "I'll be hopin' three to the beat."

"Okay," Willie said briskly. "I want you to do three laps around the reservoir in the morning and be down to the gym at two o'clock." He paused. "This Burke is a good boy, sign or no sign."

"I'll get the flesh fine, Mr. Willie, and pray for the generation of the Spirit."

Willie bit his tongue to keep from saying, "Leave it to me!" Aloud he said, "Okay, don't worry."

Because Willie didn't feel himself qualified to personally pester the Deity — except with an occasional automatic plea when drawing one to two pair — he went for his miracle to Three-Story Gooch. Three-Story was a well known non-tax-paying citizen with a dubious reputation for reliability. Willie found him that night, after some inquiry, in an out-of-the-way bistro discussing architecture with a suburban acquaintance. The architecture under discussion had to do with the floor plan and arrangement of drain pipes, etc., in a house in Westchester said to harbor some high-grade ore.

Three-Story Gooch was a burglar, when at liberty, of the soft — or tennis — shoe variety, and was really quite skillful at ascending a vine-covered portico, when inspired. And even a few small gems inspired him mightily.

Three-Story and his companion looked up briefly from their table at Willie's approach and acknowledged his presence with grunts. Then they went back to their art work on the table top.

"This here's the gutter?" Three-Story said, pointing with his pencil. "And the old lady sleeps in here through this window? . . ." He looked up. "Sit down, Willie," he said.

Willie sat down.

"Now," Three-Story went on, "the wall safe is under the pitcher in the old man's bedroom but he don't come home Tuesday night? He stays in his apotment in town?"

"That's right," Three-Story's friend said.

"Okay," Three-Story said. "I'll case the jernt tomorrow myself an' let you know." He lit a cigarette. "How they goin', Willie?"

"Fair," Willie said.

"Know anything?"

"My boy's got a fight comin' up. Three weeks."

"Ummm, he gonna win?"

"Yeah."

"That's good."

"You're gonna help me make sure," Willie said.

Three-Story murmured, unsuprised, "Yeah?"

"I need a miracle," Willie said.

"Use one myself," Three-Story agreed absently.

"My boy Refugee has lost his faith — his faith in the Lord," Willie explained.

"I've had mine shook, myself," Three-Story said.

"And he — well, it affects his fightin', the wrong way, if he don't think the Lord's with him," Willie explained further.

"He's a sweet boy," Three-Story said. "When he's right," Willie agreed, "but he ain't gonna be right unless the Lord gives him a sign."

"Any particular sign in mind?" Three-Story asked.

"Yeah," said Willie. "And that's where you come in."

"I'm listenin'."

"I figure it like this," Willie said. "We get us made up a little neon sign, in shape of a harp — a battery-operated one — and when I give you the office, you turn it on."

"You lost me back a ways," Three-Story said. "Start over."

"When we come into the ring," Willie said, "you tap the corner they give us, and you get at the window where we're looking right at you if we look up. I give you the office and you light the little harp up for a minute."

"What window?"

"I dunno, whatever window there is. That's up to you! On the roof some place, I guess. You oughta know about roofs."

"I know about roofs," Three-Story said, "but I'm kinda confused."

"I'll start from taw," Willie said. "The night of our go you are at the fights. You got your little battery neon harp under your coat. You wait to see what corner we draw, then you go outside and get up on the roof and get to a window just opposite, where we can look right up and see the window where you are at. I tell Refugee I'm gonna ask the Lord to give him the office. I signal." Willie paused. "I'll lean over and put both hands on Refugee's shoulders. When you see me do that you turn on the harp and let it burn for ten seconds. Then climb down and throw the harp away and pick up your dough."

# THE RECONSTRUCTION OF REFUGEE SMITH

**With fight at hand, Willie Wurtzel knew that nothing less than a miracle would bring his boy victory. But he found that man-made miracles—like prize fighters—can get out of control.**

**REFUGEE SMITH**, doubt-torn but loyal to Willie, trained well. He came down to weight. He was hard and physically sharp.

Willie, with confident reiteration of the coming sign, fed Refugee's glimmering hope.

A Third Avenue electrician fashioned a neat harp warranted to operate in any weather, and two nights before the fight Willie delivered the harp to Three-Story Gooch, gave him painstaking instructions on its quite simple operation and inquired solicitously as to Three-Story's general health, agility, etc.

Three-Story assured him that, due to a happy plan of construction, he could be at any top-row window of the arena that fortune designated in a matter of minutes, and could rest comfortably there while awaiting the call from below. "A half-wit could do it in wooden shoes," Three-Story finished.

"How am I gonna get up on the roof?" Three-Story asked. "What if they see me?"

"I thought you wasn't no amachure," Willie said disgustedly. "Don't you know your own business?"

Three-Story said quickly, his professional pride touched, "Sure, sure I can do it. If the price is right you done bought a miracle."

After fifteen minutes of spirited haggling, the terms were agreed upon. One miracle, C.O.D., three hundred and seventy-five dollars. The same to be deposited with Ed Delaney, the book, and collected by Three-Story immediately following the fight, provided the harp glowed on signal. Outcome of the fight not to affect the price.

"I'll put up the dough with Ed tonight," Willie said, "and get the harp made up and give it to you just as soon as it's ready."

"Okay," Three-Story said. "I'll go and look the place over and get my route figgered."

"Never mind the wooden shoes," Willie said. *"Just don't miss."*

"I won't," Three-Story assured him. Flicking on the harp to look under his bed for a shoe.

"Don't be wearin' out the batt'ry," Willie said, annoyed. "They're hard to get."

Three-Story retrieved the shoe, put it on. "Okay," he said. "You know," he added ruminatively, "this is a kinda awkward shape, but I might use the idea for some of my own work."

The sound of the crowd, filtering into the dressing room, told Willie Wurtzel that the semi-windup was drawing to a close. He shooed everyone from the dressing room, walked over and put a pudgy hand on the powerful black shoulder of his fighter. Refugee sat on the rubbing table, his head bowed.

"Ref," Willie said, putting feeling into his voice,

"we're goin' out there tonight with the Lord in your corner."

"I sure hope so, Mr. Willie," Refugee said. "But I ain't caught no sign."

"Don't worry," Willie said. "When the time comes, he'll deliver."

There was a knock on the door and a call. Refugee Smith stood up and, with his taped hands, pulled the old green bathrobe with the golden harp on it around him. The same bathrobe Willie had bought him for his first preliminary years ago in St. Louis. Willie grabbed his satchel and they started up the aisle.

Refugee walked with his head down, apparently obvious to the roar of sound. Willie bustled behind him, hardly hearing the familiar sounds, either. His beady eyes scanned the upper reaches of the arena. It was perfect. The top row of windows gave back to a flat, then there was a drop and another row of windows. Even now, Three-Story was probably sitting up there, unseen in the darkness but with an unobstructed view of all that went on below.

In the ring One-Round Burke grinned evilly, standing listening to the referee's instructions. "Keep yer eye offa my thumb," he told Refugee.

Refugee appeared not to hear.

"Get dirty and I'll toss you outta the ring," the referee said to Burke. "Now shake hands and come out fightin'."

And it was bad. At the end of the first round Refugee had taken a beating. Refugee wasn't bad. In fact, he was good, but One-Round Burke was better.

"He's strong, Mr. Willie," Refugee told him after the end of the second round. "He's dirty, too." He shook his head. "And there ain't no sign," he added, tears in his voice. "There ain't no sign at all!"

In the third round, Burke dropped Refugee with a whistling right cross and sank two left hooks to the black body. Refugee made it to his corner, hurt and dazed.

Willie Wurtzel leaned over his fighter, put his mouth close to his ear. "I ain't worthy," he said, his eyes closed, "but Lord, don't let this pure boy down. Give us a sign, oh Lord, give us a sign!" He put his two hands on Refugee's big black shoulders and slowly turned his head and looked up.

Refugee's brown eyes came up slowly, reluctantly. Blood shone redly in one of them, and desperate hope showed there, too.

And high in the black shadows of the rafted roof, framed by the vague outlines of a window, appeared a glow. It was small at first, but it became brighter until, like distant stars welded together, there appeared, sharper and sharper, the outline of a harp.

As it grew in brilliance, Willie dropped his eyes, and his lips formed the words: "That dunce Three-Story wore out the batt'ry and had to get another — and what a batt'ry!"

**WHEN** he looked back the light was gone, gone from the darkness of the night. But there in the eyes of Refugee Smith, the stars that had seemed to form the harp still gleamed through a mist of tears.

The warning buzzer sounded.

The warning buzzer is to tell the fighters that the gong will ring in ten seconds. It warns the handlers to get from the ring. Had it foretold to One-Round Burke what was to happen to him, he would probably have gotten out with his seconds.

Sir Galahad found the Holy Grail and it gave to him the strength of ten. Refugee Smith, his great heart full of faith and hope — with no charity for One-Round Burke — came out with the bell.

Now One-Round Burke had never been in the ring with ten dark brown middleweight fighters before. And as for ten dark destroying angels with six-ounce gloves, that was even farther from his imagination.

Ghastly were the things that happened to One-Round Burke. He caught a left jab, pulled up his hand and had a brown arm impale itself six inches deep in his vitals. He was gone, then, falling when he caught the right across to his jaw, unhinging it somewhat and moving his chin over toward his right ear.

Refugee stepped back, then, and let him fall.

One-Round Burke called for a priest when he had regained consciousness in his dressing room, before he knew the extent of his injuries, which he assumed were fatal. And when they told him he was not to die he vowed to lead a different life, that grateful he was. And so he came back to the fold.

Refugee Smith, mute with wonder and happiness, sat in his dressing room on the rubbing table. Willie was unwinding the tape from his hands. Ed Delaney stood beside him waiting.

"Great fight," Ed Delaney said to Refugee.

"I just can't talk, Mr. Ed," Refugee said, "but hit wasn't me. Nobody could of beat Us tonight." He stood up, shook off his robe and walked to the shower, strong, humble and happy.

**ED DELANEY** leaned down to Willie Wurtzel's ear. "You was so hepped about this money gettin' to Three-Story tonight I thought I oughtta tell you right away about him."

Willie Wurtzel peeled a hundred-dollar bill from a roll he took from his pocket. "And give him this, too," he said.

"But I can't," the big commission man said. "That's what I mean."

"Why not?" Willie said.

"You get it back," Ed Delaney said. "Three-Story got the finger cracking a spot up in Westchester. They got him in the pokey. Since last night."

"Well," Willie said automatically, "I save myself four hunnert and seventy-five clams . . ."

Then suddenly he fell to his knees. "I didn't mean that, Lord. I didn't mean that . . ."

Ed Delaney's jaw dropped. His eyes popped as he stared at Willie Wurtzel. "But what about the dough?" he asked.

Willie Wurtzel looked up at him and the sweat was bright on his brow. "Give it to a charity, Ed!" he breathed. Then he turned and in an anguished voice said again, "I didn't mean that about savin' the dough. Honest, I didn't, Lord."

# Other Stories of the Ring

The story of a courageous gentleman who fought a good fight.

# RIGHT-HAND MAN

**JOE MORDESTI** was smart, Ace Finley thought; he was smart, and he knew fighters. That helped; that's what would make it work. Ace Finley was standing in Jocko Humboldt's corner, watching Jocko work. He worked with a smooth precision that had not been his seven years ago, when he had been fighting for the title the first time. Seven years ago, but Finley would never forget the fight. Jocko wasn't so smooth then, but was young. He had been winning; he had had the champion on his way out.

But Joe Mordesti had been down on the champ for a lot of dough that night; and because of that, Jocko Humboldt had stumbled through the last five rounds half-blind. He had been cut to pieces. Joe Mordesti had cut him to pieces, in a way, Ace Finley knew; because Joe had been the man that paid the handler who had smeared red pepper across Jocko's eyes, in a towel. Joe Mordesti — smart. He'd changed his name at least once, we learned later; but he was smart about that as well, for we never did learn the real one.

Finley was smart too, now. Nothing like that had happened again. Jocko had been champion six years. But Jocko was getting old for a fighter; his legs weren't so hot; and his hands had always

- 88 -

bothered him. He was getting old; his last fight was only four days off, and Ace Finley had not yet kept the promise to himself to pay Mordesti off for that night seven years before.

Well, it was okay; they were ready now. Mordesti was smart and knew fighters; and they had rehearsed this thing. They had it pat.

It would help with the odds, too. And they needed that. Jocko was broke. For a moment Ace Finley wished again he had taken better care of the boy. But he forgot about it then. With the odds right, the purse and what they'd win, would do the trick. Jocko wouldn't have to fight any more. Whatever else, Finley thought, his boy would retire as the champ; he would never let him get punch-silly. This was the last fight.

Finley glanced around the gym where Jocko was working now. Mordesti was not there. He'd be along, though; he dropped by and watched the champ work out for a while each afternoon.

The round ended and Jocko moved to the ropes, walking around the edge of the ring, breathing deeply. When he glanced down at Finley, Finley shook his head very slightly in negation. Finley called time and Jocko moved in again, boxing carefully, paying attention to his feet and now and then glancing at Finley who called monosyllabic directions.

A couple of newspaper men came in and shouldered their way through the crowd to the side of the ring. Jocko waved a left hand to them and smiled. They waved back.

Three more men came in a little later. They moved unostentatiously to a point from which they could see the ring and stood there expressionless.

Jocko had been clowning for a movement for the newspaper men, and the spectators around the ring were laughing. The three men who had just come in did not laugh.

Finley had seen them standing there; so had Jocko. Now the sparring partner who had been in the ring came down, and a colored boy climbed in when Finley told him to. He was a well-muscled boy, with crinkly short hair pasted to his small skull. He was badly marked, and his ears looked like little leather buttons. The sparring partner who had just come down tossed his headgear into the ring, but the colored boy just kicked it back out again, a simple contemptuous grin on his face.

Jocko smiled and shrugged expressively. Finley called time, and they started boxing. Jocko made the heavier colored boy seem to be wading in water ankle-deep. He stabbed him twice with his left hand and moved away. The dark skinned man followed him, unconcerned. Jocko was taking it easy, clowning a little. He hit the colored boy easily and whenever he wanted to. The boy didn't care, though. He just came in or stood his ground.

Presently, in close, he drove his left hand hard to Jocko's stomach, and Jacko winced, danced away and quit clowning.

He was coming back in now, carefully. Everybody around the ring became suddenly alert, intent. The newspaper men drew their breaths slowly, and the three expressionless men in the corner kept their eyes fastened on Jocko.

**NOW** Jocko was different. He moved flat-footedly; he looked as slow as the colored boy. He carried his hands a little lower; they looked open. The colored boy was the only one who seemed to sense no change.

He shuffled forward, heavy-footed, his small round head protected halfway up his jaw by one shoulder, held high.

Jocko feinted — so swiftly that he got no reflex from the boy. But his own body had shifted, and he was already crossing his right. Everybody in the gym heard it hit. It landed on the colored boy's brow. With a pop.

Jocko Humboldt danced away; his lips were thin. His right elbow jerked twice convulsively.

Then he grinned a slightly funny grin and danced in again. He feinted again with his left; he hooked his left. His head bobbed and he jabbed the colored boy twice with his left. The colored boy backed away, grabbing the top rope. Blood was coming from a cut over his eye where Jocko had hit him. Jocko dropped his hands. The colored boy was biting at the laces of his gloves, turning for the audience to see the crimson side of his face, grinning at them. Finley was shouting to Jocko and Jocko walked to the corner where Finley was standing and then shook his head in negation to the question in Finley's eyes. And he grinned again, but to some one watching very closely that grin looked just a little odd.

Finley said: "Okay. That's enough for now. Come on down."

Jocko Humboldt went into the dressing-room for his rub and shower then. Ace Finley went with him. The three men in the corner, Joe Mordesti and his two companions looked at one another when they had gone. Joe Mordesti and his two companions were still in the gym, later, when Jocko came back out, dressed now. Ace Finley was walking beside him and talking to him rapidly.

As they passed through the crowd, Finley fell silent. He looked concerned. He grinned once, but only briefly.

Jocko was talking to the kids that crowed up, but he did not shake hands with any of them. His right hand was in his topcoat pocket.

When Ace Finley and Jocko got into a cab outside and drove off, Joe Mordesti and his two companions were standing in the door of the gym. Mordesti signaled another cab. It followed Finley's cab to an office building thirty blocks away. When Finley and Jocko Humboldt, two hours later, came from a door marked T.J. GRAYSON, M.D. — one of Mordesti's companions happened to be in the hall.

Joe Mordesti visited Dr. Grayson's office that night with a friend of his. Grayson wasn't there, but that didn't matter. Mordesti's friend was a fellow who knew a lot about locks.

**"I TELL** you," Joe Mordesti said again, "I can't be wrong." Harry Bartzo, manager of Young Roland, the challenger, took a long drag on his cigar. He laid it on the table beside him and got up and walked once back and forth across his hotel room. "What are you tellin' me fore?" he asked suspiciously.

Mordesti spread his hands. "I was going down on the champ. He was goin' to take you. You may not think so, but he'd flatten that mug of yours in four, five rounds. But he can't do it with that right gone. "Well —" He spread his hands again. "What the hell, your boy can win now. Only if you don't know Jocko can't swing his right you're goin' to tell your boy to go in there and not leave no holes for that right. If you did that the champ might just wave it at him and beat him with his left. Why wouldn't I tell you?"

"You know a hell of a lot," Bartzo muttered.

"My business," Mordesti said, "is knowing a hell of a lot. And I mean *knowing*. You've seen X-ray plates. Have a look at this one."

**FROWNING**, Bartzo took the plate and held it up to the light. He looked at it silently for a long time.

"That came out of Doc Grayson's office," Mordesti said. "It was in the file marked *Humboldt*. How it came out of there don't matter. But I'm the only one knows; I'm the only one tumbled."

Bartzo was still frowning.

"It's a break," he said. "I've seen plenty. He can't hit with that hand." He ran a hand through his scanty hair and handed the plate back. "But why wouldn't he call off the fight?"

"I'll tell you that, too. If he calls it off he'll have to let this out. He'll have to wait some months before he can fight again. His hands never were much good; they'll heal slow. And it might never heal. And he needs dough. His wife is sick. He's broke. He never laid up a dime yet. And he's about through. He figures nobody knows about this — so he'll go ahead. He knows his right is dynamite, like everybody knows, and he figures you're sending Roland in to be careful of that right. What the hell, he'll just tap with it and outpoint Roland, he *thinks*," Mordesti added with a little complacent smile. Harry Bartzo walked back to his chair and sat down. Slowly a grin spread over his face. He nodded a little. "If the boy goes in there and doesn't have to worry about that right he's a cinch. A dead cinch." Then he stopped grinning and looked at Mordesti closely. "Wait a minute; how do I know you're not stalling — that the picture isn't a fake? That you're not bettin' on the champ to win by a knock-out and this is just —"

"You know," Mordesti cut him off, "because as soon as you tell me you're sending Roland in there swinging from the bell, I'm layin' fifty grand on Roland to win. I mean fifty, see? And maybe — maybe more. And if you don't believe that — you can lay some of it for me."

Bartzo began to look very pleased.

"I guess I can stir up a few G's myself," he said. "I guess I'll get it down before you turn the odds too sour."

Mordesti stood up, chuckling. "Now you're wakin' up," he said. "You won't have to hurry. Nobody tumbled. Nobody tumbled but me when he busted his hand on his sparring partner's head."

It was a little after ten o'clock the next morning when Ace Finley came into Jocko's room. Jocko looked at him with a question in his eyes but Finley didn't say anything for a moment. He took his topcoat off.

**Everybody in the gym heard that blow as Jocko's right landed on the colored boy's brow, with a pop.**

all the money that had gone through their hands; money that could not be recalled now. Thinking about Jocko Humboldt, one of the greatest lightweights that had ever pulled on a glove. No man had ever stepped into the ring with a heart greater than Jocko, and Finley knew it more surely than ever now.

Why hadn't he put some of that dough away for him? It didn't matter about himself; but Jocko was a fighter; he had never done anything else. It'd be tough to start anew now.

"Roland is a tough boy," Finley said not turning around. "Young and tough. We — don't *have* to play it out."

Jocko said slowly: "I need the dough, Ace. It'd be — too long. We'll play it out."

Finley nodded a little and turned around. "Yeah, I guess so. It's the only way." He shook his head.

Jocko Humboldt pulled a grin onto his face. "Don't worry," he said. "Don't worry about it. Just go ahead. We'll see who's smart."

"I guess we will," Ace Finley said. "I guess we will." And he tried to grin back at Jocko, but it was a bum job.

"Don't forget," Jocko Humboldt said, "don't forget — I'm champion of the world."

"Well," he said then, "well, they got it. They got the plate. I just talked to Doc Grayson."

"Yeah," Jocko said. There was no elation in his voice. "Yeah. I thought they would."

There was silence in the room for a little while.

"Well," Jocko said finally, "did you talk to Doc Grayson about — the other?"

"Yeah," Finley muttered. "I fixed that. That's set if we have to play it out."

Jacko Humboldt smiled a little, but there was no humor in his smile. "We've got to play it out," he said.

Finley looked away from him then wandered over to the window. He stood there thinking about

> "That came out of Doc Grayson's office," said Mordesti. "It was marked *Humbolt*."
> "It's a break," he said. "He can't hit with the hand."

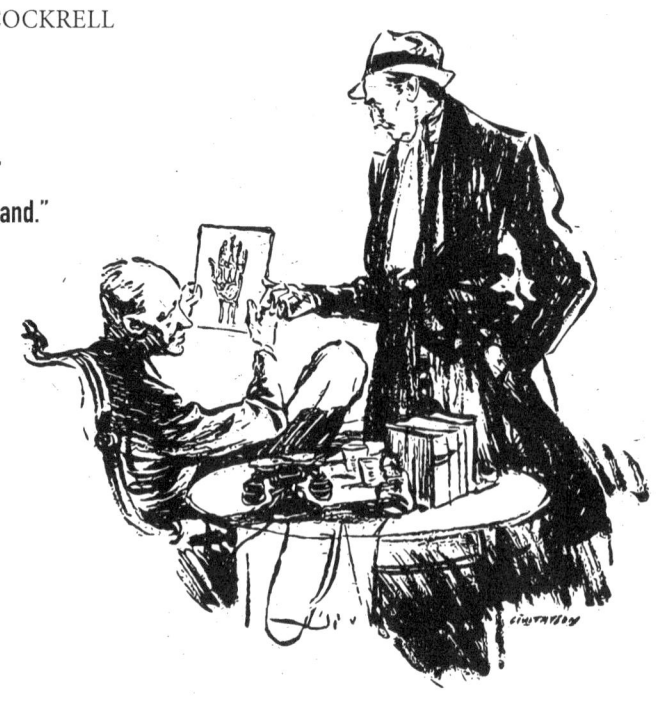

You had to manage a lot of fighters, Finley thought, to get one like this guy.

**THAT** day money which said Jocko Humboldt would not retain his title suddenly became plentiful. At the original odds of one to two, after eight hours, this money went begging. The day before the fight, five bucks would get you eight if you thought there would not be a new champion — and turned out to be right.

For rumors were flying around then, among the boys who like to bet without gambling. For Joe Mordesti was very heavy on Young Roland; and when Mordesti bet, he knew something — when Mordesti bet as he had been betting — so much that he couldn't conceal it, though he had tried.

And Jocko Humboldt had not pulled on a glove since he had worked out against the hard-headed colored boy; he had not punched the bag. The champ had never had strong hands; everyone knew that.

And by noon that day five bucks would get you nine if you thought the champ would win. *And* were right.

Ace Finley began his betting then. A little here; a little there. Some of it went out of town and came back in under another name. Ace Finley raised cash against his boy's guarantee. He bet it. He borrowed two thousand on his word; that's all he could get. Jocko could borrow fifteen hundred, and did. Ace bet it all. He bet it on the champion to win. And if he won they would have slightly over a hundred thousand dollars; for he had got good odds.

Thinking of those hand-made odds Ace Finley's thin face twisted into a grin; a bitter, ironic ghost of a grin.

**JOE MORDESTI** came into the large, ornate restaurant and looked twice around. He saw his man, caught his eye, and beckoned with his head.

Harry Bartzo got up and came over to Mordesti, who said: "Come on."

They went out of the restaurant and presently turned down a side street. Mordesti didn't say anything. They went into a small quiet restaurant and sat down in a booth. A waiter came, and Mordesti cursed him and told him they'd call him when they wanted him. Bartzo looked at him queerly and said: "What's eatin' you?"

"Nothin'!" Mordesti said bitterly. "Nothin' at all except Doc Grayson just bet a thousand bucks that Jocko wins by a knockout!"

"Doc Grayson? Who's he?"

"He's just the guy we lifted that picture from. That's all. That picture we thought was a picture of Humboldt's right hand. The X-ray. You remember?" he added with heavy sarcasm.

Bartzo was blinking. "Why," he said, "then — are you sure?" Bartzo almost whispered it.

"Of course I'm sure," Mordesti growled. "He bet it with Ike Loomis. He must not've known I know every dime that's bet with Ike and who bets it. He couldn't have known," he added, "or else —"

"Hey!" Bartzo said quickly, "Hey! I don't get this. What the hell is goin' on? Why should —"

"You know what it means, though," Mordesti said. "You know that. He's the guy that they went to see. He bets he wins by a knock-out. And Humboldt don't never knock 'em out except with his right."

"Jeeze," Bartzo whined. "Jeeze! The hand's okay. And I got five grand —"

"Five grand!" Mordesti snarled at him. "Five grand!" Listen, you goddam plunger, I got *fifty* grand on your boy. You hear? Fifty grand in cold cash and that aint all. I got twenty-five more. Twenty-five on the cuff. Twenty-five I aint got." His face went pale for a second. "Twenty-five G's, and if this falls through — I'm gone. I'm through. Out of town. I'm lucky," he finished grimly, "I'm lucky if I don't get rubbed out."

"But it's screwy," Bartzo said, pleadingly. "It's screwy, ain't it? I mean it don't make sense."

Mordesti was calm again now — calm and cold.

"It makes sense," he said. "Plenty. I been thinkin' about it. I got it all figured out. It ties together. I beat those guys one time. I beat 'em with a punk of a handler and some red pepper. And they aint forgot it. They pulled this thing for me. The whole thing. It was all a phony, from beginnin' to end, includin' the picture. Doc Grayson was in on it. He had to be. That picture wasn't Humboldt's. They were plenty smart. But they slipped up. They didn't know Doc Grayson was gonna get greedy and put his dough up; and *he* didn't know I'd find it out in time."

"Damn you," Bartzo said. "Damn you, you got me into this. Now what're we gonna —"

"Shut up!"

Bartzo heard Mordesti's flat cold voice and saw his eyes. Bartzo shut up. "I'm tellin' you what we're gonna do," Mordesti said, "and I'm tellin' you why. You just listen, see?" He paused a moment. Then he went on.

"Jocko can't go the route," he said. "They didn't do this just to get back at me. They knew I'd come tell you, and you'd send Roland in swingin' right from the bell, payin' no attention to that right. Jocko's gonna hold it. He's gonna hold it until he's got a wide-open shot. What happens? He lands once. That's all he needs. He's got Roland limber like a rag doll and he polishes him off quick. Early in the fight, see?"

"But if he don't get the shot?" Bartzo asked.

"You got the idea," Mordesti said. "I thought Jocko could take your boy okay. But they don't think so, or they wouldn't have done all this. And they know more about it than we do. Anyhow that's the only way we can figure and have a chance. Three years ago it wouldn't've mattered. Jocko would just bust in there and smack your boy's guard down. He can't do it now and still have enough left to finish him off. He can't go the route. He's old, see? So we can win. You're sendin' Roland in there and he's gonna stay in his shell. He's gonna stay there until Jocko's tired. Just box him. Till the ninth or tenth, if it takes that long. He can go on and win then. But he never gives him a shot with that right. That's what you tell him and that's what he does."

"If — if I don't tell him?" Bartzo murmured.

Mordesti stared at him a moment; his right hand came up and patted what lay beneath his left arm-pit.

"You'll tell him," he said. "You'll tell him. I'm gonna be sittin' right there in your corner. Helpin' you, see?"

Bartzo saw. He shrugged. "Okay. It's the best way, anyhow."

**SMOKE** hung in the air. Young Roland came along the aisle through the smoke and climbed into the bright lights of the ring. A roar of sound had followed him, growing as he neared the ring.

He walked around the edge of the ring now; his green bathrobe made a blob of bright color against the white of the canvas. Young Roland walked with his hands clasped above his head; he was grinning. He was young and tough and he had a lot of fights before him. He liked to hear them yelling . . . . Jocko Humboldt swung his legs off the rubbing-table and stood up. He hunched the bathrobe closer about his neck and said: "All right."

Ace Finley picked up a towel and water-bucket and motioned to a boy in a yellow sweater.

Jocko, looking at his manager's tight, lined face, said hurriedly:

"Damn you, Ace, you're thinkin' you shoulda been a wet-nurse for me and made me put away some dough. Forget it. Listen, you managed me and you made me a champ. You made me a lot of dough and if I aint got it now it's not your fault. Forget it, you hear? But don't forget this, Ace. I'm still the champion of the world. Let's go."

Jocko's face was grim and strained as they left the

room. But it was different when they were walking down the aisle, between those two walls of sound which rose on either side. It was still grim; but it looked confident now. He walked quickly through the reaching hands. He looked like a champion.

Young Roland had his orders. He had been told the why of those orders. He looked at the champ when they came to the center of the ring for instructions. The champ looked worried, but Young Roland thought he could see a little light of confidence behind the champ's eyes. Young Roland grinned at the champ. "It's tough," Young Roland said, "that this aint only five or six rounds. Huh, champ? *Ex!*" The referee told him to shut up, and Jocko Humboldt just looked back at him and didn't change expression at all.

When the bell ended the first round they were in the champ's own corner. The champ just sat down. Roland grinned, walking across the ring. He knew the champ had arranged to be in that corner. He grinned because he didn't have to think about little things like walking across the ring a few times; and the champ did. "Keep that left shoulder up," Bartzo told Roland. "Circle to the right. Airtight, remember! Never let him cross that right."

Roland laughed. "What the hell!" he said. "I could take him the best day he ever saw. He's just another fighter."

"If he bounces that right off your chin," Bartzo said fervently, "you'll think he's two other fighters."

Roland laughed again; but he remembered about that right . . . . It was a slow fight at first. But the crowd didn't boo. Some of them thought they knew something. Most of them were just watching a fight. But they felt something in the air and they didn't boo because it was slow. They just waited. There was Jocko — the champ. He smiled a little, like always. But he hadn't thrown his right. He moved slowly and easily. And that right was

**Young Roland laughed. "Let him throw that right—I can take it." "If he clips you with it," Bartzo said, "it'll be a long time 'fore you know where you took it to!"**

always cocked. But he didn't throw it. And there was Young Roland — the challenger. He was young and he was tough. He wasn't hurrying. But he made you think he knew what he was doing. He was young; he could travel the route. The champ stabbed with his left and danced away. He had Roland's nose beginning to turn reddish. Maybe by the end of the fight Roland's nose would look like an apple. But that didn't mean anything. They didn't pay off on that, and it didn't bother Roland. Maybe you sting a man, popping him on the nose, but you don't hurt him much essentially. You don't take anything out of him for those last rounds. And Jocko's belly was getting a little red, too. That meant something.

The kid was tough. The champ was old. And smart.

Between Rounds Four and Five, in the champ's corner: "Keep the right cocked, ready. Don't move away too much. Let him come in and tie him up. Break slow."

Jocko grunted. "He's good. He's in shape. He'll keep coming."

"Let him," Finley said. "Tie him up. Save your legs and feed him the left. You take these first four by a mile. A mile."

The bell brought them out again.

**YOUNG** Roland kept coming . . . . He might, ten years from now, be fighting some second-rater, taking a beating trying a come-back, and his name would be just a name. A joke.

But tonight Young Roland *was* young. He was a thick-set kid, tough; he was a hooker, moving in. He was resilient and his legs were just things that carried him close enough to punch; things he didn't think about. His breathing came back to normal between rounds.

And the champ was old. The champ had been young once, like Roland. Once, when the champ was young, he had fought five rounds blind. That was seven years ago and you have to fight seven years to know how long they can be; what they can do to your legs. Between Rounds Seven and Eight, in Roland's corner:

"Careful kid. Don't go in with both hands that way." Roland, as the round ended, had got under the champ's left and sunk two solid shots to the body and they had seen the champ wince under his grin clear back in the row named Z. But Bartzo went on now: "Don't hurry. I'll tell you when. It's a wonder you didn't get your head torn off with that right then. He knew the round was nearly over, is all."

Roland laughed. "What the hell! He's just another fighter. Let him throw the right. I can take it."

"If he clips you with it," Bartzo muttered, "it'll be a long time 'fore you know where you took it to!"

And Roland was careful in Round Eight.

There were tentative boos from the crowd now. A few catcalls. This would rise to cruel uproar in another round or so like the last seven had been. They had faith in the champ; they knew the challenger could take it. But they wouldn't watch unmitigated, air-tight boxing forever.

Jocko had his right cocked. He had it cocked all the time. It was a threat for awhile. It was a promise. But he didn't use it. He stabbed with it, now and then. He tapped Roland a few times. But it wasn't the right that had made him champ. It wasn't dynamite; it wasn't the night-cap.

Roland's face was cut up some; it was red. But that didn't hurt a man if he came through right in the last few rounds. And the champ was getting reluctant now, when he came out of clinches. He was moving flat-footed, and his right was a joke. Just a joke; not the murderous weapon of eye-defying speed which had made it famous.

And Joe Mordesti, sitting just behind Harry Bartzo, telling Harry Bartzo what to say to his boy, and listening to see that he said it, began to get a little worried, and began to wonder a little in the ninth round.

Because the champ was getting slower. He was getting slower, and never yet had he crossed that right. Never yet had he cut loose. He had had a few openings; not perfect, but good shots. And he hadn't crossed. Not like he meant it. He had just tapped. And now between the ninth and tenth rounds Roland said over his shoulder: "His right? Hah! He aint got any. What the hell! I said he was just another fighter. Let's get this over."

Bartzo started to speak, but Mordesti tapped him on the shoulder and Mordesti said evenly: "Not yet. Wait one more. I'm not taking any chances."

**IF** Jocko could throw that right, Mordesti was thinking, then why hadn't he thrown it? Because Jocko was tired now, Jocko was about through now, or else he was putting on one hell of a good act. Good? It was too good! Mordesti couldn't understand it.

But it was all right. Either way they should come out okay. The bell rang and Mordesti stopped thinking to watch, watch closely with those bright, black little eyes of his; never missing anyone. And why wouldn't he? This fight couldn't mean more to anymore else than it did to him. All the money he had; too much that he didn't have. And maybe — maybe his very — Mordesti forgot about that then. For as the round neared its end, coming out of a clinch, pushing Jocko back and disregarding that right, Roland left an opening that a first-time prelim' boy would have been ashamed of.

And all Jocko did was paw Roland's face with the right. That's what it looked like; he just pawed it. Pawed it, Mordesti thought, just like you'd wipe a baby's nose. Mordesti grinned for the first time that night.

Roland, back in his corner, was irritable. "Hell," he said. "Another fighter? Why, this guy's just another tramp. I been wasting time. Nuts with you, chief! I'm turnin' it on this time." Mordesti heard him, and looked carefully at Jocko, sitting across the ring. Jocko just sat there, slumped down. His face was pale and his body was limp under Ace Finley's anxious, punishing hands, hands that tried to punish a little life into that tired frame. And couldn't do it, Mordesti told himself. They couldn't do it. It didn't matter — the whys of this thing. It was in the bag now. Mordesti leaned forward and tapped Bartzo on the shoulder and nodded to him. "Now's the time. He can cut loose. We're in the bag. Either Finley and Jocko are dumb as hell, or Doc Grayson is a lunatic, but it don't matter which. Give him the go sign." And then Mordesti sat back and looked with satisfaction at his score card. The fight was even, up to here.

These last two rounds would do it. Mordesti knew he was right; he had kept score on too many fights and had been right too many times. The ten-second whistle blew.

**ACROSS** the ring Ace Finley, with the anguish showing plainly on his face, looked down at Jocko and then blurted suddenly:

"Damn it, I oughta be killed for tellin' you, but you're champion and you ought to know. It's these two rounds. It's even up to here, Jocko. It's these last two rounds. I oughta have my neck wrung, but damn it, you're champ, and you'd want to know."

Jocko Humboldt heard him, and came to his feet two seconds before it was necessary. His face had a strange grin on it.

"That's right," he said. "That's right. I'm Jocko Humboldt, and I'm champion of the world."

Ace Finley had to turn his eyes away from the boy. Jocko hadn't been talking to him. Jocko had been talking to himself.

The bell rang — and Jocko Humboldt, lightweight champion of the world, came from his corner, with his right cocked high, threateningly.

But Young Roland didn't give a damn for that right; Young Roland had tasted it and didn't care. Young Roland was mad because he had wasted time. He would have looked better if he had won early.

Young Roland came in and gave Jocko a shot at his jaw to prove the right was nothing, and Jocko just wiped his jaw with a soft glove. Young Roland sank a left hook into the champ's belly. The old champ. The lines in Jocko's face didn't change. He seemed to be trying to dance away and he seemed to be trying to grin; but he managed neither. Still, he was hard to open up, Roland found. But finally Young Roland got him where he wanted him. He got him around against the ropes, near a corner, and the champ couldn't get out. Young Roland set himself. Young Roland set himself — and two lefts hit him in the face. They weren't dazzling for speed; but they hit him, and they kept him off balance. And he hadn't been expecting them. Then Jocko Humboldt, with the stretched ropes tight behind him to add power, crossed his right.

Young Roland was without motion for two full seconds. Then his knees buckled. Jocko Humboldt moved to a neutral corner and stood with his arms along the ropes. The ropes sagged a little, but Jocko looked ready to come out. He watched Roland closely, except for one second. Except for one second in which he turned his head and looked down at Bartzo, in Roland's corner, and at the man behind Bartzo, and laughed a short quick laugh of triumph and derision.

Then he was watching Roland again. Young Roland was not yellow, and he proved it for good and all that night. He got up. He pawed at the second rope; he got hold of it with both hands, and then got a hand on the third rope. He got a foot under him at "seven" and got the other under him at "eight."

Jocko Humboldt moved in — and the bell rang.

**JOCKO** sat there waiting for the last round with his hands on his knees. Ace Finley was talking to him, but Jocko couldn't hear what he was saying. Jocko didn't know anything but his right hand, which was now the whole right side of his body above his waist. And Jocko couldn't remember when he had last claimed acquaintance with whatever was below his waist.

It didn't matter that he couldn't hear Ace Finley. Ace Finley didn't know what he was saying. The bell.

**IT** wasn't much of a round to look at, that last one. Roland came out shaking his head, trying to clear some of the cobwebs. But Roland was slowed down. Roland tried gamely, instinctively, to move in and work. But he was jabbed five times with a left before he ever got on balance and got in close enough to function. And then he found he was in a clinch.

He was in a clinch, and heard jeering words in his ear:

"So you're just one of those guys that believes everything he sees in the X-ray pictures, huh? You had me worried. I thought you weren't going to swallow it."

Young Roland heard that, and then he heard a malicious, happy chuckle; and as the champ moved away, Young Roland got a good look at his eyes. They were bright and they had something in them now not quite human — something wickedly eager and hungry. Something that was in Humboldt's voice also, as it taunted him, urged him, invited him:

"Well, let's make it a clean fight . . . . You've tasted it . . . . Have another nibble . . . . Let's don't leave it for a decision . . . . Let's have a kayo. Can't take it? . . . Ah, what do *you* know? Maybe it really *is* busted now . . . . Try again . . . . Have another whirl, kid . . . . It —"

Young Roland heard, and he wanted to move in, and he told himself to. But he didn't do it. He saw those eyes, he heard that voice, and saw that right hand cocked there. And as the champ had told him, he had tasted it. It was too soon; he didn't have time; he couldn't forget it. Young Roland hid his chin behind his shoulder.

Young Roland never forgot the night. He had seen what a champion looked like . . . . The bell caught him along to his right, a baffled look on his face, backing away from Jocko's occasional left.

Ace Finley was in the ring, cutting the laces on Jocko's right glove. The referee was reaching down for the slips on which the judges had written their decisions. Then he walked over and took hold of Jock's right hand and started to hold it up. Ace Finley yelled at him. Jocko Humboldt hooked his right elbow over the top rope and held it there while the referee lifted his left hand high.

Every winner in the house yelled out; and then the losers began to yell. Presently there was a complete, shrill, triumphant bedlam.

And only the next day did they realize fully what they had cheered . . . . Two cops made a lane to the dressing-room. Another cop had Jocko Humboldt's left arm, supporting him. His right arm hung over Ace Finley's shoulder. Doc Grayson, with that little black bag, walked close behind them.

In the dressing-room, Jocko seated himself on the table. He had no expression in his face. It was vacant-eyed, grey; he was just about out. The face will not react at all to the kind of pain that owned his whole right arm.

Doc Grayson had cut the bandage off and now he was jabbing a hypothermic needle into the pulpy mass which had once been a hand.

Four feet back, two feet to one side, Ace Finley was standing with tears running down his face for the first time in twenty-eight and a half years and he didn't even care. The dressing-room was full of people and he didn't know it and if he had he wouldn't have given one half-hearted damn. As Doc Grayson pulled out the needle he handed Jocko a brandy flask, made him drink from it, and then gave him another shot. This time in the biceps of that right arm.

Three minutes later then, slowly, Doc Grayson started the examination which was no more than confirmation as far as he was concerned. Handling Jocko's now numb hand very gently, and casting up through his bushy eyebrows occasional questioning and wondering glances, he presently put the hand tenderly in Jocko's own lap and stood back a step.

"THE other day," he said to Jocko softly, "I told you your hand would never heal to fight again. Well . . . . I was wrong." Doc Grayson was an old man who had been around Broadway and been around fighters until he had thought he knew all the answers. But Doc Grayson's voice caught a little bit now and he looked down. "I — good God, man," he said, "I sure was wrong!"

Then he looked straight at Jocko — his gaze very grave. "But son," he said, "I'm not fooling now. If you ever can pick up a pencil with this thing again," — and he touched Jocko's right hand lightly, — "you'll be lucky. You'll never fight again."

The brandy had got a flimsy hold on Jocko, but it was too flimsy for the way he felt. He lifted the bottle and wet his lips from it.

Then he grinned at Doc Grayson. "You're tellin' *me*," he murmured. "I — I think I'll lie down a minute," he added, and he folded back on the rubbing-table. Quietly . . . . Finley had his back turned. "He's a great guy," Finley was saying to himself. "He's all right. He's got a hundred grand now. It aint a fortune; but I'll never let him touch it. He'll be all right; him and his wife. Maybe a kid. The income will do; it's *gonna* do! It's funny," Finley's thoughts went on of their own accord, "it's funny how there's such a lot of guys they call champ. Anybody could hit a man as hard as that with a busted hand, maybe. One time. But then to grin and put on an act that convinces — that's something different. With a numb hand cocked high like you *wanted* to hit. That's what a champ does. That won the fight for Jocko."

People kept punching Finley on the shoulder, gently but insistently. He turned around.

"YOU were there," he said to the newspaper man. "You were there and didn't notice . . . . That's right. He broke it in the gym four days ago. When he hit his partner. It was just an act, but he got too damned intent about it. Too much realism. Get Joe Mordesti to tell you about it," he finished abruptly. "Know? Sure he'll know. Better than anyone in town. You'll find him. Grand Central — Pennsy — the pier of the first boat out of town. Some place like that. Just give him the password," said Finley. "He'll be glad to talk . . . . What? Oh, it's *Triplecross*. He'll know. Oh, sure he will."

Ace Finley paused a moment then, staring at the blank wall of the dressing-room. "A champion," he added, "is a funny sort of guy. A very funny sort of guy. Sometimes."

No one heard him. The reporters had gone. He didn't know that.

The kid chopped out a right to the button and K.O. Jones went down for the count.

# GLOVES FOR THE GOVERNOR

**Let it begin in 1909, said the Fates, with three babies in their cradles,
and a young pug flattened by Ketchel's Sunday punch; then skip twenty-one years
and tangle the threads to reunite the four for a final star-crossed bout with Destiny.
And who'll be champion? A unique and exciting novelet of the ring.**

**STANLEY KETCHEL** came down the aisle and climbed into the ring in the old River City Convention Hall, at nine thirty P.M. on a night in the fall of 1909. He looked across the ring at the set, pale face of Jack Fitzgerald, smiled good-humoredly, and began talking casually to his handlers and waving at the ringside....

Down in the squalor of a riverfront shack, Billy Hope was born at nine thirty-one, Central Standard Time....

Across the street from Billy Hope's home, John Jacob Minelli gave a tentative bleat, then getting no response, quieted. John Jacob was eight months old....

Two blocks over and one down, in an even meaner section of the town, four-months-old Benjamin Bagadaccio slept soundly, though wetly....

When Billy Hope was four minutes old and John Jacob Minelli was quiet again, the bell by the side of the ring in the River City Convention Hall was struck a smart blow by a man with a hard hat tilted back on his head; and Jack Fitzgerald, this night twenty-one years old, walked out to meet Stanley Ketchel for the middleweight boxing championship of the world.

When Billy Hope was twenty minutes old Jack Fitzgerald awoke, lying on a hard table in his dressing room with the fumes of ammonia tearing at his nostrils, sat up quickly and saw Stanley Ketchel, swathed in a bathrobe, standing before him. Stanley Ketchel patted Jack Fitzgerald on the shoulder twice and smiled. "I figured there was no use carryin' you, kid, he said, "and getting you marked up. I hope you feel all right."

At this moment, Billy Hope's mother died, John Jacob Minelli turned slightly in his sleep and Benjamin Bagadaccio awakened to find himself very uncomfortable and let out an imperative squall.

Jack Fitzgerald sat up and surveyed his now empty dressing room, heard the clamor of sound that came from the other dressing room and came to the conclusion that the life of a losing prize-fighter was not for him.

**ON A HOT** early-fall day in 1920 Billy Hope sold all his papers very quickly because they bore a headline that told of an attempt to blow up the House of Morgan in Wall Street that injured a hundred people and killed thirty.

That same day John Jacob Minelli shined the high tan shoes of a lithe young Negro named George Washington Jones, better known as K. O. Jones, leading contender for the middleweight crown, who fought that night in River City's new Convention Hall. John Jacob Minelli put such a terrific gloss on the shoes, and so sincerely refused to accept the proffered quarter from the brown hand that had knocked out so many men that he was offered tickets to the fight by K. O. Jones for himself and his two friends, "if I can arrange it with mah manageh, Jack Fitzgerald."

Benjamin Bagadaccio who had won eighteen cents from a couple of Irish kids down the block shooting craps with dice that weren't all they should be, on receipt of the news that he was to see the fight that night, immediately parlayed his dubiously won money back on K. O. Jones to win by a knockout in six rounds. Eighteen to twenty-three was the best odds he could get.

That night the three boys met in a drugstore across from the hall, each with a first-balcony ticket clutched in his hand.

"K. O.'ll take him easy," Jake Minelli said. "I never seen him fight but I seen him work out a couple of times and he's got a left hand like lightnin', and what's more he can cross his right hard enough to knock out anyone. He's a perfect fighter, pretty near. He's fast, a boxer, and he can hit."

"I looked up his record," Ben Bagadaccio, called "Bagdad," said, "and he figures to win in six rounds, easy. If I'd had more money" — he went on fingering the not-quite-square dice in his pocket — "I'd of bet it just like I'm bettin' what I am."

"I'm gonna be just like that K. O.," Jake Minelli said. "Not that color, but a great fighter like him. He's a cinch for the title if he'd ever get a shot at it and I'm gonna be just like him. Champ of the world."

"Well," Bagdad said judiciously, "if you're fightin' for the title sometime and I figure you to win like I do this Jones tonight, I'll have the dough ridin' on you, too. Only it'll be more likely eighteen hunnert, than eighteen cents."

"I'm gonna be a lawyer," Billy Hope said, and his gray eyes were bright. "I'll be prosecuting attorney of River City some day, and maybe governor even. I've got forty-two dollars in the savin's bank right now. I'm goin' to college."

"Jeeps," Bagdad said. "Forty-two simoleons is the bank and I coulda got six to five that the shine don't win in six rounds. Billy, I coulda had you a hunnert tomorrow."

"I'm not takin' any chances," Billy Hope said. "I'm gonna make sure."

"Let's go," Jake Minelli said excitedly. "They opened the doors a'ready, and I know a couple those bums fightin' in the prelims."

**ON A WINTER NIGHT** in 1932, K. O. Jones, the old champion, successfully defended his title against Harper Wild in a fifteen-round decision bout; and announced through his manager, a pudgy, gray Irishman named Jack Fitzgerald, that he was retiring from the ring. That same day a Japanese Buddhist priest was killed in Shanghai. Fighting on the same card with Jones, Jake Minton decisioned Spud Marsarkey in six. Ben Bagdad, part owner of a gambling house on the West Coast won twenty-three hundred dollars on Jones' win.

Billy Hope in first year law, turned off the radio as the fight started and went back to his books.

The next day Bagdad collected his winnings and announced that he was selling his interest in the gambling house and journeying East. Jack Fitzgerald caught a train back to River City where he had bought a pool hall, announcing his complete severance from the prize ring and things pertaining thereto. Jake Minton (John Jacob Minelli, remember?) began deviling his manager to get him into the tourney that would be conducted to find a successor to K. O. Jones. Billy Hope went out for the university boxing team. The coach thought he had a right.

Two weeks later the papers announced that Jake Minton would fight Dave Shields, that Max Harris would fight Sammy Booker, the two winners to meet and the winner of that bout to be recognized as the middleweight champion. The papers also announced on that day that Charles Augustus Lindbergh, Jr., had been kidnapped. Bagdad took an apartment in New York. Billy Hope won his first inter-collegiate bout, fighting as a middleweight, by a knockout.

**BILLY HOPE, L.L.B.,** now two years out of college, faced Jack Fitzgerald. "I came back here," Billy Hope said, "and opened up an office. But nothing happens and I've about decided to run for D. A. Even if I lose I'll get some publicity. People will know that I'm a lawyer."

Jack Fitzgerald folded his hands over his paunch and said nothing. He was sitting in the back room of his pool hall at a desk and Billy Hope sat across from him.

"I remember you from a kid," Billy Hope went on. "K. O. Jones gave Jake Minelli tickets to the fight, the night he fought here before he was champion, because Jake wouldn't take any pay for shining his shoes. I remember you were K. O.'s manager."

"And," Jack Fitzgerald said, "you want me to manage you, while you turn box-fighter to raise the dough to make your campaign for D. A.?"

"Yes," Billy Hope said.

"How old are you?" Jack Fitzgerald asked.

"I was born October 16th, 1909," Billy Hope said. "I'm twenty-nine."

"October 16th, 1909," Jack Fitzgerald mused. Then he laughed. "That's the night I fought Ketchel," he said.

"I didn't know you had ever been a fighter," Billy Hope said. "Neither did Ketchel," Jack Fitzgerald answered. "It wasn't much of a fight."

"What happened?"

"As well as I can remember," Jack Fitzgerald said and there was a funny little smile on his face, "he started a left hook for my belly." He paused.

"Then what happened?" Billy Hope asked.

"That's all I remember," Jack Fitzgerald said. "I woke up in the dressing room and he'd come over to see how I was. He patted me on the back and said, 'I figured there was no use carryin' you, kid, and gettin' you marked up. I hope you feel all right.' I decided then, to be a manager. Finally, I found Jones."

"He was sweet," Billy Hope said. "I remember that night; my two pals and I went to that fight. Jake Minelli had got the tickets from Jones. He said Jones was pretty near a perfect fighter. That he was a boxer and could hit."

"Yeah," Jack Fitzgerald said. "He was sweet." He paused. "But when I found him," Jack Fitzgerald went on, "he was seventeen years old. When he was your age he was champion, and slowing up."

"Then you think I'm too old," Billy Hope said. Then desperately he went on. "I don't say I can get in there and beat a Minton, I only say I fought three years on my school boxing team and I never lost a bout. I can hit and I can take it. I'm not a K. O. Jones. All I want is a chance to get in there and make a little quick money to pay my debts and finance my campaign. I'm asking you to help me because you've got a reputation of being square and you could get me fights."

"Son," Jack Fitzgerald said not unkindly, "three two-minute rounds in a college bout ain't fifteen three-minute rounds with boys that play for keeps; and an L.L.B. don't ride no punches. Anyway, what's your hurry? You got a long time to live and practice law in this town. You'll get along."

"There's a girl," Billy Hope said. "She can't see waiting until I'm a success and I can't see marryin' her if I can't support her."

"Oh," Jack Fitzgerald said, and he studied the earnest young face of the boy facing him.

Billy Hope returned his appraisal with a persuasive grin. "You can't turn down an Irishman," he said, "that has the same birthday as yourself."

"I would do it for the superstition of the thing," Jack Fitzgerald said, "if you were five years younger."

Billy Hope artfully changed the subject. "I often wondered what happened to John and Bagdad," he said. "It's been a good long time since I looked down from the balcony and yelled for K. O. Jones because Bagdad had won eighteen cents shooting dice that afternoon from the O'Reilly kids down the block and had bet it against twenty-three cents that Jones would win in six rounds."

Jack Fitzgerald looked out into space.

"I remember he was coasting," Billy Hope went on, "and when the fourth round came up he hadn't thrown a right hand. John yelled down at him between the fourth and fifth and he looked up and grinned. 'My pal has bet his roll you'll win before the seventh,' John hollered and Jones waved his hand."

"I remember," Jack Fitzgerald said.

"Where is Jones now?" Billy Hope asked innocently.

"He lives in Memphis. He's — "

"You can drive that in half a day," Billy Hope interrupted fiercely. "Let me take you down there and box a couple of rounds with *him* and see what he says."

"He'd kill you, son," Jack Fitzgerald said, "even now, if I let him go." But his eyes were narrowed as if he were thinking.

## II

**THAT SAME DAY** Ben Bagdad sought out Jake Minton in New York. He found him in the Boy Bulldog talking to a reporter. He walked up and stuck out his hand. "Hello, John Jacob," he said. "I'm Ben Bagdad."

Jake Minton jumped up. "Bagdad," he said. "It's been a long time. I'd never have known you."

"Me either," Bagdad said, "except you told me and Billy Hope one night you were gonna be champion of the world. So I looked up the champion."

"Remember the twenty-three cents you won when K. O. Jones beat that tramp out in River City?" Jake Minton asked. "Jones would never have stopped that guy that soon if I hadn't yelled at him that you had the bankroll down that he won before the seventh."

"I won four G's last time you went," Bagdad said.

Jake Minton sighed. "There ain't anyone around now," he said, "I could draw flies with."

Bagdad stood up and shook Jack Minton by the hand. "I make a little book," he said. "If any of your friends like a horse or a fighter or a golfer or anything." And he handed Jake Minton and the reporter his cards.

**BILLY HOPE** came by Jack Fitzgerald's pool hall at eight o'clock in the morning and honked his horn. Myra Bruce, beside him, said again, "I think the whole scheme is crazy."

"Darling," Billy Hope said a little hopelessly, "Mr. Fitzgerald used to be a famous manager and he doesn't think anything will come of it, either. But please, if I made a few hundred dollars and won the campaign, or even lost it but attracted some attention as a lawyer, it would be better than sitting in my office waiting for clients that don't come, wouldn't it?"

"And your Mr. Fitzgerald told you that you were too old to take up such a hair-brained scheme but you worried him so that now we've got to drive to Memphis while he watches you box with a colored man to prove that you're making a fool of yourself."

Jack Fitzgerald came out of his pool hall carrying a little satchel and walked over to Billy Hope's modest sedan. Billy Hope introduced him to Myra Bruce. "We'll make it by noon," Jack Fitzgerald said, then added. "It'll be good to see George again."

"Who's George?" Billy asked.

"The reporters put that name K. O. on him. He's George Washington Jones to me."

Myra Bruce tilted her patrician nose and said unsmilingly, "It seems a shame that Billy feels the only way he can get ahead is doing something an uneducated darky can admittedly do better."

"There's kinds and kinds of education, ma'am," Jack Fitzgerald said amiably. "Some men are educated in their heads and some are educated in their hands. George was a Ph. D. with his fists."

"Well I hope he knocks all this nonsense out of Billy's head," Myra Bruce said, still a little peevishly.

"He will," Jack Fitzgerald said, still cheerful. "He's knocked more nonsense out of more heads, I guess, than pretty near anybody."

Several hours later Jack Fitzgerald tapped Billy Hope on the shoulder and beckoned him to stop. He got out of the car, then, and walked up through the noon-time somnolence of Beale Street. In a few minutes he returned and with him was a man.

**HE WAS** a brown man, slightly gray around the temples, with wide shoulders, a slim waist and the smooth effortless walk of an animal. He was clad in white flannel pants and a green coat and shirt and the whiteness of his tie matched the whiteness of his teeth. He bowed, grinning, and acknowledged the introductions by Jack Fitzgerald.

"I'm pleased to meet you all," he said. "Mr. Jack tole of you on the telephone. I'll be obliged to box with you for a few rounds and give you my opinion of yoh ability."

"That's nice of you," Billy Hope said. "I guess Mr. Fitzgerald told you that I worried him into this."

"We want this strictly private, George," Jack Fitzgerald said. "Where do you reckon we can go?"

"There is an old ring," K. O. Jones said, "down the river at the barbecue grounds, which will be utmostly private at this time. If you all will follow me I will lead the way in my own car." And K. O. Jones grinned broadly.

"I'll take you up to the Peabody Hotel, darling," Billy Hope said, turning to Myra, "and pick you up, there, when we get through."

"Listen," Myra Bruce said determinedly, "if you think I just came along for the ride you are crazy. I came down here to see you get some sense boxed into your head and I intend to see it."

George Washington Jones looked embarrassed. "I will go get my car," he said, "and be by in a minute. It has license numbeh fohteen twenty-nine," he added.

"But I'd rather — " Billy Hope began.

Jack Fitzgerald interrupted. "It's all right," he said, "let her go." Then he added quickly, laughing: "George couldn't think of any way we'd know his car except by the license. Get a load of it when he comes by."

They heard a horn that gave a four-note bugle call only louder. Then into their vision came the car. It was long and low and the white top was down and the white wheels gleamed against the bright red body.

"He was right about the license number," Myra Bruce said, and her laughter pealed.

"He ought to have a siren," Billy Hope said laughing, too.

"He did," Jack Fitzgerald said. "The law made him take it off."

Billy Hope swung in behind and they made their way down Beale Street. "I wish I'd quit looking back for the calliope," Myra Bruce said. "This is fun."

Every dark face on the street lit with pride and recognition as K. O. Jones, retired undefeated middleweight champion of the world, led the way out of town.

At the picnic grounds Jack Fitzgerald took the suitcase out of the car and opened it. He threw the colored man a pair of shoes. "Remember those, George?" he asked.

K. O. Jones picked them up and looked at them, "Yes *suh*, Mr. Jack." He showed Billy where to change into jersey and trunks and shoes, and went to get into his own things. When they got back Jack Fitzgerald took out new gloves, broke all four in his hands and laid them aside. Myra Bruce sat in the car, her face immobile.

Jack Fitzgerald went over and sat down on the running board of K. O. Jones' car and talked earnestly and low to him for sixty seconds. K. O. Jones nodded occasionally and his ebony face was grave.

**JAKE MINTON** pushed his chair back and stood up. "Listen," he said to his manager. "I'm a fighter. That's my trade. I want to fight. Just because you can't get me a match that will fill the Polo Grounds ain't any sign I'm not gonna fight. It's a hell of a thing when the champion has to go around beggin' for matches. You get out and get me some fights.

"They don't have to guarantee me half the gross and a diamond-studded belt every time I climb in there. There oughta be plenty boys around the country that would like the challenger's cut and a chance to knock me off. You get out and get me some fights."

As Jake Minton talked in a hotel room in New York, Jack Fitzgerald put the last strip of tape on K. O. Jones' brown hands and pushed the gloves up his wrists and began lacing them.

… Ben Bagdad, sitting in a third base box at the Yankee Stadium turned and said softly to his companion, "A hunnert will get you a hunnert and a half if the Yanks don't win…."

Jack Fitzgerald walked to the center of the ring, standing in the deserted clearing on the banks of the Mississippi River and beckoned the square pale Billy Hope and the supple brown K. O. Jones to the center of the ring.

"Now," he said. "I'll ring the bell and I want you boys to go along just like you were in the ring. That's the only way we can tell anything. I want you to fight," he said, turning to Billy Hope, "just like K.O. was still champion and you were fighting for the title." He turned to K.O. Jones. "George," he said, "you have your instructions."

Billy Hope cleared his throat nervously and glanced at the still face of Myra Bruce.

"Now," Jack Fitzgerald went on. "I'll sound the bell, and I'm going to let you go three-minute rounds. Go back to your corners and come out fighting."

"Fighting with a colored man," Myra Bruce muttered bitterly to herself as K.O.Jones shuffled flat-footed from his corner to box with her fiancé.

George Washington Jones came out, standing straight, his left hand out far in front of him, moving easily in the classical pose of the Corbett-era boxer. Billy Hope carried his hands low and his shoulders hunched. He shoved in and loosed a vicious left hook for the brown body before him. But the body was turning and slithering away into space and a long brown arm, pumped three sharp leather-clad jabs into Billy Hope's nose. Rat, tat, tat, like that, and each one of them swung Billy Hope's head back on the hinge of his neck about an inch.

Billy Hope grinned and moved in. Holding his head down he swung left, right, and left for K. O. Jones' body. Two of the blows hit K. O. Jones' forearms and the third whistled by his contracted waist with a cool little swishing sound and K. O. Jones pumped four long lefts ping, ping, ping, ping, to Billy Hope's slightly red nose and glided away, a dark wraith borne on knowing feet. Billy Hope's nose was slightly redder and a little larger, throwing the grin, now set on his face, out of proportion. K. O. Jones' face was grave.

Again Billy Hope crowded in and K. O. Jones was on the ropes now, catching punches on his arms and gloves, slowly being forced into a corner.

Billy Hope had his head down, his chin hidden behind his high left shoulder and the grin was gone from his face and his eyes were narrow. And K. O. Jones was in the corner. Billy Hope swung, shifting his fire to the brown face and K. O. Jones ducked, not moving his body, but suddenly reducing his height, with swiftly bent knees and was behind Billy Hope. Billy Hope swung around, his eyes slits. He had a baffled angry look on his face and K. O. Jones hit him three times with long stiff lefts on the nose.

Jack Fitzgerald banged on the old bell at the ringside with a rock.

Billy Hope sat down on his stool in the corner, looking at the floor, not looking at Jack Fitzgerald, not looking at Myra Bruce. There were little tears in his eyes from those stinging thrusts on his nose and he took deep breaths trying to clear the hot rage from his heart.

K. O. Jones leaned down and listened to Jack Fitzgerald and nodded his head, frowning.

Myra Bruce got out of the car and came over and stood beside the ring. "When do you come to bat?" she asked Billy Hope and it pulled a grin onto his face.

"When he gets tired," he said, and Jack Fitzgerald hit the bell.

**K. O. JONES** came out as before and Billy crowded in. K. O. Jones hit him twice precisely on the nose and Billy was coming so fast that the last one started blood dripping that made a ragged pattern in the blond hair on his chest.

Billy Hope rushed in as K. O. Jones, giving ground like a reed in the wind, caught his foot in a tear in the rotted canvas. Billy Hope chopped home a right hand, and K. O. Jones was down.

He pushed himself to his hands and knees and swiveled his head to Jack Fitzgerald and signaled him with a gloved hand. And then with his head held slightly to one side, as if listening, he waited.

For a moment, all surprised, there was no sound.

Billy Hope retreated to his own corner, a look of growing elation on his face and in that instant before Jack Fitzgerald realized what the colored man was waiting for you could hear Myra Bruce breathing. Then Jack Fitzgerald knew.

" … five; six; seven; eight; nine … " he counted.

And K. O. Jones was on his feet and over him had come a subtle and indefinable change. Where before in his movements there had been only a suggestion of the cat, the stalking leopard, now it was an effort of the mind to remember George Washington Jones was a man at all.

His left shoulder had gone up higher, and his right glove had dropped. There was the suggestion of a crouch in his stance and as he moved in his feet were flat and seemed to be gripping the canvas through his shoes. He led a clumsy left, and Billy Hope brushed it down and came in. He came in as K. O. Jones crossed his right.

Myra Bruce said, "Ahhhhhh … " letting the sound come out just as Billy Hope, falling forward, hit the floor with his gloved hand held before his face.

Jack Fitzgerald started counting. "One; two; three…." The muscles down Billy Hope's sides tightened from some subconscious mental stimulus and then relaxed. He pushed one hand out to his side. " … seven; eight…." He pushed the other hand out and his knees came off the floor with "nine," walked in blindly toward K. O. Jones, his hands up, swinging.

K. O. Jones caught Billy Hope's hands and pulled him in a clinch. Over the white shoulder he said, with elaborate movement of his lips but silently: "Hit the bell, Mister Jack."

**BEN BAGDAD** took the sheaf of bills from the outstretched hands and started wending his way toward the exit of the stadium. "You can't beat a man that don't work," he told the owner of the hand, and grinned.

"You'd think them Yankees would cure me some time," the man with the empty hand said. "But I can't turn down a price."

"No bet's a good bet," Ben Bagdad said sagely, "unless you win it."

"There's plenty tank towns in this country," Jake Minton concluded, his hand on the knob of the door, "that ain't had a title fight in thirty years. Take River City, my home town. I ain't been there since I was thirteen but I remember they used to have good cards there and they drew. The country's full of towns like that. Write around to towns like that and see what you can do."

Billy Hope sat disconsolately on the running board of his car and held his head in his hands. Jack Fitzgerald was packing the shoes and the gloves in his satchel holding low-voiced conference with K. O. Jones, who was smiling and nodding.

Myra Bruce sat down beside Billy Hope. "You knocked him down," she said. "Flatter than a fritter."

"It turned out to be a mistake," Billy Hope said, trying to grin. "I thought he had hit me with a club."

"Your poor nose," Myra said. "Your poor, poor nose."

Jack Fitzgerald came up to the car, then, and put the suitcase in it. "He sure showed me the error of my ways," Billy Hope said. "I'm sorry I caused you all this trouble."

Jack Fitzgerald pursed his lips. "You're gonna cause me a lot more," he said critically.

K. O. Jones came over buttoning his coat. "I'm sorry, Mr. Hope," he said. "That I fohgot myself, to the extent I fohgot myself. But when you put me down once more I thought I was a young boy and I clean fohgot about evehthing 'cept to signal Mr. Jack I was all right and then to get up and try to beat as quick as I could such a dangerous hitteh as you'self."

"I'd never have hit you in a hundred rounds," Billy Hope said, "if you hadn't caught your foot in that hole."

"I would not have arose neitheh," K. O. Jones said, "until Mr. Jack had counted a hundred, if I had not rode the punch a little."

"I wouldn't have gotten up when you hit me," Billy Hope said, "if I'd known what I was doing."

"*Ketchel* never hit me any harder than that,"

Jack Fitzgerald broke in. "And I was out in twenty minutes."

"I put my hips into that one," K.O. Jones said, "and until now no one never did get up in time. That," he added a little ruefully, "was my Sunday punch."

"Well," Jack Fitzgerald said, "let's go. I wanna get home before dark."

Billy Hope stuck out his hand. "It was nice to meet you, George," he said, and he managed a smile and then turned his head so Myra Bruce couldn't see his face.

"I'll see you , suh," K.O. Jones said, "on Monday. Mr. Jack has asked me to come to Riveh City and try and teach you how to keep from getting' hit so much. As foh how to hit," K.O. Jones finished, grinning, "I can't teach you no more about that."

## III

**JAKE MINTON** came back from Atlanta, where he had stopped Bob Shires, unknown except in his home town, in three rounds and he dropped into a saloon on Forty-Fourth Street for a glass of lemonade and conversation. He found Ben Bagdad looking glum, sitting by himself. He walked over and sat down with him.

"Hello," Ben Bagdad said. "I see you stopped the mug in three."

"I pick up a few bucks," Jake Minton said, "I don't take no chances. I'll take bouts like that any time I can get 'em. Why not?"

"I," Ben Bagdad said, "was arrested for makin' book. I never see such a town as this in all my life to try and make a dime in. It's full of stool-pigeons and honest cops and tough D.A.'s and I am leavin' it."

"Where do you aim to go, Bagdad?" Jake Minton said.

"Jake," Bagdad said earnestly, "I am goin' back to River City. I see by the papers that Harry Harman is running for D. A. out there and I figure to go out there and talk business with him. I'll put up some dough and if he wins he lets me go. I'll open a small store and cater to the elite and settle down and get mine. River City is a town with plenty of money and yet it's small enough you can put in a fix without havin' to square the Russian standin' army."

"Well," Jake Minton said, "if you get to town let me know. And if I ever hit River City I'll look you up." And he got up and went to another table. Ben Bagdad took a time table from his pocket and started studying it.

A few days later he sought out Harry Harman in River City.

"I'm Benjamin Bagdad," he said, "I was born and lived 'til I was thirteen in this town. I remember it for a hustling city. I always liked it."

Harry Harman stroked his regal head of silvery hair. "It's a fine town," he agreed.

"Now you're runnin' for D. A.," Ben Bagdad said, "and you're runnin' without opposition. Right?"

"That's right," Harry Harman said. "I feel that I can be of service to the people of this city, representing them in our courts of law. However, you are in error to a degree. I am running only for my party's nomination without opposition."

"What the hell," Ben Bagdad said. "If you're nominated you're in, ain't you?"

"That has been true in the past," the attorney admitted. "Probably, though, there will be opposition to my nomination. There simply have been no other candidates who have got filed."

"Do you think you will win?" Ben Bagdad asked bluntly.

"I don't know what this conversation is leading to, Mr. Bagdad," Harry Harman said a little tartly. "I naturally think I'll win, otherwise I wouldn't make the race."

"Well," Ben Bagdad said. "I have done a little askin' here and there around your town and it seems as if you have the smart money on you. Such organization as there is is for you; there don't look like there's anyone that can jump in now that'll beat you."

"I'm glad to hear that," Mr. Harman said. "But I'm a busy man and I would appreciate it if you'd get to the point of … "

"There ain't gonna be no protection for no one if you win?" Ben Bagdad broke in and he curled his lip the slightest bit.

"A public office, my boy," Harry Harman said, "is a public trust."

"If someone mailed you a check for ten thousand bucks," Ben Bagdad said, "and you spent it in the right places, you'd be a gut cinch to win, wouldn't you?"

"What? Er, yes. Ten thousand. I think it would remove all doubt." Mr. Harman said and he smiled a wide and cordial smile.

"I call myself a gambler," Ben Bagdad said, "but really I try not to take no chances. Now I figure that maybe you and me can deal. I figure … "

Harry Harman punched a buzzer on his desk and to the voice that came back he said: "Tell anyone who calls that I'm out. That means *anyone*."

**NOT FAR** up the river from River City, on a deserted farm far back from the road, carpenters had thrown up a ring and in it George Washington Jones and Billy Hope labored. That is Billy Hope labored. Huge gloves were on his hands, a headguard protected his ears — but not from Jack Fitzgerald.

Jack Fitzgerald started a vitriolic sentence, remembered Myra Bruce knitting under a nearby tree and took a deep breath. "No!" he screamed. "No, no, no. Not like that. George, show him. Show him that in throwin' a left hook he does not also have to lead with his chin."

George grinned reassuringly and in slow motion made a demonstration.

"Smellin' beat our Joe," he said, "the fuhst time because of just that. Now you protect yourself like this…." And he demonstrated again.

"All right," Jack Fitzgerald said, "go ahead." They started boxing again and after a minute Jack Fitzgerald said, "That's all," and wandered over to Myra Bruce.

"I got him a fight," he said glumly. "I didn't want to tell him for a while but I can't put it off forever. Up in Des Moines."

"And he'll get paid for it?" Myra Bruce said and laid down her knitting.

"He'll get enough to pay his filing fee," Jack Fitzgerald said. "And if he wins I can get him more dough next time." And he walked off to where K. O. Jones was now polishing his car.

"George," Jack Fitzgerald asked, "did you ever see anyone come on so fast?"

"He's one hundred percent improved oveh before and he was one hundred percent betteh then, than the time before." And George Washington Jones grinned a mighty grin.

"I got him a fight," Jack Fitzgerald said, "against a boy that is supposed to be tough but dumb. I want him to get some confidence. But don't you tell him that he is getting good. It might make him ease up."

Billy Hope came out of the improvised dressing room where the scales were and said, "A hundred sixty, flat."

"Okay," Jack Fitzgerald said gloomily, then added, "I got you a fight. In Des Moines. Next Saturday night."

"Swell," Billy Hope said. "Who did you say I was?"

"I said you was Billy Hope," Jack Fitzgerald said. "You ain't so famous you can't use your own name."

"I'd just as soon, though," Billy said, "not let it out I was a prizefighter, if I'm going to run for district attorney and I *am* going to run, now." Then he added anxiously, "I'll make enough to pay my filing fee, won't I?"

"Sure," Jack Fitzgerald said sarcastically. "And pay me, and pay George for all he's done and pay for buildin' this ring. Sure, you'll make enough."

"But … " Billy Hope began.

"Be quiet," Jack Fitzgerald said fiercely. Then in a more subdued tone he went on. "You can square me and George up later."

"Then you do think I'm going to make some money. You think I'll be all right?" And hope and disbelief were both in Billy Hope's voice.

"I didn't say that," Jack Fitzgerald said, then fierce again he added: "Do eight miles in the morning and don't cut no corners."

As Billy Hope's little sedan made its way out of sight down the lane toward the highway a sigh escaped Jack Fitzgerald. "If I had him," he said turning to K. O. Jones, "when you retired, I'd have had another champion."

"If I was Mr. Crump," George Washington Jones said, "I'd just let him be prosecuting attorney of Memphis and they wouldn't be no more to it." And he gave a fender of his car an extra rub singing softly, *Mistuh Crump don't 'low no easy riders heah.*

**THE NEXT MORNING** Billy Hope, running in the park, met a small dark man walking home. The small dark man was faintly familiar and Billy wondered who he was for the space of a hundred steps until the thought of his coming fight, his professional debut; his filing-money fight, drove all else from his mind. All else but Myra Bruce.

… Jake Minton's manager said. "I got you bouts in St. Louis, Memphis, Birmingham, Des Moines, River City and Denver. I don't know 'em all, I mean, who you'll meet, but they won't run no contenders in on us, I know that. Just local talent I guess mostly. Now will you quit squawkin'?"

"Sure," Jake Minton said. "I'll quit squawkin' as long as I'm fightin' and makin' money. I'm not going to last forever, you know."

*From* The Des Moines Times Register:

*… Billy Hope, a newcomer, stopped Maxie Roth, in two. They were middleweights …*

*From* The St. Louis Globe Democrat:

*… Jake Minton, looking every inch a champion knocked out Chilly Stiegel, local sensation, in six rounds last night. It was the first of a series of tune-ups …*

Billy Hope climbed up on his sound truck and adjusted the microphone. The swelling around his eye had gone down and except for a tinge of blue beneath it he looked all right. "Last night," he began, "I became a candidate for the office of prosecuting attorney. Tonight I open my campaign. The reason I choose this corner for my first speech is because I've spent more time on this corner than any other corner in River City. I sold newspapers on this corner for five years."

Ben Bagdad standing at the edge of the small crowd swore under his breath. "It's Billy Hope," he said to himself.

Billy Hope grinned and the light from the street light glinted on his blond hair and on his white even teeth. "This is the fourteenth ward," he said.

"The bloody fourteenth. This is my ward. I was born down here and I worked down here saving my money so I could go to law school."

"Yeah," Bagdad muttered. "It's Billy, all right."

" … and I'm not an orator like Mr. Harman, and I won't have much money to spend…."

There was a pause and from far back in the now larger crowd came a booming rich voice, *Mr. Hope won't 'low no easy riders heah.*

"If I'm nominated and elected I'll take office, politically, socially and financially indebted to no man…."

Ben Bagdad turned away and moved uptown. He was talking to himself. "I ain't superstitious but Jake told me he was gonna be champion, and he is. I told Billy I was goon be a big shot and if Harman wins I will be — *but* Billy told us he was gonna be prosecuting attorney of River City, and now he's runnin' and I'm ten G's in with Harman…."

He made for a drugstore and in the phone booth dialed Harry Harman's number.

**HARRY HARMAN'S** laugh came warm and tolerant over the wire when Ben Bagdad had finished. "He filed last night," Harry Harman said. "And today I looked him up. He hasn't tried any cases to amount to anything, and he's young and inexperienced and he hasn't any money. How can he beat me?"

"I don't know much about this politics," Ben Bagdad said, "but I used to know this Billy Hope, we was kids together. And he was always hell for doin' what he said he was gonna do."

Harry Harman's voice was not so warm. "Listen," he said, "I *do* know about politics and I'm telling you we are lucky that we haven't anything worse than a kid lawyer with no money to beat. He hasn't any money and he's not going to be able to raise any with the hopeless situation that he faces."

"All right," Bagdad said, dubiously. "But if he wins…."

"You were swell, Billy," Myra said. "And remembering all those people by their names. It was wonderful."

"Honey," Billy Hope said, "I lived down there for fifteen years, almost, in business," he added grinning. "I ought to know my neighbors and my customers, oughn't I?"

"That Harman is a crook," Myra said suddenly. "I know he is. I just wish we could get something on him."

Billy Hope laughed. "I don't think he's a ball of fire," he said, "but I wouldn't call him a crook. What makes you think he is?"

"He looks too honest," Myra said firmly. "Naturally, you can't look that honest and not be hiding something sinister."

Billy Hope leaned over in his little car parked before her apartment house and kissed her. "If you find the sinister thing he's hiding," Billy said, "let me know."

"When do you fight again?" Myra asked.

"Next Thursday night I go against the champion of Arvalia County, Nebraska. We'll have to drive all night to get there in time."

"Why all night?"

"Honey," Billy explained, "I can't be mysteriously away from the city during the campaign. Maybe a day occasionally won't hurt, but I can't be away longer than that. They might make something of it."

"How much will you get for this fight?" Myra asked.

"I'm glad you asked me," Billy said. Then after a dramatic pause he added: "Two hundred and fifty dollars, or converted into two-cent stamps to put on letters to undecided voters, twelve thousand and five hundred. A nice round sum."

"Well," Myra said, "You better get on home. And if they want to make something out of this they can," and she leaned over and kissed Billy Hope on the lips.

*From the* Nebraska Blade:

*Billy Hope, one fifty-eight and a half stopped Shag Mercer last night in the fourth round of as torrid a pugilistic encounter as these old eyes have seen since the days of Terry McGovern. They hit each other with everything but the ring posts before the superior arsenal of young Mr. Hope fetched him triumph.*

*Definitely, "the quality of Mercer was strained," and in the fourth round it snapped. But not before Shag had brought the red gore of Billy Hope a-dripping from his nose and a badly cut lip. Those who like their fights rare and juicy found this one made to order. Twice in the second round….*

*From the* Birmingham Age Herald:

*The fighting champion, Jake Minton, stopped Red Robin, in the Municipal Auditorium here last night after five dull rounds. Jake took five rounds to lure Red out of his shell, and then about fifteen seconds to finish him off….*

**BILLY HOPE** climbed up on his sound truck and adjusted the microphone. "I hope you will excuse my appearance," he said. "I have been taking boxing lessons, and my instructor was a little bit too enthusiastic." He paused then and waited for an instant. "I propose tonight," he continued, "to give you my trial record. It's not bad. In fact, it's pretty good. I've tried a good many cases for a good many people. It so happens that they usually didn't have any money to pay me with." Billy paused a moment and grinned a battered grin. "In fact," he said, "I've tried more cases, won more cases, have a better won and lost percentage than Mr. Harman who today told the Civic Club that I was too inexperienced. Here's the record. First mine, then his."

Then Billy Hope in the fashion of an announcer gave the respective records.

A falsetto piped rudely from the back of the crowd: "Be careful with your language, boys. He's so pure."

Driving Myra home that night, Billy said discouragedly: "They're making it too tough for me down there. They've spent thousands of dollars down there and that's the ward we'll win or lose in. That guy that heckled me tonight was paid to do it. I know that."

"What will we do?" Myra Bruce asked and she, too, sounded discouraged.

"I need money," Billy Hope said. "I need more posters down there in the fourteenth, more workers, more cars to haul my people on election day. All that takes money. Harman's got those things. I need a big purse. Just one good big purse. If Jack could just line me up a fight that would pay me heavy dough I wouldn't care whether I won or lost. I wouldn't care if I didn't fight again. I could borrow against the purse and I could turn on the heat until election, down there."

"Why don't you tell him that?" Myra asked.

"I will," Billy said. "I'll tell him that tomorrow."

**BEN BAGDAD** came into Harry Harman's office and his face wore a bleak expression. "Listen," he said, stopping Harman's greeting half complete. "This Hope is going like wildfire. I want to know how we stand."

Harry Harman laughed easily. "I've had precinct workers out quietly checking strength," he said, "and we have nothing to worry about. A lot of noise doesn't necessarily mean a lot of votes."

"I'm worried," Bagdad said. "I don't like the looks of it."

"Don't you trust my judgment … ?" Harry Harman began.

"I don't trust nothing about you," Bagdad said flatly.

"Perhaps," Harman said with elaborate sarcasm, "you would like to withdraw your support?"

# IV

**JAKE MINTON** paced back and forth in his suite in River City's best hotel and he was reading from the papers aloud to his manager, alternately laughing and frowning.

"Bill Hope," he read, "the dashing young candidate for prosecuting attorney who receives his answer from the people tomorrow at the polls, tomorrow night receives his answer also from Jake Minton, the world's middleweight champion as to who shall hold that title. For not only is Bill Hope, candidate, and L. L. B. He is also Battling Billy Hope, aspirant to the crown."

Jake Minton read on, moving his battered lips slightly, now grinning. "For Billy Hope's whirlwind campaign for office has been largely financed by the proceeds from his bouts out of town during the campaign. Tomorrow night he gets his answers."

"It's Billy, all right," Jake Minton said. "We was kids together."

Jake Minton's manager yawned. "What of it?" he said. "He ain't fought but six times and while he's won 'em all by knockouts he ain't beat anyone that could fight their way out of a paper bag with their hands on fire — just a bunch of never was's."

Jake Minton frowned. "I know that," he said. "I ain't worried about the fight. I was just remembering … "

"Does he know who you are?" Jake Minton's manager asked.

"Naw," Jake said. "I don't suppose he does. He knew me by my real name, John Minelli."

"Let's not have no 'old pal' stuff at the weighin' in," Jake Minton's manager said. "The guys that pay their way in don't like that stuff so good."

**BILLY HOPE** confronted Jack Fitzgerald across the desk and his voice was even and cold. "So I'm the mysterious local boy, the masked marvel, the stooge? So this is why I didn't know who I was fightin' and why I was gettin' so much for it?"

Jack Fitzgerald frowned. "Son," he said, "you told me you needed a big purse and that you didn't care whether you won or lost. I got you a fight with the champion. You'll pack 'em in. We've broke publicity in every sheet in town about all your other fights and how you've won 'em all and how K. O. Jones has been your trainer. I held it off, not lettin' nobody know, not even the promoter nor Jake, who you was so it wouldn't hurt your campaign."

"Not hurt my campaign," Billy Hope grated. "Not hurt my campaign. They go to the polls tomorrow and you've got me signed to go in there and fight tomorrow night. Nobody wants a common pug as prosecuting attorney. You've ruined my campaign."

"I think you're wrong, son," Jack Fitzgerald said. "But you can cancel out if you want to and I'll forfeit the dough I've put up with the commission. If you won't go, say the word."

Billy Hope's shoulders slumped and his voice changed. "I'll go," he said. "I've borrowed and spent the money I'll get, already." Then added: "Myra has given me the pitch."

"What do you mean?" Jack Fitzgerald asked.

"I promised her that no one would ever know I'd been a fighter to raise my money," he said. "I promised I'd never let it out. She doesn't like the idea, I guess."

"I didn't know that," Jack Fitzgerald said slowly.

**BILLY HOPE** came down the aisle from his dressing room swathed in a red bathrobe, his hands already taped. He looked neither to left nor right. Waiting, sitting in the ring he paid no attention to K. O. Jones and no attention to Jack Fitzgerald whispering alternate last minute advice in his ears. He didn't look up when Jake Minton climbed into the ring and bowed, shaking his hands over his head.

The referee called them to the center of the ring. He looked at their hands, gave them their instructions. Jake Minton was grinning at Billy Hope, but Billy Hope didn't look at him. He stared at the floor.

The referee finished his instructions.

Ben Bagdad, sitting in a ringside seat, chewed his cigar. "Jake must know who Billy is," he reasoned half aloud. "Billy don't know who Jake is. Will Jake carry Billy for old times' sake? How in the hell did the election come out? We won't get no flashes here and when this is over the results will be in. I can't figure this fight."

Jake Minton, a thorough craftsman, who valued his title though he would fight often in its defense, came out of his corner with the bell. He advanced cautiously, feinted Billy Hope into a bad lead and rapped him twice with lefts to the head and then caught Billy up in a clinch.

"Billy," Jack Fitzgerald asked between rounds, "what's the matter?"

Billy Hope rinsed his mouth out and spit the water out. "Nothing," he said. "Got any returns?" His voice sounded as if he didn't care much.

"The election's over," K. O. Jones said. "Now git out there and win the title."

"I can't beat this guy," Billy Hope said. "He's a real fighter."

"You got nine more rounds," K. O. Jones said. "Lots can happen in nine rounds."

Jake Minton leaned back in his corner and took deep breaths, easily. "He's strong," he said, "but he ain't a fighter."

"Don't get careless," his manager cautioned. "He can hit. He's stopped some tough boys."

"Nice house," Jake Minton said, running an appraising eye around the hall. "I guess it's capacity." And he bit into the rubber mouthpiece his second shoved between his teeth and went out for the second round.

Halfway through the fourth round the referee warned Billy Hope to make a fight of it. The crowd was stamping their feet and the boys in the gallery were whistling the *Merry Widow Waltz* between jeers.

Jack Fitzgerald sat disgusted, not saying anything to Billy Hope between the rounds but K. O. Jones kept up his talking. "He's gettin' careless, Mr. Billy. Just go along, and remember what I told you. Crowd him more."

"I wonder what I did down in the fourteenth?" Billy Hope said dispiritedly. He heard the bell and went out.

Jake Minton was still careful but he was opening up. He cut Billy Hope over both eyes and shook him with hard rights during the sixth round.

Billy Hope went to his corner brushing blood out of his eyes with the back of his hand, walking without animation, not tiredly but as if he had nowhere to go. He sat down and as K. O. Jones worked swiftly with collodion he pushed him away. "Let it go," he said. "It'll be over pretty soon. Don't bother."

The bell brought him out for the seventh round.

**JAKE MINTON** came in swiftly. He jabbed Billy with left hands, sunk his right into Billy's stomach and swished it up with his shoulder under it and it dropped Billy Hope like a log. He was up at "six," moving in and Jake Minton dropped him with a sharp left hook.

He was up at "nine" as Jake Minton came in to finish him: but Jake Minton was over-confident and careless and Billy Hope tied him in a clinch and clung to him long seconds while his head cleared. He weathered the round but K. O. Jones had to lead him to his corner.

"I'm not tired," he said, in his corner. "He can hit," he added, as if he were a spectator. "I wonder what I did in the fourteenth. I wonder where Myra is. Good old Myra. There's a girl for you, Jack," he mumbled bitterly. "That Minton reminds me of somebody. I wonder where Myra is? Good old Myra. The Bruces are such lovely people. They couldn't make a matrimonial alliance with a common fighter. It's all right if nobody knows it, but not if it gets found out. And it's three more rounds to go. It'll soon be over."

Billy Hope came out for the ninth round and Jake Minton dropped him with a one two and the crowd was hollering for the referee to stop the fight but somebody else was hollering, too. And out of that welter of sound Billy Hope recognized the voice and pushed himself to one knee.

Myra Bruce was running down the aisle. She was running down the aisle and she was screaming! And Billy Hope could hear her.

"Five," the referee intoned and his arm came down and rose once more over Billy Hope.

"You're winning! Billy, you're winning! Myra Bruce was screaming. "You're ahead! You're winning!"

"Seven."

Myra Bruce had reached the ringside now and emotions were tangled up in her voice.

Jake Minton standing in his corner creased his brow. The girl was beating on the ring apron. "You're carrying the fourteenth! Get up, Billy, you're winning."

Jake Minton moved his lips, thinking. "She's punchy," he said to himself, "it ain't but a ten-frame bout."

Billy Hope got up. Jake Minton came in, measuring Billy Hope and Billy Hope a grin breaking his face, making his cut lip drip blood faster, feinted with his left hand clumsily, and as Jake Minton brushed it aside he crossed his right.

"Ker-wham!" George Washington's voice broke above all the tumult. "The Sunday punch."

Jake Minton went down. Nothing could be heard. Benjamin Bagdad stood on his chair and bit his cigar in two.

But Jake Minton was a champion. He got up. Billy Hope rushed in, but Jake Minton, acting from instinct, still cunning though his mind no longer worked, groped into a clinch. His knees were like water, but he was on his feet and he had Billy Hope clutched to him, his hands tied up and he was trying to remember something. Billy Hope was trying wildly to break loose, Jake Minton remembered what he was trying to remember and he spit his mouthpiece out and whispered in Billy Hope's ear: "I'm John Minelli, Billy."

Billy Hope fought loose and the sentence he had heard didn't register in his mind until he had swung again and Jake Minton was on the floor.

Jake Minton climbed to his feet at "Nine," moved back, and as Billy came in, maneuvered him with numb arms into another clinch. "I'm John Minelli, Billy," he said again. "Champion of the world. If I hit the deck again this round I'm afraid I can't get up."

**IT WAS COMING** back to Billy Hope. Coming back with a rush. Selling his papers, listening to John Minelli tell again and again his destiny. *Just like K. O. Jones, only not that color. Champion of the world.... Even with all that money Harman hadn't been able to buy the fourteenth. The fourteenth was the backbone of the nation and all that stuff. Good people came from the old fourteenth. Billy and Bagdad and John. Billy and Bagdad and John. Champion of the world was one. Prosecuting attorney was another. Just like they said. Bagdad. The big-time gambler. "I'd had you a hunnert...." Bagdad ought to be here.*

Billy Hope's chin was over Jake Minton's shoulder and he was staring straight at Benjamin Bagadaccio. And Benjamin Bagadaccio was watching that face and trying to read it. Trying to fathom what brought that expression to the face of Billy Hope and if he could fathom how to convert that knowledge into cash. The champion was out on his feet. As soon as Billy Hope got out of this clinch the title would change hands. That was plain.

Ben Bagdad took a chance. He stood up and he talked right straight at Billy Hope and he made his voice like he hoped it was when he was a kid: "I'll lay eighteen hunnert to twenty-three hunnert Minton is the winner," he said.

Billy hope heard the voice. *Eighteen to twenty-three. Eighteen to twenty-three.* Billy Hope creased his eyes and looked out into the gloom into the small dark face of Benjamin Bagadaccio.

Billy Hope shoved his arms under Jake Minton's arms and said: "Clear your head, pal. I'll hold you up."

The referee pried them apart and the bell rang.

Jake Minton was a champion. He came out

for the tenth, like he came out for the first. Careful, breathing easily. Boxing carefully. Billy Hope bounded out. Swinging, dripping blood, grinning.

The last round was fast but there was no damage done.

## V

**JACK FITZGERALD** sat across from Ben Bagdad in the back room of his pool hall and his hands were folded across his paunch. "Well," Bagdad concluded. "What about it?"

"As I understand it," Jack Fitzgerald said, "you want to rent the farm I got up the river to set up a gambling house on. Is that right?"

"Yes," Ben Bagdad said. "Billy wouldn't let his own starvin' mama run a store in this town. Your farm ain't but ten miles away and what's ten miles to a guy who wants to make two grow where one grew before?"

Jack Fitzgerald smiled. "There's a story goin' around," he said, "that you had the fix in to open a gambling place here after the election. Is there anything to that?"

"Never mind that," Ben Bagdad said and he summoned a wan grin. "I at least won a bet I made that Minton would win, when Billy had him out on his feet."

"I have absolutely no scruples about gambling by people who can afford to lose," Jack Fitzgerald said. "You cater to the carriage trade and we can deal."

**MYRA BRUCE** was sitting in the car with Billy Hope in front of her apartment house. "You were right," he said. "Harman was a crook. Bagdad came around after the fight and told me he had him fixed it if he was elected. That was before he knew I was going to run."

"I want to get married right away," Myra Bruce said, and then she buried her head in Billy Hope's shoulder and whispered, "I don't want to ever be away from you again."

Then she looked up.

Billy Hope grinned. "We'll have a wedding," he said. "With Jack Fitzgerald…."

"And K. O. Jones."

"And John Minelli, and Bagdad and…."

" … all your precinct workers…."

"How's my left?"

"Swell, darling."

"My right?"

"Perfect. In fact those gloves you used tonight are going to hang in the executive mansion — when you're governor — and I — "

Then through the night they heard a four-note bugle call. A red car swished by them and it was long and low and expensive. It had one passenger. Its passenger was singing a song. They only caught one phrase and part of another: … *I got them Memphis Blues … and Mistuh Hope don't 'low no easy riders heah.*

Billy Hope watched the taillight of the red car wink out in the distance and then he turned to Myra Bruce. "This," he said, "is my Sunday punch." And he kissed her.

# THE LAST FIGHT

**The story of a Swede who got mad.**

**HE** looked around at the dressing-room, trying to see everything, note every tiny detail. He wanted to watch the worried face of Manny, his manager, that Manny thought was so impassive — that dark excitable face with its dead cigar that made the slightly off-center dot under the exclamation-point that was a nose. He wanted to watch Manny; but still he wanted to watch the gnarled hands of Nick, his little Greek chief second and trainer, moving lovingly, almost reverently as they kneaded his heavy brown legs. Those legs that looked so thick and solid and sinewy, but were his weakness. He wanted to suck into his nostrils that pungent, faintly acrid smell of liniment and long-dead cigars and dried sweat and soap. He wished that all his perceptions were sharper, to record this scene so he could always be able to recreate it in his mind. For in his heart he knew that in its actual reality it would never be repeated. He knew, from the long years, the countless fights, the careful observations, that had kept him for ten long years champion among those men weighing between one hundred and forty-seven and one hundred and sixty, that tonight, in a few minutes, he would walk up the aisle, nodding to his friends, smiling, outwardly the same, and climb into the ring and — lose his title. Christian Sturluson propped himself up on his elbows on the rubbing-table and pressed the half-lemon in his right hand to his mouth. He looked at the three newspaper men.

# THE LAST FIGHT

**"Land, land, land!" said Manny. "Then it don't rain and—"
"it will rain again," said Sturluson.**

They were talking among themselves, preparing to leave, to go up to the ringside, where they would watch the fight. They knew. Christian Sturluson knew they knew. He knew that Manny knew, that little Nick knew. It was almost as though the fight were over — almost as if they had brought him back to this dressing-room, and he was lying here on the table, the defeated champion. There was that in the air. Christian Sturluson looked at his hands. They were big hands, heavy, competent. He had never had trouble with them. Plenty of work chopping wood, carrying as a kid two balls of newspapers that he was always squeezing. Squeezing and finally shredding, to be replaced by two more. Even as a kid welterweight pleading for a spot on a small card in some promoter's office, he remembered being laughed at as he unconsciously squeezed the two balls of paper. He had had a little more of an accent then, and that had made him funnier. They thought it funny when he solemnly informed them as a reward for a fight, he would come back and fight for them as champion. But he had. All the little clubs that had helped him, all the small promoters that had given him spots as a kid; he'd come back and fought for them — as the Champion of the World.

There were laws, it seemed — immutable laws. A man might take a sound body, and a cool brain and by never deviating from his purpose, by never for a moment relaxing his will, parlay that asset into a million dollars. He had made a million dollars. Maybe more, in the last twelve years. He had fought often, and some of his opponents had been colorful fellows who might, just might possibly, find the chink in the armor and beat him. Until tonight no man had done that . . . . But there were laws.

It was a law of the ring, a law of nature that applied to those who lived by fighting other men with gloves upon their hands for the entertainment of a slightly sadistic populace and as good a cut in the gross as their managers could get, that the legs of a man went first. The hands were there, the good strong hands. The punch was there: the devastating hook, the lightning right cross, the blows to hurt and beat the man who absorbed them. But the legs of a man went first.

And Chris Sturluson's legs were gone. Sometime between the third and fifth rounds they lost their resiliency. The extra tiny bit of elasticity, the ability to move and react instantaneously to reflex.

The reporters said something faintly cheerful to him, and one reached over and patted him on the back. Then they were gone. Manny walked over to the table. He tilted back his black derby and looked down at the long muscled body; then his eyes strayed to the thin blond hair with the bald spot in the center, and Christian Sturluson could almost see him wince.

"Take it easy," Manny said, and his voice was edgy. "Take it easy."

Chris smiled his slow one-sided smile. "As if the big squarehead wouldn't!" Manny muttered. "Nerves like a hog."

Christian Sturluson closed his eyes. His mind took him back to a night in Chicago when he had watched a great fighter stand helplessly in the center of the ring, and beckon with his gloved hand for his opponent to come in and fight. He didn't understand it then. He didn't know that when the great Jack Dempsey stood there and beckoned the back-pedaling, still slightly dazed Tunney to come to him, that he, Jack Dempsey, could not go after him . . . . The legs went first.

On the hand of little Nick, the left hand so skillfully massaging, there was a ring. In the ring there glared out, like a white and baleful light, a stone. It was once a tiny stone. The night that Christian Sturluson had won the title, Nick had bought the ring. It was really the same ring: a symbol, a symbol of success. With each succeeding defense of his title, the stone had increased in size. Now it was enormous. Would it shrink when he had lost tonight? Would the diamond get smaller, and with each pitiful come-back attempt, get smaller still until it was gone? Because there would be come-back attempts. Yes, there must be. Maybe if he showed well, a return go with the champion.

**CHRISTIAN STURLUSON** was broke. This night, at the age of thirty-four, he would step into the ring with his end of the purse already gone. Borrowed on and sent after that other money, all those dollars that he had made, and had tried to invest so carefully in the land — land that would produce, that they could not take from him. That would be his always, that he could live on and love, and raise blond boys on, now that he had found their mother. She was sitting up there now. Sitting in a ringside seat, her big eyes serious and calm, with faith in her man shining out of them. She had never seen him fight, but she would see him fight tonight. His girl.

See him step out under those lights against a boy, smooth black hair glistening, white teeth shining, who could move like the wind and hit like a piledriver. A Latin lad who would be an old man at thirty-four — but a lad who tonight could stay clear of Christian Sturluson for a few rounds, and thus be crowned.

He would have loved to fight this boy in the old days. This flash, who looked like nothing so much as swift flickering light as he flowed around the ring. This dark lad who would tantalize with long left hands, the tired bald Swede who plodded after him — and in the old days would have caught him. Would have caught up with him sometime in the middle of the fight, and then begun a methodical campaign to bring him down, a quivering husk, in the thirteenth or fourteenth round. He could see that fight; he could plan it, lying here now. He could feel his muscles warming and loosening as that fight progressed. He could feel himself getting stronger and faster as he piled on the pace. He could almost see the dark face getting desperate as he kept crowding in. That was as it would be in the old days. But tonight he would be through,

practically, sometime around the sixth round; and tonight he could not catch this lad in six rounds. Then he would be beaten. From sometime near the sixth round until the fifteenth, he would be beaten because he could not move.... If the fight went fifteen rounds. Manny Roberts threw down his dead cigar. He cocked an ear, hearing the applause above him in the stadium. "It won't be long now," he said. Then he turned to Christian Sturluson lying there before him, and added viciously: "Why couldn't you listen to nobody? Land, land, land! The good earth! Then it don't rain, and the damn' stuff blows away. You don't catch no clothin'-store nor no saloon, nor no apa'tment-house blowin' away because it don't rain."

"It will rain again," Christian Sturluson said placidly. "And the taxes must be paid."

"A million bucks! A cool million bucks you've kicked off! You ought to have your head examined."

"I have some splendid farms," Christian Sturluson said. "They will be fine when it rains again."

"He owns half the dust-bowl," Manny Roberts said, to little Nick. "He's the la chumperoo de luxe, when they talk dirt to him."

"I did not expect the men to cheat me," Sturluson said, "about the land."

He would do his best—he would try to beat his age.

"He never tells me what he's doin' with his dough. All these years he never tells me. I got a brother makes pearl buttons in Joisey. Doubled his money, I woulda. But no, don't tell me. I'm just his manager. Now he has borrowed on his purse and bought the rest of Oklahome, and paid the taxes that he owed on Kansas."

Nick looked up and grinned. "Why not he should sella some of his land, and then he has money, and his taxes, it's smaller?"

"I do not sell land," Chris said shortly. They didn't understand, of course. How could they? They didn't — "All right," a voice from the opened door said, and four men filed in. Two were from the camp of Angelo Lazia, and one was from the Commission. They watched solemnly, in silence, as Nick began bandaging Christian Sturluson's big hands. There were no complaints. Manny had gone to watch the bandaging of Angelo's hands. Christian Sturluson stuck his arms into the armholes of his heavy white bathrobe, and pulling it around him, began walking toward the door. He said no word.

Then he was in the aisle, and a mighty roar went up. It warmed him as it welled and followed him up the long aisle, and he felt he knew all these people.

He had fought many times for them, and each time he had done his best. And each time he had won. Tonight he would do his best. He would go all out to try and beat his age. But his heart told him that he couldn't. . . . Then he was in the ring. Angelo Lazia half smiled, half sneered across the ring at him. Christian Sturluson smiled back. He felt relieved. It would be over soon. The gnawing realization that had first come to him, when he started training for this fight that he was old, and he was glad, almost, that it would soon be over. Just one regret — just one regret! He needed money. He needed money to get started. He needed money to bring his farms to profit, to tide him over until the rains. To get married on. He would like to get married tomorrow, and go out to his land, lying in one magnificent square of countless rolling acres, and get to work on it himself. He hated the idea of the come-back — the come-back that never came off. He had viewed with pity champions who had tried it in the past. Now he must do it . . . . This — this would soon be over. Sitting on his stool, he looked down at his legs. Manny had taken off his bathrobe, and Nick had laced on the new gloves. The bathrobe was draped over his shoulders now, and he was waiting to go to the center of the ring

**"Kill the big squarehead, Angelo!" Anna Nelson screamed.**

for his instructions. Then he was in the center of the ring. The referee was an old friend of his. He smiled at him, and he smiled into the face of Angelo Lazia. The referee seemed to be giving special attention to some matters of heeling, and rabbit-punches. Chris Sturluson looked up, mildly surprised, but he saw that the referee was directing his remarks chiefly to his opponent. Angelo Lazia grinned at the referee. "And that's how I knew that Old Man Mose was dead," he sang. Somebody in Angelo Lazia's corner laughed. Christian Sturluson hardly heard. He was looking down into the big gray eyes of Anna Nelson sitting in a press seat, beside Williams of the *Blade*. Anna smiled at him; and her smile hurt him, it was so full of quiet certainty.

Then he went back to his corner. He came out slowly with the bell, the thought in his mind that he must go the route to get a return flight. Angelo Lazia glided in and flicked him twice with long left hands, and tempted him with feints and deceptive half-openings to follow him.

Chris bore in, but Lazia was gone, and he smiled at his stupidity. They wanted him to move — to follow this wraith until his legs were tired, and then it would be soon over.

**BUT** that was the only way he knew to fight — to crowd. Fifteen years of fighting, and never a backward step. He must try to unlearn that, make Lazia bring the fight to him; that was his only chance. But Lazia didn't do it.

And so Chris moved in. He had to. Some compulsion to crowd, to get in, to fight, made him move forward. When he went back to his corner, Manny hissed bitter words into his ear. "Let him come to you. Don't chase him. You won't be able to stand up, by the sixth. Make him come to you, and work on his belly. Tie him up. Hold him, ride him. And for God's sake, don't play tag with him." Chris Sturluson nodded. He knew Manny was right. But what difference did it make? Manny didn't know that already, as he sat there, he could feel a telltale tiny tremble in his right calf. He went out with the bell. He wasn't warm yet, really. He hadn't got loosened up, and yet his left leg trembled slightly when he sat down. Standing, going out to meet the man before him, it felt all right. How long would it feel all right?

Christian Sturluson felt uneasy for the first time in his life.... He crowded in, knowing he shouldn't and jockeyed Lazia to a corner and hit him a short solid right above the heart. Lazia's face let a funny look cross it before he danced free. But in an instant he was smiling his insolent smile, dancing provocatively away. Chris Sturluson smiled to himself with the knowledge that five years before, he would have murdered this rather ill-mannered lad. That punch had hurt him. Chris Sturluson moved in. With the bell, he allowed his eyes to drift to Anna Nelson, and he smiled into her eyes with what he hoped was reassurance. Angelo Lazia saw that by-play. He laughed to his handlers. "This," he said, "is gonna be fun."

"Please," Manny was pleading. "Please get it through that billiard-ball of yours that you can't beat this boy in no foot-race. Let him come to you. You'll get tired, and he'll cut you to ribbons —"

"I know that," Chris Sturluson said. "I'm sorry. I can't change my way of fighting." He paused. "I guess," he finished, "I'm too old." He said it calmly. And Nick, rubbing his stomach, noticed that there was a tiny tremble in his legs.

The bell brought Chris out.

Manny looked helplessly at Nick. Christian Sturluson moved doggedly forward. "He knows," Manny said. "But he aint got the nerves of a good well-bred hog."

Angelo Lazia noticed that something was not as

it had been. Christian Sturluson came into him, and he worked into a clinch. The old man was fading early, Angelo decided. He would have some fun.

"How come," he said into Chris' battered left ear as the referee came to part them, "you rate a classy dame like that? I got a good notion to take her over too, along with the title."

Chris smiled to himself at this awkward attempt to upset him, and pushed free of the clinch. It amused him to think of this conceited boy and Anna. How she would hold up her proud head if this boy with the greasy hair would make so much as an attempt to speak to her. But still it gave him a funny feeling, and he broke from the clinch, and his effort to swing a right left him open, and Angelo Lazia hit swiftly and opened a cut beneath Christian Sturluson's left eye.

Manny didn't speak to him when he went to his corner. Not for ten seconds. Then suddenly he asked: "What was you gabbin' about? Who could run fastest?"

He worked with swift expertness on the eye. "What was you thinkin' about when he clipped you?"

Chris answered the first question methodically. "He was teasing me about Anna," he said. The bell prevented his answering the second. The tremble was in his legs, and he could feel the presence of these thousands of people that he would disappoint. He could hear them. The working press at the ringside, the gamblers. He knew the welling sounds that had come so often to his ears; but he moved forward, because he had to move forward.

He looked at Anna, and he saw that Manny was talking to Anna. And that Williams of the *Blade* was nodding and smiling. All this with the corner of his eyes; and he bored in, trying to catch on shaky legs the man who was not there.

Angelo Lazia taunted him from long range. With long lefts and with words.

"A bald-headed old man like you shouldn't have a dame like that," he said. "After I knock your ears off, I figure I'll just move in."

**SOMETHING** entirely unfamiliar welled up in Christian Sturluson's breast when he heard that; and he rushed in, swinging wildly. Then suddenly he was sitting on the floor, and the referee said *"Four."*

And above the tumult and the shouting, he heard a voice — a voice he could not mistake. "Kill the big squarehead, Angelo!" Anna Nelson screamed.

"Five," the referee intoned. And from that point on, Chris ceased to think methodically. A thousand thoughts welled in his brain. And though the pink haze that came before his eyes, he saw only the pretty face of Angelo Lazia, and thought of the pretty face of Anna Nelson. Angelo Lazia's face would change. He would change it. Anna Nelson

"How come," Angelo said as the referee came to part them, "You rate a classy dame like that? I got a good notion to take her over too."

he hated. He rose at nine with some animal cunning, and swaying, feigning grogginess so well that he brought Angelo Lazia toward him for the kill. Then Christian Sturluson, who in all his thirty-four years had never before been mad, moved to meet his rival, and the crowd came to its feet in sheer hysteria.

Christian Sturluson went in clubbing. Both great arms swinging, wide open. He caught a hard right that cut his eyebrow and sent blood dripping, and he shook his head and went on in — both hands down, swinging murderously, amateurishly, awkwardly. But with power.

Angelo Lazia danced away, and a long right whistling far behind his head reached him as he drew back and set him on the floor.

Christian Sturluson stood over him and cursed him in long words rich with consonants, and the referee dragged at his arm to get him to a neutral corner. He turned, almost hit the referee, in unrecognition; and Angelo Lazia got to his feet and fled. But he couldn't get out of the ring.

Christian Sturluson shook his head with a mad rage when he turned and saw his quarry gone. He lowered his head and turned around. Then he plunged, his hands low, at Angelo Lazia; and he made a slight designed for terror. Bald head, blond hairy chest matted with blood, and incarnate fury in his square and battered face.

Angelo Lazia stood back and tried desperately to box. A clubbing long left hook sent him crashing down. And Christian Sturluson would not move. The rich Scandinavian profanity rolled out of him and welled out above the uproar of the crowd. The referee dragged bravely at his arm, and finally Chris remembered something, and moved to a far corner.

And there he stood.

Angelo Lazia wasn't out. He had been hurt, but he wasn't out. But he wouldn't get up. He cowered on the floor, and his eyes begged protection from all that he could see. And he was counted out. People were climbing into the ring now: Manny, screaming; a policeman; and the referee was reaching for Christian Sturluson's arm to hold it aloft when Angelo Lazia, deeming it safe, got up.

Christian Sturluson threw the referee aside and moved swift as a striking snake. In an instant he had Angelo Lazia in his hands and above his

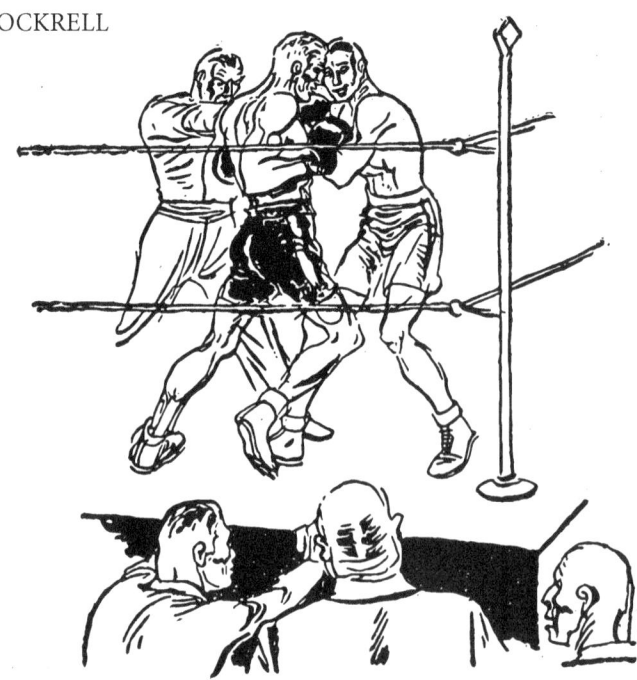

head, and he walked to the ring apron and threw him through the air at Anna Nelson as a man would throw a rotten apple; and to Anna Nelson he directed a fierce remark in his native tongue as Angelo Lazia bounced crazily on the upraised hands of the reporters. Then the policeman had him.

**CHRIS** was lying on the table, and he knew that he had lost. But he was glad that it was over. No more anything. He was through. He looked up at the face above his, and heard the great tumult in the dressing-room. Anna Nelson smiled at him. Christian Sturluson smiled back his slow and crooked smile. "Something happened to me," he said. "It was something about you. Something like a bad dream. Did I fight well? Did I lose like a champion?"

Anna Nelson couldn't say anything. Manny Roberts was beside her and little Nick, and they were looking at him. It was little Nick who finally spoke, who said the words. "The morning papers is out," he said. "They say heavy general rains all over the Middle West." And on his right hand, as he rubbed Christian Sturluson's leg, his great ring gleamed bigger, it seemed, and more baleful than ever.

Wham! K.O.'s hand snaked around Hassard's neck and smacked against the ring post.

# SWEET-TALKIN' MAN

**K.O. was too old to fight but he claimed he was tough as an alligator—and even an alligator will battle when some no-account slicks him out of his supper.**

**K.O. JONES** stood first on one foot and then the other and his grin was sickly. Jack Fitzgerald said again, more sharply: "Come on, George, don't stand there grinnin' like an ape. Tell me what you came up here for."

"You sure hit the nail on the head, Mistuh Jack," K.O. Jones said enthusiastically. "Yes, suh, you sure hit the nail on the head."

Jack Fitzgerald brushed a fly exasperatedly off his bald head and looked at K.O. Jones. "George," he said evenly, "you've come clear up from Memphis to tell me somethin'. Now you might as well get along and tell it. Don't give me any more of this nail on the head business and stop scufflin' your feet."

"I was just agreein' with you, Mistuh Jack," K.O. said, all contrition. "I was just agreein' about me bein' an ape. Well," he amended, "maybe not *exactly* a ape. More like a monkey, maybe."

"Listen to me, George Washington Jones," Jack Fitzgerald said slowly, "I've known you for twenty years. I've known you since I picked you up on the street shinin' shoes when you were sixteen years old and I knew you when you were the middleweight champion and I managed you all that time and I know you.

"You got somethin' on your mind, and you might as well tell me and get it over with."

"Mistuh Jack," K.O. Jones said desperately, not smiling now. "I'm busted." Jack Fitzgerald got up from his desk in the little room behind his pool hall and he walked over and looked at a picture on the wall. The picture was of a lithe young Negro, gloved hands up, beautiful in fighting trucks. Jack Fitzgerald went back and sat down at his desk. "How much do you need?" he asked, finally.

"Mustuh Jack," K.O. Jones said softly, "you know I never come askin' no charity."

Jack Fitzgerald said quickly: "I know that. I thought maybe a little loan. To tide you over . . ." Something about K.O. Jones' expression stopped him.

"Mistuh Jack," he said, "when we parted company I had forty thousand dollars and I had me a good house and a good car. But I met with a sweet-talkin' man who said he was from Chattanooga who wanted to use my money for a little while and then give it back. He was gonna help the colored folks of Memphis and then give my money back."

"Why didn't you let me know about it, George?" Jack Fitzgerald asked. "You promised me you'd leave your money where it was unless you let me know."

"The man," K.O. said, "was in a terrible great luxury. He said that if'n he didn't get it right then and there pretty near that day, that he wouldn't be able to swing the deal."

Jack Fitzgerald thought sadly of this for a moment. "So you let him have it?"

"I let him have it, Mistuh Jack, after I had talked to my lawyer. He tole me to let him have it."

"Your lawyer was a crook?"

"He could follow a snake's track and never hurt his back," K.O. Jones said.

"Who was the one that got that money? Who was the sweet-talkin' one?"

"He didn't rightly tell me his real name. I come to find later from Hoppy Hall, who runs a gambling parlor on the gay way, 'cause when I told Hoppy of the man he says his name wasn't Alvin Miller like'n he tole me but known in the Big Town as Maxie Mataxa."

Jack Fitzgerald snorted. "You lived twelve years in Harlem, George," he said. "And you saw gamblers and gunmen and thugs every day of your life. You were a fighter in the big time. Didn't you learn anything?"

"You taken care of me in them days," K.O. Jones said logically. "An' except for four bits or a quarter on a policy number I had dreamt strong I never misbehaved myself to speak of."

"If you don't want any money," Jack Fitzgerald said, "What did you come to me. . ." he stopped then. "Uh-huh," he said.

**K.O. JONES** walked around the desk and he reached out and the fly that Jack Fitzgerald had slapped from his head and was now droning busily over the desk suddenly appeared wriggling between the brown right thumb and forefinger of K.O. Jones' right hand. "Fightin'," K.O. Jones said, "is the onliest trade I know. Please, Mistuh Jack."

Jack Fitzgerald walked over to the wall and pointed to a picture. "Who's that?" he asked.

K.O. Jones spelled out the name laboriously under the picture of the massive figure with the big left arm straight out in front of him. "James J. Jeffries," he said slowly. "The ole boilmaker."

Jack Fitzgerald pointed to another picture. K.O.'s face lit in immediate recognition. "Jack Johnson," he said. "Li'l Arthuh hisself."

"Jeffries tried to come back," Jack Fitzgerald said. "He fought himself into an air-pocket. He didn't have any one to whip. So he retired. When he came back he fought Johnson. It was pitiful. I don't want you to look pitiful like that, George."

"I've heard you speak of the old days Mistuh Jack," K.O. Jones said slyly. "An' who do you think was the best middleweight of 'em all?"

Jack Fitzgerald looked at him a moment, puzzled. "You or Ketchel," he said finally.

"Uh-uh, Mistuh Ketchel. Uh-uh. Say another one."

Jack Fitzgerald grinned. "Oh," he said. "Fitzsimmons. But he was a freak. He was big as Dempsey in his shoulders, he was a freak."

K.O. Jones gazed innocently at the ceiling. "How old was Mistuh Ruby Bob Fitzsimmons when he won the heavyweight championship from Mistuh Gentleman James J. Corbett?"

Jack Fitzgerald smiled. He didn't want to smile but he smiled anyway. "They say," he said, "he was thirty-eight years old."

"He was the light heavyweight champion, the middleweight champion and the heavy champion, at the same time when he was the age of forty years old, or so you've told me, Mistuh Jack."

Jack Fitzgerald grunted. "I told you he was a freak . . ."

"I'm pretty freaky myself," K.O. Jones said and he was grinning then, a happy grin. "Like an old crocodile. You know a crocodile ain't gettin' his growth good till he's two, three hundred years old. I'm like an old crocodile."

"You may have something there," Jack Fitzgerald said. "They skin crocodiles. Their skin is very valuable." He picked up the phone on the desk in front of him. "Or maybe its alligators," he said. He gave a number and talked briefly, then, to someone on the phone.

"Sit down," he said to K.O., holding the receiver of the phone down, "and look like a crocodile." Then he picked up the phone once more and put in a long distance call to Memphis. And K.O. sat down.

**WHEN** Benjamin Bagadaccio came through the door from the Fitzgerald Billiard Parlor into the little office, he walked over to the desk, tossed his head slightly toward K.O. Jones sitting in a chair by the wall and let his eyebrows go up a fraction of an inch.

Jack Fitzgerald stood up. "This is Bagdad, George," he said. "Bagdad, this is K.O. Jones, my old fighter."

Benjamin Bagadaccio turned his five feet five and one hundred and ten pounds on his heel like an automaton, took K.O.'s extended hand limply and dropped it. He bowed slightly. He didn't say anything. K.O. Jones sat down. Jack Fitzgerald went on genially: "George is just an ole crocodile, Bagdad." He paused. "Who's Maxie Metaxa?" he asked.

Bagdad's expression didn't change but he took one delicate, well-manicured hand from his beautiful jacket pocket and waved it across the desk once, thumb down.

Jack Fitzgerald picked a cigar carefully from the box on his desk, lit it and took a deep puff. He nodded his head, then slowly, "I see," he said. Then added. "Will he gamble?"

Bagdad spoke then for the first time. His voice was very soft. "No," he said. "He won't gamble."

"Will he bet?"

Bagdad took a cigarette out of his pocket like a magician and lit it. "He'll bet a poor widow woman," Bagdad said softly, "that the sheep won't kill the butcher." He took a drag from his cigarette and let the smoke come out his nose and mouth without propulsion as he finished. "If he gets odds."

Jack Fitzgerald turned to K.O. Jones. "How old are you, George?" he asked. "Honest?"

"I ain't right sure, Mistuh Jack, but I judge near thirty-two years old."

Jack Fitzgerald sighed heavily. "He was a pretty good welterweight then when he was eleven," he said to Bagdad with heavy sarcasm. "That's when I picked him up."

The phone rang then, and Jack Fitzgerald picked it up. "This'll be Memphis," he said. He talked quite a long time on the phone and all the time Bagdad stood, not changing expression. K.O. Jones' face changed expression, each time he heard Jack Fitzgerald mention a name he knew. Almost all those names were distasteful in the extreme to K.O. Jones, fetching back to him memories of his house, now gone, and his fine long red car, idle in a garage with a large storage bill against it. Finally Jack Fitzgerald put down the phone. "It's all legal, probably," he said to neither in particular. Then he turned his attention to Bagdad. "Maxie clipped George for forty Gs. All I saved for him in twelve years' fightin'."

Bagdad nodded.

"Down in Memphis," Jack Fitzgerald went on. "Very simple. Simple things for simple people." He paused again. "I can get together about twenty thousand dollars. I'd admire to have you with me in this thing, Bagdad, because it's gonna take a fine Italian hand."

"What?" Bagdad said. Jack Fitzgerald looked up. "I'd like to get it back from him," he said. "And some for you, too."

"I don't have to have a cinch," Bagdad said then. "But I'm a gambler, too. I want a lot the best of it."

"All right," Jack Fitzgerald said. "All right. You come see me tomorrow mornin'. I'll be ready to talk to you then."

Bagdad turned and walked to the door. "Okay," he said, then paused, with the door open. "Sesame will win the fifth at Bowling Green today. Take a hundred for yourself but don't let in your friends."

"How can you be so sure, Mr. Bagadaccio?" Jack Fitzgerald said with genial sarcasm. "Because," Bagdad said, and for a moment K.O. thought he was actually going to smile, "he ain't Sesame."

**JACK FITZGERALD** moved the desk a little and then he moved the chair a little so that it was in what light there was in the room behind his pool hall. "Sit down, George," he said and he snapped the scissors together experimentally.

K.O. sat down in the chair with trustful docility. "Bagdad," Jack Fitzgerald said, "he got a sort of Indian look about him. Give him a high chair cut and a droopy mustache and we can bill him the Indian Terror and nobody knows no different."

Benjamin Bagadaccio moved a little to one side and contemplated K.O. Jones with a hard impersonal stare. "They've done it to horses," he said.

Jack Fitzgerald waved his borrowed tools. "He's got a pain like a Yaqui Indian then let's give a look."

"He ain't a horse," Bagdad said logically.

"Hell's fire," Jack Fitzgerald said. "Lemme try my hand for once. I can make him a Yaqui Indian easy. Anyway, whatever we make him, we got to cut off his hair. He's getting gray as a badger."

K.O. Jones squirmed in the chair. "What you doin' to me, Mistuh Jack?" he asked. "I don't want to be no Wacky Indian. Can't you just get me a couple go's as K.O. Jones, ex-middleweight champion?"

"You want," Jack Fitzgerald said, heavy sarcasm weighing each word, "to fight semi-windups for five hunnert a go and have all the old-timers feelin' sorry for you?" Jack Fitzgerald snapped the scissors twice. "You're forty years old if you're a day, and I don't aim for you to get in there and disgrace yourself under your real name."

K.O. Jones moved his head slightly, dislodging the clippers. "I won't disgrace no one," he said. "I want to fight as K.O. Jones. We beat the best of 'em like that, Mistuh Jack."

"Hold still, George," Jack Fitzgerald said. And he warmed his clippers and ran confidently up the side of K.O.'s face.

Jack Fitzgerald gave no sign he heard. "This barberin' is a cinch," he said, and he gave his attention to the back of K.O.'s head. "We'll get him a couple go's with tankers," he said to Bagdad, "and make him look bad but win. Then we'll throw him in there with some strong young kid he can beat and we'll take Mr. Metaxa like Grant took Richmond."

"You got it too high," Bagdad said. "Too high on this side. Lemme have the scissors for a minute. Maybe I can fix it."

Jack Fitzgerald handed Bagdad the scissors. "It's gonna take some doin' though," he admitted to himself. "Have you figured an angle?" he added to Bagdad.

"What I'm tryin' to do," Bagdad said, "is kind of feather it off. How come it comes out in scallops like that?"

Jack Fitzgerald looked up. "Whoa!" he yelled. "George, he's ruint you. Bagdad, lemme have those clippers. You got your side higher'n mine now by half an inch and it still looks boxed off."

Bagdad stepped back reluctantly. "I was thinkin'," he said, "about a guy around town I know. Named Willie Shoshone. He's a real Indian and he looks kind of like K.O. He was a pitchman. There's a lot of actor in him."

"An angle?" Jack Fitzgerald asked.

"Well," Bagdad said, "maybe we could get him to say he was one of K.O.'s tribe. Give him a flash roll to play around with and maybe they'd take him for a chump. Lot of them Indians down around Oklahoma got plenty dough from oil."

"How is he for honest?" Jack Fitzgerald said.

"He'd have to be watched," Bagdad said. "But I could do that." He took a cigarette quickly from his pocket and lit it. "Hold on, Jack," he said suddenly. "Look what you're doin' to this side."

Jack Fitzgerald stepped back. "It *is* a little higher'n yours," he said. "George could train out at your place, couldn't he?" he concluded.

"Jack," Bagdad said, "let me have those clippers. You got it now so high he's gonna look pretty funny." He took the clippers and worked delicately over K.O.'s right ear; far over it. "Yeah," he said. "He could train out to my place. Nobody is there except at night. And it's good and off the road."

"Well," Jack Fitzgerald said, "if we could get a couple local kids that would keep their trap closed; we could have him train back here and only fly him east to fight. That oughta work all right, at least for two, three flights." He surveyed K.O. speculatively. "Bagdad," he said. "You're way too high, way too high." He walked once around the chair where K.O. sat. Finally he stopped. "Work up some lather," he said to Bagdad, "we got to go whole hog now."

"Whole hog?" K.O. asked faintly. "What you mean, Mistuh Jack?"

"Bagdad has got your hair in such a shape," Jack Fitzgerald said sadly, "that we're gonna have to shave your head. But don't worry. That's what we want to do, fix you so nobody will know you."

"Oh, Lord," K.O. Jones said. "Oh, Lordy, Lordy."

"I'll drive him out to your place when I finish with him," Jack Fitzgerald said to Bagdad. "You get hold of that Indian you was talkin' about and bring him on out. We'll start K.O. right in this afternoon. He can do a little wood chippin' and road work before we need any sparrin' partners."

Bagdad looked at K.O. "You got him lookin' like a Turk, now," he said. "He looks like Yussuf Goulash himself. You wouldn't never know him."

K.O. gave a soft moan. "I could have got me a W.P.A. job," he said. "I surely could."

**THERE** is a restaurant in New York where men who would be discontented with six percent per annum on their investments are wont to loaf and eat. In fact, most of these men like something at even money that wins in the fourth round or something that pays six, two, and even and canters in many lengths ahead. It is a self-evident fact, to them, that this is better than even ten percent per annum. Maxie Metaxa was a habitué of this place, and even Benjamin Bagadaccio was not unknown there, having made trips to the city himself in his day.

There was considerable discussion among a number of those gentry one morning as to the relative merits of some steeds that would perform that afternoon at Belmont but when Willie Shoshone came in the door, all discussions ceased.

Willie walked to the bar and demanded whiskey. He demanded it in loud and perfectly understandable American. And finally after some discussion with the proprietor as to the laws applying to inns and restaurants in the Commonwealth, he got it. Now his entrance and the argument created a quiet among the ones who had been discussing the horses because Willie's costume was sort of a cross between a burlesque comic's and a North Hollywood cowboy's and naturally took precedent in interest over a mere horse, even a shoo-in at eight to one. But the interest in Willie that had been reasonably intense was downright ennui compared with the interest that was created when Willie fetched forth from his pocket the wherewithal to pay. Because the wherewithal consisted of something that looked like a large handful of very big bills. And it was.

"Haven't you anything smaller, sir?" the bartender asked, now deferential.

Willie looked at the bartender with a look that should have withered him and after some searching through the inside of his money, found a fifty. "Keep the change," he said. And turning on his heel, he departed. Maxie Metaxa was the first one to say anything. Finally he got it out. "Gawd," he said.

Ten minutes later Bagdad burst into the restaurant. We waved to a couple of people he knew, but didn't stop. He rushed up to the bartender. "Has there been a crazy Indian in here?" he asked, not too loudly. "In a screwball getup?"

The bartender admitted that such a one had been gone only ten minutes. Bagdad cursed and started out. Maxie Metaxa intercepted him. "Hello, Bagdad," he said genially. "How're tricks?"

Bagdad stopped. "Lousy, Max," he said. "I'm ten minutes late for a fortune."

Maxie Metaxa kept his face blank. "How come?" he asked.

Bagdad looked around him. "That Indian," he said, "is the same tribe that has got an old has-been named Al Gator. This Al is supposed to be a fighter. He goes tonight at the Uptown A.C. against Bennie Smoot and that Indian is willin' to bet that he beats Bennie."

"Oh," Maxie said. "Where . . . . ?" But Bagdad was gone.

"I gotta find him," Bagdad yelled from the door. "I have gotta find him."

**THE** Uptown A.C. was packed. It hadn't been

packed since Ruby Goldstein fought there, on his way up, but tonight it was packed. Word of mouth had done it. It was known that Maxie Metaxa had, in plain sight of many people bet sixty thousand dollars against Chief Willie Shoshone's forty thousand dollars that Bennie Smoot would go the distance. And that was what packed the Uptown A.C. Willie Shoshone was at the ringside, and Bagdad was at the ringside. Maxie Metaxa was complacent. Willie Shoshone was drunk. His work done, he was relaxing. Willie was very drunk. The semi-windup was over and the announcer was in the center of the ring. "There has," he said into the amplifier, "been a slight rearrangement of tonight's card. I know it will meet with your approval. In place of Bennie Smoot, popular young middleweight, who was injured only this afternoon in an automobile accident, we are substituting Joe Hassard, leading contender for the middleweight crown." And there went up a tremendous roar. It isn't often you see Joe Hassard for a dollar sixty-five tops and these people knew it.

Maxie Metaxa leaned forward before Bagdad had a chance to get around the ring and he asked Willie Shoshone in tones both loud and clear: "Is the bet still on?"

And Willie Shoshone, drunk now, carried away with his role of wealthy plunger leaned back in his seat and said so everybody heard him, "Never heard of 'nyone name Hashard." Then in tones even more clarion he bellowed, "Let 'er ride. Let the bet ride."

Benjamin Bagadaccio stopped halfway around the ring where he was running and his face went perfectly white. Then slowly he started down the aisle, toward Al Gator's dressing room. Maxie Metaxa leaned back. "That cost me two grand," he said to his companion, "but I figured if Rain-in-the-Puss was crazy he was clean crazy and now I don't take no chance at all."

It smelled like liniment and stale cigars and dried sweat in Al Gator's dressing room and after Bagdad had told his story, Jack Fitzgerald waited for almost a full minute before he spoke. Then when he spoke, he spoke to the brown figure lying on the rubbing table.

"George," he said slowly, "you're fightin' tonight against a guy that you would have trouble with the best day you ever saw. And George," he added, "if you don't stop him, we're all broke."

K.O. Jones rolled over. His shaved head made him look ludicrous. "I thought I was fightin' a young boy," he said, "that was a sucker for a right cross."

"There has," Jack Fitzgerald said slowly, "been a change. You're fightin' Joe Hassard, and you're fightin' him for the biggest purse you ever fought for. A cool hundred grand. And you got to stop him."

K.O. Jones puckered his forehead. "I'll try," he said.

**K.O. JONES**, alias Al Gator, came back to his corner at the end of the fourth round and he was breathing hard. "He's shifty," he said, "and he can hit, and I can't stop him when he boxes me and stays on that bicycle." K.O. Jones looked down at his brown legs. "I can't catch him on these here legs like I once of could."

"George," Jack Fitzgerald said tensely for the hundredth time, "you've got to make him come to you."

"He's a Fancy Dan," K.O. Jones said. "He won't come in." The bell rang and K.O. Jones went out.

Joe Hassard danced in, stabbed two long lefts at K.O.'s shaven head and danced away. K.O. Jones followed him doggedly, slowly. Joe Hassard stabbed him with a long left and retreated half across the ring. K.O. shrugged his shoulders to the crowd and followed him. When K.O. came back to his corner Jack Fitzgerald leaned over and said something to him. It was quite a long speech for Jack Fitzgerald and he could see that K.O. didn't quite understand. Desperately he said: "He's right down at the ringside. It's the sweet-talkin' man from Chattanooga. He's gonna break me and Mr. Bagdad, too."

K.O. Jones thought this over for a long moment, but the bell took him out before he could reply.

The sixth round was even duller. It was a fast, shifty boxer conservatively out-pointing a tired old man. Al Gator was definitely slowing up and there was a frown creasing his forehead and he seemed preoccupied. When he went back to his corner he said: "Tell me that again, Mistuh Jack."

"It's an old trick," Jack Fitzgerald said, "but it may work. If it don't we'll all be broke. The sweet-talkin' man from Chattanooga will have all my money and all your money and all Mr. Bagdad's money."

Jack Fitzgerald added, trying to keep his voice calm: "You can do it, George. Crowd him to a corner and swing careful, but make it pop."

"He'll come to me then, won't he, Mistuh Jack?" K.O. Jones said trustingly.

And Jack Fitzgerald answered him: "Yes, George, he'll come to you, then."

K.O. Jones came out of his corner for the seventh round fast, and swinging. Joe Hassard danced away, behind a long left hand but all at once Joe Hassard found himself in a corner and he could see a looping right, swung from the hips coming, and he ducked.

K.O. Jones' right hand swung around Joe Hassard's neck and you could hear it pop against the ring post in the forty cent seats. K.O. Jones backed away and his face was drawn and dirty looking. His right hand was pulled against his chest and his face was vaguely contorted with poorly concealed pain. He stalled through the seventh round but he never moved his right. And Joe Hassard came to him in the last moments of the seventh round and Joe Hassard was grinning as twice he left openings and the right cross didn't come.

Jack Fitzgerald kept his instructions low and calm as he talked between the rounds but the pride was in his voice: "Perfect," he said. "Perfect. He thinks your hand is broke. I never saw a better job of actin'. He'll come to you now and try to knock you out, and he ain't afraid of the right any more. But stall another round and then when he gives you that openin', let him have the Sunday punch."

K.O. Jones didn't answer his manager. He just sat there in his corner and his right hand wasn't back on the ropes but clutched to his side.

Twice in the eighth round K.O. started a right and both times he stopped the punch halfway to its target and it was evident to everyone that the right hand of Al Gator was useless.

Joe Hassard saw it, too. And Joe Hassard knew a knockout would look better on his record than a decision and so Joe Hassard, young and contemptuous, came in swinging.

Bagdad saw what happened. Bagdad saw it all. Jack Fitzgerald couldn't see it because K.O. Jones was boxing straight away from him and all he could see were the big muscles bunching under K.O. Jones' right shoulder blade as Joe Hassard came in to add another knockout to his record.

K.O. Jones swung his right.

Joe Hassard was coming in, fast, disregarding the right hand that K.O. Jones had broken on the ring post. Joe Hassard was finally setting this old man up to knock him out. This old man who had a funny lot of savvy in close but who had been clumsy enough to break his hand against a ring post.

And Joe Hassard caught that right right on the whiskers.

K.O. Jones walked over to the ropes and stood there, big tears he couldn't stop hurting his eyes, as he listened to the count. "Seven, eight, nine, aaannnddd *out!*"

"Mistuh Jack!" he said.

**JACK FITZGERALD** had him, then, around the shoulders and down at the ringside the stakeholder was paying off and a cop was in the ring and Maxie Metaxa was screaming something. But Bagdad was taking big rolls of bills from the man who had been game enough to hold the stakes and Bagdad had one hand under the front of his beautiful jacket as if he were reaching for something deep in his lower left vest pocket and Willie Shoshone was giving what he later said was his tribal battle cry. K.O. Jones was talking half to himself, half to Jack Fitzgerald. "I done all right," he said. "I done all right."

Jack Fitzgerald took out his knife then, knowing, and cut the glove from K.O. Jones' right hand.

K.O. Jones' right hand was blue under its black hide and there was a little blood oozing from a crease that ran from wrist to the joint of the thumb down to the *v* that thumb and fingers made. "I ain't much of an actor," K.O. Jones said. "I really broke it on the post."

And Jack Fitzgerald, looking at the hand, said calmly: "The cartilage is gone and it will never heal. And you'll never play the banjo with that hand." And then his voice got a little low but K.O. Jones could hear it. Above the tumult in the ring and the tumult of all the voices. "But give me a break," Jack Fitzgerald said, "and let me shake it."

You want a good stooge, champ? Take a half-blind, slap-happy pug and kick him around all you want, but when you ask him about the jangling noises in his head— don't smile!

# RESERVATION ON QUEER STREET

**MIKE SUTTON** was half blind, but that really made it better because there are jokes that can be played on a person who can't see very well that won't go with a man who can. They could wire a chair and he wouldn't be able to see the wire that ran to it and he would jump in a very satisfactory manner when the current struck him. There were lots of gags like that. They all worked fine. The Champion, Louis Arnovich, was the one that played most of the jokes and the cruelest, which, I suppose, is natural because when a man is rounding into shape and gets drawn pretty fine he gets very irritable. The heavy quiet of the upstate training camp got on his nerves and practical jokes were an outlet for him and of course Mike was the natural butt of the jokes. Mike was about forty-five and he hadn't been really a top-notch fighter. He'd taken so much punishment around the head that his ears rang dully most all the time and sometimes he thought he heard things jangling in his head. But it didn't disturb him much because this had gone on for a long time. Louis Arnovich was a lightweight and champion of all the world in that division. His manager, a tight-lipped little man called Foxy McGinnis, had him upstate now training for his outdoor bout with Baby Face Gannon in the Stadium. It was very beautiful at the training camp, a little cluster of cottages and a training ring and a barn where the punching bags and other equipment were kept. Down in the thick green valley there was a sliver of water that was a lake.

But Arnovich, the champion, wasn't really much interested in that.

There were four sparring partners at the camp. Two undistinguished light-weights named Smith and Coon; Slip O'Dowd, a pretty fair ham-and-egger who could simulate Gannon's style; and a very fast colored featherweight named Billy Harvey. Harvey and O'Dowd were fighting preliminaries on the same card with Arnovich and Gannon. The sparring partners got fifteen dollars a day on the days the Champion boxed, but Mike Sutton wasn't paid anything at all. He got his meals and a place to sleep and Foxy McGinnis would sometimes give him old clothes. Foxy was about the same size as Mike.

Mike rubbed down the Champion after his workouts and ran errands, but mostly he was valuable as a stooge. As a butt for the jokes that the Champion and Foxy would figure out.

And in a way, he had a real value to the Champion.

Louis Arnovich didn't read and he didn't listen to the radio. After he had done his road work in the morning and worked with the bags and skipped rope and boxed a round or two with each of his sparring partners in the afternoon, he had nothing to do. While he would play a little pinochle or maybe listen to one program on the radio, it bored him and he would be like some caged animal pacing around his cottage, all his splendid vitality boiling up in him. Too, Louis Arnovich was no longer exactly a natural lightweight and it was more trouble as time went by for him to make the weight. It increased his irritability to be always hungry and for his mouth to be always dry; when you are trying to take off the weight, you must go easy on liquids.

So each time Louis Arnovich trained for a fight Foxy McGinnis would have Mike Sutton around for Arnovich to play cruel and elaborate jokes on. This would take up some of the Champion's idle time and ease his tension and provide a few laughs for everyone.

Mike didn't mind so much. He didn't hate the Champion for being cruel to him because he couldn't remember things long enough anymore to keep on hating someone. Besides, it was worth almost anything to sit in the evening and look down the long green valley and hear the little things in the woods making chirping noises that drowned out the buzzing in his head and made him feel at peace. If Louis Arnovich gave Mike the hotfoot or sent him walking clear to the village for a left handed monkey wrench or a pipe stretcher and Mike discovered it was a joke, he would think it rather natural, remembering dimly that fighters were mean when they were getting fine. He would take it as a good sign of Arnovich's condition and then forget it.

**ONE** thing scared him though; it made the things jangle loudly in his head and the sweat pop out his brow. It was something that Arnovich would do if he was feeling mean. He had done it many times. And it was perfectly simple. "Mike," he would say, "some day they're gonna get you. They come for you in uniforms, not like coppers, but gray uniforms and they take you away to the booby hatch."

Then Arnovich would tip off Foxy or maybe it would be the other way around; maybe Foxy would say it first about the men in uniforms. That evening they would sit on the porch and one of them would remark casually: "I saw a couple of guys in gray uniforms down at the village, they were headin' up this way."

Mike wouldn't be able to hear the things chirping in the green woods, he wouldn't be able to think of anything for a moment, and then he would slip away. Sometimes he would hide until midnight, and all that time he would be crouched out in the woods or under the ring, and the effort of thinking, of watching for the men in gray uniforms, would drive the buzzing in his head to unbearable crescendos. Finally he would come back and the next morning it would be only a vague fear far back in his jumbled mind.

But it was there.

As the day of the Gannon fight came nearer, Louis Arnovich became more worried. Gannon was young and very good. Louis Arnovich realized this and he was worried because he hadn't saved his money and he was getting older all the time. He had sometimes thought of retiring undefeated, but he always seemed to be short, to be needing most of his share of the next purse just to get things straightened out. The Gannon fight was only eight days away now and Arnovich weighed one thirty-nine, which was four pounds more than he must weigh the day of the fight. He knew he would have to dry out to make the limit and that is a disagreeable process.

The jokes he played on Mike became more

frequent, more pointless, more cruel, and the sparring partners suffered, too. He was fine now and his punching was very sharp. The day the two important reporters came up he dropped Slip O'Dowd twice in one round and cut Billy Harvey's eyebrow in spite of the heavy helmet the colored boy wore.

Louis Arnovich came out on the porch after his shower, where Foxy was fixing a drink for the newspapermen. Mike was sitting on the steps, looking down the long valley at the little bit of lake, noticing how the setting sun on the water made it shine. His face under its tissue of scars was serene.

Louis sat down by the wall. "Foxy," he said, "did you see them guys in them gray uniforms down by the lake today?"

"Yeah," Foxy McGinnis said. "I saw 'em. The ones with the ropes."

"I guess they'll be getting up here in a few minutes now," Louis Arnovich said and he yawned.

Mike Sutton looked around. His face was pale and working.

"How are the bells, Mike?" Foxy McGinnis asked. He turned to the newspapermen. "Mike's got bells in his head. He's punchy."

"If something scares him," Louis Arnovich said, "it makes the bells ring louder."

Mike Sutton stood, looking fearfully around him. Then he wheeled and ran stumbling around the cottage.

Foxy McGinnis turned to the newspapermen and over Louis Arnovich's laughter he asked: "How's the kid look?"

"All right," one of them said. "He is a very strong kid. What made Handsome run away?"

"The Champ will cut him to pieces," Foxy McGinnis said.

"The Champ was great today," Slip O'Dowd said and he looked at the colored featherweight sitting over by himself on the banister with the strip of tape very white over his eye. "He was great today, wasn't he?" O'Dowd said again, looking directly at the colored boy.

"Yes," the colored boy said. He got up off the banister and walked around the house.

"What made the old guy run away?" the newspaperman said again.

"We tell him there's a couple guys in gray coats lookin' for him to take him to the nut house," Louis Arnovich explained. "It scares the hell out of him. He'll hide somewhere." And he laughed again, more softly.

"The Champ's heart was eighty-one after the last round," Foxy McGinnis said, "and it went down to fifty in three minutes. I guess that shows the kind of shape he's in."

One of the reporters stood up. "Let's go down to the village and get some beer," he said flatly.

"This Baby Face," the other said, "they say he beats his grandma, but I guess he's a pretty nice boy. I only hope he's as strong and tough as he looks, that's all I hope." And as they walked away down the path to get into their car they heard the colored boy's soft voice out in the woods.

"It's all right, Mike," the colored boy was calling. "It's all right, Mike. They ain't any men, they was lying to you. It's all right, Mike, they was lying."

**SLIP O'DOWD** was fighting the semi-windup and Billy Harvey, the colored boy, was fighting a preliminary. Billy Harvey was out there now. The sound of the crowd was like a great mosquito down in the Champion's dressing room under the stands; a great mosquito that flew close and then drifted away, but never quite out of earshot.

Louis Arnovich was lying on a table with a heavy towel bathrobe wrapped around him. The bones in his cheeks looked very sharp. He had made a hundred and thirty-five with great effort, but the two-pound steak he'd eaten after weighing in that afternoon had helped his disposition. He was lying quietly, sucking a half lemon, waiting calmly until it was time for him to go up.

Mike Sutton sat on a folding chair over in a corner. His good eye gleamed and he was making little noises in his throat because the smell of the dressing room and the distant roar of the crowd pleased and excited him. He knew they wouldn't let him go up to the ring and watch, but he didn't mind that. Sitting down here with the familiar smells in his nose and the familiar sounds in his ears was enough. He just waited and took it all in, and thought it was like the old days. And it was. Foxy McGinnis was pacing aimlessly around the room chewing an unlit cigar and one of the newspapermen who had been up at the camp was standing looking down at Arnovich. "Did it weaken him to make the weight?" the reporter asked Foxy McGinnis.

"He was awful mean in camp the last week," Mike said, suddenly intelligible.

Nobody paid any attention. "He is strong as a bull," Foxy McGinnis said. "Best shape of his career."

"The meaner a guy is . . ." Mike's voice trailed off as he forgot what he was going to say. The sound upstairs was suddenly greater and presently Billy Harvey came through the room, going back to the showers. He stopped and patted Mike on the shoulder. "I give him a lacing," he said. He went on then, not speaking to anyone else. Somebody called at the door and Slip O'Dowd went out the door, skipping a little and lifting his arms as if the muscles in his shoulder were stiff.

Foxy McGinnis walked over and looked at Louis Arnovich. "You've seen all his pictures," he said. "Just keep your left hand in his face and box him. Circle him to the right and keep your left hand in his face."

"He's a hitter," the reporter said, "and he's a kid that just keeps on coming. It ought to be a good fight." He walked to the door then, without saying anything more, and went on out into the stadium. There was a long silence. "He didn't wish me luck," Louis Arnovich said finally.

"He musta forgot," Foxy said. "But you don't need luck. Just think, box him, watch his right. Box him and circle to his right. Keep your left hand in his face."

Then all at once a man who would work in Gannon's corner was in the room and he was watching Foxy bandage the Champion's hands. Then there were some more people in the room and somebody was laughing and a voice said: "Slip got stopped in the first."

A minute or two later, just as suddenly, the room was emptying. Mike came over and grabbed Arnovich's taped right hand. "Good luck, Champ," he said and his voice was thick with sincerity.

"Thanks, pal," Arnovich said and a little sardonic grin played across his face. "Don't let nobody get you while I'm gone." And they were gone.

**MIKE** heard the sound roll down the aisle with the Champion as he made his way toward the ring. When the sound told Mike that the Champion was in the ring, he walked over and closed the door. He looked carefully all around the room, half fearfully, then smiled a little and sat down. He turned his mind to envisioning the scene in the ring.

He could see it all quite clearly. Now they would be introducing the old champions and the challengers, and now they would be clearing the ring and the referee would be giving them their instructions.

Mike got up and shadow boxed slowly for awhile. Then he went back and sat down on his chair. Round one would be over now. The Champ had probably felt him out that round. He'd probably walked around him like a cooper 'round a barrel stabbing him with his left hand, finishing the round in his own corner, his sharp dark face expressionless.

Mike stood up and stretched. Then he heard the voice. It was at the door.

"Let's try it, it oughtn't to be locked. Let's pick up a slug in here."

The other voice answered. "Okay," it said. There was the noise of the door opening and the two ushers came into the room furtively. One was reaching for the bottle in the hip pocket of his gray uniform. Mike Sutton stood up and looked wildly around. Then, summoning all his courage, he dived past the two men and through the door and was running down the interminable distance to the ring. Twice he fell and twice he felt hands that tried to catch him, but each time he tore free. Finally he was there, his face white at the apron of the ring and his voice shrill. "Champ!" he screamed. "Oh, God, Champ, don't let 'em take me!"

Louis Arnovich boxing cautiously at long range against the stocky blond youngster who was boring and turned his head, recognizing the voice subconsciously.

And in that split instant, Baby Face Gannon came up with his right.

The roar of the crowd drowned out even Mike's shrill screaming. Louis Arnovich came up at *nine* and Gannon dropped him again with a left hook a shade too high, that broke Arnovich's nose and splattered blood across the clean canvas. Arnovich, his arms hanging at his sides, climbed to his feet without a count and stood there swaying, glassy eyed. Then the bell rang.

Mike Sutton felt himself seized; he saw with a sob of relief that these arms were clothed in the dark blue of the cops. They were dragging him, all three of them backing up the aisle. The cops wanted to watch the fight. They were stalling, wanting to see how Louis Arnovich came out for the next round after that pasting he'd taken.

Mike saw Foxy working feverishly with ice and brandy and ammonia. Louis Arnovich was coming around. His body was responding, but his eyes were still blank. He came out solidly at the bell, and walked in and started slugging, fighting Gannon's fight. That was all Mike saw.

**"THEY'RE** waitin' for me in the dressin' room," Mike said, above the ringing in his ears and the noise of the crowd. "In gray uniforms just like the Champ said."

"Who?" the oldest cop asked. Mike tried desperately to get away. "There's one now," he said as an usher came down the aisle. "There's one of 'em."

"He's an usher," the cop said. "They's a gang of them guys around. Ain't any usher gonna bother you 'less you crashed in."

"I'm with the Champ," Mike said. "I was waitin' in the dressin' room when they come for me."

The oldest cop let go his arm. "You go back to the dressin' room," he said, "and don't run down yellin' no more. We want to get back and see the fight. Them guys is ushers, they won't hurt you."

"All right," Mike said. He walked back up the aisle, found his way to the dressing room and sat down on his chair by the wall. The place was empty and he sat there alone for a long time. There was no room in his head for anything but dull pain and sound gradually easing. He didn't know how long he waited, but suddenly the room was swarming with people. The Champion came in, walking by himself very straight, and lay down on his table. He was badly marked.

The Champion lay there and Foxy worked on his cuts and his chief second gave him a drink of brandy. Then they cleared the room. Foxy McGinnis looked around and abruptly he walked over and hit Mike in the face with his soft fist. It didn't hurt.

Mike got up and got his bottle and went over and started rubbing down the Champion's legs. The second was working on the cuts. Louis Arnovich looked up and winked at Mike. "I'll be glad when the fight's over," Louis Arnovich said. "These woods give me the willies." He closed his eyes then.

"He won in the eighth," the second said, "but he went up queer street when the guy dropped him in the second and he's still up queer street."

Louis Arnovich heard and looked up. "Eighth?"

The second looked down at him. "Yeah," he said. "It's over; you stopped him in the eighth."

Louis Arnovich creased his brows and made the blood start flowing from one of them. "Not Gannon?" he said. "Yeah." The second grinned. "He don't look like no Baby Face now."

"No?"

Louis Arnovich lay back and closed his eyes again. Suddenly he sat up and his eyes were wild and pleading. "Mike," he said, "what's it like?" And he shook his head back and forth quite hard.

Mike went on rubbing him, looking at his face. "It's kind of like a buzzing and that goes away and then its kind of like a jangling sometimes later on. I never noticed it until one night in the old Garden I was lyin' just like you and I'd . . . I'd. . ." Mike stopped, trying to remember. Foxy McGinnis came over and looked down at the Champion. "It was. . ." Mike began again.

Foxy cut him off. "Boy," he said, "did they love it when you walked in there and slugged it out with him? We'll let 'em angle us into another fight with that boy and we'll draw a half a million."

"It was like a buzzing," Mike said again, "at first. . ." He looked down at Louis Arnovich's face and though he had remembered what he was going to say this time, he didn't say it. Vaguely he wondered why.

---

"Would you," Cyril yells, "rather I knocked him out or boxed his ears off?"

# A FIGHTER HAS TO FIGURE

**Saga of a very scientific pugilist who could analyze every angle of his profession—except a cheering house.**

**I'M AN** old guy, see? I been around a long time. A long, long time. It said in the papers I was his manager, but I wasn't. He paid me a salary. So much a week, rain or shine; fight or not. He did all the managing that was done. He made his own fights, picked his own spots.

I was his second. He hired me because I am one of the best seconds in the world. I can do a lot for a guy in that time you get to work between rounds. That's why he hired me. He always hired the best he could. Why, two or three times he had sparrin' partners could beat the guy he was training for.

He hired me because I was one of the best seconds in the country, but that didn't matter. I never told him anything between rounds and he never come back to his corner in trouble, but once. He reminded me of some of them in the old days. Because he was no stumblebum. You say they all got to get hit a lot and hurt a lot? Not all of them. Did you ever hear of Young Griffo? He couldn't punch his way out of a paper sack with his hands on fire, but they never hit him solid when he was right. Packy McFarland fought ten, eleven times once in a month and was sore because he wound up with a black eye. And if Jim Corbett had a mark on him from fighting, I never saw it.

His name was Cyril Brady. He was a natural middleweight. Weighed a hundred fifty-eight and never varied more than a pound or two in or out of training. He won thirty-two straight in the amateurs out on the Coast and there was a lot of guys trying to sign him up but he never listened to them. First time I ever talked to him was one morning the phone woke me up at my hotel and he asks if he can come up and see me. He told me who he was but it didn't mean anything. I told him to come on up.

He came in the room; I was still in bed. He walked over and sat down in the chair and I tried to place him. He was a sallow-faced fellow and he looked like any clerk though he was kind of tall.

"You're Mr. Danny Fayden, aren't you?" he asked, and he didn't sound any more like a fighter than he looked. I admitted I was.

"Well," he said, "from what I am able to read and observe you are probably the best man in the world for a boxer to have in his corner during a contest."

"Maybe I am," I said, grinning.

"I am anxious to make some arrangement with you," he said. "Theoretically," he went on, "a situation could arise where the competence of your second could be the deciding factor in a fight."

"Leaving the theory aside," I told him, "there are Joes will tell you that me and Whitey Bimstein and Ray Arcel have won more fights than any three guys in the world."

"I came to you because you are older than those you mention —"

"Came to me for what?" I interrupted.

"To be my second," Cyril said. "I can beat any man in the world under a hundred and sixty pounds."

"Oh," I said. "Who have you beat so far?"

"Nobody but a few amateurs," he said. "I came here to New York to get some professional fights. I think I can get along here faster. There is more money and more talent."

**HOW** could you take a guy like that serious? I grinned a little wider. "How many rounds for instance," I asked, "would it take you to stow away Mr. Eddie Kincaid?" Mr. Eddie Kincaid being the champion.

"I could beat him in fifteen rounds," Cyril said, "but I'm not ready for him." He paused. "But that hasn't anything to do with it. How much would you take to be my nominal manager for the next five years and always be in my corner when I fight and work with me in training and so forth?"

Now things have not been so good. I am not a manager and I am an old duck and have been around a long time. There are Joes will tell you that I am not as fast as I used to be and that I am strictly a windbag that talks about the old days.

"Oh," I said aloud, "a hunnert and expenses — that's a week — and I guess we could deal." This I say very offhand and sarcastic, see?

This Cyril takes out a sheaf of paper from his pocket. They are typewritten papers and he takes a pen off the desk and makes a few fill-ins. "I am taking Law," he says, "by correspondence, and I have drawn up this contract myself, leaving the spaces blank for salary and so forth. I have filled in one hundred and expenses. Will you sign here?" He points to the line.

Now I take a little pause, as they say. I look over the papers. They read all right to me and I am not so sleepy. "This is all right," I tells him, "but what about binding the bargain?" And I am not grinning so wide.

He fumbles around in his pocket for a few seconds and brings out a billfold. He peels off ten twenties and hands them to me. "Here are two in advance," he says. "Will you sign?"

Good money, see? Strictly Uncle Sam's finest. I sign. Maybe I ain't woke up. "I will take the contract with me," he says, tucking the papers back in his pocket. "I will be fighting a six-round semi-windup at Eagan's Upstairs Fight Palace in Queens next Tuesday night. I will expect you to be there." He starts to go, then stops at the door. "Here is your expenses," he says, "get off at Hunters Point." He hands me a nickel for the subway.

I am out there all right. I am out there with my kit and a new sponge and my lucky bucket. I am there right on the dot. Cyril is sitting down in the booth they call a dressing room with two, three other bums. They give me plenty looks — I am famous, see, and I don't work nothing but the Garden and such spots as a rule. Marcus Books is there. I figure he owns most all the fighters on the card. "Hello, Danny," he says, "I see you got the reincorporation of Stanley Ketchel settin' over there. How does it feel to be back in a champion's corner?"

I got to dummy up, see? I don't know nothing about my boy. The two C's got me out here. I look around.

Cyril is sitting in a corner reading a thick book. He has a new towel robe around him and he is sitting on a little stool. I ease over. "Who're we fightin'?" I ask. He looks up from the book. "Hello," he says.

"Who we fightin'?" I ask again, feeling silly.

"Oh," he says. "A fellow named Blunder Roos. It doesn't matter."

"No?" Now this Blunder is a very good trial horse a couple years ago and while he has gone way back to be over here, I remember him as a monkey with plenty of moxie and strong in close.

"No," he says. And then we get our call and I go on out behind him.

We get up in the ring and the referee looks a little bugeyed when he sees me in Cyril's corner, but he don't do more than grin.

"Blunder Roos," he says pointing like Joe Humphreys used to, but still not no more like Joe than nothing. "Hunnert fifty-nine and tree quarters."

Which is a damn lie. Blunder has got a life-saver around his belly and he had trouble making sixty two years ago. "An, Cyril Brady, one fifty seven and tree quarters." And he cuts his hand like Joe used to do, pointing and marking the weight, though the worst seats in the house was closer than you could get in the Stadium for eleven-fifty and they could have heard him if he was talking natural.

**CYRIL** goes out and I go with him. Billy Moore is third in the ring and he tells the boys the same thing he has told the boys always: "Break clean and come out fightin'," Billy finishes. We go back to the corner. "This Blunder is a hooker," I says from habit, trying to tell my guy right. "Give him a long left hand and wait a round or two."

Cyril don't even look like he heard me. He stands up and looks out at the crowd from his corner. "Would you," he yells, "rather I knocked him out or boxed his ears off?"

It was wonderful. Really wonderful. They hate over in Queens like they hate the Giants in Brooklyn. Boy, they started hating that Cyril right then. This Brady, he is a long drink of water without no muscle showing on him and he is sallow as a cheap candle. When he hollers that, they really start hating him. "Kill 'em, Blunder!"

"Gut him!"

"Murder him!"

It never got to Blunder. They ain't anything got to Blunder for a long time. But he grinned when they yelled at him and came out bounding. I was out of the ring like twenty years ago, fast.

Cyril comes out and he is all oil, he's got a left hand that is long as a clothes line and thin so you can't hardly see it. He stabbed this Blunder forty-two times more or less right on the nose and he never got cooled off from Blunder fannin' him. He went away like Tooney in the seventh at Chi that time, but prettier, and you couldn't have bought a tomato for a quarter at Washington Market as big and red as Blunder's nose, come the bell. Cyril sits down in the corner and I give him a little conversation and a little ice on the back of his neck. He shoves me away. "I'll tell you what I want you to do," he says. "Just leave me alone until I need you and when I need you I'll tell you."

I'd like to tell him, the stupid, that when he wants me and needs me he won't be able to tell me. But not tonight. I get down slow, halfway out of the ring with the ten-second buzzer and there is C. Brady standing up talking to the crowd. "I don't want to hurt him," he yells, "so I'll knock him out this round."

And he did. He stiffened Blunder with a right cross about halfway through the round and poor old Blunder was groping for the rope trying to pull himself up at *ten*. They tried to spit on Cyril going down the aisle to the dressing room. "What," I asks him as he is putting on his clothes, "was the idea of the speeches?"

He looked at me. "People will come to see you hoping you'll win or hoping you'll lose. I want to get everybody hating me so they'll come to see me lose, then when I win they'll hate me worse and come again when I fight."

"You don't expect ever to lose, I suppose?" I says.

"Oh, no," he says.

The promoter bustles in the door then. He pays

Cyril off. It is thirty-five bucks. "I'll see you next Tuesday," the promoter says. "Yes," Cyril says. "How long would you like the fight to last?"

Jimmy Eagan is the promoter and he looks at Cyril. "You're fightin' Billy Haynes," he says, "and I hope Billy kills you."

"You're paying me seventy-five dollars," Cyril says, "according to our agreement, as if I beat Blunder. Well, Mr. Eagan, you hope Billy Haynes beats me so bad, how about paying me a hundred and fifty if I win and nothing if I lose?"

"You damned well right," Jimmy says.

**EAGAN** scaled his prices up forty percent and the joint was packed. They started booing Cyril when we started down the aisle. But he didn't pay any more attention to them going up the aisle this time than if the place was empty. Tonight he is playing cold silent contempt.

Now Billy Haynes is a pretty good fighter and was on his way up. He is young and tough and very enthusiastic. That is, he is very enthusiastic for two rounds. By that time he is cut up so bad that the referee stops it.

Cyril looks out at the crowd and shrugs his shoulders like, "Well, it's not my fault he was so over-matched." The next day there is a little in some of the papers about the fight and one writer comments on Brady's lack of sportsmanship.

Brady is up in my room talking to me when I show him this. He looks at it and smiles. "I wonder why they think it is a sport," he says.

"There are some guys," I say, "that treat it like a sport. That —"

"Yes," he says, "the Blunder Roo's." He goes on then. "I have a chance to fight a windup in Jersey for two fifty. It is a week from Friday. I don't believe I'll take it."

"No?" I says.

"No," he says, "I made some mistakes against Haynes. I don't think I want another fight for a month."

"Some mistakes? I didn't see any mistakes. It looked to me like you done about perfect."

"No," he says. "He hit me twice in the first round."

"Oh," I said. "You think this is a mistake?"

"Yes," he said. "While it didn't hurt me, if Eddie Kincaid had had those shots it might have been serious."

I just grunt.

"I am in this business to make money," he says, "not to get hit."

"That is an angle," I say.

"Listen," he said, "I work two years, three hours a day hitting a bag on a long rope with my left. I didn't just happen to be able to stab a guy when I wanted to. I worked with the best boys that were in the gym and would work with me for two years.

"I saw every picture that Eddie Kincaid and all the other topnotchers ever had taken of their fights twenty, thirty times. I know every move they make by heart. I carried paper wads in my hands squeezing them all the time for months to strengthen my hands.

"I worked with the heavy bag four rounds a day. I sleep every night, I eat very carefully. I'm not a natural. I prepare for a fight the way a good lawyer prepares for a case. This stuff of acting mean, that's just to make people hate me so I'll be worth more at the gate."

Now this is something; a little all right. A guy that wants to be a fighter and learns to fight. That is certainly a little different.

**AND** like he says he gets into the money. In the ring he taunts his opponents and out of the ring he taunts his opponents. He offers to fight them winner-take-all. He treats the crowds like morons to come to a fight so uneven as him fighting somebody.

And the time comes, finally, when he gets Kincaid.

It is like this. He makes a match for himself with One-round Finnegan, who is supposed to be the contender and he agrees to fight Finnegan for nothing if he gets Kincaid as and if he beats Finnegan.

This gets into the papers and it packs the joint. They really hate this Cyril by now. He murders Finnegan and they have to stop it in the seventh.

And so he gets Kincaid. He gets Kincaid in an outdoor shot for June. You think he don't know what he's doing? Let me tell you how he trains for this one. In the first place he does all his boxing at night under the lights. "I fight under the lights," he says, "why not train under them? Your body is a thing of habit. If you get used to working your best at two o'clock in the afternoon that's when you are going to feel the best. These guys that train, going to bed at nine for a fight that's gonna be held at ten at night, they get into the ring half sleepy."

So he gets up at noon, does his road work, eats breakfast at two-thirty, lunch at six-thirty, does his boxing at night and eats dinner at eleven, goes to bed at one-thirty. Everybody thinks he's crazy, but he's not crazy. If you think about it a little you'll see he is right.

Anyway, he gets Kincaid. And he comes up for Kincaid very sharp. But he does not seem to be thinking about the fight and this worries me. Kincaid is a fighter. He is a real, sure-enough champion. He is a short, wide guy very tough, a hitter.

The fight draws very well and the boos we get coming up the aisle make Cyril smile. But still it is a funny smile like he only hears them with one ear and he is thinking about something else. He goes out with the bell and starts stabbing Kincaid, softening him up, working on his eyes. Eddie Kincaid has a lot of scar tissue on his face and he cuts easy. Cyril knows this very well. Eddie Kincaid just grins and bulls in. He likes to get his shoulder under a guy's chin and fire at his belly with both hands. But he has never dealt with a man that can go away like Cyril and still punish you going away. The first round is Cyril's by a mile. But I am uneasy. Brady acts like he is worrying about something. Like he is not thinking about the fight. He proves it in the second round.

Eddie rushes him into a corner and Brady ducks, sits down on the second rope and instinctively throws his hands out. Before he knows what is going on Kincaid has smashed his nose over to one side of his face, and dropped him with a left hook to the chin and Cyril is getting up, not taking a count, and Kincaid is rushing in, slugging his best and scoring plenty.

Brady goes down again. This time he doesn't get up right away because he can't. He's got a mouse over one eye as big as a egg it looks like. He makes it up at *five* and gets into a clinch some way and weathers out the round. I go to work. He has to be led to his corner, and it takes me a second or two to get him there. I cut the mouse with a razor blade, suck out the blood, get some collodion over it, get his mouth piece out and rinsed, throw an ounce of brandy down him, clean up his nose and in the five seconds before the buzzer pour some ice water down his spine. He sits there all the time like he is still out. Then he gets up off his stool with the bell and with a mean look on his face and both hands down, cocked, he marches out.

**BOY**, what a brawl. He gets slugged a couple of times, but he has got Eddie backing up, bleeding and half-way through the round he drops Eddie, but he forgets to go to a neutral corner right away and Eddie gets about fifteen seconds rest.

He comes back with the bell and sits down. "That guy hurt me," he said, kind of resentful, "while I was thinking about my bar examination."

"Bar examination," I holler. "My God!"

"It's tomorrow," he says. "And I am not quite sound on torts."

"Box this guy —" I begin.

The buzzer sounds. "Box him," he says. "I am going to knock him kicking so I can get some more studying in tonight."

He goes out. He is a pretty sorry-looking sight in spite of the work I have done on him and he gets sorrier by the minute. But he is giving as good as he gets and the crowd is standing up and Eddie Kincaid is backing up. Cyril catches him with a right cross and drops him. But Eddie, he scrambles right up and comes bulling in. He gets his shoulder under Cyril's chin and belts him twice in the belly and Cyril goes pale and grunts. The bell rings. Cyril comes back very shaky. "That man," he says, "he can be sued for defamation of character for what he called me in a clinch. I never hit a man like that and had him get right up," he added.

He is a very tough tomato," I tell him, working like crazy. "Box him —" The buzzer sounds and I climb down.

"I'm about halfway mad at that fellow," Cyril says and he marches out.

He acts like it. He starts boxing, and when he's boxing he's pretty. But he steps into one and it drops him again.

"Take nine!" I scream.

He looks over at me, climbing up on one knee and nods. But when he gets up he walks in and starts slugging. They stand out there and slug and the crowd is crazy. They both got blood all over them by now, but they ain't backing up. Finally Eddie is the one to give ground and Cyril is after him, hooking for his head, getting his measured. Finally he cuts loose with a right and Eddie goes down. The bell rings. "You got all night," I say. "Take your time and keep away from him."

"I am going to beat his head off," Cyril says a little thickly.

All the preparation and all the study and all the training is what saves Cyril. He is in a little better shape than Eddie and Eddie starts slowing down and Cyril piles on a little pace and pretty soon he gets Eddie set up and he lets him have a one-two and the right drops him. The referee could have counted a hundred.

You should hear them howl. They are standing up and really yelling. The ring is full of cops and they are trying to get Cyril to say something over the radio and he is sitting there in his corner with a dumb look on his face.

"Are they cheering me?" he says finally, in a low sort of voice.

"I say they are," I said. "You are a dead game boy and they always cheer them."

He feels his face with one hand as they cut off the glove. "You fix me up, didn't you, Danny?" he said. "You saved me."

"That's what you pay me for," I said.

"I'm going to cut you thirty-three and a third out of this gate," he says, "and I am not going to take that examination tomorrow."

"Oh," I said.

"I'll take the examination sometime. Sometime when I am getting along and can't fight. But to tell you the truth, Danny, to hear 'em yell like that, that is pretty nice. "And," he goes on, "and I need a manager, I need a manager awful bad."

"I'll get you another match with Eddie," I said, grinning. "We'll cut the champion's end."

"Do that," he says, "I won't get battered up like this the next time. And —" he adds, "I'll murder the bum."

"Sure you will," I tell him, "And anyway," I add, "there's a jillion lawyers but there's only one of you. Champion of the world."

Suddenly, Joe had it ... they spoke to him and it was clear. He must do his best. The best that lay within him.

# FOURTH MAN IN THE RING

**IN** the old days he could wring something more from himself, in the clutch he could call from his entrails, from his being, some burst of energy, a spark, a quick kick-up of his amperage and that was what made him a champion.

And a champion still he was. For a little while, a few more rounds. *What round is this? The second. Eight more rounds — twenty-four minutes.* The Kid came to him behind a good left hand, stabbing him and going back away and to his left; very sharp, his left, and he moved good, economically, but fast and sure. He was a supple kid, a lithe young man, a fancy-dan, unmarked, the sweat glistening on his olive skin making him look fine. Joe Wilder followed him stolidly, with wanting interest, but the kid made a tactical error on the ropes, misjudging where they were, and Joe curved a left hook under his heart that should have slowed him down but didn't. The kid stabbed him with his left, and stung, crossed a high right and opened a little cut under Joe Wilder's eye and laughed at Joe, going around to Joe's left, back to the center of the ring.

Joe Wilder grinned back at the kid. He liked him. But it seemed funny to be fighting in silence, hearing the great roars of the crowd like the little noises you hear out in the woods at night when you think it is so still and then begin to listen. Joe Wilder — Sergeant Wilder — was very deaf; that and some stuff they had dug from his hip (but left it as good as new) had finished him in the Army — in the Army, where so rarely was a sudden burst of latent power called upon, but where it paid a guy if he could go a route.

Arnold Baronski moved to him again behind that fine left hand, and Joe saw a coming repetition of events that he was completely powerless to hamper.

But Arnold Baronski suddenly dropped his

hands and turned and started for his corner with a little triumphant skip because he knew he would be a champion soon; Joe, too, turned, realizing the bell had rung, and moved toward his own corner, looking out over the crowd blankly, and walking to his corner.

He sat down and Coco closed the little cut with neatness and great speed, and Joe leaned back and rinsed his mouth and let the breath go clear down into his guts, moving the great muscles loosely, and looked out again over the crowd. The house was full and tonight Joe Wilder would make thirty-seven and a half per cent of the gross; and he needed that. He thought of his wife listening to the fight, sitting there with her mother — her mother drinking coffee, moving around, saying little silly things . . . . Lorna lying in her bed. He saw Charley Cook's face looking up at him from the ringside, and he winked at him absently, thinking of little Lorna, his little Lorna lying in her bed, the doll beside her she had clutched while falling off to sleep.

Those things he knew were there — would be there. Those things had made a difference in larger, darker fights . . . . He watched the timekeeper now, and got up with the bell.

**BARONSKI** came to him, still careful; he would be careful. There was a red mark on his midriff from the left hook he had suckered himself into in the last round; but he was in good shape; it hadn't slowed him, just made him doubly careful, even surer.

Joe liked Baronski. Arnold was a nice kid, modest, a fine clean fighter. But there were men he *loved:* His Captain. Like Lorna, or like his wife, almost. The Captain asked you not to die for him if there was dying to be done. Joe had come down behind him from the mountains, thirty minutes after they had brought him down; and he had been lying there like a kid asleep, but asleep too deeply — with no doll to clutch upon the morn.

Joe had stopped and knelt beside him, there where he lay with the helmet they'd brought down with him, to hide what the bullet had done. And Joe had said aloud, respectfully:

"I loved you, sir." And then he had stood up and saw two other soldiers standing there, and he had flared, ready to fight — he could have called up that great spark then; but he saw that they were quiet; and one of them said: "Take it easy, Joe. We loved him too." Baronski had a left hand like a jointed snake with a hard chunk of leather for a head; it was in Joe Wilder's face and he moved in close, but Baronski tied him up, and he could see Baronski's lips moving though he heard nothing and could not read what they had said. He

Joe had stopped and knelt beside him and had said aloud, respectfully: "I loved you, sir."

clubbed Baronski in the belly, getting free because he was an older hand, and strong, and had more savvy in close, but he didn't hurt Baronski. Baronski stabbed him with the left and went to his left, circling, sure and pretty, a fancy-dan because he didn't waste his motions.

And then somebody said something in Joe Wilder's ear, in a normal tone of voice, not loud but he could hear it and he almost looked around before he realized that it was his Captain's voice and it was unintelligible, though loud and clear enough. Joe Wilder stopped, shaken, then moved on toward Baronski and he would have hit Baronski after the bell if he hadn't been looking down at the timekeeper with the corner of his eye and seen him hit the gong.

He went back to his corner. His Captain lay at Anzio, and his Lorna lay asleep, her doll beside her, and his wife sat by the radio, and listened to this fight.

Coco, a round little man but wonderful in a corner, cupped his hands around Joe's ear to shout: "Crowd him — feed him a little pace!" And it came through to Joe as a sound far away and not like the words that he'd heard from his Captain. His Captain hadn't shouted. Yes, he loved men, some men, and some were still . . . . Corporal Roscoe Hammond was a loved one. A big strawhead from Kansas, of all places, but he didn't get excited.

Roscoe was the only person Joe had ever known from Kansas though he remembered a lightweight years ago name Rocky Kansas, a champion for a while; but Rocky really was Italian.

Kansas, as a place to live, was as improbable as Utah or those other funny states. But Roscoe wasn't improbable or funny and he didn't get excited and that had saved them all — that is, all that were saved. Coco gave a lemon to bite, and he watched the timekeeper and went out when he rang the bell. Baronski came to him, but not clear to him, in left-hand range, moving to his left, stabbing him and ready to go away.

**COCO** yelled for pace, but it wasn't there. He could plug in, but he was rusty; he was strong but he was rusty. You couldn't come back and defend your title against a roundheel. He could beat this guy, just maybe, if the go went twenty frames, but a tenner, like this, he was getting himself stabbed silly. And he didn't care.

Baronski threw some rights, sharp rights, and that was all right, because Baronski got mauled a little in exchanges. Joe got to sweating good and moving better, but Baronski took heed from what had happened when he tried to punch it out and reopened the cut below Joe's eye with skill and accuracy and went back and away, always to his left. Joe stopped, stock still, and grinned at Baronski but Baronski just grinned back and didn't come back close and Corporal Roscoe Hammond said something in Joe Wilder's ear — clear, easy, not yelling, and it was plain and it was the same thing that his Captain had said, the round before, but Joe couldn't tell what it was. Joe could almost cry because he couldn't tell what it was, and the referee came in front of him when the bell rang, because the referee, the third man in the ring, knew that Joe was deaf; but the fourth man in the ring, the one who spoke to him, the one who could speak through to him though not raising his voice, he was his Captain, he was Roscoe. . . . But what was it that they said?

"I'm getting punchy," he said to Coco, working on the eye again. "I hear guys sayin' somethin' to me out there."

"The guy ain't hurt you," Coco yelled. "Bull him around, work him to the corners."

They were proud of Joe Wilder in the Army, a champion. And they kidded him a little bit about it sometimes: "Put up your dukes . . . . Let's go a couple rounds, Joe!" But they were proud of him. And that was silly. There were no champions in the Army. There was no company of vaster potentialities than any other company, no regiment, no division better than another regiment or division.

Some were better trained, better this and better that; but the human heroism and human weakness was there in equal quantities. Not, perhaps, in individuals; but among two hundred men who called America their home, who knew the things that were there for them to return to if they returned, among those two hundred men, or fifteen thousand men, there would be those things of value in the collective human spirit to level that of another equal number.

Baronski came a little faster now. Sixth round?

Joe wasn't sure, but he would make a fight if he could move to this boy.

**HE** went to Baronski, working him toward a corner, his hands down, cocked, and he took sharp punishment and there went the cut again, now bleeding freely, and Baronski was too smooth, a fanciful-daniel, maybe, like Loughran in the old days — who would finish the round in his own corner and then just sit down, smiling with the bell. He heard a voice, clear and cool, mature; it said the same thing. *What did it say?* Joe got close to Baronski, finally, and shook him with a sharp right cross and the little sounds out there came into a faint wave. Well, they used to call him a crowd-pleaser; he would make a fight of it, but the sharp unhurried words that came in his ear were in the voice of his Captain . . . . No, the things they said weren't all the same things, they just meant the same things. They were saying something to him and he couldn't understand.

This fight, this unimportant fight, if he didn't have to go ahead and try against this lad with too much youth and too many gloves, maybe then he could hear what they said to him. But he wasn't there, and there were eighteen thousand paid admissions here tonight, and he had to try and work his trade.

He slugged with Baronski in a corner and got the worst of it, and that was bad. The kid boxed his ears off, and then outslugged him. The referee pulled them apart at the bell and Coco worked and swore about the cut because the cut was now two cuts, another one above the eye. Joe looked down at the ringside and saw some uniforms there and he felt as though the crowd were already crowning a new champion.

But he went out. Coco was yelling. Joe knew not what. The fight was unimportant, that was the trouble. He could summon no great burst of fury to fell a foe, a nice kid that he liked. It was not important that he win or lose; not like his Captain lying there in the cool moonlight. He had lost — or had he? Joe suddenly hoped not and he thought of Lorna and her doll, lying asleep now, but to rise again upon the morrow.

**BARONSKI** was there before him, always, always moving to the left away from Joe's right hand, his left shoulder well up, hiding his smooth chin, his long left hand like a well-managed ramrod stabbing at Joe's cuts. The blood came down again and the eye it ran into lost its effectiveness, but Joe Wilder bobbed his head and moved on in, wishing the fight was over.

He didn't place the voice, though it spoke to him concisely, and Joe was not now surprised. He didn't place the voice, because he had only heard it once, and if it hadn't had a vague similarity to Corporal Roscoe Hammond's voice and thus called up associations, he might not have placed it at all. It was a slightly Kansas voice, and it was Eisenhower's.

It was concise, precise . . . . But though the words seemed clear and plain, Joe couldn't understand just what they were. He thought; he tried most desperately; he *must* know what was said to him by that fourth man in the ring.

He took it that round bad; preoccupation rode him and he lost effectiveness.

And between the rounds he sat and thought, harder than he had ever thought in his life. And suddenly he had it, and felt he could understand if they spoke to him again. Because now he knew *who* they were, and knowing who the composite fourth man was that stood beside his ear, he felt if that man spoke again he could understand. And when Coco punched him and he knew the bell had rung, he went out eagerly now, not eager for the fray, but eager for the word, the word that if it would come now, would be within his ken.

Baronski moved upon him, swift and silent, punching, and Joe rode out the flurry, waiting. And they spoke to him, and it was clear. They spoke again to him, in turn, and they said it differently but they said the same thing.

They told him that from one champion to another, he must do his best, the best that lay within him. The Army told him that, one champion to another.

They told him. The Army was a corporal and a general and a colonel and a captain, with the best-loved one lying dead there in the dark. It was a force, and as a force it did its best. Cowards, heroes, millions of men, doing its best.

**Baronski was there before him, always moving to the left away from Joe's right hand, his left shoulder well up, hiding his smooth chin.**

**THEY** told him, plainly — they told Joe Wilder, old champion, discharged from the service, that he had to do his best — not for them, or for his wife or for his little girl; but if he took up the fight, he must give it all he had. Call up the reserve that lay within him. Give to the contest all there was to give. There could be no compromise with his utmost capabilities.

And — as one champion to another — they truly loved a winner.

Coco fixed his eye so he could see, and Joe Wilder sat there on a little stool and asked himself if he could fetch something from his vitals to batter down this lad.

"I heard what you said to me that night," his Captain said quite clearly, "and I love you too, because that night you gave your best, and I did too, and that you must always do."

And Joe Wilder knew that from somewhere he would summon that last resource that he hadn't tapped. A man can love a man, as a man and as a symbol, and sometimes as both. A man can love his country, and his daughter and his wife. And a man can almost love himself if he always does his best.

Coco punched him in the back, and Joe Wilder went out once more into the lonesome center of the ring.

Fury, not insensate but calculated fury, dredged up from his bowels in the clutch. Joe Wilder summoned that, and he met a smooth young man, slightly careless now, and crowding, and that made it easier. Baronski came to him, and Joe Wilder met him moving in, and he took some punishment to get Baronski where he couldn't go to the left, and he shook Baronski up with a right and sunk a left hook to the body halfway to his wrist. The fact that Baronski buckled, and then fought back with more savagery than reason, was not important. Joe Wilder was fighting now, his utmost level best.

That he dropped Baronski for ten fateful seconds a short time later was not even so important, though as one champion to another the Army loves a winner. But that he could give as he gave, that was important. In his dressing-room, with the thing hooked in his ear that made him hear almost as well as anyone, he told Baronski what had happened — not all of it, just a little of it.

Baronski, like the nice kid that he was, had come by and said, baffledly, that Joe *was* a champion — and what about another match?

"Kid," Joe Wilder said, "you're too good for me. Tonight I had a fourth man in the ring."

Coco shook his head in sympathy, and Baronski went on out. But the next morning playing with Lorna, his little girl, Joe Wilder seemed all right again, as sane as anyone.

With the ropes at his back and the bells in his head, the champ came back for one last round—for the fight of another guy's life! Sporelli promptly knocked him down with a dynamite loaded right...

# THE RIGHT GUY

**DOC PAINTER** sat in the chair and looked at his fighter. It was hot in the hotel room, hot with the windows open, the fan droning. A grittiness was in the air. Doc Painter ran a palm across the table beside him and felt the grittiness beneath his hand.

Kid Richards lay in his shorts on the bed. Lean and balding, old for a fighter, not much marked. Lean and mean, and broke. Making the weight had been hard and though the weighing-in was past and he'd eaten a big steak, he was thirsty and he'd stay thirsty until after the fight.

"I was in Florida once," Doc Painter said, "right before a hurricane. It was like this, edgy weather. Makes you feel —"

"Shut up," Kid Richards said and then he swore at his manager half-heartedly.

Doc Painter sighed. He didn't want Richards feeling jolly. He wasn't supposed to feel jolly. He wanted him mean. But he'd rather he didn't call him those names. Kid Richards was a louse, a heel, formerly a gold-plated heel, but now, still champion, a broke and aging heel, but a good fighter. A sometimes great fighter.

Doc Painter got up and walked to the door. He stood in the open doorway a moment and looked at his watch. "Five, almost. We'll leave here about nine. Try to sleep."

"I guess you're gonna go down and have yourself a coupla beers." Kid Richards called his manager four short names of incredible obscenity.

Doc Painter looked at him, expressionless, closed the door and walked to the elevator. He didn't see the girl who stood watching the door.

Where Kid Richards was old at thirty-one, the girl, selling her beauty in chorus lines, was running a little to fat. She was ancient at twenty-seven. The last year or two she was down to working places where you drank with the customers between shows. She couldn't act and she couldn't dance. But she had courage of a kind. She came from her hiding place down the hall and opened the door to Kid Richard's room and walked in.

Kid Richards didn't get up, didn't move. He looked at her, not moving except for the muscles in his left forearm that crawled a little bit. "Get out of here," he said.

"I just come up to bring the letter, the letter in your box, and wish you —"

Kid Richards got up and on stealthy bare feet moved to her. She stopped her sentence in the middle, watching him in a kind of trance, but without surprise.

He took her hair in his right hand with a cat-like sweep, cut his left hand around, slapping her across the mouth hard with the palm and then the back of his left hand. He moved her toward the door, still holding her by the hair. "Get outta here! Leave me alone! Leave me alone, you hear? I'll —"

The girl didn't cry. As she passed the table, propelled toward the door, she dropped the letter on the shiny part of the table where Doc Painter had lately wiped his hand. She said, "I know they ain't anything. I don't want nothing from you. I just come up to wish you luck."

Kid Richards pushed her out of the door and shut it and locked it. He walked over to the bathroom, went in, ran the water in the basin, leaned down and washed out his mouth, holding his mouth under the stream, ignoring the glass. He spat the tepid water in the basin and cleared his throat.

He felt better.

Doc Painter opened the door silently and came in. "Come out of there. Come away from that water." Doc Painter was a gaudily dressed little man, lean as a whippet with a whippet's face. He spoke with cold authority.

"Doc," Kid Richards said, coming out of the bathroom, feeling pretty good, feeling a little breeze with the hint of dusk outside, "do you think I'd be so stupid I'd drink a lot of water four hours before a fight? You think I'm a dumb guy, don't you? Well, I been champion for eight years." There was hate in his voice now. "Eight years. And I don't drink no water before a fight." He looked at Doc Painter. "You think I'm that stupid?"

Doc Painter said, "Yes." He sat down, noticed the letter the girl had left. "I saw a frail in the hall," he said. "Looked like a frail used to ride your arm, the one that the papers said you were going to marry."

"Doc," Kid Richards said, "you been with me eleven years. You know I never told that stupid broad I was gonna marry her."

Doc Painter shrugged. "Lie down and try to sleep." He picked up the letter.

It was addressed in pencil to "Kid Richards, Esq." He put a thin hard finger under the flap, ripped it and pulled the sheet from the envelope and read the letter.

*Dear Mr. Kid Richards:*
*My name is Welford Meek and I am writing you to ask you to do me a favor. If you would just as leave, would you please k.o. that challenger (haha) Sporelli, in the fourth rd. I am in a place where the lights has to be out, the radios off by ten-thirty, no matter what. I have read about you since I could read. About how they call you Kid Richards, The Lion-Hearted, and how you are still single as the right girl has not come along. Please give that fighter (haha) Sporelli the old lethal right in approximately the 4th rd.*

*Your ardent admirer*
*Welford Meek*
*10 yrs of age.*

Doc Painter's face didn't change expression. "Welford," he said moodily. "Funny name." He lit a cigarette and said, "Want to see the letter?"

"Who's it to?"

"You."

"Some broad?"

"No, a kid. Must be in an orphanage. A kid with a peculiar name — Welford Meek."

"Orphanage?" There was a trace of expression in Kid Richard's voice. "Ain't there a address where it come from?"

Doc Painter turned the envelope over. "Yes," he said. "Orphanage all right, over in Jersey."

Kid Richards said, "Hell, I ain't gonna get no sleep."

"You never do," Doc Painter said.

"Lemme see the letter. Some kid in a orphanage, huh?"

Doc Painter handed him the letter.

Kid Richards studied it for a long time, breathing with occasional little snorts through his nose.

"I don't think he's so funny with those ha-ha's about Sporelli," Doc Painter said.

"Hell, Sporelli's a bum."

"Sure. A nice young bum who can knock your head off with either hand. Some bum."

"I guess you think he's gonna beat me?" Richards said.

"You don't want me to tell you what I think?" Doc Painter said. Kid Richards picked up the letter and read it again. It took him longer this time. Finally he put it down. "Same damn place I was. Never let me stay up till no ten-thirty."

Doc Painter went over to the window and flipped his cigarette out. "Try to get some sleep," he said automatically.

**THEY** rode out to the stadium, leaving the hotel at nine, and there was some hurrying in the dressing room because the semi-final ended in a second-round knockout. They were walking up the aisle at ten minutes of ten.

Doc Painter kept his fighter bundled up, stood looking down at him in the ring, not talking to him. "Nice house," he said at last. "Run sixty, sixty-five jesters for you before taxes."

"I can use it."

Anthony Sporelli was a dark smooth young man who had the weight. He was out of his robe, limbering up in his corner, letting the people see his smoothness, the smoothness of the next champion.

"You know," Doc Painter said, looking down at his fighter and telling him how the fight was coming out. "You know, Kid, it's a damn shame you fluffed off all your dough."

"What'd you do with that letter?" Kid Richards said, sullenly.

"It's back at the hotel."

"Kid's name was Welford Meek. Funny name, out there in Jersey."

"You better think about Sporelli," Doc Painter said. They went to the center of the ring and heard the referee's instructions.

The fighters came into the center of the ring at the bell and Sporelli, to erase all doubt in his own mind and in the mind of Kid Richards, the Lion-Hearted, feinted a left, chopped a right and broke Kid Richard's nose.

Doc Painter watched, expressionless. Now that his relationship with Kid Richards was about to end he was glad. Every time Sporelli beat the aging Richards to the punch, every time he heard Richards grunt above the roaring faceless chumps that Doc Painter knew as the crowd, it gave him satisfaction. Eleven years. Eleven years of associating with a heel. A guy that wouldn't give the time of day to his mother — if he'd had a mother — a guy that never did a thing for anybody else.

The bell sounded to end the round, and Doc Painter moved. He was in the ring, ministering, talking — a great handler, a wise head giving advice where no advice would serve.

Automatically he moved with the warning buzzer, but to the face that Sporelli had marked up more in one round than a hundred others had in a thousand, he said, "Some bum."

Kid Richards went out from his corner, full of fight, game, deadly game.

It's a peculiar kind of animal courage, Doc Painter thought. Tonight it is no good. But they, the fans, think it's good, think that it's really courage, when it's stupid, insensate driving that pain and blows can't numb.

Sporelli made him miss, but himself didn't miss. Sporelli moved in close and tied him up and proved that he was stronger. He was having fun, savoring his strength, showing himself and Kid Richards, the champion of the world, that he was stronger. A good young man, good to his mother, a youngster who had found the right girl. Doc Painter worked hard on Kid Richards to get him out there for the fourth. He had to. And at last he leaned down and yelled at the bloody, pulpy face of Kid Richards. "It's time for Welford Meek to go to bed. What about —" The buzzer drove him from the ring before he finished.

But Kid Richards looked at him and his expression changed.

Sporelli promptly knocked him down with a dynamite-loaded right, because Kid Richards moved in with such haste. But Kid Richards got right up and Sporelli looked at him and all at once he was worried. He'd won the fight and still it wasn't over. Kid Richards bulled him to the ropes, grunting, and dropped Sporelli with a lucky right and wouldn't go to a neutral corner until the referee half-dragged him there, and it gave Sporelli more time than he should have had. Kid Richards came again to him, hands low, like a mad, stupid beast in its heart. Sporelli was suddenly afraid.

Kid Richards backed him up until he reached a corner, because now he was afraid and he wasn't thinking. There Kid Richards dropped him and moved off to the neutral corner, walking into the ring post with a jolt.

"He's clean up Queer Street," Doc said. "But Sporelli can't get up."

And so Doc Painter, at the count of ten, went out and got his fighter.

They brought the microphone. The ring was suddenly full of people. They held the microphone and Kid Richards took it in his two leather paws and said, "Did I do all right, Welford? Welford Meek over there, make 'em let you listen. I'll take him the next round for sure."

**DOC PAINTER** sat and watched his fighter lying on the bed, the next day's light upon them, a man lean and mean and balding, cut to hell and bandaged. "How do you feel about Welford Meek, Kid?"

Kid Richards, the Lion-Hearted, thought it over as best he could. Finally he said, "Who?"

"Welford Meek. You went up Queer Street last night and after the fight you said into the microphone that you would win for him, this Welford Meek, ten years old."

"After I'd won?"

"Yeah." Doc Painter lit a cigarette. "I've been fooling around fighters for thirty years, and you for eleven. Kid, you're the only one I ever saw that never cared for anything but yourself, was selfish all the way. And yet you finally did something for somebody else and win a fight you rate to lose from here to yonder."

"You mean I ain't such a heel if I'm out of my head?" Kid Richards asked. Then after a long time he said, "I remember about the kid."

"You do?"

"Doc, I was orphaned out, folks died. You know that, Doc." There was a little pleading note in Kid Richards' voice and it grated with reluctance and sounded sad as he went on. "I'm sorry I been selfish, Doc. I'm sorry about the way I been. I really shouldn't slapped that tomato around yesterday."

"You were edgy, thirsty."

"You oughtn't to slap no broad around because you're thirsty," Kid Richards said accusingly. "I done it for Welford Meek, all right, won over Sporelli, even if —"

"Even if what?" Doc Painter asked. "I started to say, even if he was a bum, but he ain't no bum. He ain't no ha-ha Sporelli. He's a whole lot better'n me."

"You must still be wheely," Doc Painter said. "You're still the champ."

Kid Richards said thoughtfully, as if he hadn't heard, "I think I'll make up with that twist I slapped around. Her and me used to have some fun. Her and me'll go out and see Welford. Funny, him in the same place I was."

Doc Painter said, "Want another beer?" He got up and opened a bottle on the opener by the door, and handed it to Kid Richards and went on out the door. He went down in the elevator and into the bar. The girl was sitting in the bar and he went over to her and sat down at her table.

"Look," he said, as if they were resuming a conversation. "He's talking now about you and him going out to see this Welford Meek. He's still changed all right, maybe still up Queer Street. But he's different, though he may not stay different."

"You think I could go and see him?"

"Well," Doc Painter said, "right now it's safe." He lit a cigarette. "But we'll have to think of something, how to tell him. If he stays this way it'll be all right." He drew from his cigarette and moved two thin lines of smoke from his nose. "We'll tell him Welford Meek wouldn't want to see him until the bandages are off and he don't look so mangled and chewed up."

"Tell him what, then? I don't get it. Tell him what?" the girl asked, giving him a look of puzzlement. Doc Painter looked at them, his eyes flat and tender. "I'm through with him. He ought to quit. I got to get me another bum, a young bum. But what I mean is, he's got to be told that there isn't any Welford Meek. I wrote the letter with my left hand, myself. It really don't make a damn. He did something for somebody else even if he was punchy, did it in good faith. Something for somebody else and it changed him."

"You wrote the letter?" the girl said. "Why? You hated him."

"I don't know for sure, honey. I been messing with fighters for thirty years. I guess I always try to help them win. And to tell you the truth, I never quite hated him, honey."

Kid Richards came into the bar then, in his shirt sleeves, bandages and all. He came over and sat down and ordered a beer. He looked closely at the girl's face. "Honey," he said, "did you ever do anybody a favor? It makes you feel funny." He turned his new emotion over slowly in his mind, looking at it in wonder. "It makes you feel good."

He looked up and said, "Where you goin', Doc?"

Doc Painter, whose steadily growing astonishment at the recent behavior of Kid Richards was now tempered by the realization that his fighter would pretty soon find out who did write the letter, reached for his pearl-gray derby.

"South America," he said.

Tiger's voice was flat. "Let me sit here alone for a minute," he said.

# COUNT OF TEN

### A city waited while Mattie learned . . . It wasn't losing, but losing like a champ that mattered.

**HIS** name was Charles Tipton, and he had retired from the ring three years before and married Mattie Todd — then Delores Dubois, working in the chorus line at a night club — a condition of the marriage being that he would never fight again. Which was fine with Tiger Tipton. He had earned some money as a fighter and had bought a restaurant when he retired, for his name was a draw in his Midwestern home city — since he had been a pleasing, honest workman at his trade.

But now he moved down Main Street, a big man, thirty-five years old, seeking his old manager, Nick Pulaski, moving like a sad and portly cat, his heart cold, a weight in his chest.

He had called Mattie *Delores Dubious* in the old days, before his last fight, when he was courting

- 149 -

her, for she had doubted that he'd quit the ring. He had been inordinately pleased with his little pun, for he was not the kind that thought of things like that. But now she lay, the girl of his heart, in the big hospital uptown, and Tiger Tipton was broke. She was alive through the efforts of the best doctors in the city; by transfusions and other costly devices that Charles Tipton did not quite understand. He only understood the money. And he was out of that. The doctors had told her that she mustn't have a child, but for Mattie there had to be a child. A Tipton cub to make this shining marriage all complete. He couldn't understand a woman who was willing to risk her happiness on such a long shot. He didn't understand, and he had protested.

"Who's dubious now?" she'd said, and laughed. "I'll be fine." But no; not fine. Not close to fine. A racking pregnancy. A stillborn child, who otherwise would have grown into a man. And now Mattie Tipton didn't want to live.

That he understood. Not the why of it, but the fact of it. The doctors said she didn't want to live. But perhaps, with certain measures. . . Measures that took money. He understood the money. He was out of that. He found Nick Pulaski in the Markwell Bar, and Nick came back to a booth with him. Nick was tense and bald and fifty. Charles Tipton had hardly spoken half a dozen words when Nick raised his right hand protestingly.

"Nonononono!" he said. "First off, the champ would assassinate you, and second off, Mattie would assassinate me."

"You know how sick she is?" Tiger Tipton asked. "She's sick enough to die, and the tab up there is three or four hundred bucks a week. I'm broke, Nick. I've borrowed all I could on the restaurant."

Nick Pulaski said, "They'll give her what she needs, dough or not —"

"I don't go for no charity, Nick, long as I can fight."

"And so you want me to match you with the Champion?"

"He's on a swing acrost the country," Tiger Tipton said. "Fightin' no-decisioners, exhibitions. Even two years on the shelf I'd outdraw anybody in town with him. Maybe pick up a score, like, say, three grand or so. That'd carry the tab at the hospital for a while."

"Mattie reads about it, hears about it over the radio, it'll kill her, Tiger."

"I thought of that," Tiger Tipton said. "I'd ask the boys to keep it from her."

"Ohohoh! The Champion of the world comes to town for a fight and you're gonna suppress it. Does she think Dewey's President?"

"She ain't out around," Tiger Tipton said slowly. "She looks at the paper some mornings she's feeling good, and they could take the radio away part of the day. I'd tell the newspapers when her radio ain't in her room."

**NICK PULASKI** didn't answer, and his eyes went blank, and then he looked back to the Tiger and said, almost half to himself, "What a sob-sister story."

"I could train in town," Tiger Tipton said. "Go up and see her just like always, wear everything but a catcher's mask so I don't get scuffed up sparrin'. I don't want no pity or no charity. I just want to work a little at my old trade and not let my wife know it."

"They get the ball park for a night in June; it ought to draw Cappa City. Cut you ten, maybe twelve and a half, per cent. Oughta be a fair score," Nick Pulaski mused.

"What story?" Tiger Tipton asked.

"I'll call New York and then talk to the local guys. If we can set it we'll have a press conf'rence. I'll handle that." He paused. "Of course, the colored boy's gonna murder you."

"Oh," Tiger Tipton said, "I ain't so sure." Then he added, "I would make it a fight."

Nick Pulaski shrugged. "The person who knows the least bit about fighters is fighters."

"What story you talkin' about?"

"I'll phone you up in a few days," Nick said. "Be the screwiest deal that ever was."

Mattie Tipton was a tall, very beautiful woman, and lying in the hospital bed she was still beautiful. Her husband's throat tightened as he sought for words, looking down at her. He smiled, no words there, feeling the tight bitterness in his chest mixed with the bitterness of his own inadequacy.

"How are you, honey?" Tiger Tipton said. "You look wonderful."

Tiger Tipton looked at the radio on the table

beside the bed. "Listen to the radio much, hon?" He felt that the question was sudden and awkward, and added, "Is it a good one? Stuff comes in clear?"

"It's fine," the girl said, and unaccountably began to weep. "I gotta go downtown," he said. "I'll see you tonight."

The girl said, between her little sobs, "You never call me Delores Dubious any more."

"Ah, honey, I wore that joke out. Why it used to make you annoyed I used that lousy old joke so much."

"Lying up here," the girl said through her tears, "I guess I got sentimental about that joke."

"Okay, Miss Dubious, see you tonight." Tiger Tipton came over and put his great hands under his wife's shoulders and kissed her. "See you tonight."

"But I'm *really* Mrs. Tipton, aren't I?"

"You sure are, baby."

"But what's the use of that?" The reporters in the promoter's office looked up at Tiger Tipton as he came in, and he said hello to them. Then he walked over to a chair and sat down.

Nick Pulaski cleared his throat importantly. Nick was dressed his sharpest, and he stood up and rapped on the desk with the promoter's paperweight. "Fellows," he said. "I'm gonna lay it right on the line. Tiger, here, is gonna fight the Champion next June, gonna make the most glorious comeback in the annals of boxing, only he's gotta make a condition: The news that he's fightin' can't get to his wife."

**THERE** was a ripple of laughter, and Nick said slowly, "It ain't a joke, son. Mrs. Tipton is real sick uptown in a hospital — so sick if she hears the Tiger's fightin' again it might — it would maybe make her a lot worse." He paused. "Maybe it would cause her to not get well," he added. "But if the radio boys will spot their stuff at certain times, we can rig it so the radio won't be in her room when they're talkin' about the fight. We'll fix the paper some way."

"Is the Tiger broke?" Joe Johnson sports editor of the local paper, asked.

Tiger looked at him and nodded.

Nick said, "Yeah, and the stuff they're doin' for Mattie runs big money."

Joe Johnson had seen Tiger Tipton fight many times and he had known him a long time. He knew a story when he saw one. So he said, not knowing whether it was possible or not, but knowing a story. "We'll run off a special edition of our sheet. Just for her. Just one paper every night with nothin' in it about the fight."

"When is it safe to mention the fight on the air?" a radio newscaster asked. "If she listens to me, I'll never mention the fight."

And so a little city in the Middle West ganged up to keep a sick ex-chorus girl from learning that her husband was going, once more, into the ring. It was, of course, a great human-interest story, worth to the paper (in those editions that Mattie Tipton did not see) reams of avidly read space. And circulation, too. But all the little people that kept the word from Mattie Tipton — well, they just did it . . . . Tiger Tipton went into training.

Thirty-five summers and thirty-six winters had come and gone for Tiger Tipton, and the training was a chore, a drudgery that came hard. His old skills and stamina came back very slowly, and only part way back, at that. They never do come all the way back. That is for the book. But still he had been a good fighter, always in the best of condition; a slow starter who piled on pace, and he had a record of wins that was dated with many late round technical knockouts.

The Champion was a young Negro, big-boned and lean, an explosive puncher, and Nick Pulaski thought that perhaps in the old days, when the Tiger was at his peak, he might have given the colored boy a good fight if he could have survived the first six rounds. Now, of course, it figured to be no contest. The Champion would assassinate him. He said as much a few days before the fight, for Nick was a realist. "Of course," Nick said in the little dressing room watching the Tiger standing on the scales, "you aren't goin' into the tank for this kid, but, after all, there's no percentage in getting your head knocked lopsided . . . . You remember what Baer told Artie Donovan when Artie was countin' him out after Louis had teed off on him and Artie thought Max oughtta get up?"

The Tiger was thinking about his wife, who was growing steadily worse, and he answered absently in the negative, looking sadly at the figures on the scales.

"Maxie said, 'These people paid to see a fight, not a murder.' I always thought Maxie showed real good sense."

The Tiger turned and looked at his manager and nodded.

"And you trainin' like for your life. You'll get your dough just the same."

The Tiger said slowly, thinking, "This is a little town and everybody in this town has helped me not let Mattie know about the fight. I can't cheat them."

"Cheat them!" Nick said. "What will you be doin' for them lettin' them watch you lose bad and bloody?"

The Tiger was preoccupied and he answered, after a while, "I don't know," and stepped down from the scales and walked to the shower. . . .

**THAT** night in the hospital they didn't let him stay but a few minutes, but long enough for Mattie Tipton to say, "You're getting thin."

It scared him for a minute, and he grinned falsely, trying to think of something to say. "I miss your cookin', honey," he said finally.

The girl tried for an instant to smile, for she had never cooked but once. Just one time, and with the traditional results of funny-paper brides. But now she spoke of that time, trying herself, recalling details of that fiasco as if trying to relive it, and Tiger Tipton guessed, then, that his wife knew she was dying. And that she didn't care. The morning they weighed in, the morning of the fight, they told him she was resting; no change. The big colored boy, the Champion, asked politely of her, and Tiger Tipton muttered something, and then was afraid he'd been rude and added, "She's about the same, Champ."

The Champion spoke of how his own mother had once been so sick the doctors gave her up, but now lived hale as anything in New York. Nick Pulaski said, from old habit, "The Tiger's in the greatest shape of his life. He's goin' in there strictly to win. He aims to make the Champ jump outta the ring."

Tiger Tipton frowned at him, and the colored boy grinned to show he understood that Nick was talking for the late editions and the gate. "I hope your wife gets well real soon," he whispered.

**TIGER TIPTON** was afraid to go by the hospital that day, and so he tried to rest, lying in the hotel room, waiting for the night. Nick Pulaski came and checked the clear weather from the window and asked him how he was. The Tiger said he was all right.

"Nobody knows where you are," Nick said. "I didn't want nobody to bother you."

It was warm, and the Tiger looked down at his now lean, naked length, remembering all the sparring, all the roadwork, all the rope-skipping, all those arduous chores behind him now forever. He raised his arms and sat up a little way, ridging the muscles of his stomach. "I came around pretty good," he said at last.

Nick Pulaski said, "Wonderful." He added, "If you was even five years younger you'd give him a bad night. I'd bet my end of the purse you went the route."

"Ain't you already bet he'll stop me in two?" Tiger Tipton asked wryly. Nick Pulaski called him a dirty name, his voice a little husky with emotion, for they had known each other many years. "I've got no end," he said. "You get it all, clean."

Charles Tipton closed his eyes and said over to himself the Lord's Prayer, and then stopped, realizing he did not want that God's will be done unless God wanted Mattie to get well. And how could he be sure of that? So he began, "And now I lay me down to sleep," that being the only other prayer he knew. At the end he asked only that God bless Mattie; but thinking, after, of Nick not taking a cut but giving it all to him, he threw in Nick, too. It was the best he could do.

"The moxie I got," he thought. "I never asked Him to do a thing about the Champion's left hook." And then, lonely and scared, he cried one dry-eyed sob and got up and sat in a chair.

It was a long, long time until ten minutes of nine . . . . In the dressing-room Nick was gone to watch them bandage the Champion's hands, meticulously observing the formalities, like it was really for the title and The Tiger had a chance — that it wasn't just a one-night stand on a barnstorming tour for the Champion.

There was a battered pay phone on the wall of the little dressing-room and now it took on the aspects of a face, black and accusing in the eyes of Tiger Tipton, and he took a nickel from somebody and with his hands awkward with bandages dialed the hospital.

Waiting for the answer, he turned to the room: "I want to thank you, Joe, and your boss for puttin' out that edition for Mattie, the days the fight was in the paper." He looked at the young radio reporter who would give the fight on the local station from ringside. "Thank you, too. Mattie's never tumbled."

It got so quiet the squeaky voice of the girl who answered could be heard, and then there was a pause and the muttered question from Tiger Tipton.

He pushed the earpiece against the broken cartilage of his left ear, and nothing could be heard but the crowd outside and above watching, buzzing suddenly like a great bee and then subsiding.

Tiger Tipton turned a putty color and dropped the earphone, not putting it back in the cradle. Lines fell into his face, and he didn't say anything for a moment, but when he spoke he heard his voice flat and even: "Let me sit here alone for a minute."

Nick Pulaski moved swiftly and hung up the phone and said, "Blow, fellows," and he went out with them and stood just outside the door.

Tiger Tipton sat there and balanced his mind like a cracked egg. Mattie was worse. Much, much worse . . . .

**THE** nurse saw the radio was there but tonight it didn't matter. Mattie Tipton lay silent. Oxygen tubes were in her nose and there were bottles swung cleverly above. Mattie Tipton said in a childish, shallow voice, "Turn on the radio."

The nurse moved automatically and flipped the switch, then flipped it off. Mattie Tipton said, "Leave that — the fights . . ." The nurse went for the doctor.

The doctor came and looked at Mattie Tipton from where he stood at the foot of the bed. He looked at her for thirty seconds, and then he nodded to the nurse, and the nurse went back and turned the dial on the radio. The doctor stood still, looking down at Mattie, and the nurse moved into a far corner and sat down, taking up as small a space as she could and holding herself quite still. The new voice came into the room like hailstones on the roof . . . . Tiger Tipton got up and walked to the door and out of the door and started up the long aisle to the ring, and Nick fell in behind him, and sound moved with them as they came.

The stars which were millions of light years away, and which Tiger Tipton guessed Some One had put there, looked down upon them, and the little flaring stars nearer at hand were cigarettes being lighted by the bleacherites in the little ball park. "And I guess it's all the same," Tiger Tipton thought fuzzily and began again. "Now I lay me down to sleep . . ."

In the ring, when the Tiger was introduced, Nick had to punch him, and he stood up and made one revolution on his heel and sat down again . . . . The disembodied voice came into the hospital room with the sharp urgency of gunfire: "And now Mattie Tipton's man comes back once more to fight for the money that may make her well again. She doesn't know this. Yours truly has never mentioned it. The paper ran off special editions that didn't mention this fight just for Mattie Tipton . . . . But here's the bell . . ."

**THE** Champion came out quickly, and, from old habit, Tiger Tipton moved to meet him. The Champion was a little embarrassed. This thing had built into a fight, a real fight, and he felt sorry for the man he met, and thought to end it quickly. He stabbed with his great left hand, and then feinted with his right and hooked the left explosively. But it took Tiger Tipton too high on the cheek, though it opened a cut on the eye and dropped the white man.

Tiger Tipton rose at seven, and the referee moved to rub the resin from his gloves where he had pushed himself up. The blood dripped from his face and caught in the thin, blondish hair on his chest. Tiger Tipton knew he had never faced such a man as this, and all the futility, all the uselessness of the whole long, painful training, all the hopelessness of this fight, came and sat upon his mind.

He stalled out the round, clinching and

cowering, and made it to his corner with the bell. Nick Pulaski said, "Take ten next time or I'll throw in the towel."

Tiger Tipton shrugged and turned a gory mask to his manager. His face was blank with despair.

"What is there?" he wondered. "Nothing, now." And then another errant thought came to him: "I can't fight death." And he made up a phrase that he would never put into words, for Mattie had been the only one to whom he could say those things. But there was Nick, and you could say anything you wanted to when you were dying inside, too. "Death," he said aloud, to Nick. "You can't fight death. He's a process server can walk right in through the walls." Then he went on, "But you can fight a colored boy — What if he *is* the Champion — he puts on his gloves one hand at a time."

The bell rang then. He wanted to say some other things, though he knew it would take him time to arrange the words. He wanted to say that there was pride of workmanship and that there was gratitude for all the people who hadn't let Mattie get hurt knowing he was fighting. But mostly he wanted to say that when you did what you could — just as the doctors had, just as everybody had — you did it your best — if you were a man. He remembered just in time. "No towel, Nick, ever . . ."

The doctor at the foot of Mattie Tipton's bed hadn't moved. He looked down, still, upon the girl who lay there on the bed, and the announcer's crisp, excited words came into the room like the voice of conscience, though not so still and small. ". . . I was down in the dressing-room, and the Tiger called the hospital, and now *we* have checked. Mattie Tipton is much worse, she is dying, and so Tiger Tipton, fighting for the money that might make her well, came into the ring tonight with *his* fight already lost."

The announcer's voice was a tense whisper now: "But something happened to the old Tiger. He went out like a man in a trance, and the Champion almost stopped him in the first round. They started to throw in the towel from his corner, but Tiger Tipton wouldn't let them. And then something happened . . . . Oh, he's magnificent out there tonight, ladies and gentlemen! With nothing to fight for, he's fighting like a champion, anyway. Red as his own blood clean to his trunks; but Nick Pulaski has got *both* the Tiger's eyes open now and he's taking the fight to the Champ, piling on the pace. What held him up these early rounds? . . . And now here's the bell for the last round."

**THE** doctor saw the tears come down the side of the girl's face, out of the outer corners and move down to the pillow. "You understand?" he asked.

The girl nodded. She looked different.

"I won't throw in the towel," she said. "And I understand so much." She moved her hands together on her chest as if hugging to her all that she understood . . . .

". . . This was a no-decision bout, an exhibition, really. But it turned out to be a tremendous fight. Here's the Champion!"

The familiar panting drawl came over the air: "I'm lucky. He's a great sportsman, ladies and gentlemen, and now."

The Tiger came in late that night, his face a hasty patchwork of bandages. He came into the room. "She heard most of the fight," the doctor said.

"She's better?" Tiger Tipton whispered.

The girl opened her eyes and looked up at her husband. "Isn't he beautiful?" she said.

The tears came down under Tiger Tipton's bandages, salty and stinging in the cuts.

"I didn't hear the decision," the girl said. "No decision," Tiger Tipton said thickly. "Newspaper's gonna call it a draw."

The girl hugged her chest drowsily, happily. She spoke once more to the doctor, and she wrapped up all her pride and love and all the things she understood in the phrase. "I'm *Mrs.* Tipton," she said. "The Champion's wife."

Tiger Tipton came around and knelt by the bed.

The doctor looked at his watch, but he couldn't see it. "At a time I could not tell," he thought, "Mrs. Tipton passed a crisis and began to get well."

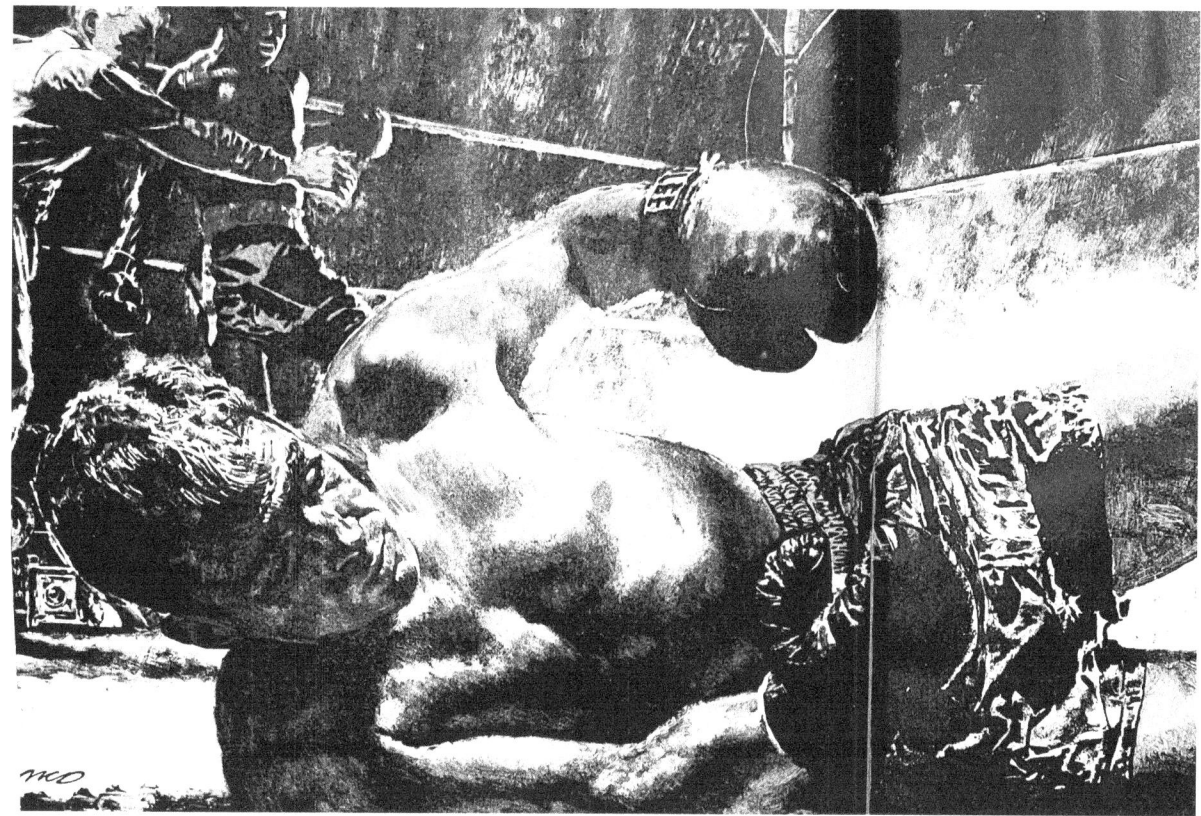

Through the fog, he heard the referee: "Six .... Seven." Lou thought: I'm okay. Now I gotta get up and fight him.

# THE EAGLEBIRD

**There are two kinds of fighters: gladiators and eaglebirds. (Champs and also-rans, to you.) It was Lou Badzik's night to show the howling, hostile ring worms which of the two he was.**

**HARRY FOX WAS GONE.** He had said his piece matter-of-factly and gone away. He hadn't put on any pressure and he hadn't asked for anything. He hadn't looked prosperous, but he hadn't asked for anything.

Lou Badzik pondered what Harry had said and he squirmed. Everything had been very orderly. Not going so good for dreams but going very good for life. Very, very good for life.

There was Joey, thought Lou. And thinking of Joey. Joey came in from the kitchen where Lou had sent him when Harry showed. Joey was his sister's kid. Joey was going on seven.

Joey pulled at his pants leg just the way kids did in funny papers. "What's a gladiator, Lou?" he asked.

Lou Badzik said, "Leave go my pants. Can't you ask a question without pullin' on my pants?"

"Sure," Joey said, turning loose. "I ain't got hold of your pants. What's a gladiator?"

"Leave me alone, Joey."

"Was that Uncle Harry? What'd he want? What's a gladiator?" Joey asked.

"An olden time fighter."

Joey had heard a good deal of reminiscence from Harry Fox. "Was Walker and Greb gladiators?" Joey asked. "Was Dempsey a gladiator?"

"Leave me alone, Joey," Lou said. "No, they

wasn't. I mean way-back fighters, Roman times. They fought with iron gloves and swords and stuff and killed each other. Now leave me alone."

Joey lay down on the floor.

There was Ruth, thought Lou. And this was as good as a dream. Better than a dream. He loved her in a way that choked him. Soft and lovely and beautiful; but hard and wise-thinking for his good. Hard and wise for his welfare.

Joey said, "Where's Ruth?"

Lou looked down in annoyance. He knew Ruth would be coming by soon, but mixed with his love for her and wanting to see her was a faint dread. He didn't want to tell her Harry Fox had come by.

Joey said, not looking up. "What'd Uncle Harry want?"

"Nothin', nothin'." Lou was almost shouting. He checked himself. "He didn't want anything," he added lamely.

**BUT RUTH** came in anyway, as was her wont on her way home from work. She was a tall, blond girl, she worked in a cafeteria — "and will until we get married." The wedding date was set. Six weeks away.

She spoke to Joey, put her purse and a paper bag on the table.

Lou kissed her but she turned from him and sat down and said almost at once, "What's the matter, honey?"

"Nothin'."

Joey said, "Uncle Harry was by."

Ruth said quickly, "How was he, Lou?"

Lou Badzik shrugged. "Okay." Then he went on earnestly, looking at the floor. "Harry's a brave man. He's a real brave guy. He never made it big because he wouldn't play ball with the mob. But he stuck with me and made me a lot of money and then got me out before I got hurt."

"Sure," Ruth said. "He made a lot of money off of you, too."

"He ain't got it now," Lou said.

"What did he say?"

"He wants to buy a boy out in K.C. A young light-heavy. He can get his contract for twenty-five hundred. Says he'll be a fighter."

"But your money's all tied up in annuities."

"I know that," Lou said impatiently. "He was talkin' about a fight. His end would make it —"

"You?"

"You needn't sound so like it was jumpin' off the Chrysler building. I'm a fighter."

"Look, honey — Harry himself got you out." She paused. "Harry himself."

"Okay. I told him I wouldn't do it." He flexed his hands. "It was a TV shot," he added. "That's why it'd be such a good payday."

"If Harry'd stay away from the race track …" Ruth said.

"Sure. And if he hadn't found me gettin' my brains beat out as a preliminary boy."

"Lou, you're thirty-four."

"It ain't eighty," Lou said. "Marciano's thirty-three."

"But you told him you wouldn't do it."

"Well, no," Lou Badzik said. "But I will. He's comin' back later." He thought a moment, then he added, "I love you, darling."

"And I love you," Ruth said. "I like Harry. Harry is a good man. He was awful good to you. But you're out; you got your annuities coming up. You're not all beat up." She paused. "You're a wonderful man."

"Gladiators," Joey mused from the floor. "They killed each other. If you didn't win you were dead."

Ruth stood up. "I'll fix dinner for you all," she said. "I brought some stuff." She looked down at Joey. "What's this about gladiators?"

"Just heard," Joey said.

"The emperor sometimes let the loser live," Ruth said. "He turned his thumb up if he wanted the loser to live."

"Well, I'll be goin' to hell. I mean, that's very innarestin'," Joey said.

The girl looked down at the little boy and started to say something, then shrugged and walked into the kitchen.

**LOU** kept the conversation away from Harry Fox during dinner. He argued amiably with Ruth about the wedding. Only Joey mentioned Harry Fox. He asked when he was coming back.

"You'll be in bed," Lou told him. "Tomorrow's a school day."

Joey didn't answer.

Ruth washed the dishes and Joey went reluctantly to bed. Lou sat on the sofa. He wished Harry Fox wasn't coming back. He hated to say something Harry might not want to hear, but it was hard to worry about Harry. Of anybody Lou had ever known, Harry seemed the best able to take care of whatever needed taking care of. Including himself.

Ruth came in and sat down beside him and Lou put his arms around her and pulled her hard to him and kissed her, trying to get into it how much he loved her. Trying to communicate to her the inexpressible feeling he had for her.

Ruth squirmed. "You'll muss me up."

Lou Badzik said huskily, a little hurt, "I'm sorry."

Ruth smiled. "Don't be." Then she added, "When's Harry coming?"

Lou felt it then. She wanted him to tell Harry no dice. She wanted to wait and hear him tell Harry; then she would kiss him.

He felt vaguely that it wasn't fair. But then it was woman-fair, he guessed. It was for him. For his own good.

Harry rang the doorbell and Lou let him in and he came in and shook hands and spoke to Ruth and sat down in a straight chair. He looked at Ruth and spoke to Lou. Harry Fox was a bald, skinny man. He had always seemed exactly the same to Lou. But he must have changed some through the years. He must be sixty now.

Harry said, "Don't say it. You don't have to say it."

Lou Badzik shrugged. "I'm sorry, Harry. If you want the dough we could probably figure to borrow it around. The two of us."

Harry Fox laughed. "Three-horse parlay and all my worries are over."

Lou looked quickly at Ruth and frowned. She managed not to say anything about people who played the horses.

But Harry didn't leave. He sat and chatted and reminisced and told a couple of jokes and took a present out of his pocket for Joey. It was a knife you could set up housekeeping with in the woods.

"He'll cut himself," Ruth said.

And Harry said sure.

Ruth yawned.

Harry said, "Have you set the date? The wedding, I mean."

Ruth told him the day and Harry smiled wryly.

"The date of the fight," he said. "That's the same day the fight's gonna be."

"There isn't going to be any fight," Ruth said.

"Oh, sure. There'll be a fight," Lou said. "It just won't be me bein' half of it." He paused. "This Cuban boy, Kid Gila. He's young. He'll be fightin' for a long time."

"He'll be champion," Harry said without feeling. "Lou woulda been," he added, "if he hadn't come along right when he did." He went off into a long story.

Ruth said with a little edge to her voice, "I believe I'll go on home. Will you call me a cab, Lou?"

"I'll take you," he said. "I'll —"

"No. Just call me a cab."

"I'll go down and whistle you up one," Harry Fox said and he got up and walked out of the apartment door.

Lou took the girl in his arms when she stood up. It was better than any dream he'd ever had. She kissed him back and whispered, laughing a little. "I wish Harry hadn't come. Tonight."

"There'll be a long, long time," Lou said. "All good."

Harry Fox came back. "Hack's downstairs," he said. He sat down.

Lou walked down with Ruth and paid the cabby and kissed her again shyly, standing in the street. The cab left.

When he came back to the apartment Harry Fox said, "She's a swell girl. You're a lucky fellow."

Sure, thought Lou, my sister and her husband were killed a long time ago and I got a little boy to raise, a real wonderful, ornery little boy, and I got money starting in pretty soon, and I got a wonderful girl that's going to marry me, and I got no bells in my head.

Lou said, "A lot of worry goes into livin'. You never know what's right. I'd like to write a letter to Joey sometime and maybe when I'm dead he could open it and see how much I wanted it good for him and how I never knew for sure what was good."

"You never know," Harry Fox said. "And words don't mean much. You pick up the paper and find a line in fine print and it says: *Joe Balloon beat Joe Doakes tko 8*. There's forty books, maybe, of words in that. Or you take a little old line like: *The war's over.*" Harry Fox paused. "You'll never write a letter to Joey and it won't matter. When he grows up he'll maybe know it or maybe he won't. Best you can do is live with yourself as clean as you can all day and try to forget the rest."

"I appreciate everything you've done," Lou began.

"Forget that," Harry Fox said. "I'm glad you didn't take the Gila go. They just wanted you on his record."

Lou said, bristling, "You mean they thought I'd get out of there; go four or five frames and get out of there for them."

Harry Fox looked at the floor. "They got to have a big indoor fight for Gila and there ain't anybody much but you. You never retired. Officially, you know. You're still ranked. You just haven't been working for a while, that's all."

"You didn't answer me, Harry," Lou said.

"You got a swell girl," Harry said. "You got a swell kid."

"Knock it off," Lou Badzik said. "Did they think I'd get out of there for this Cuban?"

Harry Fox looked around as he always did for something to do with his cigarette. "Maybe if Joey starts smokin'," he said, "you'll have an ash tray around here once in a while."

"Harry."

Harry Fox's smooth face didn't change. "Lou," he said. "I been around awhile. I never had a stable — just a boy or two I tried to do correct by. I also been playin' the horse races since a filly won the Kentucky Derby, and in the old days there used to be a boat race every once in a while. They'd fix a race — they wouldn't fix it exactly —" He stopped. "What I mean," he went on, "was, say they was three horses figured to win it, they'd arrange for two of 'em not to. This was in the days of the legal books when a price would hold. The books would pay what they had chalked up." He pressed out the cigarette and put it in the cuff of his pants.

"What the hell you tellin' me about horses for?" Lou Badzik asked. "I don't know anything about horses. And from you and them I don't want to know anything about 'em."

"It's a great diversion," Harry Fox said. "But that wasn't what I was gettin' at. Like I say, they arrange for two horses not to win, where they figure three are in the contention. Then they chunk it on the third one." He paused and lit another cigarette.

"But there's maybe ten horses in the race. So there's seven of 'em they don't bother with. They had a name for these horses. I never knew where they got it. They called them eaglebirds."

"Look," Lou Badzik said in irritation. "This is all nothin' to me. I don't know what you're talkin' about. I asked you a simple question."

**HARRY FOX** looked up. "I'm trying to answer you," Harry said. "They figured you an eaglebird, Lou."

"They knew they couldn't put in any fix with you and me," Lou Badzik said indignantly.

"They never bothered to try," Harry Fox said patiently.

"So I figured a cinch loser," Lou Badzik said levelly. "I've seen this kid a time or two on TV and —"

"You can't tell how rough he is on TV," Harry Fox said. "You are smart and you know your way around in there. I figured you could make us a good payday and not get hurt."

"*You* figured he'd beat me."

"Look," Harry said. "It's off."

"But you figured he'd beat me?" Lou Badzik said.

"Yes," Harry Fox said. Then in apology he added, "It would be your last fight. I didn't think it would —"

"You make me sore sometimes, Harry," Lou Badzik said. Then he muttered, almost to himself, "Eaglebird."

"This boy is young and very strong," Harry Fox said. "He's a gladiator, Lou."

Lou Badzik stood up, the word hanging hot in his mind. "Joey was askin' me …" he stopped. "What the hell do you mean by that? A gladiator."

"Drop it."

"You come up here to ask me could I fight on my wedding day. You're the busted horse, layin' one that's hustlin'. What do you mean: 'He's a gladiator?'"

"I should louse up your wedding, louse you up with your girl. I told you I was glad you turned it down." Harry Fox paused and lit a cigarette and knocked the ashes on the floor. "But I'll tell you what I mean. With Gila, fightin' ain't a trade. He comes to win, or else. That's why I said he was a gladiator."

"And I ain't?"

"Outside of Robinson, you're the sweetest in your division I ever saw."

"But I don't come to win — or else."

"This Cuban," Harry said, "if they don't get him out of there — and they won't — he won't be worth throwin' away ten years from now. But he's mean in there now. Nobody can beat him now."

Lou Badzik thought about Ruth, and his love for her was a wave of choking tenderness; and he thought about Joey and how he wanted it for him. And then, finally, he thought about himself. "Harry," he said at last, "we'll take it."

"But, Lou …"

"Call 'em now," he said. "Call Al now. Get him out of bed. Tell him we're going to take it."

"Not tonight."

"Yeah, tonight. Tell him we'll take it. I'll train up in the country."

He fixed for a woman to come and stay with Joey at the flat. And then there was Ruth. And finally he figured how to tell Ruth. He went to the cafeteria where she worked and got some stuff and pushed it around to the cash register and there she was. She looked up and smiled and then the smile went away. He said the speech he had rehearsed.

"I took the fight. I'm going up in the country to train. We'll get married just the same, the same day. I'll come out of the dressing room and you be there with Joey and we'll have Harry drive us down to Maryland and we'll make it so it's the same day, with luck. I took the fight for a reason."

The man behind him said, "Pay your check and get outta the way, Buster."

Nothing showed on Ruth's face. You could read shock or pity or nothing. Lou forgot the rest of what he meant to say. He put down three one-dollar bills and left the tray with the food on it and walked out, not looking back.

**HE SAT IN HIS CORNER** and looked around to find the camera. He'd never fought a TV shot before and he watched the floor after he found the camera. Joey would be watching, maybe Ruth. He hadn't heard from her. Harry had stopped by the cafeteria and she'd been nice but she hadn't sent any message.

Joey had come up week ends and he'd loved the camp as much as Lou had hated it. The cruel jokes, the boredom and the irritability and the work, and the drying out at last.

The fight was an anticlimax, something to get over with. He'd looked at Gila when they weighed in and now he looked across the ring at him again. A black and somber chunk of muscle.

Harry went out to the center of the ring with him, rubbing his shoulders. Nobody listened to the referee's instructions.

Lou thought, you can't stay mad six weeks. I took this for my pride, and it all seeped away up there in the camp. I want to get it over with.

Harry said over again, "Stab, and go to the right. Stay away; he's very strong in close." And the bell rang.

Lou saw the camera up above and then he felt a stiff left hand in his face and he slipped it partly and then he stabbed with his left and went to the right so he'd be going away from the left hooks. He stabbed and went to the right and Gila came after him and Lou let him come in and tried a long right that missed and then he tied up the black arms, but Gila tore loose and Lou felt his wonderful strength and vitality as the boy broke out fiercely; and then the left hook thudded under his heart and he felt sick; there was a tremor in his legs and a wave of nausea.

Lou Badzik stabbed and moved away, the picture fighter who knew his way around in there — just a little nauseated, a little wavery, but concealing it so well he was the only one who knew it. Who else needs to know it? he thought. And then he thought: We will get paid. I'll get hurt tonight.

The bell sounded like a Christmas carol.

Harry snatched out his mouthpiece and said, "See what I meant?"

Lou nodded and looked up at the camera and then he remembered the commercial would be on. Joey would be watching the fight.

"I was awful brave when I told you to make this one for us," Lou said to Harry Fox.

The whistle sounded. Then the bell clanged.

You can stay away, but you can't go home until it's over. And you can't stay away so good when you are fenced in with ropes. Lou Badzik was working at his trade — the beautiful left — but what was a left in his opponent's face? Only an annoyance. He almost admired the speed with which Gila started the combination. And then he heard the referee say, "Three."

I got six seconds, he thought. He wasted one looking up at the camera. Joey would be watching back there some place. Back behind the camera. They didn't have television in Roman times. And there was nobody hereabouts to turn a thumb up for him.

The referee said, "Seven."

Lou thought: I'm all right. And now I gotta get up and fight him.

He got up and the referee wiped off his gloves and the Cuban came in savagely.

Lou stepped to his left and whistled the long right cross. Everything paused for a moment as Kid Gila stopped momentarily. Then he moved again and Lou moved toward him. Gila put his head down and hooked with both hands for the body.

Somebody grunted. The left hook caught Lou too high; all it did was peel his eyebrow back, but it made a great opening for a fighter who didn't mind getting hit, and Lou wheeled the right again, and Gila went down. He got right up, though, too stupid or too strong to take a count, and came in swinging.

He didn't have to come far, for Lou went there to meet him. Put your head in the way of that left hook, Lou thought, and you can hit him with a right. And bang him very hard and he'll bleed, too. It was a relief to learn that.

He took the left hook high on his head and crossed the right and Gila went down. This time he took a five count, with his corner screaming for him to take nine.

Lou looked at Gila's corner and tried to smile. They didn't even understand their own guy. He came to fight as long as he could get up. And he could get up. He got up with a spring and came in banging. He came to win — or else.

Lou dropped his right and asked for the left hook. Again it landed. Too high to kill me, Lou thought, and he threw his own right again from 'way back.

Gila went down again, this time on his hands and knees. He clawed his mouthpiece out with his right glove and spit out some blood and pushed himself up and came to the wars.

The referee grabbed him.

**AND** Harry Fox grabbed Lou. He held his mouth to his ear and yelled, "They had to stop it on three knockdowns."

Lou walked uncertainly toward the Gila corner where there was screaming in shrill Spanish. Gila threw his arms around Lou and said, "Fight again?"

Lou Badzik looked at him, a block of ferocity, and smiled. "No," he said. "Thank you very much — but not again."

On the rubbing table the house doctor sewed his eyebrow and then Lou Badzik walked out of the dressing room door and looked up.

"Sure, I'm here," Ruth said. "How did you think I loved you?"

Joey pulled at his pants leg, just the way kids always did in jokes and funny papers. "I saw it with Ruth from the ninth row."

Lou Badzik patted him abstractedly on the head.

"I didn't want to bother you," Ruth said, "until after the fight. I don't love you less because you think you are an ancient gladiator."

"Car's on the Ninth Avenue side," Harry Fox said. Then he looked at Ruth and saw her smile and he picked up Lou Badzik's right hand and handed it to her. "Some eaglebird," he said.

# Find Volume I of
# THE MASTERPIECES OF EUSTACE COCKRELL
# in bookstores and at Amazon

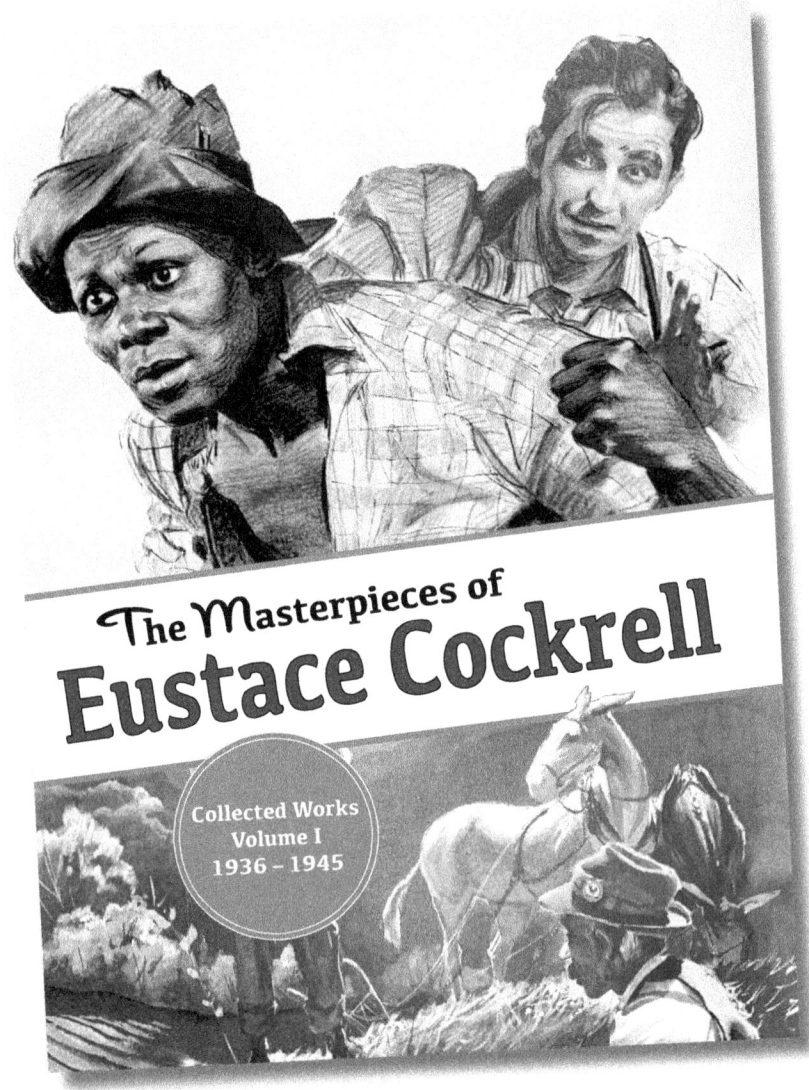

*Eustace Cockrell was a gifted writer for whom everyone, even the most hardhearted and downtrodden, received a second chance. Hope came not from the wealthy or powerful but from the innocence of children; the integrity, particularly of women; and the insights of those often on the fringes of society. Though he spent most of his life in New York and Los Angeles, Cockrell maintained his small-town values and lived with the same sense of honesty, humility, and fair play that infused his writing.*

*The discovery of Eustace Cockrell's "lost stories" is now available as a collection in* **The Masterpieces of Eustace Cockrell***. Here the reader will find the same insights and quality of writing that later brought Cockrell respect as a pioneer writer of television scripts.*

—ROGER COLEMAN, Editor, *The Masterpieces of Eustace Cockrell,*
   *Vol. I and Vol. II*

# Find Volume II of
# THE MASTERPIECES OF EUSTACE COCKRELL
# in bookstores and at Amazon

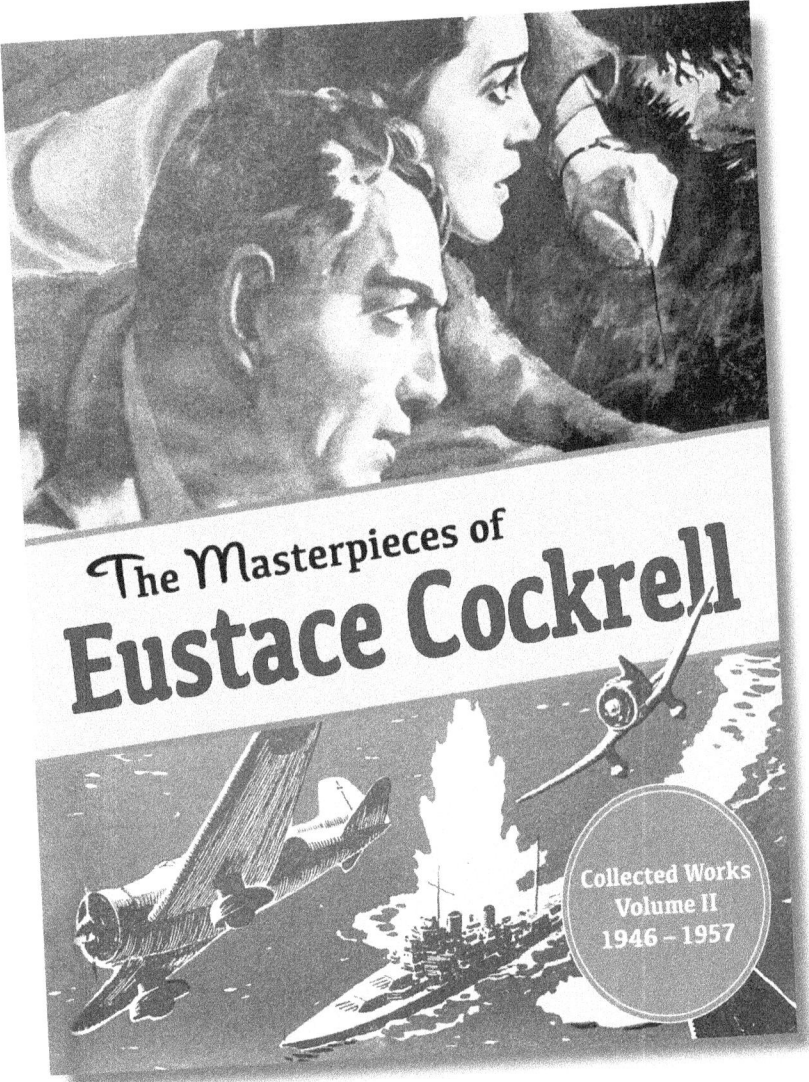

*Eustace Cockrell's stories are filled with memorable characters, the population of a lively era: jockeys, politicians, newspapermen, girls-about-town, mediums, and even St. Peter. They struggle against expectations, the worst instincts of their fellows, and often enough of their own inclinations, to arrive, somehow, generally a bit worse for wear, at a life in some way renewed. First published in magazines from* Argosy *and* Blue Book *to* Cosmopolitan *and* Collier's, *these stories constitute a time portal to the middle years of the twentieth century.*

—AMANDA COCKRELL, niece of Eustace Cockrell, and author of *Border Wars*

Lightning Source UK Ltd.
Milton Keynes UK
UKHW032239300322
400851UK00002B/45